"RICH, SENSIT... **NG MOST DECIDE**...

World

Janelle found her ... dark brown eyes. The ... as if the tide were drawing her out to sea.

"Good morning, Lieutenant. I understand you hurt your hand?"

"Sure did. Too bad I had to run a nail through the center of my hand just to get to see you again."

"Very funny," she said lightly, drying her hands on a sterile cloth.

"Scout's honor." Lance lifted his good hand, three middle fingers pointed up.

Taking his injured hand in hers, she pulled it closer, leaning so near she could feel the heat rising from his body. She turned the hand over. "When and how did this happen?"

"You don't buy my story that this wound was intentionally inflicted in order to see you?" His lopsided grin became an expansive, heart-melting smile.

God, you're a charmer, she thought, realizing how easily and swiftly he had pulled her in. . . .

Anita Richmond Bunkley

WILD EMBERS

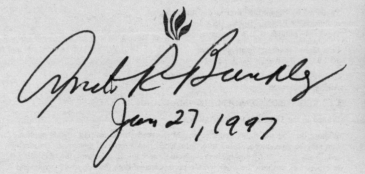

Anita R Bunkley
Jan 27, 1997

A SIGNET BOOK

SIGNET
Published by the Penguin Group
Penguin Books USA Inc., 375 Hudson Street,
New York, New York 10014, U.S.A.
Penguin Books Ltd, 27 Wrights Lane,
London W8 5TZ, England
Penguin Books Australia Ltd, Ringwood,
Victoria, Australia
Penguin Books Canada Ltd, 10 Alcorn Avenue,
Toronto, Ontario, Canada M4V 3B2
Penguin Books (N.Z.) Ltd, 182-190 Wairau Road,
Auckland 10, New Zealand

Penguin Books Ltd, Registered Offices:
Harmondsworth, Middlesex, England

Published by Signet, an imprint of Dutton Signet,
a division of Penguin Books USA Inc.
Previously published in a Dutton edition.

First Signet Printing, February, 1996
10 9 8 7 6 5 4 3 2 1

PUBLISHER'S NOTE
This is a work of fiction. Names, characters, places, and incidents either are the
product of the author's imagination or are used fictitiously, and any resemblance to
actual persons, living or dead, events, or locales is entirely coincidental.

This book is dedicated with much love to:

My husband, Crawford B. Bunkley III
My sisters—Barbara, Carol, Mary, and Tracie—
and my brother, Cliff

I would like to acknowledge and thank the following people for their assistance:

Ms. Annie Brown, Macon County-Tuskegee Public Library, Tuskegee, Alabama

Colonel Herbert E. Carter (ret. and a member of the original 99th Fighter Squadron), Tuskegee, Alabama

Sergeant Champ, Alief Army Recruiting Station, Houston, Texas

Maperal Clark, Macon County-Tuskegee Public Library, Tuskegee, Alabama

Charity Adams Early (first black officer in the Women's Army Corps [WAC]), Dayton, Ohio

Linda Hengst, Ohioana Library Association, Columbus, Ohio

Colonel Roosevelt Lewis, Tuskegee Flight School at Historic Moton Field, Tuskegee, Alabama

Ms. June Powell, National Afro-American Museum and Cultural Center, Wilberforce, Ohio

Ms. Barbara Richmond Wells, R.N., Houston, Texas

PART I

How much longer, in our defense preparation, are we to gamble with the safety of the nation while we indulge in the luxury of our antipathies? How soon are we to be done with the irrelevancies and trivialities which prescribe to color of skin and refuse to recognize instead the industrial skill and competence of those whose labors are necessary to complete the job ahead of us?

—Emmett J. Scott,
Pittsburgh *Courier,* 1941

CHAPTER ONE

The argument started late in the afternoon, flaring up in harsh words that Janelle had hoped she would never have to speak. The ugly confrontation eventually settled into an uneasy tolerance that permeated every inch of the house. When Perry slammed out the door without saying good-bye, Janelle had actually wished her brother would not come back.

Janelle hated the situation she had created but did not regret her words. Perry had flaunted his arrogant independence in her face for the last time, and she would never apologize for what she had said.

Now, staring into darkness, temporarily soothed by the warmth she'd created in her cocoon under layers of threadbare blankets, Janelle listened to the winter storm raging outside. She burrowed more deeply into the middle of her mattress, tugging the covers tightly over her shoulders, but the clatter of freezing rain that pummeled her bedroom window could not distract her from her thoughts about Perry.

Perhaps she shouldn't have put so much pressure on him. Perhaps she should have listened to their mother and let Perry have his way. But his irritating ploy to draw sympathy from their mother had without warning pushed Janelle over the edge. In scathing honesty she had finally told him exactly what was on her mind, what had been eating at her for the last twelve months, since the day their father died.

Distressed to the point of tears, Janelle turned onto her stomach and pressed her face into the pillow. Feelings of guilt nudged her more fully awake. She had intentionally hurt Perry yesterday, and when he had callously smirked at her, trying to put her off, she had allowed her resentment to turn into a hardened kernel of resistance. No longer would she even try to see things his way, no matter how much their mother pressed for peace.

Well, it *was* time for Perry to pull himself together and begin acting like a man, she thought. He ought to be working or at least going to school. Mourning for a year! He should have moved beyond his grief. Perry wasn't the only one who had been traumatized by Garret Roy's sudden passing.

Out of habit, Janelle leaned up and groped toward the luminous glow of her dome-shaped clock, tapping the small red button on top to shut off the alarm before it came on. Then she tuned the radio to WBNS to catch the morning weather report.

The prediction of sleet and more snow for central Ohio did not surprise Janelle, but she shuddered and rubbed her arms when the announcer said that residents of Columbus could expect a high of nineteen degrees on this, the second day of 1943.

Stretching as she sat up, Janelle let the blankets fall away from her brown torso and pulled her twisted flannel gown from beneath the warm press of her firm, heavy breasts. She sank back on the bedcovering, tilting her hips slightly forward as she flexed one slender leg in catlike languor.

The deep, throaty voice of Lena Horne settled over the room, sending out a mournful message of lost love while stormy weather indeed raged outside the window.

Janelle swept her mahogany-colored hair from her face and tucked it behind her ears. Thick and glossy, now freed from the mesh snood Janelle usually wore, her hair cascaded in waves that reached the middle of her back.

She sat and blinked her eyes, adding a few extratight squeezes that she firmly believed would help maintain the smooth, taut skin over her high cheekbones. Lowering her chin, she gave her shoulders a deep shrug, then reached toward the cottony fluff of her favorite old robe and pulled it over her arms.

Her ten-hour shift as a private-duty nurse at the Werner house didn't start until seven o'clock, but Janelle always got up at five. If there was one thing she hated, it was being rushed or being late, and she had an uncanny internal clock that seemed to keep her on schedule naturally.

By rising early, Janelle could sit alone, drinking black coffee as she watched the morning sky change from dark purple to rose while the sun either pushed its red globe over the horizon or lingered as a shadowy presence behind snow-laden clouds. It was the only time she had to sit still and really think, and lately she'd had a lot on her mind.

Lowering her feet to the floor, Janelle slipped her toes into ice-cold slippers, shivering as chilblains covered her legs. She gently pulled aside the old yellow quilt she had hung over the window last night. It certainly had helped keep the draft at bay.

Frosty vapor clouded her view. Crystals of ice gathered in delicate clumps on the pane. With the palm of one hand, Janelle rubbed a small circle in the cold white mist and looked outside.

Sometime during the night, rain had turned to snow and settled silently along the fences lining Oakwood Alley. In places it had drifted into waist-high mounds that eerily reflected the moon. As she gazed over the beautiful predawn scene, Janelle's anger at her brother began to ebb away.

Perry had better get a job this week, Janelle thought as she tied the cord of her robe around her slim waist and headed for the bathroom at the end of the hall. God knew she was tired of supporting him. After all, she had been shattered by their father's death, too, but she hadn't let it paralyze her. She still went to work every day.

At the foot of the stairs Janelle stopped, surprised to see a yellow strip of light glowing at the bottom of the door to the kitchen. She was not in the mood for a conversation with anyone. Especially not with Perry.

Placing her hand against the edges of peeling paint on the kitchen door, she eased it open. The glare of the overhead bulb, hanging naked from the ceiling without its long-ago-broken frosted glass globe, made Janelle flinch and narrow her eyes.

The thin wash of pale blue paint her father had layered over the uneven walls, along with her mother's collection of blue and white dishes did help brighten the pitiful kitchen. At the gray- and blue-flecked Formica table, face buried in the crook of his arm, sat Perry. Fast asleep. A scattering of hand-lettered pamphlets littered the floor.

Janelle stood rigidly in the doorway looking at her only brother, her heart aching for the misery she knew he was in, her soul desperately wishing he could find peace.

Three years her junior, in Janelle's eyes Perry was still her baby brother. In sleep, his face had softened. The taut muscles usually tensing his sharp jawline had eased, giving him back the boyish appearance that Janelle hadn't seen for months. His soft coffee-colored skin, which matched her own, glowed with a deep copper tinge. Though now twenty, he rarely had to shave, having inherited his father's baby-smooth complexion, along with his stocky, muscular build. The deep brown eyes that had pierced Janelle in angry defiance just yesterday now lay gently shuttered against his sister's stare.

As she looked at him, Janelle struggled to summon a big dose of unconditional love. It was very difficult. If only they could turn back the clock one year to the time when the Roy family had been happy and whole and had lived as if their future could not possibly encompass anything as horribly devastating or ugly as death. Or war. Or the threatened breach of familial love that now hung between Janelle and Perry.

Janelle's first thought was to tiptoe around the kitchen and not wake Perry up, but she was tired of the coddling act. She turned on the faucet and let the water run full blast, then rattled the coffeepot noisily as she opened the percolator to pour the ground coffee in. With a clatter she set the pot down on the stove, struck a match, and lit the gas flame.

Perry moaned sleepily and raised his head.

Janelle turned from the stove to face her brother.

"You been there all night?" she asked, knowing he had not been home at twelve-thirty, when she and her mother had returned from Union Station.

Perry rubbed his eyes, put both hands behind his neck, and lifted his jaw from the wool collar of his navy peacoat. "Yeah, I guess so." His voice was rough with sleep.

The strain of yesterday's argument lingered, interrupted and unresolved like a radio program turned off in midpoint. Janelle didn't like it one bit.

Moving toward the cabinet on the other side of the room, Janelle turned her back to Perry, thinking about what to do. Start right in where they had left off yesterday? Ruin her day before it even got started? Or let the whole affair slip down into the eroding crevices of family discord, to be forgotten and forgiven over time.

Unexpectedly the shrill blast of the telephone kept Janelle from saying anything.

At the stand in the hallway she picked up the telephone.

"Yes? . . . This is Janelle. . . . Oh, hello, Flora. . . . That's all right." How odd for the Werner housekeeper to be calling her so early.

"Flora? What's the matter? You sound like you're crying." Janelle frowned, biting her lower lip as she listened. "All right. . . . Yes. . . . Yes. I understand. I'll take a taxi. Listen carefully, Flora. Call Dr. Carter and tell him what's happened. I'll be there as soon as I can."

* * *

The taxi driver skirted a pile of week-old snow banked against the curb, slammed on the brakes, then flipped the gearshift into park. Janelle gripped the armrest at her side to keep from pitching forward.

"Seventy-five cents," the cabbie said bluntly.

"What did you say the fare was?" she asked again, wishing he would turn the radio down.

The man scratched his head through his woolen stocking cap, sighed, and repeated, "Seventy-five cents."

"It's always been fifty cents," Janelle stated firmly. "I make this trip often enough to know." She caught the driver's eye in the rearview mirror and stared directly into his face. Arguing over the inflated fare was not what she wanted to do, not at six o'clock in the morning.

The man only blinked, acting as if she had not spoken, and leaned over to turn up the volume on his radio. The heavy car idled loudly at the foot of a dark, narrow driveway as the newscaster on the radio announced: "Lantree Aviation's open call for men . . . and women is expected to bring more than two thousand hopeful job seekers to its plant over the next three days. As the war effort intensifies, it appears there will be plenty of work for all."

Yeah, Janelle thought wryly as she fumbled with her purse. Plenty of work for white men and women. Lantree's president had already announced that Negroes need not apply. Thank God she didn't have to stand outside a dirty factory waiting for someone to offer her a job.

Freezing rain sluiced over the hood of the taxi, spilling into gutters clogged with chunks of murky ice, eating away at the remnants of December's last snow.

He could at least pull into the driveway, Janelle thought, knowing that if she were a white woman, he'd be breaking his neck to let her off in the driest spot he could find. She pulled her raincoat more fully over her crisp white uniform and took three quarters from her change purse.

Janelle scooted forward. The pungent smell of cigarette butts, along with the odor of the driver himself, swept up and nearly gagged her. She considered tossing the money onto the front seat, but when the driver raised his hand, Janelle carefully dropped the coins into his upturned palm, taking pains not to let her fingers touch his.

After checking the buckles on her sturdy galoshes, Janelle forced the door open and had barely slammed it shut when the cab lurched away from the curb. Dirty water splashed over her thick white stockings.

"Dammit!" Janelle cursed, straining to see the license plate on the retreating car. D-375. "He's getting reported," she vowed, making up her mind never to use City Cabs again.

The relentless downpour gathered strength. A flash of lightning lit the road, illuminating a border of dense, thorny bushes growing wildly along Sunbury Road, a natural barrier that discouraged curiosity seekers from venturing onto the Werner estate. Janelle looked up at the redbrick house looming before her.

Built years before the Civil War, the Werner house dominated Sunbury Road, competing in grandeur with the network of stone structures above the ravine that made up St. Mary's of the Springs. Sitting across from the Catholic college, the mansion rose on the west bank of Alum Creek, its slate roof glistening in the pearly sheen of moonlight. Its deep wraparound porch looked like a dark, gaping mouth. Two small windows on the second floor of the house glowed softly yellow, punctuating black lacy shadows cast by trembling leafless oaks.

Janelle had passed the Werner mansion many times as a child, relishing the shocking tale her mother told of the mysterious death of Randolf Werner and the lengthy estate trial of his motherless daughters. When the judge awarded the stately mansion to Cordelia, and the fortune in cash to her sister, Sara, he had initiated a feud that continued to this day.

Clutching the scrolled iron railing running from the street to the front door, Janelle mounted the ice-covered steps. She hesitated for a moment, staring at the rose-colored stained glass panels set in weathered oak, then decided to knock. She wouldn't go around to the back door. Not this morning. She tapped the brass knocker loudly three times, then stood waiting until Flora pulled the tall door open. Light flooded the porch. A burst of warm air spilled out.

"Oh, Miss Roy. Thank goodness you're here." Flora's watery blue eyes opened wide with relief as she wiped a plump finger over perspiration that had beaded on her upper lip.

"How is Miss Werner doing?" Janelle rushed to ask as she entered the house, pausing to stick her dripping umbrella into the rosewood stand near the door.

"Better. Much better. She calmed down and even drank a little tea. I sat with her until she fell asleep." Flora opened the closet door for Janelle, watching as the nurse took off her rain-soaked coat. "Oh, Miss Roy," she went on, "Cousin Cordelia had such a bad night. Off and on she'd wake up, complaining of terrible nightmares and a pounding headache. When she started tossing and turning, jerking around, I was terrified. She acted like she was in some kind of a trance. I don't think she heard a word I said."

"Did you talk to Dr. Carter?" Janelle asked, kicking off her stiff galoshes, unmindful of the dark water spots left on the old Oriental rug. Shoving her coat and boots into the closet, she headed toward the stairs.

"No. I couldn't get through. The line to Dr. Carter's house is dead." Flora hurried along behind Janelle. "It was probably knocked out by the storm."

Janelle's mind whirled as she rushed down the wide upstairs hallway, which was lined with gilt-framed portraits of Werner ancestors.

Bedridden with rheumatoid arthritis, Miss Werner did suffer constant pain, but Janelle had never heard complaints of headaches or bad dreams. She wondered if the new sedative Dr. Carter had prescribed yesterday had something to do with this.

Flora, whose absentminded chatter sometimes grated on Janelle's nerves, continued her lament. "I sat with her until she fell back to sleep, but I'm worried, Miss Roy, real worried."

Pushing open the bedroom door, the two women stared across the richly decorated room. Their charge lay in the center of a mahogany bed draped with white satin panels. Trailing grapevines and raised oak leaves were etched across the headboard, the footboard, and down all four posters, which soared up toward the fifteen-foot-high ceiling. A mound of lace-edged pillows surrounded the sleeping woman. Her snow white hair, usually pinned neatly behind her ears, hung in limp tendrils over her forehead, nearly covering her withered face. She looked dangerously fragile and pale.

Janelle and Flora exchanged glances. Unspoken concern for Cordelia Werner bound them in a tenuous acceptance of each other. Day in and day out they went about their duties, managing small talk threaded with courtesy and respect, their common mission centered on Cordelia Werner's well being. Now, as their eyes connected briefly, each silently comforted the other.

The raspy sound of Cordelia's shallow breathing filled Janelle with dread. She had unexpectedly grown very fond of the eccentric, wealthy spinster who preferred the company of her timorous cousin and her colored nurse to the presence of her only sister, Sara Werner Johnson, who had hired Janelle.

"She looks so drawn, Miss Roy," Flora said.

"She certainly is pale," Janelle replied moving to her patient's bedside, picking up her liver-spotted hand. As Janelle took her pulse, she saw Cordelia's eyes flutter open. Then Cordelia smiled up at Janelle.

"Miss Werner?" Janelle waited until her patient's eyes connected with hers. "Flora tells me you had bad dreams last night?"

Cordelia nodded weakly and placed her fingers to her temple.

"A headache? You have a headache?"

"Yes," Cordelia whispered.

"All right. Just relax. I'll give you something for the pain after I've checked you over." Janelle was warmed by the unexpected press of Cordelia's hand on hers.

Then, moving with professional assurance, Janelle checked Cordelia's heart rate, pupils, temperature, and blood pressure, listened to her lungs, and examined her arthritic joints for new swelling. Nothing out of the ordinary. She touched her gently and spoke. "Everything seems fine, but I still want to talk to Dr. Carter."

"I'm glad you're here," Cordelia managed to say, before closing her eyes, sinking back on her pillows.

"Don't worry," Janelle replied, "just rest." Inwardly she smiled, pleased that Cordelia Werner had grown so fond of her. Private-duty jobs like this one didn't come along very often, especially for colored nurses, and the recommendation she would get from Sara Johnson would secure her future as a private-duty nurse in the wealthiest circles in Columbus.

"Is Cordelia going to be all right?" Flora asked.

"I see nothing to be alarmed about so far," Janelle replied, stepping away from the bed as she put her stethoscope in her pocket. "Her vital signs are stable." She watched Flora's expression sink into a somber half frown, a look Janelle had seen before.

"I'm sorry I panicked," Flora muttered, visibly ashamed of her actions.

"No, Flora. You did the right thing. I'm glad you called," Janelle said reassuringly, wishing Flora had a little more confidence. "There's no reason to apologize. Now I wish I *had* stayed over last night." She hated to hear herself say those words, remembering her adamant refusal to live in when offered the job.

"I didn't call Sara," Flora said. "I started to, but I know she'd have gotten herself in a real twit if I woke her up for no reason. The last time I called when Cordelia wasn't feeling good Sara made it clear not to bother her. She said to telephone Dr. Carter."

Janelle kept her face still, eyes lowered, not doubting for a minute that Flora spoke the truth. Sara Johnson wanted only one thing: to get her hands on the deed to the Werner mansion as soon as her sister died.

"I do the best I can," Flora said, tears emerging at the corners of her eyes. "I begged Sara to hire a night nurse—somebody trained to help Cordelia. Like you. But she refused."

"We've managed fine, Flora," Janelle said. "Luckily Miss Werner doesn't need much attention at night."

"Perhaps, but I'd sleep much better knowing someone like you was here in the house." Flora edged to the foot of the bed. "Sara will never forgive Cordelia for not moving out when she married Dr. Johnson. Sara wanted this house . . . oh, how she coveted Cordelia's right to live here. But that was so long ago. Now she ought to do better by her sister. She can well afford to bring in extra help."

Janelle agreed, but it was not her place to comment on the well-publicized power struggle between the Werner sisters. She deliberately changed the subject.

"Did Tyler's pharmacy deliver the prescription Dr. Carter called in? He told me yesterday he would be changing Miss Werner's medication."

"Yes, late last night. It came long after you left, Miss Roy."

"And you gave it to Miss Werner? Just as I instructed?" Janelle stepped back to better observe her patient.

"Yes. Yes," Flora said. "Four pills every two hours. Started at ten o'clock. I made sure she took them on time."

Janelle dropped the bottle of aspirin she was holding and stared at Flora. "How much did you give her?" she asked, just as the sick woman's right hand fluttered to her throat and rested like a faded lily beneath her skeletal jaw.

Flora picked up a small brown vile from the table where Janelle kept all the nursing supplies and said again, "Four tablets . . . every two hours."

Snatching the bottle, Janelle stared in disbelief at the label. Febrahyde. The new medication. "*Two* pills every *four* hours, Flora. See, on the label. Two pills! Not four!" Now panic rose in Janelle's throat.

"No. No. I'm sure you said four," Flora protested, her mouth gaping open in horror.

Janelle sank down beside her patient and tried to rouse the sleepy woman. "Miss Werner," she said clearly and firmly, "it's me, Janelle. Open your eyes. Wake up." Janelle tipped the water pitcher on the nightstand and soaked a small towel, then placed it on Cordelia's brow. Cordelia suddenly began to thrash around, pitching left and right, tangling the heavy cotton sheets around her body. Janelle moved to the edge of the bed to keep from being struck as Cordelia flailed arms that appeared manipulated by demons.

"Call White Cross Hospital. Have them send an ambulance," Janelle yelled. "Flora! Call the hospital. Now!"

"Oh, Miss Roy. You mean, I—"

"Get an ambulance!" Janelle jumped up to face the flustered housekeeper, motioning toward the door, then turned back to Cordelia, who had suddenly calmed and lay quietly, her raspy breathing coming in ragged gusts.

Janelle tucked the sheets around Cordelia's skeletal body, smoothing wrinkles from the thick satin spread. In a burst of strength, Cordelia tore free, her unfocused eyes springing open. Their vacant, disoriented gaze chilled Janelle, and she turned from the bed, yelling into the dim hallway, "Flora! Try Dr. Carter again." She could hear Flora talking on the telephone but could not make out her words.

When Flora reappeared at the doorway, Janelle muttered, "How in the world did you misread the prescription?" not really expecting an answer. "You've given Miss Werner her night medication so many times before. Flora! What happened?"

"I don't know. She always took four of those other pills, you know? I guess I was nervous . . . the storm . . ." Her words trailed off, and she covered her lips with stiff fingers.

Janelle lunged forward as Cordelia rose up and threw back her head in a convulsive spasm. "Hand me that tongue depressor! A ball of gauze! Anything! Hurry!"

The situation was worsening.

Flora fumbled around on the table, grabbed a flat wooden stick, and thrust it at Janelle, who immediately wedged it between Cordelia's yellowed teeth.

Arching her back while pressing her head violently into the pillows, Cordelia rocked the heavy antique bed. Janelle and Flora could do no more than stand and watch in horror until the old woman stiffened like a papier-mâché puppet and lay staring at the ceiling, her face frozen in a twisted mask.

Flora sobbed, "I've been watching Cousin Cordelia go down a little more each day for fifteen years. I knew her last days were coming on, but I never thought that it would be like this or that I would be the cause."

"Hush, Flora," Janelle said softly. "Don't say that." She focused on the housekeeper now, giving her a puzzled look. "Anyway, I can't believe that the medication would bring on seizures like this."

Febrahyde. A new drug, it was released on the market just last month. Dr. Carter had assured her it was an extremely mild sedative, much weaker than the lowest dosage of chloral hydrate. "Something else must be going on," Janelle concluded. "Regardless, Miss Werner must go to the hospital."

In the calm moments following the last attack, Janelle gently wiped Cordelia's face. "Better go telephone Sara Johnson now," she told Flora. "Tell her to meet me at the emergency room at White Cross Hospital."

"I can't do that, Miss Roy," Flora refused, sucking in her cheeks until her lips pouched out. She remained firmly rooted at the foot of the bed. Straightening her rounded shoulders, lifting her oval chin, she said flatly, "She made me swear on the Werner family Bible that I'd never break her rest again, and I don't ever want to be on her bad side."

Janelle reached over and took Cordelia's hand in hers. Holding it firmly, she told Flora, "Well, I'm not leaving Miss Werner. I can call Sara from the hospital."

CHAPTER TWO

The heavy double doors of the ambulance burst open. Two uniformed attendants jumped inside, grabbed the gurney at the foot and the head, and wheeled Cordelia Werner out. Janelle hurried along behind the men into the brightly lit corridors of the emergency wing.

Caustic odors of disinfectants, antiseptics, and potent pharmaceuticals swept over Janelle, jolting her back to the days of her practice nursing in the emergency room of Belton Park, a bustling hospital, much like White Cross, that served the east side of town.

A calm, efficient-looking nurse stopped Janelle. "Is this the Werner patient?"

Janelle could only manage a vigorous nod.

"All right"—the nurse spoke to the attendants—"room six is open. The staff doctor is already in there." She turned to Janelle. "I need some information from you; then you can join your patient." Noticing the distress on Janelle's face, she added, "Don't worry, Dr. Reid himself will be coming down to oversee this case."

Dr. Reid! So the name Werner had drawn the chief of staff of White Cross Hospital into the situation. Janelle shuddered, then stiffly followed the nurse to a counter and began to answer questions, though her thoughts were far from Cordelia's personal statistics and medical history.

Four pills instead of two. Could the overdose of Febrahyde have caused the convulsions? Didn't Dr. Carter say it had an anticonvulsive agent? He had told her it was extremely mild. If only she had stayed long enough to administer the medication herself. Janelle's mind whirled with possibilities.

"Who is Miss Werner's attending physician?"

"Dr. Thomas Carter," Janelle replied, going on to give the nurse phone numbers, addresses, and next-of-kin information.

Absently she checked her watch: six forty-five. She decided to call Emma, knowing her nursing school classmate, who supervised the drug dispensary at East Side Clinic, could quickly answer her questions. New pharmaceuticals emerged every day, and Janelle had to admit that working private-duty did keep her out of touch. Whenever she needed information, she turned to Emma, whose job demanded that she be informed. As Janelle rummaged in her purse for a nickel, the nurse's voice stopped her.

"That's all I need right now, Miss Roy. You can go in with your patient." Janelle snapped her purse shut, walked down the corridor, and slipped into room 6.

Cordelia lay ashen and slack on the examination table, her shallow breathing barely moving the white sheet drawn over her chest. Janelle stood rigidly alert, leaning forward, trying to hear what the staff doctor was saying as he checked Cordelia over.

Suddenly the door flared open, and in strode Dr. Benjamin Reid. A gruff-looking man with bushy white hair, he had the reputation of heading the most efficiently run hospital in the city, though it was widely known that his stern demeanor masked a generous, sympathetic heart. One charitable organization or another was always honoring him. The Urban League had recently applauded his decision to send the White Cross mobile unit into the poorest areas of town.

Letting the door swing shut behind him, the physician crossed the tiny cubicle and went to stand by the draped table where Cordelia Werner lay. He looked over the young doctor's shoulder, listening intently to the precise summary of findings as two nurses checked the patient's vital signs.

"The pupils are unequal, Dr. Reid," the staff doctor said.

"Let me see." The chief of staff accepted the ophthalmoscope handed him.

Janelle stared at Dr. Reid's towering form, suddenly feeling small and shabby in his presence. She glanced down at the splatter of mud over her uniform and grimaced, recalling the frantic rush to get Cordelia into the ambulance. Even Flora had ventured outside, wading through icy mud to hand Janelle her galoshes. *Oh, God,* she prayed silently, closing her eyes for a second, *let Cordelia pull out of this.*

"You're the Werner nurse?"

The words interrupted Janelle's prayer. Her eyes flew open to meet Dr. Reid's questioning stare.

"Yes, Dr. Reid. I'm Janelle Roy, Miss Werner's nurse."

"Um-hmmm." Dr. Reid watched Janelle closely. "Tell me, has your patient been complaining of headaches? Blurred vision?"

"No blurring of vision, but headaches, yes. The housekeeper said Miss Werner woke up complaining of pain during the night. When I examined her this morning, she also indicated that her head was hurting."

Dr. Reid nodded. "Did the housekeeper give Miss Werner anything to help her rest? Any medication for pain?"

"Yes." Knowing it had to be told, Janelle rushed on. "Dr. Carter had recently prescribed a new sleeping medication."

"What is it?"

Janelle pulled the small brown vial from her purse and handed it to Dr. Reid.

"Febrahyde," he read aloud. "When was the first convulsion?"

"At about six-fifteen this morning." Janelle fought to subdue the tremor in her voice.

"Has she had any other medication in the last twenty-four hours?"

"Only aspirin," Janelle answered, hurrying to explain. "I don't live in at the Werner house. Unfortunately the housekeeper who is with Miss Werner at night inadvertently doubled the prescribed dosage of Febrahyde."

Dr. Reid's bushy eyebrows drew together in a frown, and he examined the vial even closer. He opened the bottle and spilled a few pills into his palm. "This a fairly new sedative. Very mild dosage here." He pursed his lips, put the pills back, then capped the bottle with a twist. Just as he turned his head to look over at Cordelia, the young doctor called out, "She's coming around. Here! Here! Dr. Reid. She's conscious. Let's get a—"

Before he could finish, Cordelia arched her back, thrusting her narrow chest toward the glaring fluorescent tubes overhead. Her ice blue eyes rolled back into her head, creating the appearance of a hollow-eyed mask. One of the nurses reached over to hold the IV pole to prevent the intravenous tube from being ripped from the patient's arm.

Janelle rushed forward. "Miss Werner! Miss Werner! It's Janelle. I'm here." She gripped the cold stainless steel railing and bent over her charge.

"Better step back, miss," the staff doctor cautioned as he maneuvered closer to Cordelia. "Two hundred milligrams of Dilantin. Stat!" he called out as Cordelia's body stiffened, then relaxed.

"Mouth gag! Suction!" The team worked frantically.

Dr. Reid came up behind Janelle and put a hand on her shoulder, guiding her toward the door. "I understand how you feel, Miss Roy. But our emergency team is top-notch. We'll get your patient stabilized. Better step outside. As soon as I can, I'll let you come back in."

Janelle lifted tormented eyes to Dr. Reid's sympathetic face.

"Don't worry," he added gently, "we'll get to the bottom of this."

As the door thudded shut, Janelle knew she had better

call Sara Johnson. She hurried down the hall toward the admitting desk.

"Where is a telephone?" she asked the nurse.

"Second floor. Top of the stairs."

"Thanks," Janelle said in a rushed tone. "Will you let me know if there is any news on Miss Werner's condition?"

"Sure," the woman replied.

Oh, God, Janelle thought. She was not in the mood for a grilling from Sara Johnson. She followed a sign pointing to a short flight of stairs where rest rooms and telephones could be found, then crossed to the far side of the corridor. She stopped near a window at the front of the building.

With the venetian blinds up, Janelle could look out over the hospital parking lot. The rain had ceased, though a flurry of light snow continued. The sky had lightened, and the day was emerging dismally overcast. The slick black tops of automobiles looked like a cluster of water bugs on a cement floor.

Nervously Janelle paced the floor, wondering what was going on in room 6, putting off her call to Cordelia's sister. Finally, she pulled her dog-eared address book from her purse, checked the number, and dropped a nickel into the slot. Sara answered on the second ring.

"Mrs. Johnson?" Janelle held her breath, then plunged ahead. "This is Janelle Roy. I'm afraid Miss Werner has taken a turn for the worse. I'm at the emergency room at White Cross Hospital." She waited for Sara to respond.

"Yes.... Yes.... That's right. White Cross."

Janelle tensed, her insides shrinking in taut apprehension as Sara's curt words stung through the telephone line. "Is this *truly* an emergency, Miss Roy? Did Dr. Carter advise you to call me?"

"I could not get in touch with him, but I assure you this *is* an emergency, Mrs. Johnson. Miss Werner has had a convulsive episode."

"Convulsions? Oh, my. Of course. I understand."

Janelle could hear the rustle of silk bedcovering being pushed aside.

"What brought this on?" Sara wanted to know.

"We're not sure, ma'am, but Dr. Benjamin Reid is with your sister now."

"Good." The word was smugly stated. "I'll be there as soon as I'm dressed."

The mention of the chief of staff's attendance seemed to satisfy Sara. "Please hurry, Mrs. Johnson," Janelle advised. "Come to the emergency wing. Room six."

"I'll be there within the hour."

Janelle hung up the phone and sank down onto a bench near the window, pressing her shoulder against the sill, feeling as if she had been walking the corridors of the hospital all night. What had gone wrong? What if it *was* the overdose of Febrahyde? The thought was numbing, forcing Janelle to consider the ramifications of Flora's blunder. After all, *she,* not Flora, was responsible for Cordelia's medical care, though Sara Johnson had made it perfectly clear that Flora would be in charge at night.

Janelle stood up and deposited another nickel into the pay phone. Her mind went blank for a second. What was Emma's number? She had dialed it hundreds, maybe thousands of times over the fifteen years they had known each other. Now it escaped her completely.

Janelle inhaled deeply, forcing herself to calm down. Even if Emma could not tell her much about Febrahyde, just hearing her levelheaded opinion about the situation might keep Janelle's imagination from running wild.

AD-2145! It came to her. She could barely get her trembling finger to stay in the flat black dial.

Busy! The line was busy. "Damn." Janelle fumed as she held the phone to her ear a moment longer, hoping the line would break free. Emma was probably talking long-distance to her boyfriend, Kenneth, who was taking aviation mechanic training at Chanute Field, hoping for an assignment at Tuskegee Army Airfield.

Friends since grammar school, Janelle and Emma managed to stay in touch, but their demanding jobs kept them snatching bits and pieces of conversation over the counter at Tyler's drug store, in the parking lot at church, at the checkout stand in Albers—wherever they happened to meet. The last time Janelle and Emma had spent time together was almost two months ago, when Emma had fixed her up on a blind date with a distant cousin. The double date with Emma and Kenneth had been a disaster, the cousin a boring disappointment.

Settling onto the bench, kicking off her heavy rubber boots, Janelle recalled the day, three weeks ago, when Kenneth had left for Illinois. Emma had feigned high spirits until his train pulled out, then had fallen into a dangerously despondent mood. Not surprisingly she began talking about volunteering, too, since the Army had finally begun recruiting colored nurses.

The idea sounded crazy to Janelle. Her first impulse was to tell Emma she was out of her mind. Volunteer for nursing duty at a segregated Army base in the Jim Crow South? It sounded like a self-imposed trip to hell. But Janelle had said nothing, convinced that her opinion would make very little difference to Emma. On her own since she was sixteen, Emma always did as she pleased, with no one to answer to but herself.

Janelle shifted on the hard wooden bench, watching traffic in the deserted corridor begin to pick up. The night shift was going off. The day shift was straggling in. She glanced up into the face of a young nurse passing by.

The red-haired woman stopped at the top of the steps, rubbed the muscles in her neck, then stuffed her tired fingers into fur-lined gloves. Janelle could almost feel the nurse's weariness. How anyone could work the graveyard shift night after night, year after year was beyond her. Taking orders from snippy, overworked supervisors and brusque doctors in the middle of the night was not something she wanted to do.

Her six-week practice nursing in the crisis center of Belton Park had been enough. It had been the most grueling, demanding, and terrifying experience of her life. Blood all over the floor from gunshot wounds, stabbings, and near-fatal beatings. Tense moments resuscitating barbiturate and heroin overdose cases. Delivering babies in crowded hallways while gawking strangers milled around. The stint at Belton had tested Janelle's skills as a nurse, while measuring her physical and mental endurance. The ghastly pressure to save a life, often with slim odds of succeeding, coupled with long hours and the prospect of low pay, had convinced Janelle to make her living nursing elderly patients at home.

Impatiently Janelle tried Emma's number again. No answer. She'd missed her. Unable to wait any longer, Janelle turned toward the steps and headed back to the emergency wing where she entered room 6.

Dr. Reid stood over Cordelia, his stethoscope pressed firmly against her chest. Janelle watched as he removed the instrument.

"Blood pressure?" he asked.

"Dropping sharply, Doctor," the nurse reported.

"Pulse?"

"Weak and thready."

Janelle held her breath, clasping her hands tightly, remaining just inside the door.

"Dr. Reid," she said.

He turned to face her.

"What's the prognosis? Has Miss Werner regained consciousness?"

"No," the doctor answered. "She's had two more convulsions, and her condition is very serious."

"What's causing this?" Janelle pressed her tongue to the roof of her mouth, anticipating his reply.

"I don't know." Dr. Reid relinquished his spot at the side of the bed to the staff doctor and approached Janelle. "Her symptoms suggest trauma to the brain . . . a tumor perhaps. Has anything like this ever occurred before?"

Janelle shook her head and murmured, "Never."

"Her pupils are unequal. Not a good sign. We're going to try to—"

"Dr. Reid!" the staff physician interrupted. "Another seizure. Here! Watch that IV, Nurse!"

Janelle gasped as she watched Cordelia's frail body jerk and twist on the white hospital sheets. Not a sound escaped lips that were pressed into a thin gray line. When her arms flew up over her head, then fell limply onto the pillow, Janelle sensed the worst. Cordelia's withered form became perfectly still, and Janelle felt the sting of tears.

The younger physician quickly pressed his stethoscope to Cordelia's chest, listened for a moment, then began external heart massage. For a few long seconds the room was deathly silent. Then the doctor stepped back from the bed.

"I'm sorry," he began, folding the instrument as he nodded to Dr. Reid. "She's gone."

"Oh, no." Janelle heard her own voice from afar. "It can't be."

"I'm afraid her heart was too weak to hold up under the strain," Dr. Reid explained.

Janelle stared numbly at Cordelia, not wanting to accept her death, feeling strangely hollow and afraid, acknowledging the extent of her affection for her patient.

With a loud crack the door banged against the wall and Sara Werner Johnson charged in. Her steel gray hair rose up in a pompadour lacquered so thoroughly it appeared to be made out of wood. Her full-length mink coat shimmered with drops of snow that quickly melted under the bright hospital lights.

"What has happened to my sister?" she demanded, walking directly to the table where Cordelia lay. The nurse who had started to cover Cordelia's face stepped back, the sheet still clasped in her fingers. She watched Sara peer down at the body.

"She's gone?" Sara asked, dramatically placing a hand to her throat.

"Yes," Dr. Reid replied, nodding in sympathy as he

gently guided Sara Johnson away from the gurney by the elbow. The nurse finished covering Cordelia's face.

"I'm Dr. Benjamin Reid, chief of staff."

"I am Mrs. Sara Johnson, sister of the deceased." She spoke as if her haughty, pride-filled voice could elevate her above the mundane trappings of the emergency room.

Dr. Reid tugged his graying beard, squinting at the woman before him. "My condolences, Mrs. Johnson. Your sister's condition deteriorated very rapidly."

Sara raised one shoulder slightly as her lips turned down at the corners. "Exactly why and how did my sister die?" She eyed Janelle as her precise businesslike words lay like a challenging gauntlet.

"Right now I have to admit that I don't know." Dr. Reid turned to accept a clipboard from the staff physician, signed his name at the bottom of the chart, then returned his attention to Sara.

Janelle stepped forward and addressed her employer. "As I mentioned on the telephone, Miss Werner had several seizures."

"That's right," Dr. Reid said. "And in order to ascertain the cause of death, I would like to have an autopsy performed."

"An autopsy? Is that really necessary?" Sara stripped off her soft kid gloves, revealing a blaze of diamonds on each hand. "I do not want Cordelia cut up and examined. What a horrible thought."

Janelle stared at Sara in surprise, taken aback by this sudden tone of concern for a sister she rarely even spoke to.

"There should be an autopsy, Mrs. Johnson," Dr. Reid began. "There is a question about the medication that was given to Miss Werner shortly before the first convulsion. It's a new sedative, and I want to determine if—"

"Medication? What was wrong with Cordelia's medication?" Sara shifted her focus to Janelle, her fleshy face quivering as she spoke. "What happened? You didn't say anything about Cordelia's medication."

The fierce pounding of Janelle's heart brought on a wave of nausea. She clutched her purse to her chest and swallowed hard to suppress the fright rising from her stomach. "There was a misunderstanding . . ." she said, her words a mere whisper. She felt hot, trapped, shrinking under the penetrating glare of everyone in the cubicle. She tugged in agitation at her stiff white collar.

"What kind of misunderstanding?" Sara's chin rose two inches with the question.

"Flora thought the dosage was four pills."

"Flora?" Sara threw back her head with such force that her gold and sapphire earrings swayed rhythmically. "Flora! What could she possibly have to do with my sister's death?"

The back of Janelle's throat felt like sandpaper. Her words lay caught behind her lips.

"Answer me! What does that simpering cousin of mine have to do with any of this?"

Opening her mouth, Janelle let her explanation tumble out.

Sara put her hands on her hips and squared her shoulders. The front of her mink coat fell open to reveal a red silk suit. "You and I had better have a private talk," she said through clenched teeth. After raising an eyebrow at Dr. Reid, Sara stepped out into the hall. Janelle took a deep breath and followed the woman across the hall to an empty cubicle.

Sara Johnson was flushed as red as her vibrant silk suit from her thick neck to the severe widow's peak at her hairline. The door swung shut. Janelle waited.

"I know exactly what is going on here, Miss Roy." She crushed her expensive gloves between her fingers. "I won't let you take advantage of Flora and blame her for your mishandling of Cordelia's care."

"I am not trying to blame Flora for anything," Janelle said. "She gave Miss Werner twice the prescribed dosage of her medication. It's the truth. Ask her."

"And where were you?"

"I was off duty. The medication arrived well after my shift."

"*You,* Miss Roy, should have stayed to instruct Flora on the proper way to administer the medication. By leaving, you did not discharge your duties in a professional manner, and you are *not* going to drag Flora into this little scheme you are attempting to perpetrate on my family."

A quiver of fear shimmered over Janelle. The entire episode was twisting out of control. "Scheme? What are you talking about?" She gritted her teeth, determined to keep her voice steady.

"It's your word against Flora's, Miss Roy. Are you foolish enough to believe you can get away with this?"

"Don't you dare imply that I deliberately did anything to harm Miss Werner." Janelle cringed to hear herself threaten Sara Johnson. "You cannot prove anything. Flora has been administering your sister's medication at night for years. We discussed the situation. You knew it!"

"Such a cowardly thing to do," Sara said, blatantly ignoring Janelle's argument. "To cast blame on Flora! That's despicable." Sara's face shifted into an exaggerated mask of disgust.

"Mrs. Johnson, there has been a grave misunderstanding. Flora and I both spoke with you about the need for a night nurse. You said, 'How difficult can it be to give an old woman a few pills?' Those were your words. Exactly."

"I *never* said anything like that!" Sara raised her hand as if to slap Janelle but seemed to think better of it and dropped her arm. Stepping closer, she hunched down as if to position herself for an assault. "Let's get a few things straight, missy. I know all about how you maneuvered yourself into good graces with Cordelia. Flora told me that Cordelia had been mumbling about putting you in her will. But let me assure you, you will not inherit a dime."

"I know nothing about that!" Janelle cried. "Miss Werner never discussed her personal affairs with me."

"Just a phone call to Cordelia's attorney. That's all it will take to erase my sister's unfortunate lapse of good sense and expose your dirty little plot."

Paralyzed by Sara's accusation, Janelle froze at the words. Her fingers flew to her mouth, and she pressed hard to keep from saying something she'd regret. Resentment bubbled up and nearly choked her, but she knew better than to utter the words that crowded her mind.

"I should never have hired you," Sara went on. "If Betty Cincinara hadn't recommended you, I'd have never brought you into my sister's home." The flame of anger in her eyes grew more intense.

"I did nothing to harm her," Janelle protested.

"Well, we'll let the authorities determine that," Sara said. "Because of your greedy maneuverings, Flora and I must suffer through the humiliation of another public investigation. Reporters will be hounding me. There will be delay in settling Cordelia's estate!" Sara's voice rose higher with each word.

Janelle heard Dr. Reid clear his throat loudly before entering the cubicle.

Sara did not let Dr. Reid's presence stop her. "You are the cause of this dreadful situation. . . . You!" Her ringed fingers pointed straight at Janelle.

"Be careful," Dr. Reid warned. "If you are making a formal charge of misconduct against Miss Roy, such a charge is not based on my findings. Only an autopsy will determine the truth."

"I don't need to wait for the results of an autopsy to keep this nurse from doing harm to other innocent families. She'll never work again in Columbus. Or in the state of Ohio, if I can help it." Sara yanked her coat fully at the throat, clutching the soft fur with a plump fist.

Janelle appealed to Dr. Reid. "How soon will the autopsy report be completed?"

"In a matter of days, I suspect. No more than a week."

"Good," Janelle said curtly. "I want the record perfectly

clear." Moving toward the door, she shook out her damp, wrinkled raincoat and locked eyes with Sara Johnson. "I'm not afraid of the truth, Mrs. Johnson. And I'm not afraid of you."

CHAPTER
THREE

The sound of water draining through the upstairs pipes alerted Perry that his mother was up. As Alice Roy's muffled footsteps thudded above his head, Perry began to feel uneasy, dreading the gentle yet firm reproach he knew she'd bring downstairs.

Perry always chafed under the unnerving way his mother chastised him with only the tone of her voice. Her subtle reprimands stayed with him for hours, even days, eating at him, making him wish she would come right out and yell or curse, venting whatever was bothering her. His mother's gentle approach was effective; Perry could not recall her ever raising her voice to him, or anyone else, for that matter.

Instead of going down into the basement to put more coal in the furnace, Perry lit the gas oven and left the door slightly ajar. Waiting for the room to warm, he cut himself a slice of cold apple pie, then sat at the table again, listening to his mother's feet tapping the uncarpeted steps as she headed down the stairs. The screen door whined when she opened it to retrieve the morning paper.

When the kitchen door moved, Perry pushed himself upright, turning to face his mother, noticing that her flowered housedress, crisply starched and pressed, fitted her slim figure like a uniform. The finger-waved hairdo she had recently adopted certainly made her look younger than forty-five.

"Good morning," Alice said, shaking a light covering of snow from the paper, spreading it out on the table. She went to the refrigerator and took out a carton of milk.

"Mornin'," Perry replied, leaning over to read the headline of the morning edition of the Columbus *Dispatch*: NAVY DISCLOSES MORE DETAILS OF PEARL HARBOR ATTACK.

An unexpected sadness surged up as Perry scanned the page. Eight battleships, ten other warcraft sunk or damaged. The USS *Arizona* a complete loss. More than two thousand officers and enlisted men killed. It seemed as if it had happened just yesterday, not a little more than a year ago.

The sobering captions leaped from the paper, drawing Perry into the full page of testimonial pictures that had never been published before: fighter planes lying on the flaming airfield, their propellers twisted, bellies split open like discarded rubber toys; billowing clouds of jet black smoke rising from capsized battleships that were crippled and sinking, their majestic bows aflame.

Perry used to think the war was so far away that America would never get involved. It had had no personal connection to him. But since the bombing of Pearl Harbor, and his cousin Frank's enlistment, he sensed his draft notice would show up any day.

"I'm glad you're still here," Alice Roy said, settling in at the end of the table, the only place in the kitchen Perry had ever seen his mother sit. Now no one sat opposite her, in the seat that had been his father's. At times Perry could still smell the pot roast and gravy that had been on the table the day his father collapsed and died, the stroke taking him quickly, propelling the family into a crisis that still simmered within the house. Perry remembered that it had taken his mother and Janelle three days to clear the table.

"We need to talk, Perry," Alice said in the tone he had heard her use with her piano students who never practiced.

Perry swallowed, licked his lips, and nervously fingered one of the pieces of paper on the table. "About what?" He acted as if he were genuinely in the dark.

"About the strain between you and Janelle." Alice went to the stove and poured herself a cup of coffee, which she laced with milk. "You've got to try to see things from your sister's perspective. She wasn't criticizing yesterday. She's worried. I am, too. It's time you got over your daddy's death—"

"I don't want to talk about it, Mom." Perry cut her off, knowing he was being extremely rude, not caring if he hurt her feelings. The slow burn of her disapproving frown heated his back as he lowered his head to spear a piece of pie with his fork. He stiffened when his mother returned to her seat and picked up one of his flyers.

Alice let her eyes flit over the notice. To her, it looked like all the others Perry had been passing around town for months. He reached up and took the handbill from her.

"Lantree's hiring again. A three-day open call." He changed the subject as he picked up his steaming mug. "Did you read what the president of Lantree said?"

Alice shook her head. "I was at your aunt Dedee's all day yesterday, helping her get Frank ready to leave."

"On the front page, Mom. Big as life." Perry reached into the battered leather satchel that had belonged to his father and pulled out a crumpled copy of yesterday's paper. "Listen . . . 'Lantree Aviation has been awarded a defense contact for 57 new AT-6's. The president, Howard Long, urges all skilled welders, draftsmen, and machinists to come to the main gate or post their qualifications on the board in the interviewing room. However, he cautioned that Negroes need not apply, for no unskilled positions are available.' "

Perry slammed the paper down to the table so hard his coffee splashed onto the shiny Formica surface. "No unskilled jobs! What the hell does *that* mean? Does Howard Long think all colored people are janitors? My God! How can he hope to get away with this?"

Placing a folded napkin to the spill, Alice pursed her lips and nodded. "I know. I know. The government needs to put pressure on that plant."

"The government?" Perry shot back. "If the federal government cared about the situation at Lantree, it would never have awarded them that contract!"

"You going over there?" Alice asked, her eyes drawn back to the flyer. Before Perry could answer, she added, "Is Reverend Crossley going?"

"Yep," Perry muttered, now gulping his cooled coffee. "Along with some people from First Church. We'll have more whites than ever joining us this time. The NAACP, the Urban League, and the Negro Committee on Defense are sending representatives, too." He began gathering up his papers. "I'm gonna be at the head of the line."

"What time is all this starting?" Alice asked in a distracted tone, putting aside the flyer, now casually perusing the full-page ad for Lazarus's January white sale.

Perry watched his mother trying to act uninterested, as if she didn't really want to know about his activities, and that awful sinking feeling he always got when he disappointed her began to gather strength.

"Seven o'clock," Perry answered. "And I'm already late." He shoved the protest notices into his satchel, anxious to escape the house. After pulling on his heavy wool coat, he stood. "Gotta go." With a flourish, he flipped a green-and-brown-plaid muffler around his neck.

"Be careful," Alice said, not lifting her eyes from the advertisement.

"I will." He hesitated, then awkwardly bent down and brushed his lips across his mother's forehead. "You worry too much, Mom."

Alice looked up in surprise, locking eyes with her son for the first time that morning. She reached over and put a restraining hand on Perry's arm. "I mean it, Perry. All this rabble-rousing. Such carrying-on. It's dangerous." She pressed her fingers into the rough wool of his coat. "Why don't you put in your application at Swift today? I heard they're hiring colored."

Perry pulled away from his mother. "I'll *never* work at Swift. I'm not going to stand around in cow manure and pig guts all day for sixty cents an hour." *Here it is,* he thought. *Here comes that goddamn lecture about getting a job.* He frowned deeply and turned away.

"Sixty cents an hour is better than nothing, son."

Her placid, even-tempered reprimand cut to the core of Perry's resentment. "You sound just like Janelle!" His words, biting and sharp, sliced the air. "You know what? I'm getting sick and tired of Janelle's attitude. Always digging at me. I know what she thinks and what she says to you when I'm not here." A fullness came to his cheeks as he swung around and glowered down at his mother. "She thinks she knows everything. Miss Perfect . . . just because she got a full scholarship to nursing school . . . and that cushy private job. She's sure livin' in a dream world. Buttering up to those society types who wouldn't even speak to her on the street. Without that uniform she's no better'n any other colored girl walking around Columbus."

"Watch your mouth," Alice admonished him, her tone stern, her voice low. "Janelle works hard and loves her work. Without her salary you know we would be out on the street, the family torn apart. Be thankful your sister got an education."

"Well, I'll *get* a job," Perry stated with conviction. "Soon. And it will be a good one, paying at least sixty-five a week." He grinned, flashing two perfect dimples at his mother. "If I can get a job in a defense plant, I'll be deferred."

"Don't wait too long, son. Your name'll be coming up soon." She looked away, then back. "It would have been nice if you had come to see Frank off yesterday. Your aunt Dedee had a hard time. She asked about you."

Perry's face fell with shame, but he took a deep breath and tried to make light of it. "Well, it was Frank's choice, Mom. He enlisted, remember."

"But it was only a matter of time before he'd have been notified."

"So? It was still Frank's decision." Perry put his hand on the doorknob and looked back at his mother. "I'd never

volunteer to fight in this white man's war, and I'm not going anywhere unless I'm drafted. Maybe not even then."
Hunching down against the blast of cold wind that rushed
into the kitchen, Perry turned up his collar and left.

Alice sat staring after her son. What the devil did Perry
mean—not serve? If he hadn't dropped out of that mechanical drafting course at Ohio State that she had paid
$127 for, he just might be in a position to get a job at
Lantree. With no training and only a high school diploma,
how in the world did he plan to get an industry deferral?
Pipe dreams. Stupid pipe dreams. And he had the nerve to
criticize Janelle.

In frustration, Alice balled up the newspaper and pushed
it across the table. Sure, it would be hard to let her only
son go off to war, but his father had served in World War
I—as a field cook, but at least he had served. His honorable discharge, framed in smooth ebony, was hanging in
the living room above the piano. Not serve! Garret Roy
must be twisting with shame in his grave to hear such
words coming from his son's mouth.

Alice shivered, reaching forward to pull the oven door
fully open, letting hot air sweep across the kitchen. She'd
have to go down in the basement and add coal to the furnace herself.

The bright orange bus ground to a halt at the side of the
road, stopping directly across from Lantree Aviation. Perry
looked out the window, scanning the crush of hopeful job
seekers for at least one dark face. None. He scribbled his
observations in his black leather notebook, then shoved it
under his jacket. "You're on, Counselor," he said, nudging
the slightly built white man at his side.

Dalton Graham removed his tan felt hat, stooping as he
made his way to the front of the bus.

He flipped back a shock of coal black hair hanging over
one blue-gray eye, removed his horn-rimmed glasses, and
wiped them. The women in the crowded bus sat up

straighter, adjusted their hats and scarves, eager to hear what he had to say.

Perry grinned, knowing Dalton, who could be coldly calculating in the courtroom, reveled in the attention of women. All kinds of women. Whether he was out on the road at a picket line or in a church basement planning protest strategies, Dalton's elegant manners and passionate, principled intelligence seemed to win over people of both sexes, black and white. Scooting down in his seat, Perry propped his feet against the footrail, leaning back to listen to Dalton.

"I want to thank Reverend Thaddeus Crossley and Perry Roy for organizing Protest for Jobs. My name is Dalton Graham. I am an attorney with the legal department of the National Association for the Advancement of Colored People, and I am happy to be here to represent the NAACP. We want to support your efforts in every possible way."

Dalton resettled his glasses on his nose and shoved his hands into the leather-edged pockets of his brown trench coat before continuing.

"The NAACP has vowed to keep the pressure on facilities like Lantree until all doors are open for equal employment. As most of you know, last June President Roosevelt issued Executive Order eight-eight-oh-two and authorized the Fair Employment Practices Committee, the FEPC, to end discrimination in defense industries."

Muffled applause rose from the group.

"And what good has it done?" Perry prompted, wanting Dalton to be the one to clarify the situation.

Dalton stretched both hands forward, palms facing the protesters as he waited for the noise to subside. "On the surface, I know it sounds encouraging, doesn't it? Unfortunately some plants, like Lantree, refuse to comply. This facility employs six thousand workers. Not one of them is colored."

The people began to murmur under their breaths.

Dalton went on. "We are here to bring publicity to

Lantree's blatant disregard for the law. We will force the federal government to take punitive action against this plant. Doors must be open to all qualified applicants."

"All right."

"Amen!"

"That's what we're here for."

The rickety bus vibrated with expressions of enthusiastic agreement. Placards on long wooden sticks swayed with a barrage of protest messages. Dalton remained at the helm of the assembly, silently nodding in approval. When the roar settled down, he continued.

"Many thanks to Perry Roy for making the placards and for distributing the flyers that brought you all out. Taking on Howard Long, the president of Lantree, is a bold move, and Protest for Jobs is fast becoming synonymous with the struggle for fair employment. This is my second time working with Perry, and let me tell you, his courage has not gone unnoticed. You should be proud to have him leading your fight for jobs in the defense industry."

At these words Perry grinned, half rising from his seat. Applause and shouts of approval burst out.

"Now," Dalton went on, "I believe Perry is going to give you instructions about what to do—and what not to do. Please pay attention. It is very important that we conduct ourselves in a manner that is legal and proper." Dalton signaled for Perry to come forward, then took his seat and joined in the dull clapping of gloved hands to welcome their leader.

"Okay. Okay." Perry calmed the group. "Listen up! There are close to a hundred people already in line out there, and it's only—" He looked down at his watch. The darn thing had stopped again. Cursing under his breath, he shouted, "What time is it?"

"Nine o'clock."

"Thanks. Well, by noon this crowd will more than triple. Lantree expects two thousand applicants over the next three days. We must be careful. Do not strike back if you are pushed, shoved, jeered . . . anything. We didn't come here to start a riot. We're here because we need jobs, and we're going to protest Howard Long's statement that Negroes need not apply for positions at Lantree Aviation." He waited for a moment, gauging the effect of his words. If any hotheads had come out, spoiling for a fight, they might just as well go on back home. "All right. Let's count off."

The men and women enthusiastically called out their numbers.

"Okay," Perry shouted. "Odd numbers, stay on the bus. Even numbers, march for thirty minutes. It's too cold for us to last the day if we all go out at the same time." Murmurs of agreement filtered through the crowd.

"Most important! When you start marching, stay at least ten feet from the gates!" Perry shouted. "Reverend Crossley's group will cover the south entrance. My group will stay here in front." He stopped talking to assess his supporters.

Housewives and laborers. Students and clerks. Veterans and teachers. Clutching their homemade placards, eyes glittering with hope, they were anxious to get on with the march. Even Mr. Perez, the deaf Puerto Rican gardener who tended the grounds at First Church, smiled broadly and nodded as if he had heard Perry's words.

"Any questions?" Steamy silence hung over the bus. The odor of damp wool and mothballs drifted up to Perry. He snapped his fingers, signaling the bus driver to open the door. He boldly stepped out first.

Catcalls and boos shot out of the crowd at the gate. One man stepped from the group that was milling around the main gate and threw an ice ball at Perry. He ducked and kept on walking.

"Clear out of here! Troublemakers!" An angry voice pierced the frozen air.

"Ain't no jobs here for colored. Go on back where you came from!"

Perry ignored the remarks, falling in beside Dalton Graham to make his way toward the high chain-link fence surrounding Lantree Aviation. Twenty-five protesters, bundled against the freezing temperature, fiercely clutching their placards, followed him in sober resolve. Another group of twenty-five trailed behind their clergyman leader, heading toward the entrance on the south side of the sprawling plant that looked like a military compound.

Perry came to an abrupt halt and turned to address his group. "Remember. No shouting. No talking. No crossing this line." Using the stick holding his sign, he carved a deep furrow in the snow. "If you cross this line, you can be arrested. If you are arrested, Protest for Jobs has no funds to get you out. You're on your own."

Several in the group raised their eyebrows, shrugged their shoulders, then lifted their signs even higher.

"Let's go!" Perry shouted, taking his place at the head of the line. Inhaling deeply, he lifted his chin, pulled his muffler more snugly around his neck, and began circling the area in silence. As the others fell in behind him, the crunch of footsteps grinding the frozen ground was the only sound filling the air.

CHAPTER FOUR

"You practice that piece," Alice called out to the pudgy girl standing on her snow-covered porch. "When you come back next week, I want you to play it from memory. From memory, you hear?"

Peggy Lee Dawson stuck out her bottom lip, clumsily rolling her practice book into an uneven tube before stuffing it into her coat pocket. "It's too hard, Mrs. Roy. Couldn't I play something else for the recital?"

"No." Alice held firm. "That's the piece you are going to play." She forced a smile, then began to ease her door shut. She wasn't about to stand there negotiating with a ten-year-old, letting all the warm air out of her house. "Just practice, Peggy Lee. You'll do fine." Alice pushed the door shut with a thud.

She stepped back into the hallway and peeked through the window, watching her student, nose wrinkled, start off down the steps. Exasperated, Alice sighed. She had given the girl the easiest piece in the beginners' book, and the recital wasn't until March. As much as she liked teaching piano, there were days when Alice just didn't feel like being bothered. At least today there would be only two more classes.

Reentering the front room, Alice noticed that water had leaked through the window again, adding fresh watermarks to the network of brown stains running the length of her beige jacquard drapes. She'd get Perry to push the red plush sofa and matching armchair up to the window to help make the room more presentable. No use even thinking about repairing the splintered frame.

At the piano Alice cleared away the primary books, preparing for her next student. The assemblage of framed photos sitting atop her Hackley upright always comforted her. She and Garrett on their honeymoon in Harlem. Janelle in full nurse's uniform on the day of her graduation. Perry standing with Frank and Dedee in Franklin Park. Her family. If only Garrett were still alive.

Alice picked up his photo and studied his face. Not a particularly handsome man, she admitted. But sitting proudly at his workstation, the seal of Ohio centered directly above his head, one arm resting atop his cluttered desk, he struck a pose of serious importance. Some people had called Garrett Roy arrogant, but Alice never used that word. Dignified. That's how she always described her late husband. Dignified, demanding respect.

She missed him terribly, often dreaming of him two or three nights a week, waking to find herself flooded with memories of the difficult side of the man she had married. For Alice, it was troubling to have unwanted memories of the early years of her marriage seep out from the past now that he was gone. As a new bride Alice had chafed under her husband's expansive, domineering presence, until she resigned herself to the way things were going to be.

Life in the Roy household always centered on Garrett, his desires, his displeasures, his ambitions. He came and went as he pleased, often disappearing for days at a time. Business, he told Alice, business she couldn't possibly understand. He had not believed a wife should work and had prohibited Alice from doing anything more than give piano lessons. She believed he allowed her to do so in order to show everyone what a cultured woman he had married.

He liked to brag about Alice's musical talent and boast that his children were not only handsome but smart, convincing himself that what strangers thought of his family made him who he was. Fortunately Alice cared little about what passed through others' minds, finding satisfaction in her music, in keeping control over one little piece of her life, and in raising her beautiful children. She even got to keep the money she earned, though it was never much, five dollars a week at most. Now time had finally begun to erode the solid image of her husband she had worked so hard to create.

Garrett Roy's job as a city health inspector had shaped his sense of self-importance. He had gone about his duties, enforcing city health codes, entering restaurants, private clubs, and the best hotels in town, demanding and getting respect. He had had access to people and places few Negroes ever hoped to get, and he had relished entertaining his friends and family with vivid stories about his experiences. A high point for Garrett had come quite unexpectedly when the mayor of Columbus had visited his home.

During the city-wide elections of 1928, Garrett had done his part, walking the streets and the alleys from Champion to Taylor, registering people to vote.

The mayor, after campaigning heavily all over the city, had ended his tour on the east side of town. There he had made it a point to seek out the Roy family. He had stayed for dinner, eating meat loaf with macaroni and cheese while graciously chatting with anyone who stopped by to shake his hand. Janelle, especially, had been very impressed.

Alice knew that Janelle had told her third-grade classmates at Mount Vernon Elementary School that her father was a good friend of the mayor's and that she had a personal invitation to visit His Honor at City Hall.

Her brash announcement had elicited skeptical remarks; everyone at Mount Vernon believed that Janelle and Perry deliberately exaggerated their father's importance. But when she took that autographed photo to school, her classmates were surprised and envious.

Alice picked up the picture taken so long ago. There was Janelle, standing beside the mayor, his hand resting lightly on her shoulder, the state flag unfurled behind them. In her red and white dress with the big sailor collar, Janelle looked like a soldier snapped to attention. Her long brown pigtails, usually hanging down her back, had been gathered into a regal crown of braids, threaded with taffeta ribbon, arranged across the top of her small, round head. Janelle's dark eyes sparkled as if sprinkled with fairy dust. It didn't surprise Alice that the haughty pride radiating from her little girl was a younger, female version of Garrett Roy's expression.

Alice knew the experience had changed her daughter. The next day Janelle had told her of the privileges being extended to her in school. She got extra time in the closet-size library, was often excused from doing the dreaded jumping jacks and deep knee bends required in physical education class, and began to ferry messages and materials between teachers and classrooms at the request of the principal herself.

As the years passed, Alice had watched Janelle fall under Garrett's influence, and she cringed every time she saw her child mimic his airs of superiority. Janelle had taken her father's words of encouragement to heart, struggling to please him by rising above her classmates. His loving praise had fueled Janelle's high opinion of herself while strengthening her desire to live and work in the white world—the world her father brushed shoulders with in his job.

As Alice set Garrett's photo down, she felt a rustle of worry stirring her soul. It didn't seem right that her daughter spent so much time talking about a way of life beyond her reach. *Just like Garrett,* Alice thought, blowing a film of gray dust off the top of the piano, shuffling the picture frames around to pull Janelle's toward the front.

The unexpected sound of a key in the lock startled her. Gripping the piano, she leaned over and peered into the hallway.

"Janelle!" Alice was shocked by her daughter's disheveled, rainsoaked appearance. "What are you doing home in the middle of the morning? and what happened to your coat? Your shoes?"

Janelle let the weight of her body close the door as she slumped against it. Water dripped from her mud-splattered coat, across the floral carpet. Tilting her head back against the doorframe, she pushed matted locks from her forehead, staring at the ceiling.

"What's wrong?" Alice asked.

"Cordelia Werner died this morning."

Alice felt her breath catch in her throat but did not panic. Saying nothing, she reached over to help Janelle out of her coat. "Come on back to the kitchen," she said, putting a comforting arm around Janelle. "Tell me what happened."

As Alice sat across from Janelle at the kitchen table, listening to everything that had transpired that morning, she knew it was time to speak her mind.

"Well, it's very hard for me to say this," she said, "but I think you would be better off working at St. Anthony or Belton Park. This notion you've got in your head about making a lot of money doing private-duty work isn't worth the complications that come with it." She hated the damper she knew she was putting on her daughter's dreams but felt too strongly about it to keep quiet now. "Money isn't everything, you know."

"Right now it is to me!" Janelle said. "I don't want to live like this forever."

"Like this?" Alice tensed, girding herself to hear what was on Janelle's mind.

"Face it, Mom. This house is about to fall down around us. Sure, we're managing, but how long can we hold things together? The front windows are about rotted out. The plumbing in the bathroom is shot, and now there's a leak in the ceiling in Perry's room."

"You think I don't know that?" Alice's voice was level as she watched her daughter pull the mesh snood off her hair, letting it fall loosely over her shoulders.

Janelle began toweling her damp hair as she went on. "I

need a car. The buses don't run out to the areas where I can get work, and taxis are getting too expensive."

"All in time, Janelle. But you must think seriously about what I said. Private-duty work puts you inside white folks' personal business. In their houses. In their lives. You set yourself up for whatever they want to do to you. It is not worth it. We can manage just fine with less."

Janelle bit her lip, then nodded, murmuring, "But I don't want to, Mom. You know what I mean?"

Alice pressed her palm over her daughter's cool fingers. "Yes. I know what you mean. And if there was anything I could do to make things different, I would." Alice hated to see tears easing from beneath Janelle's lowered lashes. "You're a good nurse. You graduated at the top of your class, even got a special citation as the outstanding student nurse in your class. You worked hard for that, and Sara Johnson can't take it from you."

Janelle laid the towel on the table and began pacing the tiny kitchen, her heavy brown hair swinging with each step.

"I think I'm going to need an attorney, Mom. The things Sara Johnson said can ruin me."

"Sounds like it," Alice agreed.

"I wasn't negligent in my duties."

"I know you weren't . . . you're right. You better get a lawyer." Alice checked the kitchen clock. Her next student was due in five minutes. She flipped through the pages of the green lesson book she had absently brought to the kitchen, trying to remember where Johnny Ingel was to begin. She glanced up at Janelle. "Harry Lawson might be able to help. You remember him. He's the attorney who got Dedee out of that mess when Woolworth's accused her of shoplifting."

"Lawyers from the Werner estate would eat Harry Lawson for lunch. He's small-time, Mom, and this is a serious situation. I need a good attorney. One with some clout."

"Those cost money, more than we could manage."

Absently Janelle picked up the heavy teakettle, poured

some hot water into a cup, and began slowly dunking a teabag up and down.

Money for an attorney? Alice thought dully, wondering if they even had enough to pay the water bill.

Looking over the table, she noticed one of Perry's flyers partially hidden under the newspaper. "Call your brother. He's friends with all those legal types who march and protest with him."

Janelle's glum demeanor lightened. "Yeah. That's right. The NAACP. The Urban League. The Negro Committee on Defense. They have good lawyers. Colored and white. They could advise me about what to do."

"The NAACP ought to help you. Your daddy practically founded the local office here. He worked with them to register more colored voters in 1928 than anyone had ever done before. The mayor was impressed, remember?"

Janelle nodded absently.

"Garrett spent nearly as much time working for the NAACP as he did for the city of Columbus. They'll remember." She squeezed Janelle's hand. "Your daddy's reaching out from the grave to help you now."

"Where is Perry?" Janelle asked.

"Protesting over at Lantree Aviation. The NCD put it together."

A knock at the door signaled Alice's next student. She got up and started toward the door. "Leave a message for Perry at the NCD office. He's so busy trying to change the world, maybe he can help save his sister's reputation."

CHAPTER
FIVE

The familiar sound of "Sweetheart Sonata" floated up the stairs. Janelle rinsed out the bathtub and shook out her towel, listening to child-size fingers fumbling to reach the right keys, the three-quarter tempo mutilated by stops and starts. She could see her mother now, eyes narrowed, standing above her student, the metronome ticking away. Both she and Perry had struggled through "Sweetheart Sonata," eager for their mother's nod of approval.

In her bedroom Janelle sat at her dressing table, a heavy Victorian piece she had rescued from a pile of discarded furniture left for the trash man behind the Werner mansion. After parting her damp hair, Janelle made a sleek roll across the top of her forehead and secured the pompadour with two wire pins. With an expert twist, she swept the rest of her hair toward the nape of her neck and smoothed it into a soft chignon.

The circles under Janelle's eyes contrasted sharply with her flawless tan complexion; the cruel events of early morning had left her exhausted, though it was only eleven o'clock.

Could be worse, Janelle thought, assessing her reflection, opening a tin of Cleopatra Bronze powder. She dusted her nose, then put on a little lipstick and dressed in a pair of tan gabardine slacks and a pink angora sweater. She headed down the stairs.

The telephone rang, and she grabbed it, stretching the

black cord as far as it would reach, pulling the telephone into the kitchen.

"Emma! You must be psychic! I tried to call you this morning." Janelle shoved a chair into the doorway between the hall and the kitchen and sat down.

"My God, Janelle! I heard about your patient," Emma said. "I don't have time to talk right now, but I had to let you know how sorry I am."

"Thanks," Janelle said, relieved to have Emma on the line.

"Is there anything I can do to help?"

Janelle didn't hesitate. "Yes. What do you know about a drug called Febrahyde?"

"Its new," Emma answered, "and I don't think it's in stock here at the clinic yet. That's what Miss Werner was on?"

"Yes, and I need all the information you can get on it."

"No problem." There was a pause as Emma turned from the phone to speak to a client. "Look. I've gotta go." She sounded rushed. "I work a half day tomorrow ... let's have lunch. Why don't you meet me at H. L. Green's? I'll bring the information about Febrahyde."

"Great," Janelle said. "See you about noon."

Early winter evening shadows had begun to gather at the base of the windows when Janelle began peeling potatoes for dinner, her mind far from the task at hand. What if the autopsy proved that the overdose of medication had contributed to Cordelia Werner's death? Would Flora take refuge behind her cousin Sara's power and wealth, letting Janelle take the blame for everything? Her stomach sank.

Absently wrapping the damp potato peelings in newspaper, she was startled when the door burst open and Perry entered, the sting of frigid air sweeping in behind him.

"What's up?" he asked before he even said hello. "I got a message that you called." He gave Janelle an odd look. "What are you doing fixing dinner? Mom sick or something?"

Janelle wrinkled her nose at her brother. True, she seldom had the time or the energy to do much cooking, but she certainly knew her way around the kitchen.

"No. She went over to Samuel's. Settling the bill." Janelle lifted a heavy iron kettle from the stove and began to fill it with water. Her mind seemed cloudy, crammed with mixed emotions. So much had changed since that early-morning phone call interrupted her conversation with Perry.

"Any job prospects?" She tried to sound genuinely hopeful.

"Could be." His words were clipped with confidence. "I think I'm gonna get an interview at Lantree. Probably tomorrow." He pulled off his gloves and threw them on the table. "If I get on at Lantree, I'll be deferred. Then I can stay here and keep on working for the NCD." He rubbed his hands together as if the deal were done.

"Sounds good," Janelle said, perplexed by her brother's political activism. It all seemed hopelessly tiring and boring to her, and she doubted Perry's efforts would make a bit of difference in the way men like Howard Long ran their companies.

"I hope you get a real job soon, Perry." She paused and gave him an even look. "Because as of today I'm unemployed, too." She watched him closely, trying to assess his reaction. Was it fear or surprise that flickered over his face?

"What are you talking about?" Perry thrust the words suspiciously at his sister, stepping slightly away from her as if he didn't particularly want to hear her explanation.

"My patient died today," Janelle said in a calm, unemotional voice.

"Well, I don't want to sound cruel, but so what? I mean, you'll get another position, won't you?"

"Maybe. Maybe not. Everything hinges on the autopsy."

"Jeez. Sounds serious."

"It is. I've been accused of mishandling my patient's care. I'm going to need a lawyer. A good one."

Perry threw one leg over the back of the blue vinyl chair and sat down. "I know a couple of lawyers who might be able to help." He reached inside his coat and pulled out a pack of Lucky Strike. "You didn't do anything wrong, did you?" he asked, shaking out a cigarette, cocking his head to one side.

"No. Nothing."

"Good." Perry shrugged off his coat and sat back. "Didn't I warn you about believing that those rich white people really care about you?"

Determined not to get into another argument, Janelle just shoved the bundled potato peelings into the garbage can. "I don't need a lecture, Perry. I need a lawyer."

"Okay, I get the picture. Too bad you got yourself mixed up in this one, Janelle." He went on, lighting his cigarette, blowing smoke toward the ceiling. "Why don't you work at Belton? Or St. Anthony. It's right around the corner. They don't have enough nurses over there to keep the free clinic open a full day." He shook his head. "You oughta leave those snooty society types alone. Take care of your own people. That's what Dad would have wanted you to do!"

Janelle's eyes widened in amazement. "How can you say that? All Dad wanted was for me to make a living. A good living. My money is holding this family together." Infuriated, stung by Perry's criticism, she felt herself trembling. "And if you want to talk about what Dad wanted . . . what he *really* wanted was for you to finish drafting school!" As soon as the words tumbled out, she regretted them.

Perry's face went blank, the slap of truth bringing him up short. He stared questioningly at Janelle.

Feeling the wounds open up, the tenuous balance of their shared grief tipping sadly, she murmured, "I'm sorry."

"I *will* go back to school," Perry said flatly, blinking to disguise his pain. "Maybe later. Not right now."

Janelle opened the refrigerator and took out a box of

oleo. She dumped the snow white lump into a bowl, broke the small vial of yellow coloring over it, and began smashing away at the lumpy mass with a potato masher. With each thrust, her irritation grew. The oleo, folded and whipped, began to take on the appearance of butter.

Perry rubbed his index finger along the bridge of his nose. "Janelle, I know I've been hell to live with this past year, but you know, it's been tough." He opened his mouth as if to say more, then stopped, clamping his jaw shut. "I'll do what I can to help out."

The contrite expression that swept over his face instantly calmed Janelle.

"But don't press me about going back to school," he added. "I can't do it. Not now, but I will."

"I believe you, Perry," Janelle said. "I guess I'm tired . . . and, I have to admit, a little frightened. There's a lot of pressure on me to make sure everything around here gets taken care of." Her voice quivered with nervous exhaustion. "But I can't be responsible for everyone! I can't!"

Perry's words slipped out, low and halting. "I want to work, Janelle, I do. But I don't want to work in a packing plant or down in a limestone quarry. You know? I have pride, dreams, too. I want to do work that has meaning."

"I *do* understand." Janelle reached over to touch Perry's arm. "You want to be respected. Important, like Dad. Organizing and leading things, that's what you want. But it may not be in the cards, Perry. Not yet. With me out of work, you can't be choosy." She stopped stirring the yellow cream and scraped it off the masher with a knife.

Dismayed, she watched Perry's jaw tense as tears brimmed in his eyes, then rolled down his cheeks. She was shocked. She had never seen him cry, not even when he was little. He would whimper and whine but never shed tears. As far as she knew, Perry hadn't cried when they buried their father. If he had, he had done it in isolation.

"Perry," Janelle nearly whispered, her face flushing with shame and regret, "I'm sorry I yelled at you yesterday, but your pain is no greater than mine, or Mom's, or Aunt Dedee's. You isolate yourself, making up excuses to avoid anything you don't want to deal with." She swallowed the bitter taste that filled her mouth and plunged ahead. "You really should have come to Union Station last night."

Lifting one shoulder, Perry expressed his indifference.

Courage gathered on the tip of Janelle's tongue. "Mom, Aunt Dedee ... and especially Frank were disappointed you didn't make the effort to be there."

Perry shifted, turning his handsome profile to his sister, the veins in his neck visibly pulsing.

"Aunt Dedee held up well," Janelle went on, growing annoyed by Perry's sullen silence. "But she was hurt that you didn't come to see Frank off. It was important for her, you know?"

Now Perry's feet thudded to the floor. "So, what's the big deal?" His voice had a hard, raw edge. "Frank *chose* to go into the Navy! He wasn't drafted. Why is everyone acting like he's been sent to federal prison?"

Exasperated, Janelle threw the metal masher into the sink. "Frank is our cousin. Our father's sister's only child. You two are as close as brothers. How in the world could you *not* see him off?" Her eyes widened in challenge. "He may not come back for God's sake! Anything could happen to him."

"Frank didn't need me at the station," Perry managed to say. His full lower lip quivered and turned downward in a contorted attempt to gain control.

To Janelle, he looked like a miserable ten-year-old boy, and her anger began to lessen. "Oh, yes, he did, Perry." Her words slipped out in soft rebuttal. "Frank needed you to tell him good-bye."

"Why? He knows how I feel. I *didn't* need to be there."

"Don't you see how you hurt Mom and especially Aunt Dedee? You always want things your way. Don't you ever think of anyone but yourself? Our family is small. We need to stay close."

"Well, I'm sorry I disappointed everyone," Perry replied. "Don't act ignorant, Janelle. You know exactly why I couldn't go." The control he had so fragilely maintained dissolved and fell away, leaving his misery and confusion starkly exposed. "I'd never let Frank see me cry."

"Life doesn't work that way," Janelle said. "You've got to pull out of this slump, Perry, and get a grip on yourself."

The apprehension on Perry's face told Janelle her words were hitting home.

"I miss Frank. And Dad," Perry muttered, pressing his eyes shut. "It was all too fast. . . . Sometimes I imagine Dad will walk through the back door and start hollering for us to come into the kitchen."

"With a sack of hamburgers from Bobby-Joe's under his arm?" Janelle said, her face softening at the memory.

"Yeah. Remember how big those things were?" Perry smiled. "I never could believe Dad could eat three of them at a sitting." He looked up at the ceiling, holding on to the memory. "It's not right, him being gone. Without him, how can anything get back to normal?"

"This *is* normal, Perry." Janelle bluntly planted the words in front of her brother. "You think I've forgotten how close you two were? How many times you cruised Lake Erie in that old half-rotten boat and stayed overnight in Blendon Woods hunting rabbits and pheasants and ducks? All the baseball games at Red Bird Stadium?" She reached out and touched Perry's arm. "I miss Daddy as much as you do. But things have changed. And they'll never be the same. You've got to put the past behind you and move on."

"That's easy for you to say! You just put Dad out of your mind and went back to nursing that white lady who treated you more like a slave than a nurse. You acted just like a robot . . . as if you had no heart at all. You are cold, Janelle, really cold." Perry put the dark blue wool of his sleeve to his face and wiped his cheeks roughly.

Deliberately turning her back on her brother, Janelle fiddled with a stained heart-shaped potholder she had carefully hand sewn for her mother in fifth grade.

"No, I'm not cold." Janelle turned back to face Perry. "It's called accepting reality. Believe it, Perry. Our family as we knew it is gone! Daddy's dead. Cousin Frank is on a ship in the Pacific and may never come home. And we're left here. We've got to carry on."

"Yeah," Perry whispered, pulling a long breath into his lungs. "I know."

Freezing rain pummeled the kitchen windows, and Janelle worried absently that her mother had not taken her umbrella.

"Can you help me?" she asked, moving off the subject that threatened to start her crying too. "Do you think I can get a lawyer from the NCD?"

"Naw, not them," Perry said, shrugging tension from his shoulders. "They don't have the clout. The NAACP has the man you need." He reached into his satchel, pulled out a piece of paper, and began scribbling. "Here. Call this number. Ask for Dalton Graham. He's about the best lawyer the NAACP has on staff. He can tell you in a minute if you've got a problem or not."

CHAPTER
SIX

It made no difference which city he was in or how many times he entered a jail, each visit to a correctional facility brought Dalton Graham a sense of pain. Believing that the majority of inmates now serving time had been given their proper day in court, he concerned himself with those who had bungled the task of holding on to their freedom, and unfortunately, wound up behind bars.

This morning Dalton threw his trench coat over his arm, picked up his bulging attaché case, secured its buckles, then spoke to the young man fidgeting nervously before him.

"If everything you told me checks out, Danny, I can file a habeas corpus tomorrow morning. You'll probably see the judge by midday." He paused, mentally calculating the time needed to move his request through the tangled legal system. "If things go smoothly, you might be out tomorrow. Late afternoon at best."

"I hope so, Mr. Graham. This is all a big mistake. I didn't have anything to do with that stolen car the police found in my driveway." Danny wiped perspiring hands on the front of his county-issue overalls and frowned. "My momma said she heard some noise in the night. Probably some guys from the Bottoms out joyriding. Got scared and dumped that car at my house. That's what happened, Mr. Graham. It happens all the time in Poindexter."

"We're checking it out, Danny. In the meantime, try to

relax. Just go along with the program here. Don't make waves. If you're innocent, I'll get you out. I promise." Dalton pushed a dark lock from his forehead and pulled on his tan felt hat, tugging the brim down over one eye. "You'd better not be lying to me, Danny. Understand?"

The frightened young man nodded vigorously. "No, sir."

"All right. I'll check with you in the morning." Dalton signaled for the guard. "Get some rest, Danny," he suggested as the iron bars swung open, then shut behind him. He hurried down the dim corridor, left the jail, and started toward the courthouse.

Walking with his head slightly bent toward the ice-covered sidewalk, Dalton fought the sharp January wind. Putting the Franklin County jail behind him, he turned north. At the corner of Fulton and High, he paused, waiting for the light to change, hoping Danny White had told him the truth.

The little punk would be sorry if he were trying to bamboozle him, Dalton thought. But something in his guts made him believe Danny's story, and Dalton Graham operated a lot on hunches, gut reaction, and hope.

At thirty-two he'd been practicing law for seven years, doggedly representing poor people, sick people, out-of-work people whose hopelessness had become second nature. Many of his clients were Negroes or immigrants caught in the web of an unfamiliar system, mired in racial and ethnic inequities that plagued a nation that was, ironically, immersed in a fight for freedom halfway around the world.

A year ago, after he had won a much-publicized case that prevented the city from taking over an elderly Negro woman's property—prime real estate near the center of town—Dalton's name had become synonymous with "champion for the underdog" and "voice of the people," tags the press quickly hung on him. When his mailbox began to overflow with pleas for his assistance, Dalton made the decision to join the legal department of the NAACP, making his commitment to civil rights official.

Dalton Graham had been born on the west side of Cleveland, and his playmates had been a Puerto Rican boy who lived across the street, a pair of West Indian twins next door, and his Polish cousins, who occupied the other side of the duplex where he and his parents lived. An only child, Dalton spent most of his time in the streets, going from one back door to another, eating huevos rancheros in one kitchen, couscous in another, or playing an intensely competitive game of mah-jongg with the Chinese laundress, Mi-Chin.

Remmy, the Gypsy fortune-teller who lived at the end of the block, used to let Dalton hide behind her smelly fringed drapes and eavesdrop on her ethereal predictions. Afterward she'd let him sit in front of her shiny crystal ball and drink her thick peach wine.

In the summer Dalton caught crawdads in the ditch behind his house and sold them for a penny apiece to the Jamaican woman three doors down, who always shared her gumbo with him.

And then there was Rickey Louis, who constantly wore boxing gloves, unless he was in school, and swore Joe Louis was his first cousin. He must have been telling the truth, because now his mother walked through the neighborhood telling the same tale, carrying an autographed picture of the Brown Bomber.

The community where Dalton grew up gave credence to the term "Melting Pot," and Dalton loved everyone in it.

His father ran a deli in the front section of the corner grocery store while his mother taught third grade at Elmer Hughes School. Growing up, Dalton never heard his parents discuss money, and there always seemed to be enough for whatever they needed, with some left over to help anyone who fell on hard times on their block. His mother even sewed and remade old clothes and distributed them through their church. The entire family had gone to Florida every summer for a two-week vacation. That's where his parents now lived.

The light changed, but Dalton didn't move. He stepped

back from the corner, fumbled in his breast pocket, then pulled out a small black notepad. Quickly he scribbled a few words as pedestrians streamed past. They jostled him, muttering under their breath as they made their way to the curb.

Dalton paid no attention, balancing his pad on his attaché case as he concentrated on jotting down his thoughts. Grinning, he flipped the notepad shut and stuffed it inside his pocket. A smirk of satisfaction touched his lips; his next case was already won.

A bus splashed by, roaring around the corner, leaving a trail of exhaust fumes in its wake. The light changed again, and Dalton joined the surge of people stepping off the curb, crossing Fulton Avenue, heading up High Street toward Mound. He glanced at the big round clock in front of Hartford Insurance. He had exactly five minutes to get to court.

PRESIDENT ROOSEVELT DECLARES THAT NOTHING LESS THAN UNCONDITIONAL SURRENDER WILL BE ACCEPTED FROM THE AXIS. Janelle scanned the front-page story, pretty sure she knew where Casablanca was but frustrated that she had only vague understandings of the other locations mentioned in the article. She'd have to drag out her high school atlas and look up Tangier, Oran, Algiers. The President's declaration meant the end of the war was not at all in sight. More men, more planes, more guns would be needed, and Janelle wondered how long it would be before Perry got his notice to appear before the local draft board.

As Janelle's eyes traveled to the bottom half of the page, the story she'd been looking for appeared: WEALTHY COLUMBUSITE DIES. The article detailing Cordelia Werner's passing ran three columns and featured her picture, an old one taken many years ago, when her hair was still blond and curly.

Janelle held the paper in trembling fingers, devouring each word. The story covered the celebrated trial of the sisters, the fortune Randolf Werner had left to his daughters, and Sara Johnson's unsuccessful lawsuit against Cordelia Werner when she tried to break the will to get the house. It listed the many charitable organizations that had benefited from Werner money over the years and included excerpts from an interview with Sara Werner Johnson in which the wealthy widow told about a new wing of the Columbus Museum that she was personally endowing.

Janelle read with trepidation, holding her breath, and when she came to a quoted remark from Sara Johnson, she gripped the paper so hard it tore in half in her hands.

Unfortunately funeral arrangements are still pending, and my sister's will has not been read, due to an unexpected complication. Her private-duty nurse, a colored girl named Janelle Roy, authorized an untrained nonmedical person to administer my sister's medication only hours before her death. A mix-up in dosage occurred, and Cordelia went into seizures. This incident has precipitated an autopsy and has caused me unbearable strain. I plan to file formal misconduct charges against Miss Roy for all the damage she has done to me and my family. Her unprofessional conduct brought this tragic set of circumstances about.

Stunned, Janelle stared in disbelief at the story. The smear campaign had started. A surge of heat rose inside, making her sick to her stomach, pushing her apprehension to a boiling sensation in the middle of her body.

Janelle threw the paper aside, took the steps two at a time, and flung her bedroom door open with such force it smashed against the wall, forcing a china vase from her dresser. It crashed to the floor and splintered.

"Janelle? That you?" Her mother's startled voice came from across the hall.

"Yes, it's me!"

The desperate edge to Janelle's words forced Alice from her bed.

Janelle grabbed her purse and frantically emptied it onto the patchwork quilt.

Alice appeared in her robe, hair clamps still in place, peering sleepily into her daughter's room. "What's all the racket, honey? What are you doing?"

"I'm looking for that phone number Perry gave me last night." She searched through the pile of papers, cosmetics, and change on the bed. "You should see the story in the paper, Mom. It's terrible!" Her voice was strained and thin. "I really need a lawyer now. I've got to defend myself."

The judge cracked his gavel loudly and hunched forward, piercing Dalton Graham with a stern look. "Approach the bench, Counselor," he ordered.

Dalton got up, looked over at his client, then circled the table and promptly presented himself before the judge.

"You have new evidence to submit?"

"Yes, Your Honor." With a flourish Dalton handed the judge a legal-size sheet of paper covered with lines of names. "This is the registration list for the civil engineering state exam given at Ohio State University on November tenth, the day my client, Sam Jupiter, is accused of illegally entering Smith Jewelry."

The judge took the document, looked it over, and allowed it to be entered into evidence. "Call your next witness," he told Dalton.

"I would like to call Ernest Hayes, the proctor on duty at the time of the examination."

The frail-looking man who took the stand was adamant in his testimony: The man now accused of breaking into Smith Jewelry at 9:00 A.M. on November 10 had been sitting in Howard Hall, classroom 24 at that time, and had remained there until exactly 12:30. Hayes had signed Sam Jupiter in and out that day. Even photo ID cards had been checked.

A short recess was called. The validity of the sign-in list

was established. Then two more instructors testified that they had seen Sam Jupiter on campus that day.

By noon the case was all over, thrown out of court, the charges dismissed, the young man set free.

As Dalton Graham pushed through the swinging doors of the courthouse, the prosecuting attorney, Charles Revel, called out, "Wait up, Graham." He ran up behind Dalton and stuck out his hand. "Congratulations, Counselor. I have to admit your client had an airtight alibi that time. Couldn't have done better myself."

"Thanks, Charles," Dalton said to his former roommate at Case Western Reserve. "Nice of you to say that."

"You still over there at the NAACP?" Revel asked, rushing to add, "You have too much talent to waste it on *those* people."

"Those people?" Dalton didn't break his stride. He was due at the office in twenty minutes to help plan a protest rally in Cleveland. "Who do you mean by 'those people'?"

"You know. Colored." Charles made no effort to hide his negative feelings. "Why are you so dead set on representing them?"

Dalton flinched at the sting of Revel's pointed remark but clamped his teeth together and did not reply.

"There's an opening coming up in the state attorney general's office," Revel went on. "You should go for it, Dalton. Very big job."

Now Dalton stopped at the foot of the expansive pink granite steps and turned to face his colleague. "When I was eight years old, somebody stole my bicycle. I ran all over the neighborhood looking for it. Never did find it. I cried for three days."

Revel fiddled uncomfortably with the stack of legal papers under his arm, wondering where Dalton was going with the story.

"Finally," Dalton went on, "the West Indian lady who lived next door came across the yard and told me to stop crying. She said, 'You ain't lost nothing but a bicycle. My boys never had one and probably never will. There are more important things you could have lost.' I remember looking at her as if she were crazy. Then I asked her, 'Like what?' She said, 'Your freedom, child, your freedom.' "

Charles pulled his coat collar up and smirked. "So what? You can work for freedom for white people, too."

"Yes," Dalton said, "and I do. Every time I win a case for the NAACP, it's a victory for everybody. Even you." Then Dalton gave his colleague a mock salute and headed off down the street.

At the newsstand on the corner Dalton bought a copy of the *Dispatch*, then walked two blocks to get his car. As he swung away from the curb, Charles's question hung in his mind.

Dalton had been asked that question many times before, but not quite so bluntly or in such a hostile manner. Lots of Negroes asked him why he worked for the NAACP, why he wanted to represent them.

When asked, Dalton told them the very same story about his West Indian neighbor—because it was the truth and because her words had summed up what life was really all about. Freedom. The space and chance to live without interference. Without it all you do is survive.

The morning after his bicycle was stolen, Dalton's parents had decided to get their son a red Schwinn Flyer with a basket and a bell. He told them not to bother, that he didn't want it, and he never had a bicycle after that.

Convinced that freedom should never be defined by color, Dalton certainly knew that it was, and he remained firm in his belief that people never suffer in isolation. Whatever wrong was done to one group or class of people in time would bring repercussions to others. Maybe not right away but later, and the pain would be vast, felt by everyone. As Dalton worked his cases, he watched freedom happen, his conviction strengthening, his confidence increasing.

A statuesque woman with a multicolored scarf around her head passed in front of his car. Dalton tensed, gripping the steering wheel, as if the sturdy leather-covered ring would keep him from the yawning pull of his past. His eyes followed the attractive stranger while the smiling face of Tahti Lantina flashed clearly into his mind.

Beautiful, exotic Tahti, the Brazilian flower he had boldly and foolishly reached out to embrace, eased under his skin in that moment. Tahti. Skin the color of rich burned cinnamon. A voice so lyrical she sang when she spoke. Queenlike in her posture. Childlike in her love for him. She was the only woman who had ever come close to capturing his heart. Dalton kept his eyes on the stranger in the colorful scarf until she disappeared into the lunchtime crowd.

Tahti. God, he thought, trying to push back the memories beginning to surge through his mind. The tightening in his chest was familiar, and he didn't want to feel it again.

The man behind him honked his horn, and Dalton looked up. The light was green. He relaxed, letting air drain from his lungs. Two years ago Tahti had been the center of his life. Now she was gone. Really gone. A letter from her sister in São Paulo had recreated, in detail he hadn't wanted to read, her last days, describing the plague that ravaged her hillside village and swept her away in its wake.

News of Tahti's death had forced Dalton to search his soul. If he had been able to make a commitment to her, she might have stayed in the States, might still be alive, might have become the mother of his children. But he had ended it all by not remaining faithful. Now he sighed, thinking back, knowing his wandering eye had been the culprit, yet realizing little had changed. A pretty girl, no matter what her race, religion, or political persuasion, could still turn his head and get his blood racing. Dalton jerked the car into a turn and swung around the corner.

Dismissing the restrictions his peers were content to live by, Dalton never regretted or apologized for any of his relationships. Those who didn't approve of the women in his life were summarily dismissed from his thoughts. Dalton Graham considered himself a man without color or class, a citizen of the world, and he damn well would experience it as he wanted.

Pulling onto Gay Street, Dalton maneuvered past dirty snowdrifts, thinking about the upcoming rally in Cleveland. Anticipating the masses he expected would gather on the steps of city hall next Monday brought on the familiar bristle of excitement that kept him pushing for justice. It would be the biggest rally he'd organized so far.

He guided his blue Plymouth into the trash-filled alley behind his office, avoiding a pile of broken glass, then parked the car and got out. Rock salt crunched beneath Dalton's feet as he circled the redbrick building, climbed a short flight of steps, and entered the glass-paneled door.

Norma, the receptionist, sat at the front desk, a phone pressed to her ear, while a man and a woman argued nearby.

Dalton nodded to her, rolling his eyes toward the ceiling. She smiled and put her hand over the mouthpiece.

"Glad you're here. Things are crazy this morning. Cleveland's really shaping up."

"Any messages?"

Norma put the caller on hold and picked up a stack of pink slips. "Let's see. Mel Parkin called. He wants those papers on the Thruman case as soon as they're ready. Then Darlene West called. Twice." Norma waved the two message slips in front of Dalton. "Isn't that the cute little blonde you brought to the Christmas party?"

"The same," Dalton admitted.

"Well, she wants you to call her today, no matter how late." Norma propped her chin on one hand. "Do I smell troubled waters beginning to rise?"

"Nope. As far as I'm concerned, the river is dry. Norma, I only went out with her a few times."

"Maybe, but I think this one is determined to hang on."

"Whew! What can I say? She's pretty, and clever but *never* stops talking. Drives me crazy!"

"Maybe you shouldn't be so charming," Norma said, smiling up at Dalton, her eyes traveling from his blue-gray eyes to his mouth and back. She flipped her hair off her shoulder with an exaggerated gesture and shook her head back and forth as she handed Dalton the rest of his mail.

Dalton leaned down and playfully kissed Norma on the cheek. "If you weren't my secretary, I might turn my charm on you."

"Oh, yeah? Don't even try it, Counselor. My husband played football at Central State, remember?" Norma laughed and pushed the button on her phone to resume her interrupted conversation.

Dalton thumbed through the slips of paper as he walked down the corridor toward his office.

Telephones rang throughout the building; snatches of conversations filtered through every doorway. The crowded offices of the NAACP were charged with activity, creating an air of urgency as the hardworking staff and motivated volunteers came and went like soldiers called to duty.

Dalton pushed his door open, switched on the overhead light, then tossed his hat toward the hatrack in the corner. He missed. It fell to the floor. Frowning, he went to retrieve it.

"Always said you white boys can't throw nothing but a fit."

Dalton whirled around to see Oscar Green leaning against the doorjamb, laughing.

"Oh, yeah? Catch this!" Dalton grabbed a ball of twine from his desk and hurled it at Oscar, who ducked and hollered as the ball whizzed past. It hit the wall and rolled away.

"Man, you coulda hurt me! Better stick to the paperwork, Counselor." Oscar chuckled, laugh lines wrinkling his caramel-colored skin. He came more fully into Dalton's tiny office. "How'd that case turn out this morning? You get Sam Jupiter off?"

"He's probably back home right now, eating a ham sandwich at his kitchen table," Dalton replied, loving the feeling sweeping over him. Another frightened person had been liberated, exonerated. There was no other feeling in the world like it and Dalton knew that he was doing exactly what he had been called to do. "The judge threw the case out. Sam Jupiter walked out of the courtroom and went home." Dalton nodded as he said, "Good thing the university came through with that registration list so fast. If they hadn't, this case could have dragged on for weeks."

"And what beautiful young lady did you sweet-talk to get hold of that list in record time?" Oscar pointedly asked, openly envious of Dalton's method of operation.

Dalton smiled slyly, gave Oscar a wink, then answered, "Claudette Lewis. Remember her? I helped get her grandfather's immigration papers in order so he could apply for citizenship."

"Yeah, I remember that case. But I never got the impression you were in any hurry to wrap it up."

"Well, she works for the engineering department at OSU." Dalton flashed a brilliant smile.

"Wonder boy." Oscar punctuated the words with a chuckle. "That's the rep you're getting around here, Graham. Wonder boy. The white miracle worker."

Dalton brushed a lock of hair from his forehead, a faint blush rising on his neck. "Just doing my job, Oscar. That's all." He opened his attaché case and took out some papers. "What's up? How are the plans for the rally coming along?"

"All set. Think we've got the mayor's car by now. Anyway, he's been warned to get to his office early on Monday, before a crowd gathers and blocks his way. I don't know if those colored sanitation workers will let him through unless he admits they have rights to overtime pay, just like the white guys. Don't worry. Things will go fine."

Dalton spread the telephone messages on his desk. "Got a slew of people to call back. The phones must have been hot this morning."

"Matter of fact, here's another one." Oscar held out a small pink slip. "I was just bringing this to you." He waited until Dalton looked it over. "This one's kinda interesting. She said to tell you her brother is Perry Roy and for you to read the story on the front page of today's *Dispatch*." Oscar raised one eyebrow. "I already read the story, and I think this lady really needs your help."

CHAPTER
SEVEN

The snow had stopped, leaving the sun to languish behind gray clouds, creating a sheet of hazy fog over the city. From her seat at the front of the bus Janelle surveyed downtown Columbus, a city of nearly 350,000 that seemed rather small to her. She knew every block of the city from visiting hotels, schools, parks, and churches with her father as he made his Saturday rounds to inspect kitchens and galleys for the City Health Department.

She loved the wide-open feeling of the city, with its Doric Capitol building planted at the corner of Broad and High. Today the snow-covered lawn stretching out in front of the multicolumned building was not even marred by tracks from the cheeky squirrels that wintered inside the huge craggy oaks that lined the iron fencing along the sidewalk.

Heavy black cars and taxis rolled past, threading through the surge of pedestrians crossing the busy intersection. People went about their business, heading into and out of the stately white stone buildings and ornately carved red-stone structures that were scattered throughout downtown.

The Chamber of Commerce Building was Janelle's favorite. Turreted and arched, it seemed exotic in its medieval grandeur. Her father had entertained her with stories about the building. His last one, told when Janelle was about twelve years old, had been about an African princess he said dwelled alone in the spiked tower, believing she was too ugly to face the world.

A twinge of loneliness struck Janelle as her father's jovial face snapped into focus. Beardless, dusky, and smooth, his youthful visage had matched his buoyant personality. Janelle allowed the comforting memory of her father to sweep over her, knowing her sense of loss equaled Perry's. Why couldn't he understand that out of necessity, she had camouflaged her pain with a facade of practicality?

When the bus stopped in front of the Deshler Hotel, she glanced down Broad Street toward the arched bridge spanning the frozen Scioto River, which divided the city into east and west. She could see the football field at Central High, where she and Perry and her mother and father had cheered her cousin Frank to touchdown victories on many a Friday night.

Janelle fingered the velvet collar of her mother's broad-shouldered coat, slowly running her palm over the nubbly green wool. Daddy's last Christmas gift to Mom, she remembered, thankful her mother had let her wear it today since her raincoat was still very damp.

When her father was alive, he had brought home pretty things for her, too. Now, Janelle thought glumly, there was barely enough money for nursing uniforms, caps, shoes, and white stockings, which were rising in price every day.

The bus slowed at the Palace Theater, where a cluster of soldiers in drab green overcoats that touched the tops of their boots stood talking on the corner, vapor streaming above their heads. Janelle watched as a soldier broke away from the group, rushed across the street, and embraced a tall girl in a shocking red coat. A flowered scarf, casually knotted beneath her pink cheeks, caught a gust of wind and flagged a gentle welcome. Janelle watched the girl lay her head on the soldier's shoulder. Then he pulled her, almost roughly, into the shadowy doorway of a closed shop and pressed her against the glass window with a kiss.

Janelle bit the inside of her cheek, hating the envy she

felt. At twenty-three she had yet to fall in love or even deep infatuation. Sure, she'd like to find a man to love and build a life with, but despite Emma's urgings, she had no intention of settling for just anyone—the way Emma had when she got engaged to Kenneth Shawn, a skirt chaser who didn't try very hard to keep his affairs secret. Janelle wondered how long that relationship would last now that Kenneth was so far away.

A surge of pedestrians blocked her view of the couple, and Janelle let her eyes roam toward a huge recruiting poster featuring an unfurled American flag. Again she thought about Emma, hoping she would not make good on her plan to enter the service. But now that black nurses were finally being accepted, many were rushing to enroll, desperate for the opportunity to serve. Janelle bristled at the thought that only fifty-six would be accepted. It was hard for her to understand why the Army would enforce a racial quota at a time when the nursing shortage was so intense.

As the bus neared her stop, Janelle began to anticipate the kinds of questions Dalton Graham might ask, aware of the importance of her mission. Forty minutes after she hung up the telephone, Graham's resonant voice still echoed in her ears. He hadn't thought she was crazy, or overreacting, or exaggerating the seriousness of Sara Johnson's remarks. In fact, he had been anxious to meet with her as soon as possible. She just hoped he would not leave her sitting in a stuffy hallway all afternoon while he tried to squeeze her in. Didn't lawyers for organizations like the NAACP have masses of desperate people waiting to see them?

The noisy bus swung onto Front Street and proceeded north several blocks, then lurched to a stop. The pneumatic doors whooshed open, and she gripped the shiny chrome pole at her side, rose to her feet, and squeezed past a teenage girl who flounced down the aisle carrying a shopping bag-size purse.

Janelle turned to stare after the girl, whose fluffy white

fur hood and matching muffler blended oddly with her pale white skin. The eye-catching outfit got Janelle's attention because she had tried it on last Saturday at Morehouse Martens. It cost forty-seven dollars. With tax. And to think she had seriously considered buying it.

Descending from the bus, Janelle felt her spirit begin to weaken. She was unemployed, with a tarnished reputation and a fight on her hands. Frivolous pretties like furry white hoods and mufflers were definitely out of the picture.

Hurrying down the block, Janelle searched for the address she had scribbled down, thankful Mr. Graham had not wanted to come to her house. She certainly didn't want him to see the deplorable neighborhood where she lived, or the stains on the drapes, or the cracked plaster sifting down from the front room ceiling. Besides, this was her affair, and she would handle it, the way she did everything else. She'd clear her name, set everything straight, and be back doing private-duty work before the end of the month.

In front of a five-and-dime store Janelle stopped to check her appearance in the window. Her hair was very unruly today, strands slipping out from beneath the flat brown hat that nestled behind her smooth pompadour. Assuming a posture of confidence, she walked to the redbrick building, mounted the salt-covered steps, and entered the bustling office.

Norma hung up the telephone, raising both eyebrows in question. "May I help you?"

"Yes." Janelle tucked a flyaway strand of hair back into her chignon. "I'm Janelle Roy. Mr. Graham asked me to come down for an interview."

"Dalton? Just a minute." Norma picked up the phone, punched a few buttons, and spoke into the heavy black mouthpiece. After a few seconds she fluttered her bright pink fingernails toward a short flight of stairs. "Second floor, third door on the right." The phone rang again, and she turned away to answer it, glancing back to watch Janelle disappear at the top of the stairs.

The door to Dalton Graham's office stood open to the musty passageway. Still wearing his brown trench coat and tan felt hat, he sat amid a clutter of papers and files, his attention riveted on a thick book lying open on his desk. A narrow stream of dull sunlight filtered between the open slats of the cracked venetian blind behind him, illuminating scrolls of gray smoke that drifted up from an ashtray.

"Excuse me."

Dalton raised his head at the sound of Janelle's voice. "Miss Roy?"

"Yes, I'm Janelle Roy. We spoke on the phone."

"Good. Glad you could come down." He stood, peeling off his coat, his smile setting set off a network of laugh lines around his handsome mouth.

"I'm glad you could see me today," Janelle said, coming into the room, accepting Dalton's extended hand.

He took it, enjoying the silky touch of her skin beneath his palm, pleasantly struck by her beauty. He could feel the familiar tingle of curiosity growing as he squeezed her hand firmly in his.

"Please sit down, Miss Roy," Dalton said. "I just got back from lunch and got caught up in this brief." Watching as Janelle unbuttoned her coat, he was startled by the tailored blue and white suit that hugged her narrow waist and flattered her shapely bosom. Intrigued by her hourglass figure, he parted his lips ever so slightly and gently sucked in his breath. She sleekly lowered herself into the cushioned chair in front of him, and Dalton picked up his horn-rimmed glasses, put them on, and drank in the dramatic combination of sophistication and innocence she presented.

The radiator hissed and gurgled beneath the window, and suddenly Dalton felt warm. "Well, Miss Roy, I read about your plight in the paper. Quite a disheartening thing to happen." Where was the prim, starched person he had visualized while reading the story? It would take all his concentration to get through this interview.

"Yes, it was. I'm still very shaken by the incident," Janelle answered.

"Let's see what we have here," he said, riffling through stacks of papers, pulling out a folder, realizing this young woman was unusual. She moved and talked and looked as if she had class, style—qualities he liked in the women he dated. Dalton opened the folder and took out a copy of the story that had appeared in the paper, then set it aside and placed both hands flat on the desk.

"Would you like a cup of coffee? I have a little hot plate here where I brew my own." He chuckled, a sparkling sound, his voice light with self-indulgence. "I like it strong and bitter. No one can make it the way I do."

"Really? I like it that way, too," Janelle said.

Dalton noticed that her glossy lashes made dark crescents on her satiny cheeks. He lowered his eyes as Janelle crossed one shapely leg at the knee and leaned over to accept the heavy china cup.

"I must have interrupted your schedule," Janelle said, and pointedly surveyed the stacks of legal volumes, court papers, and notepads piled high on his desk.

"No, not at all," Dalton quickly replied, pulling his eyes away from Janelle's legs. He took a legal pad from his attaché case. "I like to meet with my clients as soon as possible after an incident has occurred. You know? Most people who need a lawyer are worried about something, usually very upset. I've found it's much easier to capture details if recalled early, here in my office—away from the scene of the crime, so to speak."

Sensing he was talking too fast, he stopped and pulled out his fountain pen. With a tug he uncapped it, then sat with it poised over a blank sheet of paper.

"That's very kind of you, Mr. Graham. I understand what you mean. Perry says you are the best attorney in the city."

"He's exaggerating." Dalton laughed. "Your brother and I have spent quite a few hours on picket lines together." He gave Janelle an earnest look. "Do you mind if we use first names? We're going to have to speak rather openly and honestly about your situation, and I feel as if you are not really a stranger." Why hadn't Perry told him how good-looking his sister was? he wondered, unsure if he should be thankful or upset.

"That's fine with me," Janelle said.

Dalton went on. "You have a very dedicated brother. He is doing a lot for the cause, you know? I'll bet you're proud of him."

Janelle flinched, and Dalton watched her eyes fall into hooded shields that blocked further discussion of the subject. She raised the coffee cup, curled her full bottom lip to the rim, and took a sip.

"Tell me what happened," Dalton said, puzzled by Janelle's reaction. "In your own words, step by step. Don't leave out a thing. I'm in no hurry."

"Where do you want me to start?"

"Any place you want to," Dalton said, patting his shirt pocket, looking around. "Mind if I smoke?"

"Not at all," Janelle said.

Dalton smiled and nodded, pulling his pack of Old Gold from beneath a tablet. He offered one to Janelle. She refused. He flicked his silver lighter open, lit his cigarette, and, inhaling deeply, sat back, swiveling his creaky wooden chair back and forth.

"First, tell me about yourself." Dalton let his eyes travel over her face before he reached forward to flick ashes into the ashtray. With his elbows propped casually on the pile of papers before them, he allowed his eyes to connect with Janelle's. "How did you wind up doing private-duty nursing?"

Janelle smiled and shrugged, as if the reason were quite simple. "My father wanted me to be the first in our family to get a college education. But when my senior year rolled around, the money wasn't there. Then, on a dare from my best friend, Emma Brown, who had already been accepted into the nursing program at Belton Park Hospital, I submitted my name for a full scholarship. I got it.

It was between a nurse or a dime store clerk. I chose the scholarship."

"So you were never the little girl dreaming about becoming a Florence Nightingale?" His amusement and sincere interest brought a glow to his clear white skin.

"No, not at all," Janelle said with certainty.

"If things had been different, what would you have become?"

Janelle sat back, relaxed. "An architect," she said bluntly, bravely, watching Dalton closely.

He showed no surprise or derision.

"My father used to take me around town and show me old buildings and make up stories about them. I always thought it would be wonderful to design elegant skyscrapers or fancy Victorian houses, then watch them come to life when the people moved in."

"The thrill of creation?" He gave her his most charming smile. "Any regrets about your decision to take the nursing scholarship?"

Janelle shifted slightly in her seat, smoothing a wrinkle from her skirt. "No," she answered, looking directly at him. "I've always wanted to be in a position to take care of myself, to better myself, and I've learned a lot about getting what I want out of life by doing private-duty work." The words rolled easily off her tongue. "I'm sure I made the right decision."

"Getting what you want? I'm curious. What exactly is that?" He knew he should be moving on to the case, but he hoped she would open up, let him know more about her.

"To move easily in society. Work and live wherever I want. The white world, to be specific—the world my father moved in and told me I had to understand if I planned to make a success of myself."

"Um-hmmm." Dalton laid down his fountain pen and clasped his hands together behind his head. Intrigued by the honesty of her response, he doubted Janelle would have any problem scaling whatever obstacles might be in her way.

If only Tahti had had that attitude, he suddenly thought. They might have made a success of it together. He pressed for more. "Don't you believe that nursing in a hospital setting would also prepare you to enter the white world? If that's what you want."

"Not really. I want—no, need—to make as much money as I possibly can, and private-duty nursing seems the answer."

"Hmm," Dalton murmured, beginning to sense that Janelle and Perry walked two different paths. "I can understand why people are willing to risk disapproval to get what they want out of life. I do it all the time."

"That's right," Janelle said, her confident words almost sounding curt. "My father had a very prestigious job with the city. Some of his friends were jealous. He knew it, but he never let it stop him. He could go and do whatever he wanted. I was proud of my father. In my opinion, he lived his life as any man should, proving to everyone he was not second-class."

"Sounds as if he had a lot of guts, confidence," Dalton said, wondering what this passionate defense of her father was all about.

"He did, but he died before I graduated from nursing school. He had been insured for fifty thousand dollars, but there was a big mix-up in his insurance papers, and the city refused to honor his policy. That left my mother flat broke."

Dalton sympathized but was taken aback by this story, for Perry had said the family was broke at the time of his father's death. He wondered which story was true.

Janelle went on. "My mother was so devastated by my father's death she could no longer give piano lessons to earn a little money. Luckily she managed to force a small pension from the city."

As much as Dalton hated to admit it, his gut reaction

was that the beautiful woman sitting before him was fabricating her story.

"So," Janelle continued, "everything fell to me. I became the breadwinner."

"It's just you, Perry, and your mother?" Dalton asked.

"Yes," Janelle said. "And I've had my hands full maintaining the house, paying the bills. Everything. At least the house is paid for. It's a huge old place, out East Broad, near Taylor. My father bought it when he married my mother. Five bedroom, three baths, fourteen-foot ceilings. You know. Well, while my father was alive he did all the repairs—kept everything in tiptop shape. Now it's difficult. Very expensive to maintain."

Dalton hesitated to reply, wondering why the devil she way lying. He'd dropped Perry off at his house more than once, and it hadn't been anything like the place she described. Dalton sat watching Janelle in awe. Then, loosening his tie, he leaned back in his chair and crossed his arms on his chest, disturbed and fascinated by her mix of pride, insecurity, and blatant ambition. She certainly deserved his undivided attention.

"How did you meet Sara Johnson?" he asked.

"She hired me to nurse her sister, Cordelia Werner," Janelle said, lowering her leg, crossing her ankles as she straightened her shoulders, obviously eager to get down to business.

"Did you and Mrs. Johnson have a written contract? An agreement that spelled out your duties?" He hoped she'd at least be honest with him about the details leading up to her situation.

Janelle began to flex her fingers, opening and closing her fists. "No. Our arrangement was verbal. Though I did jot down her instructions during the interview."

"Do you have those notes?"

"No. I'm sure I threw them away."

"Was there a witness to your conversation—the housekeeper, perhaps?"

"No." Janelle's voice was wispy and low.

"Too bad. A written agreement or a witness to your conversation would really help your case."

He knew his words, though gently spoken, might sound like an admonishment to Janelle. He was not surprised to see her face fall in disappointment.

"I'm sorry, Janelle," Dalton rushed to say, "it's the truth."

She said nothing for a moment, then blurted out defiantly, "I trusted Mrs. Johnson. I thought her word was enough."

"Let me give you a little advice: If you plan to continue doing private-duty work, approach it like a business. I know you don't like hearing this, but it's always best to get specifics down in writing. No matter how trivial you may think something is, if it's an agreement for work to be done, the conditions and responsibilities ought to be clear, just like any other type of contract for work."

"You don't understand. I can't go around waving contracts under white people's noses. I was lucky Sara Johnson took me on at all. You don't know how hard it is to get a job like the one I had!"

A wry grin preceded Dalton's words. "I work for the NAACP, remember? I think I have a pretty good idea of the obstacles you face." He stubbed out his cigarette. "How do you view the opportunity you had to work for Mrs. Johnson now—in light of what's happened?"

"This may sound strange to you," Janelle went on, "but I am glad I got to work at the Werner mansion. I won't let this incident shatter my plans to continue my career."

"What exactly do you want me to do for you?"

"I want you to help me clear my name so I can move into another position right away. Without a reference from Mrs. Johnson, the good private jobs are out of the question, and I don't want to do shift work at the charity hospital."

With unreserved annoyance, Dalton folded his shoulders inward, piercing Janelle with a critical gaze. "Why not?

There's a war on. Your talent and training are very valuable. You could help many unfortunate people."

"That may be true," Janelle admitted, "but I have to think of my family, too. If I have to leave Columbus to work private-duty, I will. I must make more than the standard wage paid by most hospitals. Besides, I don't think I could stand being trapped in that maze of regulations and shift work, walking the wards, taking orders all day long."

Dalton put the fingers of both hands together, pressing until his fingertips lost their color. Clearly Janelle had no idea how self-serving her attitude appeared. In a rigid voice he told her, "You may be in for a rude awakening, Janelle. Life doesn't always give us what we want."

"I know that, Mr. Graham." Her brow knitted into a frown. "I just want to clear my name and get a retraction and a reference from Sara Johnson so I can secure another position." Shifting closer to the edge of her seat, Janelle asked, "Do you think you can help me?"

"I'll do the best I can," Dalton said, knowing he could not turn down her request. "As long as you tell me the truth, I'll be happy to try to work this out."

CHAPTER EIGHT

66 You ready to order?"

"I'm waiting for someone," Janelle replied absently, accepting the glass of water the waitress set down. "But I know what we'll have." Checking her watch, annoyed that Emma was fifteen minutes late, she decided to go ahead and order. "Give me a bowl of chili and a ham and cheese on rye for my friend."

Nodding, the waitress walked away.

Janelle placed the glass to her lips, sipping, her eyes fixed on the revolving door at the front of the store as midday shoppers and midtown employees streamed into H. L. Green's. Running her fingers over the moist sides of the cool glass, she waited. Emma had an obsession with being on time. She would show. An emergency must have occurred at the clinic for her to be so late.

Emma had always come through for Janelle ever since they met in Miss Williams's third-grade class, sitting in a reading circle on a checkered tile floor. Too frightened to ask to be excused to the bathroom, Janelle had squirmed and shifted, hoping she could hold on until all the children went to the rest rooms together.

But Janelle hadn't been able to wait and had burned with shame when in spite of all her effort, a puddle began to seep from beneath her candy-striped skirt. Horrified, she had squeezed her eyes shut, unable to raise her hand. When the story ended and all the other children stood up to go to recess, Janelle had remained behind, terrified of the punishment she knew was coming.

How clearly she remembered Emma stepping back from the line to ask what was wrong. Seeing Janelle's predicament, she had whispered to the teacher that her friend had had an accident.

Her friend! Just that easily and quickly Emma had decided to be her friend. With no reprimand, and a great deal of sympathy, Miss Williams had handed Janelle a towel and a pretty floral apron, sending the two girls off to make repairs. From that day on they were inseparable, and Emma, in the fifteen years Janelle had known her, had never mentioned the incident again.

Janelle took out her compact and touched up her lipstick, letting her thoughts turn to Dalton Graham. She was intrigued by the smart, handsome lawyer, heartened by his pledge to help her, and his image kept appearing in her mind. She had pumped Perry for all he knew about Dalton's personal life, getting little for her effort. All Perry would readily admit was that Dalton was a bachelor, and he warned Janelle of his open flirtation with every pretty girl they encountered.

Perry's remarks only heightened Janelle's interest. She wanted to get closer to Dalton; spend time with him outside his office, and assess his attraction to her. She sat back in the booth, letting her curiosity take over, loving the sense of challenge that daydreams of a future with Dalton Graham inspired.

He may be the man I've been waiting for, Janelle thought, *the key to the kind of life I'd like to have.* It was not that she wanted to marry a white man, but she couldn't deny it: She wanted the chance to move out of the dreary, constrictive world trapping her now. She felt as if there were an invisible line dividing what she had and what she wanted that sometimes was vague, other times so clear-cut she could imagine herself living in a big stone house in Bexley, shopping for shoes in Russell's or hats in Manco's, the most exclusive salons in the city. What would it be like? Dining and dancing at the Club Cartuff, swimming in the tropical indoor pool that was rumored to be at the top of the Deshler Hotel. No one she knew had ever seen it. Dalton had seemed critical of her refusal to work in a hospital, but she knew it had nothing to do with race. He was the least prejudiced person she had ever met, and his attraction to her was unmistakable—

"Sorry I'm late." Emma's words startled Janelle.

"Oh! Hi there." Janelle set her glass on the table just as the waitress arrived and plunked down their order.

"Great," Emma said, slipping into the booth. "Glad you ordered. I'm starved."

The waitress splashed more water into Janelle's tall glass, then asked cheerfully, "Anything else for you two?"

"No, thanks," Janelle said, suddenly feeling a surge of exhilaration as a mixed race couple took the booth in front of her. Sure, unofficial segregation existed in lots of places in Columbus, but things were changing, gradually improving, moving toward a more open future that Janelle could imagine being a part of.

"I'll have coffee," Emma told the waitress, raising her voice above the noisy clamor of lunchtime shoppers strolling through the five-and-dime.

Janelle unrolled her napkin and spread it across her lap as the waitress moved to the next booth and picked up a pile of dirty dishes.

Emma pushed up the sleeves on her cable-knit cardigan and reached into her purse. She took out a sheet of notebook paper and laid it beside her plate. "I got the scoop on Febrahyde," she said, opening her sandwich to spread mustard on the bread.

"What do you think? Could it cause seizures?" Janelle leveled her gaze at Emma's small face, watching her jet black curls bounce at her cheeks as she went about preparing her sandwich. Janelle watched her every move, knowing that Emma would start at the top of the piece of bread, first smooth the mustard around the edges, then work her way to the center. The precise movements used to drive

Janelle up the wall, but now she smiled to herself, comforted by her best friend's familiar routine.

Though only two months younger than Emma, Janelle always thought of Emma as much older than she. Her confidence in Emma's take-charge ability and her way of putting problems into perspective kept Janelle turning to her for advice. Listening to Emma's blunt, thoughtful assessment of a situation made anything seem solvable.

"I talked with the head of the school of pharmacy at OSU this morning, and from what he said, Febrahyde was probably not the culprit. *Probably* not." Emma sounded confident.

"Probably? Come on, Emma, give me the negative side."

"What was the prescribed dosage?"

"One hundred milligrams."

"Your patient was given two?"

"Yes," Janelle said.

"And it was the first time she had taken it?"

"Yeah."

"Well"—Emma drew out her response—"I really doubt Febrahyde had anything to do with that. Listen." She picked up the notebook paper and read. "Belongs to the barbiturate group. It is used to provide sedation in a variety of tension and anxiety states. Adverse reactions include headache, nausea, vomiting, drowsiness, vertigo." Emma took a bite of her sandwich. *"But"*—now she widened her eyes, tilting her head to one side—"restlessness may be produced when given to patients in severe pain."

"Umm," Janelle murmured apprehensively.

Emma continued reading. "Tolerance and dependence may develop when taken repeatedly, and sudden discontinuation of Febrahyde, after prolonged use, may provoke withdrawal symptoms of anxiety, insomnia, tremors, weakness . . . and convulsions."

"She took it only once," Janelle replied, almost defensively.

"Right, so we're not talking withdrawal here." Emma

reached over and put her hand on Janelle's arm. "God, you're jumpy. Don't get yourself all worked up so soon. There are obviously a lot of holes in Sara Johnson's case."

"I guess so." Janelle sighed, beginning to feel uneasy.

Emma put the paper down and sipped her coffee. Scowling, she set the cup back in the saucer and added a spoon of sugar. "So, tell me about this lawyer. From what you said on the phone this morning you seem more impressed by his resemblance to Rory Calhoun that his ability to represent you." A faint smirk curved her lips as the ends of her short bobbed hair sprang to life, waving in fluffy curls around her honey bronze forehead and cheeks.

Janelle did not answer right away, keeping her face lowered toward her bowl of chili. She stirred it lazily with her spoon.

"Come on now, Janelle. Give me the scoop. What does Mr. Graham plan to do? Can he get you out of this mess?" Emma's question came in rapid, clipped words that pricked Janelle out of her daydreams. "And what about the autopsy? When are the results due in?"

With hand in midair, Janelle stopped toying with her food. "Okay, okay. Slow down." Feeling oddly pressured by Emma, she tore open a package of crackers. Flat-chested and rail thin, Emma was a petite bundle of energy who loved to talk, was always in motion, and never shied away from giving Janelle her honest, though sometimes brutal, opinion on any subject. Janelle always thought that instead of nursing Emma should have studied law, where her methodical mind could have been used to sway a judge or a jury.

Theirs was a relationship of contrasts. Begun while young, it had run hot and cold as they matured, eventually settling into a comfortable understanding that their differences were what made their friendship worth preserving.

"Dalton is going to call Sara Johnson and arrange a meeting to discuss what happened. Then—"

"Oh, it's *Dalton,* is it?" Emma interrupted. "Pretty fast work, Janelle."

"Well, that's what he asked me to call him," Janelle replied, a little surprised at her own defensiveness. Maybe she had made a mistake, telling Emma about her attraction, about the unsettling effect Dalton Graham had had on her. At times Emma could act somewhat narrow-minded, especially when it came to interracial relationships.

"He's been working with Perry on the protest activities. You know that, Emma. So it's not as if the man is a complete stranger." Janelle put her spoon on the saucer under her bowl, leaning forward. "As far as the autopsy is concerned, let's see, today is Thursday. It probably won't be available until late next week—Friday, maybe even later."

Emma lifted her chin, shrugging her small shoulders back. "This is really a mess, you know? Is he aware of the power the Werner family wields in Columbus?"

"Oh, yeah," Janelle said, placing her fingertips to her cheek. "But don't look so worried. You make me nervous. I've got no choice but to trust him. He believes that truth always rises to the surface, burying the lies in the process. Dalton seems very confident that he'll get to Sara Johnson. I think he's moving in the right direction."

"I hope so," Emma said.

"You really should have seen him." Janelle sighed, tired of the discussion about the situation. "He is gorgeous!" Why try to hide the impact Dalton had had on her? Whom else could she confide in but Emma?

"Please! Are you looking for a lawyer or a lover?" Emma's mouth remained open, her brow knit in suspicion.

"Relax," Janelle said, smiling. "And stop with that look I know means you think I'm crazy. All I said was that he's gorgeous."

"Um-hmm," Emma murmured.

"You should have seen me. I was proper, dignified. I did not let him see how interested I really was. And no, I didn't try to seduce him."

"Um-hmm," Emma murmured again, in that infuriating

way she had of not committing herself to approve or disapprove of what Janelle was saying.

Janelle squinted, saying, "I *do* want to get to know him. He's a very unusual man." But in her heart what she hoped was that Dalton Graham had found her interesting—interesting enough to make a move. "He took me completely by surprise," she went on. "Not at all what I imagined he would be. I was shocked when I saw him."

"What did you expect, Quasimodo?" Emma giggled, flashing Janelle an impish glance. Last Saturday at a special repeat showing they had huddled in the dark balcony of the Ohio Theater watching Charles Laughton covet Esmeralda from the bell tower.

"That's not funny, Emma. What I'm saying is, I guess I had some preconceived notion that any white man who would dedicate himself to the NAACP must be a dull, bookish, failed lawyer, unable to get work anyplace else."

"Well, he proved you wrong, didn't he?"

"Boy, did he ever!"

"When are you going to learn? That's exactly why it didn't work out with my cousin Robert."

"No, it wasn't," Janelle said, cringing at the memory of the disastrous evening and the boring, insecure young man.

"Well, hadn't you already made up your mind that you would not like him before you met him? Isn't that why the whole evening was ruined?"

"No," Janelle said. "But when you told me he worked as a dogcatcher in Zanesville before he moved to Columbus, I have to admit my interest kind of faded."

"Yeah, you made up your mind not to like him."

"That's not true, Emma. I didn't say I didn't like him." Janelle hadn't meant to hurt Emma or her cousin, but there definitely hadn't been the least spark of attraction. "I only said that we didn't have anything in common, that's all. Robert's a nice enough guy. Just not my type."

"He fell hard for you, though. He still calls me, just checking in, he says. Always asks if you're still single.

You ought to give him another chance, Janelle. He's one man you're going to regret not holding on to. He's enrolled at Wilberforce University, taking business administration classes. He plans to open his own breeding kennel for Irish setters someday."

"Good for him," Janelle said, swallowing a spoonful of chili. "I hope he finds someone at Wilberforce who is as enamored with dogs as he is. I certainly wasn't." She made no attempt to hide her distaste. "How to catch a rabid dog humanely, how to tell when a bitch is in heat, and how to keep fleas out of your house are not topics I care to discuss on a date."

"Don't be so smug. He's ambitious. He's good-looking."

"Tolerable, Emma, just tolerable," Janelle corrected.

"You could do worse." Emma squared her shoulders for her next remark, one she seemed to need to gird herself to say. "Don't try to deny it, Janelle," she said, "as many times as I've fixed you up on dates, you've never been as enthusiastic about a single colored guy as you are about this white attorney."

The remark took Janelle by surprise, and her body stung with guilt. Emma's assessment came close to hitting the mark, though she didn't want to admit it to Emma.

"It's got nothing to do with color," Janelle said. "Dalton Graham *is* good-looking, educated, charming, principled—"

"And I guess you could say he's *just perfect*," Emma finished, shrugging.

"No . . . not perfect, but he's so *worldly*. That's what it is. He doesn't seem to judge people, is very dedicated to quality, and he's been to Europe. Twice."

"Lots of people have," Emma said, not seeing what that had to do with anything.

"I mean . . ." Janelle struggled to make sense of her observations, wishing Emma could be less pragmatic. God, you'd never guess she was in love. "He kind of removes himself from the petty, everyday things that bother most

people. He's concerned with higher, more important issues. Causes that count, you know?"

"Well! Is this Janelle Roy talking? The Janelle that I
know has never voted and thinks all politicians are thieves
and has refused to give as much as a nickel to any socially
conscious organization in the city? Deliver me!" Emma had
to laugh. She wiped her hands on her napkin. "What did the
two of you do? Read the NAACP charter together?"

"Don't be flip now. We had a very intellectually stimu-
lating conversation."

"I'm sure you did," Emma said somewhat wryly, attempting to soften her remark.

"Dalton is totally consumed with his work. Talks about
it with reverence. It's a mission he's on, that's it." Janelle
turned and caught the waitress's eye and signaled for the
check. "I can't wait to get to know him better," Janelle
said, her face glowing with optimism.

"Oh, Janelle." Now Emma lifted a finger as if to caution
her friend but caught herself and thrust her hand into her
lap. "Don't get your emotions confused with what needs
to be done. So this guy is gorgeous. What's that got to do
with solving your problem? You went to Dalton Graham
for legal advice. Take it and get back on track. Don't com-
plicate matters by getting personally involved."

"Don't worry," Janelle said, knowing that Emma could
get downright preachy if the subject really fired her up. "If
he's not open to getting better acquainted, I'm not going to
make an issue of it. But he probably would have no problem dating colored."

"I hate to hear you say that, Janelle. You ought to find
a guy of your own race and settle down. You're always so
impressed by white people."

"I am not! That's not fair," Janelle answered. "I work
for white people because they pay well. And as far as my
relationships go, I just haven't met a colored guy who has
really impressed me. You know? A man with flair and
class and education, too."

"You've put no effort whatsoever into making yourself available or agreeable to dating any of the men I introduce you to," Emma said. "Admit it, Janelle."

"Well . . ." Janelle faltered, crushing her napkin in both hands, fishing for the words to explain what she wanted, wondering if her view of the world was all wrong. Her father had moved easily and confidently within the white world and had stressed that he wanted his daughter not to judge people by race alone. He had encouraged her to be open-minded, courageous, to fight her own prejudices and open her heart to those who were different. If he were still alive, he would understand, she thought. It was not about race at all. It was about happiness, progress, living a good life, with whoever could bring her love.

Swallowing, Janelle thought for a moment. "I don't want to miss an opportunity to find happiness, even if it might be with someone who is white."

"I understand that, honey," Emma said, "but you've got to be realistic. Columbus is a pretty liberal town, but don't press it? Go easy."

"Most of the guys I meet seem so . . . awkward. I guess that's it. You know what I mean? They act like they just jumped off the tractor and stumbled into town."

"Maybe some of them have," Emma said defensively. "So what? Everyone didn't burst to life in the heart of the big city with a college degree." She put her sandwich down. "Remember, your daddy walked from a shack at the edge of a cornfield in Lexington, Kentucky, to Columbus, Ohio, in 1910—if I remember correctly."

"That was years ago." That old story had been one of her father's charming maneuvers to be the center of attention; Janelle had never believed it was true.

Suddenly Emma began to chuckle. The serious tone of their conversation struck them, and they dissolved into a cascade of laughter, Janelle sputtering water across the table, grabbing her napkin to press to her lips. Emma broke into an effervescent giggle that quickly bubbled up into an all-out howl. She put her hand to her mouth and swallowed hard before another loud guffaw broke loose.

All the air drained from Emma's lungs in a loud whoosh. She shook her head, wiping her eyes, reaching with one hand to grab Janelle's wrist. "Enough. Enough. Let's drop the subject." Her voice resumed its pragmatic tone. "You know I want you to be happy, Janelle. If Dalton Graham *is* the man for you, I'll be the first to admit I was wrong."

"I know, Emma."

"I just don't want you to be hurt."

"I won't be."

Emma gave her friend a reassuring smile and clicked open her change purse. "Hand me the check. Lunch is on me."

After settling the bill, Emma bought a big chunk of chocolate fudge and split it with Janelle as they walked to the car.

"What have you heard from Kenneth?" Janelle asked once they were riding down High toward Broad.

"His classes are almost over. He hopes he'll be assigned to Tuskegee within the month."

"You still thinking of applying for the Army Nurse Corps?"

"I've already presented my credentials to the Red Cross. There aren't many spaces at Tuskegee. I don't know if I'll be selected."

"Gee," Janelle said, "you're going to do it."

"Yeah. Why not?" Emma checked the rearview mirror, then crossed from the inside lane and slowed at the corner. Snow had begun to fall. "I miss Kenneth so much, and there's really no reason not to try to get in the Army. Besides, I *want* to go. I want to do what I can to help end this crazy war." The car rolled to a stop.

Disturbed by the possibility of Emma's leaving Columbus, Janelle shivered. Though weeks might go by without her hearing from Emma, she knew their friendship survived on the knowledge that whenever they needed or wanted to be together, they could do it on a moment's notice.

When Emma's parents, who did missionary work for the Methodist Church, were offered an assignment in Mexico during Emma's senior year, Janelle had faced the prospect of separation from her friend. But Emma had been adamant about remaining in Columbus and had managed to stay behind, living with a cousin until she finished nursing school. Then she moved out on her own. Those years at Belton Park Hospital—moving through their nursing classes, growing into womanhood together—had molded their present adult relationship.

Janelle popped the door open and stepped out onto the slushy curb. "I'll give you a call tomorrow," she said, forcing a light touch to her words. "Thanks for getting that info on Febrahyde."

"No problem," Emma said, leaning across the passenger seat. "I've got my fingers crossed that it had nothing to do with Miss Werner's death."

"Me, too," Janelle said.

Emma pulled away, swinging west over the Broad Street Bridge. Janelle caught Emma's eye in her rearview mirror and waved, a tug of gratitude drawing her tight.

"How about grabbing a sandwich at Hugo's, Counselor?" Oscar Green stuck his head into Dalton Graham's office, an index finger pointed in question.

Dalton stubbed out his cigarette and looked up. "Gotta pass today, Oscar. Think I'll run over to the medical examiner's office and get a fix on the Werner autopsy report."

The lanky young man slouched down in the chair facing Dalton's cluttered desk. "So, you took on that case involving the nurse?" He was obviously interested in Dalton's reply.

"Seriously thinking about it," Dalton said vaguely, not ready to give up too much information. If Janelle Roy were not telling the truth, he'd be tangled in a heck of a mess. "I want to dig into a few things first. Talk with some people. Check her story."

"What's your gut reaction? I know you go on your first take."

A knowing smile played over Dalton's lips, and he shook his head. "Mixed."

"Mixed?" A wide-eyed expression betrayed Oscar's calm inquiry. He'd never heard Dalton so noncommittal. "You think there are holes in the story she told you yesterday?"

Dalton frowned. "There is something about Janelle Roy that I can't put my finger on. I want to believe her. Surely the overdose was accidental. The housekeeper must have been accustomed to giving the patient her medication at night since Janelle Roy didn't live in. But I'm going to take this one slowly."

Dalton hoped Janelle was not at fault. But after her exaggerated story about her family background, her credibility was stretched pretty thin with him.

"What about the accusations in the paper? Think the Johnson lady has a case?"

"Well, if Miss Roy is telling the truth, Mrs. Johnson will be charged with slander." Dalton grunted and shifted in his chair, wanting desperately to cast Janelle in an innocent, honest light. He'd thought of nothing but seeing her again since the moment she'd walked out of his office twenty-four hours ago. But until the autopsy report came in, he'd play it strictly by the book.

"Well," Oscar said, standing to leave, "if your gut reaction says she's innocent, she probably is." He went to the door, then turned. "I caught a glimpse of her when she came in yesterday. A real looker, huh?" He grinned so widely his white teeth seem to cover the lower half of his narrow face. "You lucky stiff. I always get to represent the crazies, the winos, the ones who smell like they've been living in a moldy damp basement, eating sardines from the can all their life."

A snort of a chuckle escaped Dalton's lips. "Hey, just the luck of the draw, Oscar. What else can I say?"

Oscar heaved a sigh, throwing up his hands. Turning on his heel, he left.

Dalton stared glumly into the hallway, the shadow of his co-worker fading from view. An odd feeling threaded with thoughts of Janelle, settled over him. He wanted to see her again, hold her hand in his again, stand so close he could smell her lilac perfume. The urge to connect with a woman was familiar, but this uneasy anticipation was different.

Dalton consciously relaxed, allowing the dull, heavy ache in his loins to come to the surface and stay there—burning, throbbing, pushing him to admit that his playful banter and scattered charm would not be enough for her. If he made a move, he'd have to follow through, but was Janelle Roy the woman who could give him enough reason finally to let down his guard?

CHAPTER NINE

Perry took a long drag on his cigarette, holding the smoke down hard in his lungs until he felt it begin to burn. That's the way he and his cousin Frank had done it, hiding in the attic in Aunt Dedee's house, after pilfering her Camels to learn how to smoke. Perry tried to picture Frank now, in uniform, aboard a Navy warship, cruising the Pacific. He wondered how the white boys on board were treating him and if he'd seen any action.

Letting his eyes sweep the festooned party room that dominated the second floor of the Regal Road Inn, Perry picked up his drink and took a swallow. For a Thursday night the place was packed. All the weekend regulars who usually sat on their barstools sipping beer on Friday and Saturday nights were now seated at long tablecloth-covered tables eating cake and peanuts, blowing noisy paper horns as they laughed and tossed paper streamers at one another.

Every year Willie Regal, the owner of the popular lounge, threw a bash of a birthday party for himself. The celebrating could go on for two or three days, so it should not have surprised Perry that the fifty-year-old honoree, who had been best man at his parents' wedding twenty-five years ago, would pull out all the stops for making the half century mark.

Perry studied the man he had always called Uncle Willie, the man who had been his dad's best friend. Perry and his father had come in and out of this place many times, helping Willie with deliveries, polishing crates of champagne glasses, listening to boxing matches on Saturday afternoons on the big floor model radio in the corner.

Perry clamped his jaw tightly shut. Lately, whenever memories of his father came to him, a dark, hungry void came right along, too. The empty space in the middle of his chest threatened to ruin whatever he was doing. Not tonight, Perry thought, deliberately dismissing the haunting specter. Nothing was going to spoil this party.

"Take the 'A' Train" blared from the jukebox, blotting out all conversation, causing the floor beneath Perry's feet to pulse and vibrate as a few energetic couples stepped out to dance. He'd never been much of a dancer, so he lit another cigarette, leaning back, content to watch the gyrations of others, sipping his bourbon and water.

Putting his elbow on the table, Perry cupped his chin with one hand. A curl of smoke drifted up into his eyes, but he just squinted, leaning closer to Alnita, taking in the familiar smell of the hair oil she used to glisten her dark brown curls. He assessed the curve of her prominent cheekbones, the flecks of dark brown freckles scattered in an uneven pattern along the side of her honey beige neck. Glancing down, he could see a swell of flesh peeping up from beneath the beaded neckline of her red wool dress. He knew that those same dark imperfections marched right across her taut, pointed breasts to the full brown aureola of her nipples.

After abruptly terminating their one-sided relationship three months ago, he had to admit he was glad to see Alnita. Sick of drifting in and out of one-night stands with two-dollar-a-night price tags, Perry was ready to stick with Alnita—at least until he got restless again.

He always did. Sooner or later Alnita Dujohn would get to talking about marriage, and then he'd walk away. After he had dated her off and on for four years, she ought to know he didn't want anything serious with her—or anyone else, for that matter. How could he even think of making a commitment to her when his own life remained so unresolved?

Perry casually laid his arm over Alnita's shoulder, letting her cuddle against him. He liked it when she did that, liked for her to feel protected and secure with him. The comforting pressure of her warm cheek under his neck aroused Perry, washing away the bothersome twinge of guilt that had been eating at him for having dumped her so callously. Hell, if Alnita got hurt, it was her own fault; he'd never promised to put a ring on her finger.

"I read about your sister in the paper," Alnita said, raising her head a few inches from Perry's chest, studying the expression on his face. Immediately Alnita saw that Perry was moodily distracted—a state, it seemed to her, he'd been in forever. His thoughts were so far from her he might as well be on the other side of town.

"Yeah," Perry said. "It's a real mess."

"How is Janelle doing?" Alnita sat up.

Perry frowned, removing his arm. With a shrug he reached toward the ashtray and ground out his cigarette. "Ah, she's all right. Got herself a lawyer. Nothing's come back from the autopsy yet."

"I know she's chewing nails over that story in the *Dispatch*. Got me upset just reading it." Alnita fluffed her hair, opened her small sequined bag, and took out a triangular vial of perfume.

"The Werners! Ha!" She tapped the bottle against her index finger and ran it along the back of one hand. "I sure as hell would be spitting fire if that old hag shot off her mouth about me like that."

Perry grazed Alnita's bare arm with a finger, the musky perfume putting him in a better mood. "Janelle says she didn't do anything wrong. I believe her. That pushy Johnson woman is just blaming my sister to keep the housekeeper's name out of it. A cousin or some kinda relative, you know?" His forehead folded into three deep creases above his brows. "I warned her to be careful about getting involved with those people."

"You did?" Impressed, Alnita flattered him. "See? Janelle oughta take you more seriously. Give you some credit. She doesn't know everything." Since high school Alnita had never really liked Janelle, finding her stuck up and distant, not one of the regular crowd. "She oughta listen to you. You have a way of cutting through the bullshit, getting to the real deal." Alnita snapped her purse closed. "Too bad, though. She had a pretty cushy job."

"So?" Perry rubbed his palms on the knees of his trousers. "She can work someplace else. That's what I told her, too. She'd be better off at Eastside Clinic or St. Anthony . . . taking care of her own."

"Well, maybe." Alnita considered Perry's words. "But private jobs are hard to find. Janelle was lucky." Alnita had been there when Perry lost his father. Softening, she added, "With all the pressure on her . . . since your dad died . . . I mean . . . well, she's got to be mad as hell about this mess."

Without comment, Perry slumped back in his chair, staring out over the dance floor. He wished Alnita didn't know so damn much about his personal life. That was one of the reasons he had cooled the relationship; sometimes it was good to be with strangers—blank faces with other interests who knew nothing about his past.

"I didn't come here to talk about my sister," Perry grumbled.

"All right with me." Alnita sighed, leaning over, trying to see into his face. "Okay. Forget it. Let's dance."

Perry shrugged. He'd have to be in a much better mood than he was right then to get out there and make a fool of himself.

Fearful she'd soured the evening, she tugged on his sleeve. "Don't go getting moody on me now. I meant that I can understand how important Janelle's job was. That's all."

Piqued at the implication that his sister was supporting him, Perry spoke in a taut, controlled voice. "Let's drop the subject of Janelle, okay?" He leveled his eyes to

Alnita's anxious face. "Even if she never works again, it's no problem." He licked his bottom lip, a half smile curving up to ease the tension. "I'm in line to get on at Lantree," he said, waiting for Alnita's reaction.

"Really?" She put her hand on Perry's knee and slowly trailed her fingers up the length of his thigh. "Oh, Perry. They don't hire colored. How'd you manage that?"

"I've been on a protest line over there all week. This afternoon I got a notice to show up for an interview on Monday." He gladly let Alnita caress his leg with firm, evocative fingers. "I'm going to talk with Howard Long, the president of Lantree. A good sign, don't you think?"

"Yeah," she whispered. "Must be something to it if he's taking time to talk to you."

"Right. There's a spot for me at Lantree. Just a matter of going through the formalities, the paperwork."

Perry's confidence soared at the thought of sitting down with Howard Long. Impulsively he moved closer. "At Lantree I can clear fifty a week to start. After sixty days it'll go up to fifty-five. Easy. So, after Monday Janelle won't have to worry about supporting me and Mom anymore. I'm going to take care of everything."

Alnita flicked the tip of her tongue over her creamy red lips, grinning approval. "Good for you, baby." She tilted her chin and hooked him with her cool brown eyes, then laced her warm fingers through his. "That's great news. You said you were gonna stir things up until you got what you wanted." She softly drew her lips together, obviously begging for a kiss.

Perry's desire for her flared at the familiar gesture. He placed one hand on the underside of Alnita's tilted chin, eased his face lower, and covered her soft, red lips completely with his. She hungrily welcomed him, pulling him closer.

Reuniting with Alnita was a good idea. Perry accepted the delicate flicker of her tongue over his, feeling an erection start in his groin. Damn, Alnita knew that drove him crazy. As he kissed her back, his need for her gathered strength. Despite the erratic nature of their union, Perry had to admit that Alnita was the only woman who could really heat him up. At that moment all he wanted was to feel her rocking beneath him with that driving, pulsating, red-hot rhythm that always continued until she screamed her release and he collapsed—groaning, spent, deliriously fulfilled.

When their lips parted, Perry relented, murmuring, "All right. Let's hit the dance floor. We came here to have a good time."

But Alnita didn't move. She reached out and placed one steady hand on the nape of Perry's neck and guided him back into their embrace. Another flush lit his insides, and he had to push her back to catch his breath.

"Hold on," he said, peeling her possessive, tempting arms from his neck. Swallowing to clear his head, he stood, looking intently down at Alnita, knowing exactly what she wanted.

"You haven't changed a bit, have you?" he whispered.

An easy, one-sided grin came over Alnita's face, increasing Perry's desire to feel her undulating beneath him again. A hint of a chuckle escaped his lips as blood raced hotly to his head. "Guess I'd be disappointed if you ever changed."

Alnita rose to stand close to Perry, her nipples, hard and prominent, straining against the red fabric of her bodice.

"Get your coat, Alnita." His husky words slipped out. "Let's blow this joint. You didn't really want to dance, did you?"

Janelle waved good-bye to her mother, then let the curtain fall back over the frosty window. She stood watching Aunt Dedee, head bent over the steering wheel, peering through the frosted window as she guided her rusty blue Dodge over the hard-packed snow that clogged the only exit from Oakwood Alley.

Every Friday morning Alice Roy and her sister-in-law made a mission visit to the Methodist Nursing Home, and

Janelle knew they'd be gone until late afternoon. Thankful for some time alone, she turned from the chilly entryway and walked toward the kitchen, thinking about Perry's empty bed.

He was probably curled up in Alnita Dujohn's two-room flat above the Paradise Grill. Why that girl put up with Perry's rudeness baffled Janelle. Their stormy relationship had been going on since they were in their junior year at East High.

Janelle went to the stove and poured a cup of coffee. They deserved each other, she decided—two insecure people, neither of whom had the guts to move on.

Sitting at the table, Janelle absorbed the morning sun on her face, loving the silence, the familiar bite of the strong, bitter coffee, the unhurried sense of time standing still, though an empty, uneasy sensation nagged at her: She should have been getting ready for work about this hour, keeping one eye on the clock, calculating whether or not her bus would be on time. Now she dared not leave the house. Dalton Graham's phone call with results of the autopsy could come at any moment.

With time to kill, Janelle plunged into the unpleasant task of defrosting the ice-packed freezer in the aging refrigerator. Balancing pans of boiling water, scraping ice, getting down on her knees to mop up spills were her least favorite chores, but by midmorning she had finished. Her sweater was damp to the elbows, and her apron was wet enough to wring out by hand.

Janelle dried her hands on a towel and was heading toward the stairs when a knock at the front door stopped her. From the end of the hallway she looked through the lace-curtained panel in the door and was shocked to see the unmistakable silhouette of Dalton Graham, lean and ebony, backed by a splash of sunlight.

How had he found her? She hadn't given him this address. What had brought him to Oakwood Alley? She considered not answering the door but knew it was too late; he'd probably seen her movement through the window.

"Mr. Graham!" Janelle opened the door. Why on earth had she pretended to live in a large, grand house? A wave of nauseating guilt surfaced. She steadied herself with one hand on the wall.

"Hello, Janelle." Dalton tipped his hat, smiling. "Sorry I didn't call before coming, but I had to drop some papers off for an attorney who has an office on Long Street."

Janelle was unable to respond.

"I have some information for you." He waited as Janelle stood staring, one hand pressed to her mouth.

"May I come in?" he had to ask.

"Oh, yes . . ." Stumbling, she backed up. "Yes. Please do."

Dalton passed her, waiting until Janelle shut the door firmly. Then he followed her into the front room.

Humiliated to the point of feeling faint, Janelle nervously fingered her damp, dirty apron, watching Dalton cautiously as he crossed the room. *Just let him say what he wants and go away,* she prayed, her mouth going dry.

Dalton remained standing, hat in hand, back to the piano, looking stiff and businesslike in his brown trench coat.

"You said you have news?" A chilly draft from the hallway spilled into the room. She pushed up the wet sleeves of her sweater. "Did you speak to Sara Johnson about retracting the story? Giving me a recommendation?"

"No, but I will on Monday."

"Is it the autopsy report?" she asked then. Was he deliberately making her squirm?

Dalton shook his head. "No, I'm sorry, the results aren't in yet, but I do have surprisingly good news."

Janelle went to sit on the red plush sofa, indicating that Dalton sit down, too. "Good news?"

"Yes." Instead of sitting beside her, he settled himself in the overstuffed chair. "I got a call from Ned Orlandy, the attorney for the Werner estate." He pulled a notepad from his pocket and flipped it open. "Seems that Cordelia

Werner mentioned you in her will. She left you fifteen thousand dollars."

"Fifteen thousand dollars?" Janelle gave Dalton an incredulous look. So much money! She could scarcely believe what she'd heard. Over the past year she *had* grown fond of Cordelia Werner, but the frugal spinster had never given Janelle reason to imagine she'd be so rewarded. Perhaps it was Cordelia's way of getting back at Sara. That thought gave Janelle a moment of pleasure until she realized it must be the source of Sara's fury.

"Yes, it is a lot of money," Dalton said. "However—"

Here comes the bad news, Janelle thought, slumping dejectedly against the back of the sofa.

"It is to be paid to you in five installments of three thousand dollars over five years . . . and Mrs. Johnson is contesting the will. She could hang the whole thing up in court for months. She not only has challenged this bequest to you but has also contested her sister's decision to leave the mansion to their cousin Flora Werner."

Janelle could not repress a smile. "Good for Cordelia." She laughed aloud, tossing her head back. The mesh snood holding her hair at the nape of her neck fell loose. Janelle distractedly tucked it back into place. "If I never see a cent of my money, I don't care. But it sure feels good to know that Sara Johnson will not get her hands on that house."

Dalton nodded. "Now don't dismiss your bequest too quickly. Just because it's been challenged does not mean you will be cut out. There's no reason to believe Cordelia Werner wasn't in sound mind when she put you in." Dalton pulled his attaché case onto his lap, opened it, and took out a handful of legal-size documents bound with blue paper covers. "I have a few things for you to sign." He fanned them over his knees. "That is—if you wish me to represent you in this matter." He laid his hands flat on top of the case. "I'd like very much to see you get the money."

Janelle lowered her eyes, shame pressing her to silence.

How absolutely unbearable to be found out like this, yet how gentlemanly of Dalton not to confront her with her lie. She bit her tongue until it hurt, wishing she had had enough sense to keep it still two days ago.

Janelle felt tears pooling, ready to spill over. "I guess you can see how much I need the money." She swept the shabby room with a despairing glance.

Dalton put his case and papers on the low coffee table and said reassuringly, "You don't have to explain anything to me."

"Oh, I do." Tears burned, threatening to flood her face. "I owe you an apology, Mr. Graham."

"Dalton, please." His eyebrows lifted at her formality.

Janelle pressed her tongue to the roof of her mouth, determined to gather her composure.

"I think I understand what happened," Dalton said.

"Do you?" Janelle asked, his resonant voice bringing a shiver to the backs of her arms. She shifted on the sofa. "How can you understand when I'm not sure I do?"

"It's not so terribly difficult, Janelle. You want and expect a great deal from life, and you deserve a chance to go after it. There's nothing wrong with that."

"I should have been more honest with you." She pressed her fingers to the side of her cheek, falling silent.

Dalton got up from his chair and sat beside Janelle. He pulled her hands away from her face.

"You knew the truth about me all along, didn't you?" Her voice was hoarse with shame.

"Yes." Dalton let go of her fingers. "I didn't come here to embarrass you. I have dropped Perry off here many times. I'm surprised you didn't know that."

"Perry and I don't always communicate," she explained.

Looking Janelle squarely in the eye, Dalton went on. "Before you walked into my office, I knew exactly where you lived and how your father died and that you and your brother have been having a difficult time. . . . The only thing Perry didn't tell me was how beautiful his sister is."

Janelle quickly stifled a small gasp of delight. Their relationship was a family matter. How dare he talk to a stranger about such an intimate, personal thing? He could show more respect for her feelings.

Cocking his head to one side, Dalton added, "I can't say that I was shocked when you embellished yourself for my benefit. In fact, I was a little flattered."

His amused, comforting manner helped lessen her misery.

"You let me ramble on like an idiot," Janelle said. Relief, shame, and humiliation rattled her like a disobedient child. "How embarrassing! You must think I'm crazy."

"Naw." Dalton's indulgent grin swept over her. "Not crazy. Just anxious to make a good impression. Trying to elevate yourself, as I am inclined to believe your father did quite well."

"Why do you say that?" My God, what had Perry *not* told this man?

"Oh, Perry's spun quite a few tales about your father. A rather flamboyant, self-promoting, and interesting character—from what I've heard."

"You think I'm like that, too?" Janelle asked, not really wanting the answer.

"I don't know, but I do think all Garrett Roy wanted was for you and your brother to be prepared to find a way in this complicated, unfair world."

As if to stop Dalton's analysis, Janelle stood and walked to the far side of the room. As she trailed her fingers lightly over the keyboard of the ancient Hackley upright, her anxiety began melting away. She kept her back to Dalton, thinking of what to say.

Finally turning, she let it all out. "So now you know the truth. I have lived right here all my life, and my mother never had a career as a concert pianist, never held a job in her life. Perry, whom you so lavishly praise, contributes nothing around here. He goes his way doing 'good deeds' for the *cause*, whatever that is, leaving the entire management of this household up to me. And now what? I'm unemployed; my reputation is threatened. How can I possibly hold things together?" She wiped a tear off her cheek.

"Janelle." Dalton stood before her. "You are a lovely, hardworking woman who cares deeply about her family. Don't belittle that! So you've had a setback. So what? It won't be the first, and you'll get through it just fine. I'll help."

The nearness of him, the sincerity in his voice, the brilliance of his blue-gray eyes ... His acceptance stifled Janelle's misgivings, increasing the attraction she felt.

Dalton continued. "The important thing is for you to stop all this nonsense about trying to be someone you aren't. Cultivate the good qualities you have. I assure you they are more than enough."

He placed his hands on Janelle's shoulders. She met his intent, disturbing gaze and swallowed the growing lump in her throat.

His touch fused Janelle to the carpet. If she moved, she knew she would shatter the opportunity he had so divinely presented. Desiring his caress, Janelle held her breath, remaining immobile, knowing the next move would be up to her.

Gingerly touching the wide, soft lapel of Dalton's tweed jacket, she stroked the fabric as she thought. His fresh masculine scent swept through her so powerfully it left her unexpectedly shaken. She prayed he wouldn't pull away.

Dalton relaxed beneath her touch, imperceptibly moving closer. "I have a confession, too," he said, his face opening up to her in mock perplexity. He spoke lowly, his words feathered with intensity. "I have not stopped thinking about you since you walked out of my office."

Janelle watched his hands fidgeting nervously at his side.

"I feel like a teenager," Dalton said. "And I hope I'm not making an ass out of myself, but I must tell you ... I'd like to get to know you better." He straightened up rather abruptly.

Janelle was mesmerized by the blue-gray eyes that

never left her face. Sunlight flooded through the window behind Dalton and cast him in a golden light.

"I've been thinking about you, too," Janelle admitted. "But I wasn't sure . . . I mean," she stammered. Suddenly there was only one way to say it. "I guess I hoped race might not be an issue." She groped for the words to express herself. "Anyway, after I lied to you, I was worried that you would find out and not want anything to do with me." Her voice cracked. "I hate myself for acting so childishly."

Dalton placed one finger in front of her lips. "Please. Don't say that." Then, with a steady, deliberate touch, he traced the outline of her full lower lip with his forefinger. "There is no reason in the world for you to believe that you can't be loved for yourself." His hand dropped away, and a smile broke the electric tension. Dalton stepped back.

Janelle felt herself blooming with joy. He wanted her! He had been thinking of her! She could see through the taut restraint on his face—the set of his mouth, the clench of his jaw, the ice-blue invitation he struggled to mask. As she looked at him, the stained jacquard drapes and the dull, shabby sofa faded into oblivion on the periphery; the man before her sparkled, outshining everything else.

Janelle stepped forward and raised both hands behind Dalton's neck. She laced her fingers together in an embrace. Tentatively, haltingly, in a silent, unsure plea, she looked up into his face.

Dalton searched her eyes as if gauging the sincerity of her invitation. "Are you sure?" he asked softly.

Janelle nodded, pressing her fingers firmly on his neck, heart pounding in her ears, now frightened by her bold, shameless movement.

Dalton placed his lips to hers. Janelle surrendered to the bliss of his skin against hers, the admission of their attraction finally out in the open.

Janelle allowed him to draw her breath until she felt dizzy. Then, suddenly, he pulled away, gently separating from her before leaning back to ease his fingers slowly to the mesh net loosely holding her hair from her face. She watched his satisfied smile as her thick brown hair floated over her shoulders.

Janelle shook her head, oblivious of the way sunlight captured and magnified the golden highlights in her hair but fully aware that her action prompted a flicker of desire. She saw it in his eyes. A shiver of longing crept over her.

Then the sound of a key grating in the lock, loud as a gunshot, pierced her. She tensed, eyes trained on the door.

It rattled open, then shut with a thud.

Dalton turned.

Janelle gripped his sleeve.

"What in the world is going on?" Alice Roy's mouth gaped as she slowly pulled off her gloves, drawing in the sight before her.

Dalton remained rooted at the foot of the sofa. He straightened his tie, tugged the lapels of his jacket.

Janelle rushed to sweep tendrils of hair from her face.

"Mom!" The word flew from her lips in a gasp.

"Yes, it's me." A stern admonishment, spoken in disgust. "And who is this man and just what do you think you're doing?"

"This is my attorney, Dalton Graham," Janelle said, humiliated by her mother's presence. To see her like this; hair loose and wildly flying about her face, moments ago pressed up against a stranger—a white man!

"Well, I am shocked at what I see, Janelle." Reluctant to enter the room, Alice stood in the hallway. "And you, Mr. Graham. What kind of lawyer are you? Making out like you want to help my daughter, only to compromise her like this?" The sides of Alice's mouth drooped down in offense. "I think you'd better be going. Janelle will get another lawyer to help her. My girl doesn't have to resort to low-class tactics like this!"

Dalton glanced at Janelle, then back at her mother.

"Mrs. Roy, let me explain. I am not taking advantage of Janelle, I assure you." Then he fell silent.

Janelle cast a furtive glance at Dalton. What could they possibly say to dispel the awful impression now branded on Alice Roy's mind?

"Mr. Graham didn't pressure me, Mom."

Alice just glared.

"This—this—" Janelle stopped. What could she say that wouldn't sound inanely juvenile? "Well, what you saw has nothing to do with my case," Janelle finished.

"I don't care what you say, it's not acceptable, Janelle. You know it! I am surprised that you would fall for whatever this man has told you to convince you to act like this."

There would be no changing her mother's mind, Janelle knew. Alice Roy's stance against interracial relationships had been clearly expressed over the years. Trying to absolve Dalton or herself at this point would do more harm that good.

"Maybe you had better go, Dalton," Janelle said flatly, wishing him gone, wishing her mother had not made her feel like a tramp in front of him. Tears pressed the backs of her eyelids and gathered thickly in her throat.

"I apologize, Mrs. Roy," Dalton began, gathering papers from the coffee table, buckling his attaché case. "My behavior was very much out of line. You have every right to be upset. I apologize. I never planned for this to happen."

"Most men don't," Alice said with a snort.

Dalton turned a blank, professional face to Janelle. "I'll leave these papers for you to sign. Just mail them to my office." He picked up his case. "You'll be notified of the outcome."

Janelle reached out to touch him, but he shrank away.

"Please, Dalton," she said, shocked at the instant cooling of his demeanor, "I'm the one who should be apologizing."

Now Alice stepped closer. "My daughter is not like all the other colored girls you're used to having your way with and tossing aside when you're finished. Not by a long shot, mister. Now you get out of my house and leave my daughter alone!"

Dalton blushed deep red under Alice Roy's blast but said nothing. Without looking back at Janelle, he moved with deliberate steps into the hallway and let himself out of the house.

Glancing nervously at her mother, Janelle could not help issuing a final plea. "I know how this looked, but I can explain." Panic engulfed her.

"You don't have to tell me what it was," Alice spit out. "This white man comes in here smooth-talking you. He knows the Werners have money. Taking your case might mean something for him."

"No. You're wrong. He came to tell me that Cordelia Werner named me in her will."

"And you were naïve enough to believe him? Janelle! Have you lost your mind? A white man wants only one thing from a colored girl. Don't you have the good sense to see it?"

CHAPTER
TEN

Taking the steps two at a time, Janelle rushed upstairs. She stomped into her bedroom and slammed the door. Tears broke loose, stinging her cheeks. He was gone! The encounter she had prayed for, shattered. She stretched out on the bed, pressing her face to the nubby chenille spread, despairing not at her mother's bitter accusations that came as no surprise but at the terrifying calm on Dalton's face when he had turned to leave.

Janelle thought about her own behavior. She had been brazen, opening herself up to Dalton Graham, chancing rejection, dismissal, ridicule. But . . . he wanted her, that was clear, and she'd be damned if she'd back down now.

After an hour of soul-searching and second-guessing and wondering how Dalton must be feeling, Janelle pulled herself together, went downstairs, and called his office.

"NAACP," Norma, the receptionist, answered.

"May I speak to Dalton Graham, please?" The tremor in her voice was evident.

"May I ask who's calling?"

"Janelle Roy."

"Hold a moment, please."

Janelle tensed, waiting. Would he be glad that she had called? Contrite? Relieved? She faltered at the prospect that he might be angry.

"Mr. Graham is on another call right now. Would you care to leave your number?"

"He has it," Janelle barely managed to reply.

"All right, Miss Roy, I'll give him the message that you called."

The line went dead in Janelle's hand.

Another hour and a half went by, and the phone remained silent. At two-thirty Janelle called again. She'd just missed him, Norma explained, and he'd be in court until about three-thirty. Why not try again at four?

She did, only to be told he'd left for the day and would not be in until Monday morning.

By Sunday evening Janelle had worked herself into such a state of anxiety she had terrible cramps in her stomach. During the night she dreamed she entered a room to find Dalton in the arms of a shapely, faceless red-haired woman and awoke with a cold sweat clinging to her body. Fearing the return of the unsettling dream, she stayed awake most of the night, tossing fitfully under the covers, listening to the winter wind hammering at the windows.

The telephone call from Dalton Graham didn't come until five o'clock on Monday. As Janelle listened to his words of apology and regret, palpitations fluttered through her in warning.

"Please, don't take my mother's outburst too seriously," she said, hoping to salvage what they'd begun. "In her opinion, miscegenation is still evil and unthinkable. She's witnessed the cruelty that comes when people cross racial lines and has told me more than once what she thinks of people who dare to try it."

"Believe me, I understand, Janelle. That's why I am obligated to respect her feelings," Dalton said. "I should have been more sensitive, more cautious." A tense silence followed. "I have no right to create hostilities between you and your mother."

"But I have the right to be with whomever I choose," Janelle said.

"Yes, that's true. But I don't want to be party to the destruction of the relationship you have with your mother."

She felt resentment rising. "You couldn't."

"Yes. I could." The finality of his tone was like a cold slap.

Despite her efforts to keep her composure, Janelle felt her confidence crumbling. "But I don't care! Dammit." Didn't he have guts enough to stick up for what he wanted? Why couldn't he risk it when she was willing?

"You do care, Janelle. You love your mother and care an awful lot about what she thinks of you."

Janelle didn't reply but pushed away the truth of his words. *All I need is a chance to hold him again, kiss him, reassure him that Mother will come around,* she thought. *His reservations will fade.*

"Perhaps I could come downtown tomorrow, meet you at—"

"I'm sorry, Janelle." He cut her off. "I'd love to see you again, really, but I have a lot of reading to do for a case that goes to court next week. Besides, right now I think it's best if we concentrate on getting you back to work, settling with the Werner estate about your inheritance. Let's not get off track. There's still a lot to do."

"You're right," she conceded. She'd play it his way—for now. "Do you have any news from the coroner's office?"

"Yes, I do," Dalton said. "The report just arrived. That's why I called. The autopsy shows that Cordelia Werner died of a slow-growing brain tumor. It had not been detected by Miss Werner's physician."

"Really?" She shuddered with relief. "A brain tumor? How odd!"

"That's right. If anything, the overdose of Febrahyde may have made Miss Werner's final hours easier than they would have been."

"That's a relief . . . Oh, God. So, where do we go from here? How can I get Sara Johnson to retract what she's said?"

"I'm going to call on her tomorrow and have a little chat. As your attorney I think I can persuade her to forget about her smear campaign. In the meantime, you need to go out and make inquiries, put in applications, try to secure another position."

"Now? Without references? I don't think I'll have much luck."

"Well, try anyway. You don't have much of a case against Mrs. Johnson unless you *can't* find a job. We've been speculating that her public statements have hurt your ability to secure a position, but we have nothing to support that fear."

"You, mean, if I get a position, there's no case?"

"Possibly. It certainly would indicate that your earning potential has not been damaged."

Janelle was silent.

"You understand?"

"Yes." The horrid ordeal was beginning to dissolve. "Will you let me know what Sara Johnson says?" Janelle asked, anxious to learn what the woman planned to do and anticipating another opportunity to speak with Dalton.

"I'll try, but tomorrow is going to be a heck of a day. I won't be in the office at all."

Janelle hoped he wasn't putting her off.

"Tell you what," he finally said. "Why don't you meet me at Hugo's, the sandwich shop next to the courthouse, at—oh, how about four o'clock tomorrow afternoon? I should be finished in court by then."

Her heart galloped. He wanted to meet her in a restaurant. He had the courage to be seen with her in public. She held her reaction under control. "I'll be there, Dalton, and . . . thank you very much."

"Don't thank me too soon." He was serious. "Mrs. Johnson is a powerful woman who feels she's been wronged. I'll have to handle her very carefully."

"I know," Janelle said, still smarting from the mean-spirited way she had been treated the day Cordelia died. She told Dalton good-bye.

Four o'clock at Hugo's. In the heart of the business district. She smiled, musing silently, hanging up the phone. *A little more time with you, Mr. Graham. That's all I need.*

You'll see that I'm right. I'm not going to let you slip away.

She went into the front room and switched on the radio, turning his words around in her mind. What could possibly be the source of Dalton Graham's fear of taking a chance with her? It wasn't about her mother's displeasure. It wasn't about race at all. There was something else bothering him that he would not admit to her.

The miniature poodle sniffing at his pants leg reminded Dalton Graham of a windup toy he had seen downtown in Lazarus's window. The pink-tinted, cottony creature nervously darted from Dalton to the doorway then back to the damask sofa where Dalton sat waiting for Sara Johnson.

The uniformed maid quietly retreated toward the back of the cavernous, opulent apartment, oblivious of the wiry little animal that nosed and scratched the red-orange Persian carpet dominating the room.

Restraining an urge to reach down and scoop the pesky thing up and toss it across the room, Dalton lowered his heavy attaché case to the floor with a thud, startling the dog away.

Its thin whine brought Sara Johnson fluttering into the room.

"Please excuse Hyacinth," she said, sweeping toward Dalton in a flurry of purple silk. "I don't receive many visitors, and I'm afraid she's forgotten her manners." Sara bent over and picked up her pet, cuddling it in her heavy arms, then extended one hand to Dalton.

"Mr. Graham, what can I do for you?" She settled her wide, square hips into a dainty tapestry chair that fronted an Italian marble coffee table. A cluster of Waterford miniatures caught the light from a nearby wall sconce, sparkling in clear-cut brilliance. The richly decorated room, with its gilt-framed oil paintings and crush of fringed velvet pillows bespoke the extent of the Werner fortune—old money bottomless and solid.

"As I mentioned on the phone, I represent Miss Janelle

Roy, the nurse you hired to care for your sister," Dalton replied. He pulled his case to his lap, opened it, and took out a paper covered with dark print.

"That's right." Sara's face lost its hospitality, and her jowls sagged in lined resentment. "And I won't mince words with you, Mr. Graham. Miss Roy's unprofessional conduct has created a very unpleasant situation for me and my family. The fact that she stands to inherit from Cordelia's estate is appalling—proof enough that she had ulterior motives. That girl deserves nothing! I'll fight it to the end."

"I have a copy of the medical examiner's report, Mrs. Johnson." Dalton jumped right in, not wanting or needing to hear more, trying to stay focused on his mission: Get a written retraction or, if possible, a letter of reference for Janelle. He pressed forward.

"According to the autopsy report, Miss Werner died of a brain tumor. It's clear that Miss Roy was not to blame."

"Perhaps not directly," Sara said, "but her lack of supervision allowed the overdose to occur. Poor Flora is utterly distraught. She's on the verge of a nervous breakdown. Oh, the strain of it." Sara shuddered dramatically, letting Hyacinth jump down from her lap. "Those rude reporters won't let me rest. My phone has been ringing around the clock. And of course, Cordelia's estate will be frozen until all this is settled. She died last Tuesday, a week ago today. The funeral has been held up entirely too long. We'll bury her tomorrow afternoon . . . God rest her soul."

Dalton gave her a nod of sympathy.

"And the will! Of all things, leaving that girl all that money!" Sara's broad shoulders quivered in obvious outrage. Hyacinth darted beneath the sofa to snuggle contentedly behind Dalton's feet.

"I understand. Losing a family member is difficult, Mrs. Johnson." Dalton chose to ignore the will. "And I know this is not a good time, but I'd like to discuss the unfavorable comments you made about Miss Roy that were published in the paper. Rather premature, don't you think, in light of how the autopsy turned out?"

"Not at all. I meant every word I said."

"Do you realize that your defamatory statements, which may have very damaging effects on the young woman's career, could be considered slanderous?"

Sara sat ramrod straight. Not an eyelash fluttered.

"Miss Roy could bring legal charges," Dalton said.

"Just let her try," Sara snapped. "She doesn't have the nerve or the resources to challenge me. And if she did, she'd never get out of court." The matron sniffed loudly and glared at Dalton. "Is that all you came for, Mr. Graham, to threaten me with a lawsuit from that ridiculous girl?"

"No," Dalton said calmly. "I came to ask you to drop your campaign to discredit Miss Roy and to give her a decent reference. Let the young lady get on with her life." Dalton doubted his words were even heard. "She's suffered a great deal over this, too, Mrs. Johnson."

"Well, she's getting what she deserves!"

Sara's words burned like drops of acid splashed on his skin. "I don't believe you mean that," he said, hoping to touch an ethical cord. Surely the woman had some sense of fair play.

In a swift movement Sara rose from her chair and glowered down at the attorney. "I think it's time for you to leave, Mr. Graham. I have nothing more to say about the situation." She snapped her fingers, and Hyacinth fled to her mistress. Sara gathered the dog up in her arms.

Dalton closed his attaché case, stood, and moved toward the door, then turned back. "It's too bad you can't see the mistake you're making. You say you want peace, no publicity, no fuss about your sister's death. If Miss Roy files a slander suit against you, the reporters will be crawling all over your family again. Think about Flora. She had a part in this, too. Would you submit her to the pressure that a legal action would bring? The Werner family problems will be fair game for the press. Exactly what you don't want." He watched her closely, noticing a shift in her posture. "Won't you reconsider your position?"

Sara stared defiantly at him, her thin lips drawn tightly into a pucker of resistance. Perspiration dripped from her hairline, creating sodden, chalky lines in her thick face powder. "I have nothing good to say about that nurse!"

"Then don't say anything at all, Mrs. Johnson." Dalton grasped the opportunity for compromise. "Just let the whole matter drop."

The purple silk caftan flowing from Sara Johnson's shoulders swayed with the force of her audible breath. A crafty gleam came to her eyes. "You tell Janelle Roy she'll get no reference from me . . . good or bad. And the only thing I'll promise you is that I will never utter the woman's name again. Not as long as I am allowed to stay here on earth." She picked up a tiny silver bell from the nearby credenza and shook it rapidly three times. "And you can also tell her to forget about getting a dime from Cordelia's estate. That will never happen, I assure you."

The maid came into the room and stood quietly in the doorway.

"Zena," Sara said, "please show Mr. Graham out." Then she leveled her eyes with Dalton's, crisply adding, "His business here is concluded."

Knowing that it was a no-win situation, Dalton pulled on his trench coat and nodded to Sara Johnson, then let the maid show him out.

CHAPTER
ELEVEN

The bitter January wind gusted around the corner, stirring up a flurry of grimy newspapers lying in the gutter at Janelle's frozen feet. Lifted in a whoosh from its filthy niche, the rubbish pitched crazily, tumbling down the shabby street.

As she stood there, trying to get her bearings, Janelle soberly watched it sail in ragged drifts before her. A blast of cold air pressed from behind, propelling her forward, making her clutch her hat with one hand, clamp her flat purse to her chest with the other, and cross the street.

Perversely welcoming the slap of frigid air on her cheeks, she wished the twenty-degree temperature could numb her mind as well as it did her raw, gloveless hands. But a cacophony of voices clamored in her head:

Sorry, Miss Roy. All of our shifts are fully staffed.

No letter of reference? I'm sorry, I couldn't possibly take you on.

Perhaps on the night shift. That is, as an aide, of course.

Four of the interviewers had immediately recognized her name, having read of her misfortune in the Columbus *Dispatch*. After politely listening to her explanation of the charges and seeming relieved that the medical examiner's report had exonerated her, they still had no positions to offer.

At Finch's Nursing Referral and Registry, she had been

interviewed by Gwendolyn Finch herself, who remembered Janelle as one of the first colored graduates she had placed.

Not many colored nurses got Miss Finch's assistance, and Janelle had entered the blue-carpeted room hoping to leave with a coveted referral slip tucked in the bottom of her purse.

It had not worked out that way, in spite of Miss Finch's genuine relief that the autopsy had cleared Janelle of any wrongdoing. No placement could be made without a letter of reference or at least a phone call from Sara Johnson.

From Finch's, Janelle had gone to the personnel offices of three hospitals, two nursing homes, and a community clinic. Nothing had been offered, no promises made. Now here she was, lost and disoriented on the south side of town after a disappointing interview with an elderly couple.

Janelle slowed her pace, ducked into the covered entryway of a shoe repair shop, and opened her handbag. Fumbling with her change purse, she counted her money, feeling relieved she had bus fare to make the trip downtown to meet Dalton and make it back home again. With a snap she closed her purse, glancing up just as a battered Buick rumbled to a stop at the snow-covered curb.

"Janelle!" Perry had rolled down the passenger window and was leaning out, calling her name. "Janelle! What are you doing down here?"

Surprised to see her brother, Janelle ran over to the car. Perry scooted back into the driver's seat as she opened the door and slipped in beside him. Hunching down, she blew on her ice-cold fingers, then began to roll the window back up.

"Whose car is this?" She glanced around the worn-out interior. "Sure smells moldy."

"Reverend Crossley's. He let me borrow it to take some materials over to the NCD."

"Oh," Janelle murmured.

Perry mentally noted Janelle's displeasure. Her lack of

enthusiasm galled him. If she spent more time in her own community, she might understand how important his activities were. Just because she had never had to fight for anything, she ought to be more sympathetic to what he was trying to do.

"What brings you to the south side?" Perry asked again. Parsons Avenue was not his sister's style, unless she and Emma ventured over to Schottenstein's to buy designer clothes at fire sale prices.

"I had a job interview," she replied.

"Where?" Perry asked. "At Children's?"

"No. A private interview."

"Did you get the job?"

"No."

He noticed that her voice seemed collapsed with fatigue. Shifting the car into first gear, he pulled away from the curb, resisting the urge to say more.

Proceeding slowly down Parsons, Perry tapped the horn now and then as he passed people he knew, lowering the window to call out friendly, bantering remarks, laughing as he crawled from one block to the next.

"Where are you headed?" Janelle asked.

"To meet Billy Engals at the *Sentinel*. We're working on an article about the Lantree protest. If the editor approves, the *Sentinel* will run the story this week."

"Can you drop me off downtown?" Janelle asked.

Because it was out of his way, Perry frowned. He didn't have money for gas, and Reverend Crossley had expected him back thirty minutes ago.

"What's downtown?"

"I'm meeting Dalton at Hugo's at four."

"Dalton? At Hugo's? Isn't that kinda chancy?" Knowing few blacks went in there, Perry raised a brow and looked straight out the windshield. Hugo's was stuffy, old guard, where the business crowd gathered, not a friendly place as far as Perry was concerned. Anyway, Dalton usually talked business in his office. Unless . . .

"I don't think going to Hugo's is *chancy*," Janelle replied. "God, Perry. Dad used to go there all the time. We *are* allowed in, you know."

"Forget it." He didn't feel like trying to make his point. He settled himself more deeply in his seat, pulling air into his lungs, composing himself.

"All right, say it. You don't approve," Janelle said.

"Well, jeez, Janelle, do you have to go and make a fool of yourself?"

Perry felt her stare warming the side of his face.

"What do you mean?" she asked.

"Oh, yeah. Act innocent." Perry flexed his fingers atop the wheel. "Mom told me what happened."

"What did she say?"

"Hell, I don't remember her exact words, if that's what you want, but she sure was upset about what she saw." Now he glanced toward Janelle. "You two having an affair?"

"No! I like Dalton, he likes me. That's hardly having an affair."

"I don't think it's a good idea for you to get involved with Dalton socially. I know him. He'll cozy up, get what he wants, and let you down hard. I'm telling you, I know all about him, Janelle. He's got a little black book the size of the yellow pages. A real Don Juan. A great attorney, but he likes chasing women as much as he likes winning a case in court. *Don't get involved.*"

"Why are you so concerned about who I spend my time with?"

"Because I know what you're trying to do."

"Yeah?"

"Yeah. You want to use him to get out of Oakwood Alley. Whew! I don't understand you. How can you do this? Mom is all upset. You know she can't stand mixing blacks and whites . . . romantically, anyway, and I agree. Besides, don't you think you've got her worried enough with this situation with the Werners?"

"I don't want to talk about it, Perry." Janelle couldn't believe she was getting a lecture from her baby brother.

"I know Dalton pretty well," Perry said, choosing to ignore Janelle. "He likes pretty women, but he's no jerk. He'd feel real bad if he caused any problem in my family. Back off."

"You talked to Dalton about me, didn't you?"

Perry shrugged and fished a cigarette out of his pocket. "We talk about a lot of things."

"You'd better not interfere, Perry. What I do socially is none of your business."

"Well, if I were you, I'd leave him alone." Shaking his head, he looked out the driver's side window, watching a man on the curb take a drink from a bottle wrapped in a brown paper bag. Without saying another word, he stepped on the gas and nudged the rusted car deeper into the stream of traffic. Neither spoke again during the fifteen minute ride toward town.

At the busy intersection of Mound and Fulton, Janelle got out of the car and turned back to look at Perry. She felt off-balance, unsure of what to say, his words still pricking her sorely, her confidence slightly bruised. Determined to keep her composure, she managed a half smile and a wave. Perry nodded, then sped away from the curb.

"He'd better worry about getting a job instead of who I want to spend my time with," Janelle muttered aloud, hurrying up the street toward Hugo's.

The chiming voices of the Andrews Sisters filtering out of the jukebox onto the street greeted Janelle on the bustling sidewalk. As soon as the brass-plated door swung open, the smells of salami, pastrami, corned beef, and grilled steak smothered her in welcome. She glanced around the room and saw Dalton. Their eyes connected briefly, jolting Janelle to hurry forward.

He stood, watching her calmly as she slipped between small tables to make her way toward his booth.

"You're on time, as usual," he said in greeting, waiting until she was settled in her seat before he sat again.

Janelle felt a pulsing begin in the pit of her stomach. "I'm a very punctual person. I hate to be late or to be rushed. So I usually wind up being early." She laughed, a nervous trill, her brown cheeks flushed from the cold.

"Well, I'm so used to dealing with people who treat my time as if it were theirs I forget what it's like not to be kept waiting."

Janelle looked around the plant-filled room that had scenes from a rustic Bavarian village painted on the walls. The diners hunched in conversation were the attorneys, bankers, merchants, and managers who worked throughout downtown. There was one other colored person in the place, the woman now standing at their table handing her a menu.

"Are you hungry?" Dalton asked, accepting a menu from the waitress.

Janelle smiled and said boldly, "Starved. I've been out in the streets all day."

"Making inquiries about a position?" Dalton casually ran four fingers through the ebony locks trailing onto his forehead, tossing the hair from his face. Then he quickly scanned the menu in a familiar manner and set it aside.

"Yeah," Janelle replied, her dark, soft eyes now lifted to the blue-gray magnetism of his. "And the results have been disastrous. Plain awful." She put the menu down. "I don't know what Sara Johnson told you, but I'll tell you right now: The alarm has been sounded. Even the registry can't help me get a job."

Dalton looked at Janelle with understanding, then said, "Why don't you order? We'll talk about your options later. Enjoy the meal. Get anything you want."

She ordered a pastrami on rye with Swiss cheese and sauerkraut. Dalton got a grilled onion and cheese steak sandwich. They skirted any reference to their ill-fated embrace, chatting about the fast-dropping temperature, the rally in Cleveland, the case of Danny White and the stolen car.

"So you believed his story?" Janelle asked, caught up in the easy, relaxed atmosphere Dalton created. He seemed so calm, she observed, pressing her trembling knees together, reveling in the acceptance he offered. Never had she felt so comfortable with any man—white or colored—and she knew he was happy to see her again.

"Sure did," Dalton said slowly, sounding as if his verdict were still not in. "I believed Danny and got the charges dropped. But that boy is covering for someone. Danny did not steal the car, I'm convinced, but I'd be willing to bet good money that he knows who did."

"And you can't get him to tell?"

"Not a chance. All I did was get him off. If the police stick close to Danny, in time he'll lead them to the guilty party. He's not squeaky clean, I suspect."

When the waitress brought their sandwiches, Janelle could wait no longer to hear about Dalton's meeting. She started right in. "Did you get to talk to Sara Johnson?"

Dalton took a bite of his sandwich and washed it down with coffee.

"Yes. I went to her apartment and met with her this morning."

"And?"

"And she said she will not give you a reference. Not good or bad."

Janelle could feel her spirits tumbling; her shoulders drooped.

"But I did get Mrs. Johnson to agree to refrain from saying anything more about you. Her smear campaign has ended."

"A lot of good that will do." Janelle's voice was husky with disappointment. "The damage has already been done."

Dalton set down his coffee cup and reached over to put his hand on Janelle's arm.

Despite the disappointing message he had brought, Janelle was buoyed by his touch. It burned through the thick brown sleeve of her dress, initiating a wondrous heavy feeling between her thighs. She looked down at his slim, tapered fingers.

"Don't give up so quickly," Dalton said. "You've been

out looking only one day. It may take weeks, but you'll get something. People will forget about the Werners, and remember, with this war taking so many nurses into the field, the need for qualified help will increase. I think getting Sara to be quiet is a victory. Let's treat it as such."

Janelle wanted to believe him, in spite of feeling that his optimism was woefully premature. "We'll see" was all she could manage. A bitter taste rose in her mouth. Pounding the pavement, having doors closed in her face, swallowing her pride and her anger at being rejected: these were new experiences for Janelle, and she did not plan to bear them much longer. Something had to come along soon.

"Persistence pays off," Dalton told her reassuringly. "You keep showing up for interviews, and stay positive. People like to help those who show determination."

Janelle laid her napkin aside and looked at Dalton as if he were a stranger; the warm feeling between her thighs had vanished. "What is it with you?" Her doelike eyes turned hard. "Are you blind? I'm a colored nurse. Out of work. And the richest, most powerful family in this city has its foot on my back. There is no work for me here. There never will be."

As much as she wanted to get closer to Dalton, she'd speak her mind, even if it drove him away. "It's easy for you to offer platitudes to keep my spirits up!" Her taut, controlled words rose to a loud whisper. "It is quite another thing to face discrimination and injustice on a day-to-day basis and stay positive!"

She slipped her arm from beneath Dalton's hand, but he clasped her fingers in a firm, warm grip.

"When you came in here," he said, "you expected me to hand you a long white envelope with a letter of reference inside it, didn't you?"

She tried to disengage her fingers from his, but he squeezed them more tightly.

"Do you think I am some kind of miracle worker?" His hard tone pained her. "Did you think that because I am a white attorney, I would be able to sway Sara Johnson to see things my way? Is that what you thought, Janelle?"

She stared sullenly, unable, unwilling to answer, embarrassed by the blunt, brutal truth.

"Well, I couldn't, and I didn't," Dalton said. "I got the best deal I could under the circumstances."

"So that's the way you operate . . . making deals?" Janelle couldn't understand the ease with which he had settled.

"Yes. Attorneys make deals, compromises. Just because the rest of the world doesn't see things my way doesn't stop me from working for compromise. That's important, Janelle. Compromise."

"You don't seem the least bit willing to compromise to give our—what shall I call it? Friendship? All right— friendship a chance to grow." Janelle bit her quivering bottom lip, sweeping Dalton with her genuine disappointment.

"Ah, well, that's different."

"How?" She had to know what it was that was holding him back.

For the first time Dalton appeared at a loss. His eyes grew opaque, as if he dreaded the effort needed to explain himself. "I felt awful leaving your house under those circumstances. Your mother's disappointment in me, in you has haunted me, Janelle. I hate that she thought I would take advantage of you. She brought it home, Janelle. She pushed it in my face and made me see all the damage my impetuous behavior could cause. I've been skimming along with some pretty shallow relationships recently, not overly concerned about anyone's feelings but my own. So I will not try to defend my behavior because I was, and still am, attracted to you."

"But?" She prayed he would say that he was willing to start over.

"But I have to make a choice, and this time I know I can't live with myself if things turned out badly. You'd wind up hating me for caring for you."

Janelle allowed Dalton to stroke her fingers. "I don't agree," she murmured.

"I feel awful that I've disappointed you, Janelle. But the road we'd be traveling would be a very treacherous one. I don't want to put you and your family through that. You can understand what I mean, can't you?"

"Yes and no." She lifted her chin. "I'm not naïve, and not particularly courageous either, but I sensed a bravery about you that I felt would protect us from this backlash you're predicting."

Dalton laughed lowly. "Brave? I don't know. Maybe foolhardy. Impetuous. Captivated by you. That much I'll admit to." He grinned boyishly, making Janelle want him even more.

Eyes lowered, she toyed with her napkin, silently wondering if Perry had undermined her chances of holding on to Dalton. She wanted him physically, intellectually, totally, and it had nothing to do with getting out of Oakwood Alley. "Are you backing away because of something Perry told you about me?"

Dalton tilted his head to one side. "What do you think he told me?"

"That I've turned my back on my race and am looking for a way to improve my lot by entering your world. The white world."

Slumping back in his seat, Dalton crossed his arms over his chest and gave Janelle a curious look "That's pretty strong!"

"Well, didn't he say something to that effect? Didn't he make me out to be color-struck?"

"We've discussed you, naturally, but he said nothing about what you wanted out of life."

"Ha! That's hard to believe," she said quickly, then added, "But I don't think you'd lie."

"No, I wouldn't, Janelle. That's why I won't make promises I may not be able to keep."

Janelle drew her shoulders up high. "Well, at least you've been honest. I appreciate that, Dalton, I do."

Dalton picked up the check and signaled the waitress, a glimmer of relief evident on his face.

"You did get Sara Johnson off my back," Janelle said. "That's why I called you; that's what I wanted. I really should be thanking you. I'm sorry. I never meant to belittle what you've done." To her horror she began to cry. She opened her purse and took out a handkerchief to wipe tears she had not felt gather. Dalton's gaze, serious and compelling, penetrated her, initiating shivers of guilt, relief, and hope. As she wiped her eyes, she told him, forcing a smile, "You certainly know how to make your point, Counselor. You are a very persuasive man, Dalton Graham, not like any man I ever met before."

"God, I hope not," he said with a devilish grin.

Janelle sucked in her breath and held it for a moment. She gave Dalton a thorough assessment. Oh, how she did want to enter his world—at his side—shielded by his optimism, engulfed in a love that could not be shaken. She tucked a stray wisp of ruddy brown hair under the sleek curve of her pompadour.

"My dad used to talk about seeing around the corner," she said. "I was very young and had no idea what he meant. But as he pushed me and prodded me through school, he challenged me not to settle for what I could see but to believe that glorious opportunities for adventure were always hidden from view. It's clearer now what he thought I should be looking for." A radiance born of understanding came to her, illuminating her face. A long-lost piece of her father's puzzling advice slipped gently and firmly into place.

"He must have been a good father," Dalton said.

"The best," she replied, swallowing a surge of useless tears that threatened to rise again, wanting Dalton to see her in a better light. "You've reminded me just how special he was."

By six o'clock the restaurant was nearly empty and Janelle had drunk so much coffee she began to feel giddy and fidgety, anxious to keep the conversation going. But

Dalton brought their afternoon to an end when he offered Janelle a ride home. She quickly declined, asking instead that he drop her at Emma's house, on the Hilltop, the same area of town where he lived.

The ride across the bridge, through the Bottoms, up the Hill calmed Janelle, precipitating a sense of beginning. She remained charged up, anxious about the future, and grudgingly thankful to Dalton for the honesty of his remarks.

Humming along with Helen O'Connell's lilting rendition of "Tangerine" on the radio, Janelle let the soothing voice transport her. It was much more fun to pretend that she and Dalton were out on a real date than to think about what would have greeted her at home, for she was in no mood for another round with Perry, or an evening of listening to *Inner Sanctum* with her mother, who remained distant yet polite, her feelings hurt, her values challenged.

The warm, dark cocoon of Dalton's car created an atmosphere of intense intimacy. Totally at ease, immersed in his presence, Janelle groaned inwardly when he pulled to a stop in front of Emma's duplex. They had gotten there entirely too soon.

When she looked over at him, with the moonlight illuminating his fair skin, sheening him in silver light, Janelle yearned to touch him, place her lips on his, but she tilted her chin up and away from him instead.

"Thank you for the lift, Dalton." Her voice seemed too husky in the darkened interior. It only heightened her desire to kiss him. "And thanks for the meal, the advice. I don't know what else to say." She lowered her eyes, fixing them on the round black buttons on her mother's green coat. "You've given me a lot to think about."

Dalton turned in his seat, reaching to touch Janelle on the cheek. "You are exquisite in this light. Beautiful." His fingers trailed along her cheek and rested near her lips. "And you're a very lucky girl, Janelle."

"Why do you say lucky?" she asked, hoping to prolong the moment.

"You're free."

She didn't dare disturb the precious sensation of his skin against hers, so she remained silent, her lips pulsing hotly under his touch.

"If the autopsy had even *hinted* at misconduct on your part, I'd be talking to you in a jail cell instead of sitting here with you in the moonlight."

For Janelle, his words rang too true, bringing her sharply back to reality. She boldly entwined her fingers through his and lowered their hands to the seat. Sitting quietly, she considered what could have been.

"I wish we could start over." How simple it was to say that, she thought, relieved to have gotten it out.

"Things happen as they do for good reasons. But I'd like to remain friends, if that's possible."

She didn't answer. She should terminate the relationship now, with no possibility of seeing him again, but she couldn't.

Longing flared, then subsided. "Let me think," Janelle said. "It may not be easy for me to be your friend."

He eased his hand from hers and placed it on the ignition.

Swallowing hard, she watched him close his eyes for a second, then take in an audible breath.

Shadows from a bank of naked maple trees towering along the avenue danced across Dalton's face, partially concealing the slant of his forehead, the keen ridge of his slender nose. Suddenly he swept Janelle with a dark, brooding look, then murmured flatly, "I'd better get going," and deftly turned the key with one hand. He loosened his tie with the other. The purr of the engine shattered the tightwire silence that had gathered volume inside the car.

Aching with disappointment that she had not willed him back to her, Janelle picked up her purse and pulled her scarf around her neck.

"Remember what I told you." Dalton's voice floated over and seductively embraced her.

"What?" she asked lightly, stirred to see a rakish dimple emerge on his cheek.

"Your drive to be special won't let you give up—on yourself or your dreams. And believe me, you won't need me to make them come true." Then he reached across her to open the door.

His hand shimmered like dark silver above her lap, and she was tempted to touch it. Instead she cleared her throat, dispersing the flutter of desire weakening her now, and said, "I'll let you know how things go."

"Please," he said easily, pushing the door open.

Janelle slipped out of the car. Peering back through the open door, making sure her eyes locked with his, she told him, "You'll always know where I am."

Janelle turned sharply and rushed up the frozen walkway to the dimly lighted porch. She rang the bell, then glanced back into the darkened street. She had hoped to catch a final glimpse of Dalton, but all she saw was two tiny red taillights beaming through a cloud of vapor rising from the back of his moving car.

CHAPTER
TWELVE

It was nearing midnight when Emma pushed herself up from the carpeted floor and stood, rather unsteadily. Blinking heavy-lidded eyes, she made her way toward the smoldering glow in her fireplace and pulled back the protective screen. A red-hot flush bathed her face. She stabbed at the logs with an iron poker until they sputtered and hissed and erupted into a colorful riot of flames.

Warm air gusted out into the low-ceilinged room that was furnished with a sofa, two end tables, and one gaudy porcelain lamp. Two bright-hued still lifes of fruit and flowers hung on either side of a wide picture window surrounded by green and white floral drapes.

"Careful there, old girl," Janelle called from her nest of blankets on the sofa, giggling as she thumped her half-full wineglass down on the end table and tucked her feet more closely to her body. Suddenly Emma was no more than a blurry specter of movement and shadow. Perhaps they shouldn't have popped the cork so quickly on that second bottle of champagne. "Let's not burn the house down," she mumbled.

"Hey, we've got to celebrate," Emma said, prodding a burning log to the center of the rate. "You are innocent! I won't have to come visit you in jail!"

"That's right!" Janelle said, watching Emma push the log around ineffectively. "Nice of you to spring for the bubbly."

"I couldn't let your acquittal go unnoticed, now could I? Besides, it's been a long time since we had a chance to *really* unwind." She shoved the flaming pieces of wood toward the rear of the hearth. "You know, I learned how to do this in Girl Scout camp, remember? Too bad you dropped out."

"Only because of the ants and the mosquitoes, my dear." Janelle's words ran together in a childish ripple. "Those damn things like to eat me alive. If Dad hadn't come to take me home, I'd have been sucked as dry as one of Dracula's victims."

"Please. Spare me the dramatics!" Emma's high-pitched giggle wafted through the room. She spun around to face Janelle, almost lost her balance, and steadied herself with the poker. Her multicolored, oversize Shetland sweater fell almost to her knees, giving her the appearance of a slightly drunken elf. Her fluffy black curls bobbed up and down as she waved a finger at Janelle. "Oh, the ants and mosquitoes weren't all that bad."

"You slept in a cabin," Janelle protested. "I got a pup tent."

"Oh, yeah. So you did." Emma pulled the fireplace screen back into place and returned to her cushion on the floor. Like an impish fairy, she pressed her tiny legs into the plush, squashy pallet, stretching the saggy sweater down to her ankles. The roaring fire flashed directly onto her face.

"Yeah. But you were bunkmates with Roberta Wimly."

"Um-hmm," Janelle murmured. "That girl never brushed her teeth the whole time we were there."

Emma's slurring whoop rang out. "Camp was fun!"

"It was ghastly," Janelle said. "Bathing in cold water. Eating burned marshmallows. Ugh! It wasn't over soon enough for me." She let her head fall back onto the sofa, staring thoughtfully at the ceiling. Golden-tinged shadows roamed back and forth, dancing on the bare white walls, bowing and curling in silhouettes that set her head to spinning. "I haven't drunk so much wine since the night before we graduated from nursing school. Remember that party at the Macon Hotel?"

"Do I remember? Oh, yeah. That's when Kenneth told me he was going to Illinois to become an aircraft mechanic."

Kenneth Shawn's rugged, chiseled face with its strong square jaw flashed before Janelle. She never did quite understand how Emma had snagged him or why she put up with his infidelity. Everyone in their graduating class knew Kenneth's reputation.

"I never told you this, but Kenneth wanted to elope that night."

"He did?" Janelle crossed her arms on her chest, waiting for more details. "You little sneak. Tell me! What happened?"

"I was too drunk and too excited about graduating to remember much of what was said. As you see, I didn't go."

Shocked and somewhat hurt that Emma hadn't confided this to her before, Janelle pulled herself upright, tugging at the uncomfortable, too-tight sweatshirt Emma had lent her. Its bold red and gray letters—OSU—strained tightly across her generous bosom. "I can't get over this. You sure kept that to yourself."

"I know. I didn't want you to know how damn confused I was back then."

"Confused about what? You and Kenneth were inseparable. I'm not surprised he wanted to run off with you, but I have to say I'm glad you didn't do it."

"That's just it. I didn't want to get married like that. I wanted to have a big wedding . . . with you as my maid of honor. In the powder blue dress we designed in seventh grade. Remember?"

"Ruffles on the neckline, tulle over taffeta. And crystal beads on the bodice. I probably have the sketches in my closet at home."

"I wanted the perfect wedding. He didn't think it was important. I—I couldn't go off to some strange city to get married without you there." Her voice wispy, she shrank back into her pillow.

"Gee, Emma." And now, Janelle thought, she'd been worrying about the same thing if Emma joined the Army.

"I wanted Kenneth, but I didn't want to start off like that. I guess I was pretty insecure, huh?" She rubbed the backs of her arms. "Sound silly?"

"No," Janelle said softly, then laughed. "Didn't Kenneth know I was going to have a great deal to say about your wedding?"

Emma chuckled. "Right. And your dad was going to arrange for the reception in the ballroom of the Deshler Hotel."

"That's the way it was going to be," Janelle said, knowing that if her father had lived, he'd have called in every outstanding favor to make sure Emma had what she wanted.

"Things will get back to normal, Emma. You and Kenneth will have your wedding."

"Not until after the war." She sipped her wine. "So what can I do? I had to make a choice. I chose to wait here. It looks like he'll be assigned to Tuskegee, and this separation could last a long time."

Janelle sat thinking, absorbing the impact of Emma's revelation. Innocently they had dreamed together, planning their adult lives as if nothing would ever surface to disrupt the routine and rhythm of their friendship. Without warning the war had intruded, taking Kenneth away, creating an unsettling imbalance that was difficult to ignore.

"Well, he's in Illinois. He's happy," Emma said. "I'm not sorry we didn't get married before he left. I think that would have made the separation even harder to bear."

The logs hissed, succumbing to the heat, turning from wood into ashes, filling the silence that descended over the two women who were perfectly at ease without conversation. Years of childhood sleepovers and their time together as roommates at nursing school had bonded the pair in familial comfort.

"Are you happy?" Janelle had never asked Emma this question before, and tonight, under these strange circumstances, it somehow seemed appropriate to bring up the subject. Her special place in Emma's life was crystallized, focused, and Janelle savored the boundaries of their friendship.

"I guess so," Emma said wistfully. "I have a man who loves me, even if he is miles away. I have my work, which I love." She ran a hand through her tangle of curls. "And I have you to keep me from going absolutely crazy." She laughed, seeming embarrassed to have defined her feelings when both knew no definition was necessary.

"Don't talk about going crazy," Janelle said, her thoughts plunging back to her father's funeral, the dark, angry days that had followed. Emma had actually moved into their house and taken over, organizing the solemn ritual for the family. Day and night, around the clock, Emma had stolidly kept the Roy family from collapsing in their grief.

"Does Kenneth like it at Chanute?" Janelle asked. "I mean, enough to leave you behind like this?"

"Kenneth? Oh, well, yes." Emma didn't hesitate before answering. "To be selected to go to Chanute was an honor. For him the opportunity to get that kind of training, then serve with the Army Air Force is worth this temporary separation."

"And after training he'll definitely go to Tuskegee?"

"We hope," Emma replied. "He can't wait to get there, but I hate to think of him down in Alabama, fighting Jim Crow, you know?"

"Humph! Where else would the Army dare station our boys?" Janelle's sarcasm was thick. "God forbid that colored pilots might accidentally fly in pristine white skies. It's almost funny. When the Germans bear down on those white boys, you think they're going to care about the color of the squadron covering their asses?" She threw off the heavy blanket and put her feet on the floor. "I don't think so."

Emma splashed more of the cheap champagne into her glass, smirking in agreement. "You sound exactly like Kenneth. Always talking about integration in the military. He says it's coming. I guess it will . . . it has to, to win this war. Yeah, I'd say he's happy."

"You still thinking about signing up?" Janelle strained to focus on her friend.

"I've got an appointment Wednesday at the Red Cross recruiting office."

"This Wednesday? You're really going to enlist?"

"Yeah." Emma sighed. "Now that colored nurses are being accepted, I'm going to apply. If I pass the physical and can prove I'm licensed, they'll take me . . . if there's space. The quotas are so low it's insulting."

"And what does Kenneth say?"

"That basic training will be horrible and I'll finally have to learn how to take orders." She smiled and shook her head. "Guess I'll also have to get over my fear of flying." Emma took a noisy slurp from her glass.

"You'd be at the base hospital?" Janelle was a bit panicky now, with Emma so sure about leaving.

"Yes. If we're not welcome on the white Army bases, why not go to Tuskegee, where we're needed . . . and wanted?"

"That's a point," Janelle said. "The government sure as hell isn't recruiting white nurses to send to Tuskegee, or Camp Livingston, or Fort Huachuca."

"Anyway," Emma went on, "what do I have to stay around here for?" Her eyes swept the sparsely furnished room. "Rattling around this place by myself. Wishing Kenneth were here. Running up horrendous long-distance telephone bills. Why not join up?"

"And if he has to go overseas, you'll be left behind on that isolated airfield in Alabama? What then?" Janelle played the devil's advocate.

"I'll do my duty and work in the hospital and pray that he comes back in one piece."

"Sounds like you've got it all figured out."

"I'm working on it, Janelle. 'Cause right now I feel like I'm just marking time."

"At least you're working," Janelle said bitterly, her voice cracking with lack of pride.

Emma quickly cautioned her. "Don't go feeling sorry for yourself. I thought we'd already hashed that through. Put it aside and take the attorney's advice, Janelle. Try to stay positive. Something will turn up."

"And if nothing does?"

"Well, why not come with me to the Red Cross on Wednesday? Sign up! Really, Janelle, it's time you started living your life for yourself. Forget about Perry! And your mother. She'll do fine. Where has she been for the past three days? At your aunt's house, right? She's always over there, and you said your aunt Dedee really wants your mother to come live with her."

"Mom would never move out of our home. Never." A wave of melancholy swept through Janelle. "Dad bought that house the day he married Mom. She says she plans to live out the rest of her life right there."

"Never say never. You ought to know that. If she *had* to, she'd go live with your aunt. And if you *wanted* to, Janelle, you could get out from some of that pressure you're under."

"You think I like it?" Janelle said.

"No, but I think you might be hiding behind it. As long as you strap yourself with trying to reform Perry—who *is* a grown man, by the way—and spend the rest of your time worrying about supporting your mother—who would probably be better off living with your aunt—you don't have to deal with getting on with your life. Now, that's close to the truth. Isn't it?"

"Ha!" Janelle's curt laugh sliced the shadowed room. "Get on with my life?" she drained her wineglass with a swallow. "I am twenty-three, unemployed, and single. And I can't even get the one man I'm attracted to interested enough to kiss me good night."

"Oh, Dalton Graham is interested, all right." Emma

pooh-poohed her friend's lament. "He's just got enough sense not to start something that will only lead to more problems for you . . . and him, too. He was right not to get involved in an affair with you. It could blow up in your faces. You ought to be glad."

"Glad!" Janelle snorted. "That's a twist. I sure don't see it that way."

"Then maybe it's time you did." Emma cast down her eyes as she added, "I think you were attracted to Dalton because he was forbidden, beyond your reach." She met Janelle's questioning stare. "More like a challenge, you know?"

"Don't go trying to psychoanalyze me!"

"I'm not!" Emma rose onto her knees. "But I'm worried for you. Your mother hates interracial relationships, and you must have known she was going to raise all kinds of hell if you got involved with a white man. Why did you dare kiss that man in her house?"

"To see if I could get him to kiss me back," Janelle said.

"Ha! You see? You were trying to prove that you could attract him, prove he'd fall for a colored girl. That's no basis for a relationship, and it sure ain't love."

"Oh, hell, Emma, I feel so empty . . . confused." Janelle's hands went limp in her lap. "Why can't I find someone who's right for me?" Desperation threaded her words.

"You will." Emma got up and stood by the sofa, looking down at her friend. "You will. Trust me, you really will. Just don't go rushing into something all wrong."

Janelle threw her legs up and slid down on the sofa until her feet touched the arm at the opposite end. She yanked the quilt up tightly around her neck and squirmed back and forth until she was settled in.

"Don't wake me up before eight," she said, cutting off the conversation. She'd discussed her life enough for one day. "I'm tired. It's been a hell of day, and I don't want to talk about Dalton Graham."

"Whatever Her Majesty wants," Emma said lightly, heading toward her bedroom. At the doorway she stopped and said, "I'm glad you're going to stay here a few days. It'll be fun having you here for a while. You're a nervous wreck, you know that? Getting out of that house will do you some good. Tomorrow we'll go pick up your clothes."

After Emma left, Janelle lay awake, listening to the faint crackle of the fire, watching the craggy logs turn orange, then pale yellow, then gray. The spark of wild embers flickering up from the logs looked like fireflies darting through the night. As the smoldering glow dimmed, Janelle allowed her thoughts to turn once again to Dalton.

Perhaps she had been trying to prove something. And perhaps her embrace might have been premature. But she had no regrets about making the first move, kissing him, feeling him kiss her back. It had been worth the sting of her mother's disapproval.

And what about her mother? Would a relationship with Dalton really force them apart, make them strangers? Drive a wedge between them that blood could never heal? The mere thought was too painful to contemplate. As much as Janelle wanted to deny it, in her heart she knew Dalton and Emma were right. Alice Roy was stubborn enough to disown her daughter and live in misery before accepting a white man as her son-in-law.

Exhausted, Janelle pressed her eyes closed; the smell of burning logs was thick in her nostrils. She needed a change in her life, to get away from all this confusion, but would leaving Columbus solve anything?

The Army? It sounded foreign and masculine—like a hugely complicated machine that sucked innocent young men into its iron craw, then ground them up until they all looked and talked alike and moved like robots toward victory. How in the world did Emma think she'd fit into that?

And Alabama? Thank God Booker T. Washington had created an intellectual oasis in the middle of the state. She'd heard enough horror stories and read enough in the newspapers about Jim Crowism in the South not to hold any illusions that colored military personnel would be warmly welcomed down there.

As fatigue claimed every nerve cell and muscle, and the champagne worked its magic, Janelle slipped into a surprisingly calm sleep, the gentle sound of her breathing commingling with the whisper of falling ashes.

Dreamless and solid, cavernous and black, sleep pressed down and stilled her soul. The banked fire dispelled the chill in the air and protected her from the January winds that squawked around the house, fighting to find a way in.

When dawn broke, leaving the sun still masked in a foggy mist, Janelle opened her eyes and lay very still, feeling totally relaxed for the first time in months.

I don't want to go home, she admitted, relishing the moments without pressure. *I don't have to face Perry, or Mother, or that damn leaky faucet in the bathroom. And I won't have to sit by the phone praying for Dalton Graham to call—because he won't. He's made up his mind not to get involved, and as far as I'm concerned, he's history. All I want right now is to lie flat on my back and stare at the ceiling forever.*

CHAPTER THIRTEEN

When the applause subsided, Dalton Graham thanked Reverend Crossley for having invited him to speak to the United Women in Christ, stepped down from the podium at the front of the church, and took a seat next to Perry.

"Your presence here this Sunday evening is evidence of your commitment to our cause," Reverend Crossley stated. "It is through the efforts of generous, caring people like you, Mr. Graham, that any progress at all is made. I just hope that our small, heartfelt contribution to the NAACP will be put to good use."

Dalton stood again, acknowledging the minister and the roomful of beaming ladies by bowing slightly before he spoke. "I assure you it will. There is much we can do to fight inequality and segregation, but the NAACP cannot do it without funds. Your support is welcome, and your concerns have been heard. I assure you we don't plan to let up at Lantree until there have been some concrete changes ... even if we have to get A. Philip Randolph down here."

A firm round of applause burst from the audience.

The Freedom Reception, a chatty, stand-around affair with punch and cookies, was held in the damp church basement and lasted thirty minutes. Afterward Perry walked Dalton to his car.

"Thanks a lot for doing this, Dalton," Perry said, falling into step beside the civil rights attorney, who was fast becoming the most sought-after speaker on the black church circuit. "Reverend Crossley kinda put me on the spot to find someone for the program. They really liked your speech, especially that part about the rally in Cleveland Thanks for coming through."

"No problem, Perry. The NAACP needs support like this, grassroots support. We always need money, but it's not numbers that count so much. Commitment goes a long way, too."

Dalton pulled out a pack of cigarettes as he approached the car. "Want a lift home?"

Perry didn't answer right away, waiting until Dalton stopped beside his car and tapped an Old Gold lightly against the back of his hand.

"Well, to be honest, I wasn't planning on going home," Perry said, his voice dropping low.

"What's up?" Dalton eyed Perry closely as he flicked open his silver lighter and lit the cigarette, inhaling, blowing smoke into the crisp twilight.

Perry leaned against the side of the car, staring at the icy ground. Not looking up, he said, "I need your advice on something."

"Sure. Shoot." Dalton was struck by the serious mood that had suddenly overcome Perry. "Something wrong?"

"Maybe." Perry hesitated, as if he had something difficult to confess. "I was just curious. Have you ever helped anybody file papers as a conscientious objector?"

Dalton's jaw clenched; the lines at the corners of his eyes sharpened. He contemplated Perry's question. "No," he finally answered. "Why do you ask?"

Perry reached into the pocket of his navy peacoat and pulled out a crumpled envelope. He held it out to Dalton.

"Got your draft notice, huh? That's what this is about?" Dalton took the form letter from Perry, scanning it in the dim street light. "Your time's about run out. According to this, you have to report to the draft board January thirteenth, the day after tomorrow."

"Yeah, I know." Perry nervously wiped the back of one

hand over his mouth. "I was hoping I'd get a job in a defense plant, get deferred. I thought things were all set for a place on the line at Lantree, but I found out yesterday it's not going to work out. That bastard Howard Long just fed me a line, then brushed me off. Guess I'm back where I started with this thing." He crushed the notice in his fist as his promise to his mother rose in haunting shame.

"Get in the car, Perry," Dalton said, tossing his lighted cigarette into a ditch at the side of the road "Let's go someplace and talk."

Perry circled to the passenger side of Dalton's blue Plymouth and stood looking at the lawyer over its shiny domed top.

"I don't want to go into the Army, Dalton. You've got to help me get out of this."

It took less than ten minutes to go from the church parking lot to the Regal Road Inn, and Perry was grateful that Dalton made small talk about a colleague at the NAACP who was up for an award from the national headquarters and held off on the serious discussion he knew lay ahead.

Once settled at a rear table in the restaurant, Perry signaled to Willie, working at the bar, and quickly secured a bottle of decent bourbon.

The place was nearly empty. Perry glanced around, unable to spot any familiar faces, glad to see that none of the regulars he usually drank with had ventured out tonight. He noticed that a bold standard-size American flag had been tacked up on the wall behind the bar, its red and white stripes and blue field of stars dominating the rustic room.

Perry remembered that Willie's eldest son had been drafted last month and was now stationed in Arizona at Fort Huachuca.

Someone at the front of the club dropped a nickel into the jukebox, releasing swing music into the room, prompting Perry to scoot his chair closer to Dalton. He drew in his shoulders in a conspiratorial manner, speaking lowly, in a voice fraught with hope, "Well, what do you think?

Can I beat the draft? I mean, legally beat it and stay out of the Army?"

After taking a sip of the ice-cold whiskey, Dalton swallowed and swirled the ice cubes in his glass. "Have you really thought this out? What you are considering is a very serious matter. Are you sure this is what you want to do?"

"Yeah. I've thought about it a lot, even before I got my notice. I can't see myself living in a tent with a bunch of men in a segregated camp somewhere in the boonies. The whole idea of a segregated Army stinks. I don't want any part of it ... if I can help it."

"What about your duty to your country?"

"What about my country's duty to me? I need a job, and I can do more if I stay here and work in a plant. Then I can keep working with Protest for Jobs, too. I can do a whole lot more outside the Army, Dalton. You gotta see I'm right."

"Sorry, I don't." Dalton's blunt reply fell between them like a rock.

"Then why are *you* still around?" Perry snapped, taken aback by his friend's cutting statement. "Why haven't you enlisted?"

"I'm classified four-F. Got a bum ankle that I broke in college. Never healed right. I couldn't get them to take me. I tried."

Perry pressed his lips together and shrugged. "Well, what about it, though? What's it take to get deferred as a conscientious objector?"

"You'd have to make a statement under oath that you are opposed to war on religious, political, or moral grounds and make a strong case for your opposition to armed combat. Even then you might be inducted and assigned to noncombatant duties, you know, some clerical work where you wouldn't have to carry a gun. You could even be assigned to work in a hospital or some other community site. You'd still be serving your country."

"What kind of proof do they need?"

"A history of pacifist activities might be a good start."

"I've been protesting and picketing for over a year," Perry said.

"Against segregation, not war."

"Well, it's about the same in my mind."

"It won't be the same to the draft board, I assure you."

Perry slumped in his chair like a little boy denied a favorite toy and lowered his chin to his chest. "I couldn't stand it, Dalton. I know I couldn't." He ran a hand over the top of his head. "I'd go nuts before I got through basic, I know I would."

"No, you wouldn't. You'd probably find out that most of the guys felt like you at first. You'd be in the same boat together. Might make a few friends, and you'd most likely rise in rank. You've got a lot going for you, Perry. Who knows what good things might come of it?" Dalton tried to lighten the mood.

"I have no interest in a military career." Perry's tone was sullen. "If I've got to go, I'm just going to serve my time and get out."

"Nothing wrong with that," Dalton replied, "but I won't help you file as an objector, Perry. It's not the truth, and you know it." He finished his drink and shoved his glass toward the middle of the table. "If you are determined to go through with your plan, find some other lawyer to help you."

Perry sat up, grabbing Dalton's arm. "You don't think it would work?"

"I don't know," Dalton said truthfully. "Maybe it would, maybe it wouldn't. But I think I know you well enough to say that if you get deferred on those grounds, you'll really screw up your life. You'd be living a lie, and sooner or later you'd regret it."

"Don't be so self-righteous."

"I'm just being honest."

"So you think I ought to show up at the draft board and walk away from civilian life?"

"Might be the best thing you ever did, Perry. You're young. You're smart. Develop a skill while you're in the military. It might come in handy when you get out. There are benefits to serving you may not have considered." Dalton pulled out a dollar and laid it on the table, then reached for his trench coat as if concluding their talk. "Let me tell you something your sister told me," he added, the memory of Janelle still very fresh. "I was really struck by the truth of it . . . it's stayed on my mind."

"What'd she say? Something cruel, I suppose."

"No, not at all," Dalton answered, wishing Perry would not assume the worst. "She said your father always told her to look for opportunities that might be just around the corner, the ones nobody else could see."

Perry swallowed the last of his bourbon. "Yeah"—he sighed—"Dad used to say things like that a lot."

"Try taking your father's advice, Perry. Go on and report to the draft board, take your physical, go into the Army, and make the best of it."

Now Dalton turned from Perry and shoved his wallet into his pocket. "I've got to get going." He pulled on his coat. "You coming?"

"Naw," Perry said, the corners of his mouth turning down. "I think I'll hang around here a little longer. Got a lot of thinking to do." Then he picked up the bottle of bourbon and poured a stiff shot into his glass.

It was dusk when Janelle got off the bus at Clarendon Avenue and started down the long block toward Emma's house. Shivering, Janelle shook fresh snow from her hair, which Emma had pressed and styled into a long, elegant pageboy.

It had been a week since she moved in with Emma, and the arrangement suited her just fine. Maybe she wouldn't go back home at all.

Crunching over the ice-packed sidewalk, Janelle struggled to hold herself together. It would be so easy to break down and cry, or scream, or lash out at somebody. Reaching down, she scooped up a handful of snow, squeezed it into a hard, round ball, and hurled it at a low brick wall across the street. She watched it splatter into a flat white disk, then crumble and fall to the ground.

Mount Carmel had had no opening for her. A private doctor had flatly turned her away, not because she had no recent references but clearly because she was Negro. Miss Finch had called from the registry with an excellent position. Janelle had tried to stall on reporting for the interview but finally broke down and admitted to Miss Finch that she wouldn't be getting a reference from Sara Johnson after all.

Tomorrow, Janelle thought glumly, she'd try the state hospital, though she'd rather face going into the Army than the prospect of working at that medieval place.

Panic began to consume her as she thought about tomorrow. Another nerve-racking interview? More humiliation? She doubted she'd be able to survive it.

When Janelle finally entered the house, the phone was ringing. She dashed to catch it on the fifth ring. When Alice Roy said hello, Janelle was glad to hear her mother's voice.

"Yes, I just got in."

"How'd it go?" Alice asked, a forced note of optimism in her voice.

"No better than last week," Janelle answered as she pulled off her gloves. "Tomorrow I'll try the state school, maybe St. Francis. Keep your fingers crossed."

"You know I will," Alice said. "Don't you go getting depressed over this temporary setback. It's all going to come to an end. Soon. Then those snooty hospital directors will come looking for you, begging you to work for them. This war is taking nurses out of the city every day. Hold on, honey."

"I'm trying," Janelle answered, thankful her mother never wavered in her support, thankful that their little spat about Dalton Graham could be put aside for this more pressing problem.

"Listen, Janelle, I called to ask you to do me a favor."

"Sure, Mom. What is it?"

"See if Emma can drive you by the house. I'm going to stay here with your aunt Dedee for another week. She's got a cold that the doctor said might turn into pneumonia, and he's restricted her to the bed for the next few days."

"What's at the house? You need something?"

"No." Alice hesitated a few seconds. "I'm a little worried about Perry. When I talked to him day before yesterday, he said he was going to stay around the house. Get the mail and the papers, keep the furnace going, you know. He must have changed his mind, though. I've been calling off and on all afternoon. Nobody's answered, and it dropped to ten below last night."

"Don't worry about him," Janelle said, her tone much sharper than intended, knowing he was probably holed up with Alnita Dujohn. "Perry can take care of himself. He is nearly twenty-one! Mom, quit babying him."

"Calm down, Janelle. It's not Perry so much as the house. If he's been gone, the furnace is not on, and we're asking for trouble."

"You want me to put coal in the furnace?"

"No. No. If it's out, just go next door and ask Mr. Henry. He'll do it. He's done it before. He won't mind a bit."

God, Janelle fumed silently, *will it never stop? I can't get away from that place for one day.* Instead she said, "All right, Mom." The least she could do was set her mother's mind at ease. "As soon as Emma gets home from work, we'll drive over."

"Thanks, Janelle. And I'll be going back home as soon as Dedee gets better."

By the time they got to Oakwood Alley, it was already dark. The streetlamps were on, but the house was pitch-black.

"Damn Perry," Janelle cursed when the house came into view. "I get so sick and tired of his trifling ways."

"Take it easy." Emma tried to ease Janelle's anger.

"He's not going to change, so don't make yourself crazy about him."

Hating the abandoned look of the place, Janelle hurried to get out as soon as Emma came to a stop, then picked her way over the icy sidewalk, mounted the steps, and put her key in the lock.

The door swung open. Janelle immediately sensed something odd about the house that she had lived in all her life. A stagnant, musty odor—like the scent of decaying wood—wafted out, overpowering her with its pungent smell. Cautiously she stepped through the door, then screamed in shock as her feet sank ankle deep into water that swirled down the darkened hallway and swept past her, out the front door.

"What the devil?" she cried, straining to see farther into the house. "Watch out, Emma," she called over her shoulder. "The place is flooded!"

Janelle inched her way toward the kitchen. When she passed the telephone, she started to grab it and call for help.

"Don't use the phone!" Emma warned. "I'm sure you'd get electrocuted—or something."

Janelle yanked back her hand as if she'd been burned, then felt her way into the kitchen, where she fumbled inside one of the cabinets until she got her hands on a candle and a box of matches. Trembling, she managed to get a flame going and held it up toward the ceiling.

"Oh, my God!" Her eyes traveled up. "Emma! Will you look at this?"

The kitchen ceiling had collapsed, leaving gaping holes, exposing pipes and beams above their heads. Soggy wet plaster had crumbled down over everything in the kitchen. Water still dripped down the peeling walls, filtering slowly along the baseboards, where it gathered in shimmering puddles or froze solid along the outer walls.

"The pipes have burst," Janelle said.

Emma came up alongside Janelle to see the damage better. "Good Lord. What a mess! This is awful. Your mother is going to be devastated."

Janelle turned away and sloshed over the sodden hall carpet toward the front room.

"Where the hell has Perry been?" Janelle grumbled, knowing he must have been away for at least the past three days. "He could have kept the furnace going or wrapped the pipes. This should not have happened."

At the entrance to the front room Janelle and Emma paused long enough to see that the stained jacquard drapes had absorbed so much water that the rods supporting them were sagging dangerously under their weight.

Janelle turned toward the stairs. "Wait down here," she told Emma.

"I wouldn't go up there!" Emma said. "The floor might cave in."

"I've got to see what's happened . . . get some of my things. If there is anything left worth salvaging!"

Janelle bolted up the stairs. At her bedroom door she stopped and thrust the candle inside. Water from the bathroom at the end of the hallway rippled past her, seeping into her room. Shoes, books, baskets, magazines, and several rag rugs floated in water four inches deep.

Janelle began yanking clothes out of the closet, piling them in the center of the bed. As she frantically emptied her drawers of cosmetics, underwear, sweaters, and stockings, she thought of the outside water main.

"Emma!" Janelle called down the stairs. "Go around to the side of the house and see if you can turn off the main line to the house."

"Okay," Emma yelled back, slamming out the door.

Janelle finished piling all her clothes on the bed, then pulled up the blanket at each corner and tied everything together in a heavy bundle.

Within seconds Emma returned, breathless at the bedroom door.

"It's frozen solid, Janelle. It won't budge." Emma frowned down at the mess swirling all around her feet.

"We'd better get out of here before something happens. I don't like the look of things. The whole top floor is going to collapse."

"Yeah. Help me with this," Janelle said, heaving the bundle of clothing off the bed. "I can already feel the floorboards sagging."

They struggled down the stairway, out the front door, managing to get the awkward, bulging blanket into the trunk. Then Janelle rushed next door to call the city emergency number to have someone come out to shut off the water, then telephoned her mother to break the devastating news.

Janelle sat glumly in the front seat of Emma's car, unable to say a word. Suddenly a terrifying, splintering, shattering sound roared from the house and filled the street. Janelle stiffened. The second floor of her home, weighted with plaster, beams, pipes, and furniture, had succumbed to the weight of the water. The impact forced a hollow boom that thundered ominously through the dank narrow alley. Beneath Janelle, the crusty ice-packed ground trembled with the implosion.

It took forty-five minutes for the Water Department to get to the house and shut off the main line. The workmen warned Janelle and Emma not to go back inside. They would report the situation to the city housing authority; more than likely the house would have to be condemned.

"What do you want to do?" Emma shuddered, anguished, feeling helpless and sad about the situation.

Janelle clenched both hands into fists in her lap, nostrils flaring slightly as she lifted her chin. Her insides were ragged, and her lower lip quivered, yet through her disappointment and grief, she managed to speak in a curtly determined voice. "I want to go to the Red Cross headquarters with you on Wednesday and present my credentials to the Army. That's what I want, Emma. I've got to get out of this town."

Emma put both arms around her friend and pressed her cheek to Janelle's warm tears. "I'm glad." She gave

Janelle's shoulders a hard squeeze. "It's going to be the best decision you ever made. You'll see. Once you get on the base and see how much the men need you and appreciate you, you'll never regret signing on."

Janelle brushed shaking fingers over her face. "I hope you're right because if I have to sleep in a mosquito-filled tent and bathe in cold water, I'll never forgive you, Emma. Never!"

"Ha!" Emma exploded, her laughter dissolving the strain of the evening "Who knows? You might be lucky enough to run into Roberta Wimly somewhere down there in Alabama!"

"Oh, God, please!" Janelle threw back her head and roared.

Emma gunned the engine and shot away from the curb. Janelle turned in her seat and looked back at her sorry little house and silently bade it farewell.

CHAPTER
FOURTEEN

The first month of 1943 ended as it had begun. Snow flurries alternating with freezing rain kept Columbusites bundled up against the sub-zero temperatures, worried about dwindling coal supplies, praying for a break in the weather. News of the war fueled conversations in every house in the city. The Service Parade section of the Columbus *Dispatch* now filled an entire page, complete with photos, and did a good job of tracking the whereabouts and fates of servicemen and women stationed far from home. It was the first section of the paper most people turned to, anxious to learn who had been furloughed, promoted, and reassigned or would not be coming home at all.

For weeks Janelle and Emma continued their routines, Emma still working at the clinic, Janelle making half-hearted attempts to find a position while the court case concerning her inheritance dragged on. After meeting all the Red Cross requirements and passing their physicals, they both had optimistic attitudes, refusing to speak of the real possibility that either or both might be passed over as low quotas for colored nurses still held. Despite protests and hundreds of letters to the War Department, the government refused to budge, and the color barrier remained in place.

On February 2 two envelopes marked "Army Service Forces" arrived at Emma's house on Clarendon Avenue.

Relief, pride, and excitement swept through them with the news that on February 10, 1943, they were to report to the Columbus induction center at Fort Hayes. There they would be sworn into the Army Nurse Corps, then sent by train to Tuskegee Army Airfield, Tuskegee, Alabama.

The day after receiving the notice, Janelle sat on the sofa in Emma's quiet living room, staring out the window, watching for Aunt Dedee's car, dreading her mother's arrival, feeling hurt that her mother had not shared her enthusiasm about the acceptance notice from the Army.

Schools were closed due to heavy snow and ice. Across the street three girls were building a snowman. When a group of boys came by and pelted them with snowballs, the girls shrieked and ran onto the porch, covering their heads with their arms. Janelle grinned, watching the children, their bodies thick and bulky in their heavy winter clothes, their innocent laughter clear as crystal on the crisp morning air. She thought of Perry, and all the snowmen they had built, remembering how their father had always come outside just in time to press lumps of coal into the frozen lopsided heads of their creations, making the eyes, noses, and mouths.

How odd, Janelle thought, to be sitting in this strange yet familiar house that she now considered home. After the collapse Perry had moved in with Alnita Dujohn until he had to leave for Camp Livingston, Louisiana. Devastated by the way the family had split apart, grieving over the loss of her home, her mother had stayed at Aunt Dedee's. A pressure of tears started building in Janelle's chest, making her nervous. She didn't want to cry, not now, not when her mother could show up at any moment.

Dedee Roy dropped Alice at the curb and kept going, promising to return in an hour. Still trying to come to grips with her daughter's imminent departure, Alice mounted the steps and knocked on Emma's door.

"Hi, Mom," Janelle said lightly, hugging her mother.

"Here's the pink sweater you wanted." Alice handed Janelle a package, frowning to see how distraught her daughter looked, in spite of the bubbling facade she put on. The strain of the past month showed itself in the dark circles under her eyes, the limp tendrils of her usually lustrous hair. Janelle, in Alice's opinion, looked entirely too thin, but she refrained from making any comment. "Good thing I had this sweater with me that night."

Janelle took the bag and set it on the dining room table, which was crowded with Emma's and her things.

"You already packing?" Alice said, eyeing the pile of clothes and open suitcases scattered about the room.

"Well, we're trying to get organized. We can bring only one suitcase apiece, and look." Janelle handed her mother a form. "These are the supplies they recommend we bring."

"Hot-water bottle, penknife, slacks, two civilian outfits for travel," Alice read. "Hmm, where will you get your nursing uniforms?"

"At the air base. We'll be completely outfitted there." Janelle busied herself refolding a blouse.

"What would happen if you changed your mind?" Alice bluntly asked.

"Nothing. The letter says if I do not show up for the swearing in, that's considered notice that I've relinquished my spot."

"How sure are you about all this?" Alice asked, circling the table, absently touching the satin hosiery bag she had sewn for her daughter years go. She was hoping this decision to go into the Army was not a result of the tiff they had had over that white attorney. She'd put that out of her mind. But she knew Janelle well enough to know that she might well take drastic action like this just to assert her independence.

"I'm very sure," Janelle answered.

"Seems awful sudden to me. And with Perry just gone. He's not even settled at Camp Livingston yet. I hate to see you do this, Janelle."

"This is what I *want* to do, Mom. I know what I'm getting into."

"Do you now? Really?" Alice had heard Janelle say that more than once, then watched as her daughter suffered the consequences. Like working for the Werners and getting involved with that attorney. For Janelle, things didn't always go as smoothly as she planned.

"Yes, really. And please don't try to change my mind."

"Oh, I know better than to try that. You're going to do what you want, no matter how it might turn out." Alice bristled. Her daughter's words sounded like an echo from Garrett Roy's grave. How many times had he told his wife the same thing, then gone out and gotten into a pretty nasty mess?

Janelle put the blouse in the suitcase and picked up a pair of slacks. Aligning the creases, she went on. "I think this is what I'm supposed to do. I feel good about this. Does that make sense, Mom?"

Alice vaguely lifted a shoulder, not committing herself.

"Remember how Daddy always used to say: 'When you're doing what you're supposed to be doing, you'll feel it in your bones. Just listen to your bones,' he'd say." Janelle chuckled. "He never got it wrong, did he?"

"Your daddy said a lot of foolish things." Alice spoke in flat tones, but there was an underlying edge to her words. "He spouted all kinds of nonsense and got people to believe him, too."

"Mom!" Janelle said sharply. "What's gotten into you? How can you say that about Daddy?"

"Because it's true, Janelle. I'm not disrespecting your father. I loved him, even though he was not an easy man to love. You're a grown woman now. You need to know a little more about what you're going to be facing."

"What are you talking about?"

Alice laid her green wool coat across the banister in the hallway, then entered the dining room. She saw a flinty mask descend over Janelle's face. "I've sat by long enough with my tongue stilled. I've been watching you covet white folks and all their trappings, striving to catch their ways."

Janelle flexed the fingers on both hands, making fists. "You're starting to sound like Perry, and I don't want a lecture, please."

"I didn't come to lecture you, honey." Alice kept her voice low, in control. "But it has not been easy for me to keep still, hoping you'd see the error of your ways, praying you'd come to your senses. Joining the Army. What's that gonna prove? That white lawyer put this idea in your head?"

"No," Janelle said. "Emma was the one . . . and I'm looking at this as an opportunity to learn more about the world, expand the realm of my experiences."

"Another one of your daddy's ideas?" Alice said derisively. "Trying to make a bad situation look good?"

"Why are you doing this?" Janelle threw a hairbrush into the suitcase, flopped down into a chair, and crossed her legs. "Why are you trying to undercut all the things Daddy taught me? All he wanted was to help me move out into the world."

"Baby, I'm not undercutting him. Just finally being truthful, after too many years. Your daddy was no saint, you hear me? He had faults and habits and ways about him that I could have let destroy my marriage."

"What are you talking about?"

Alice sighed, turned away, and went to the window, her thin, rigid back to Janelle. "I'm talking about the white woman he kept in a house over in Urbancrest."

Janelle gripped the seat of her chair, eyes wide. "Mom! What is this?"

Now Alice turned, slowly calculating the damage her revelation had done. "What I'm trying to tell you is that for the first dozen years of my marriage I had to live with the knowledge that there was another woman in my bed. In my mind. Always between me and my husband."

"Who was she? Did Aunt Dedee know about this?"

Alice tightened her slender frame as if girding herself to expunge the memories. "Now you want to know, don't you?" She managed a wry smile. "So now it's time to tell. Yes, Dedee knew. She was the only one."

"The woman?" Janelle stood, rocking back on her heels.

"Gone."

"Gone?" Janelle moved to stand right in front of her mother.

"Yeah, gone. I read about it in the *Sentinel*. A little blurb on the back page on Christmas Eve. 'Woman Burned to Death in House Fire.' I kept that paper until the day your daddy died. Don't have any idea why I did that."

"I don't believe you." Janelle took a step back, judging her mother with a critical eye. "It's impossible."

"It's true. Garrett escaped from the fire but had to go to the hospital. And don't tell me you don't remember that Christmas Eve, Janelle, the first one your daddy ever spent away from home."

"I do remember." Janelle let the words out haltingly. "You told me and Perry that Daddy was working an extra job, had gone to Cincinnati for three days. It was the worst Christmas of my childhood."

"I can't say I remember it that way." Alice spread her painful truth at her daughter's feet, glad finally to unburden herself. "All I felt was relief."

Janelle tried to leave the room, but Alice grabbed her by the shoulders, firmly but gently, like a mother cat clamping down on a kitten in its mouth. "Don't run away. Can't you see what you've been doing, what's happened?"

Janelle didn't answer.

"You've got to find out who *you* are, Janelle. Maybe the Army is the best thing for you. I don't know. Maybe going down to Alabama, living on a segregated base with only colored people who need you will help bring you back to who you are."

"That's crazy. I know who I am."

"No, you don't. And neither did Garrett. He hated who he was, what he did, where he came from, but he'd never have admitted it to anyone, so he spent his life bragging about his job, his children, his high-cotton friends. Blustering about, throwing up smoke screens to hide the shame of his lies."

"But he was good to us. We *were* happy." Janelle protested, limply allowing her mother to guide her head onto her chest, sinking into the protective comfort of her arms.

"Yes," Alice murmured, stroking Janelle's back. "In many ways he *was* good. But he didn't know how to live with who he was, and I couldn't help him. You know he never listened to me. But I can't keep quiet and let you continue as you have been and make a mess of your life."

The sounds of the children in the street, the fresh wind against the house, and the thin whine of a stray cat on the porch next door seemed to cement Alice's confession to the moment.

Janelle raised her head, running dry fingers over wet cheeks. "I wish you'd never told me all of this." Her words were tinged with defiance.

"Maybe now you do," Alice said, removing her arms from Janelle's quivering shoulders. She opened her purse and took out her handkerchief and began wiping her daughter's face as if soothing a stumbling toddler. "But you need to know that your daddy's 'aspirations' hurt a lot of people around him. I don't want you to make the same mistake."

Gently Janelle pulled free of Alice's embrace and went to sit on the sofa. Pressing a hand to her lips, she absorbed the anguish on her mother's face.

"You're so smart, so pretty," Alice said, feeling she'd stripped a heavy weight from her soul. "And you're proud. That's what's important, honey. Forgive me if I hurt you, but Lord knows, nothing's gonna keep you from getting what you want. I only hope I cleared the path a little, got rid of a few bumps in the road up ahead."

Janelle watched silently as her mother pulled on her coat. She was still reeling and upset, but she felt as if she had learned more about her family, about herself, in the last half hour than in all her twenty-three years.

Part II

"Now," the flag sergeant cried, "though death and
   hell betide,
Let the whole Nation see if we are fit to be
Free in this land; or bound down like the whining
   hound
Bound with red stripes of pain in our old chains
   again!"
Oh! What a shout there went from the Black Regiment.

—George H. Boker,
   "The Black Regiment"

CHAPTER
FIFTEEN

In the heart of the Kisatchie National Forest, fourteen miles north of Alexandria, Louisiana, hundreds of buildings, thousands of tents, and more concrete streets than most towns could claim made up the segregated Army post Camp Livingston.

When twenty-five times more Negroes entered the Army than the government expected, the solution to the question of where and how to train this burgeoning field of recruits—who had to be kept in "separate but equal" facilities—was solved by the creation of posts like Camp Livingston.

One of a series of segregated Army camps built in the South by the War Department, Camp Livingston accepted a generous portion of the government's recruitment quota for Negroes, which had been set by President Roosevelt at 10 percent of the nation's population.

The central Louisiana military complex, forty thousand acres of lush countryside, was home to more than fourteen thousand colored troops. There narrow roadways curved past artillery ranges, connected clusters of classroom buildings huddled at the edge of the dense forest, and ended at the community of Spartan barracks perched high on concrete blocks. Neatly printed rectangular signs, designating whether or not colored could enter, hung in front of each structure. In the middle of the swampy lowlands, safe from the snakes, alligators, and wild boars that roamed the thicket, black men began their military service with hopes of entering combat.

At the camp optimistic volunteers and reluctant draftees, under the command of white commissioned officers, went through four weeks of basic training, learned military codes and conduct, and were eventually assigned to technical and mechanical units destined to serve as support squadrons to white combat troops overseas.

Stretched out on top of his tautly made bed, Private Perry Roy slowly folded his two-page letter and slipped it back into its envelope. He turned the stiff paper square over and studied his mother's handwriting, the pale blue stamp, the postmark, San Diego, California.

It was hard to believe his mother had left Columbus, let alone enjoyed living in California. When Aunt Dedee had decided to move to the West Coast to be nearby when Frank got shore leave, Alice had agreed to go along, ready to put Columbus in her past.

It was also difficult for Perry to believe that his home was gone. Knocked down in less than an hour, his mother had written. Now a vacant lot remained at the address on Oakwood Alley where his mother had come to live as a new bride, where he and Janelle had been born.

The Roy home had been reduced to a tiny patch of rubble. Like a crusty, brown scab covering the lifeblood of his family, it was converted into a place where stray dogs sniffed and neighborhood kids played kickball, eventually claiming it as their own.

Perry ran a finger over the return address—a four-room bungalow on Tropicana Avenue, where his mother said roses bloomed year-round. A floodgate of disappointment opened up inside his chest.

If he had left the Regal Road Inn with Dalton after their talk, he would not have gotten so staggering drunk, would not have gone home with Alnita Dujohn. At home he would have stoked the furnace, warmed the house, prevented the disaster that destroyed the bedrock of his family, his childhood. Perry's guilt over his irresponsible behavior sometimes threatened to suffocate him when he thought about how badly things had turned out.

He shook a Lucky Strike from his half-empty pack.

So Janelle was now in the Army Nurse Corps. *Good for her,* he thought, thumbing open his lighter, squinting toward the flame. With his four weeks of basic training behind him, he had hoped Sergeant Clapper, his hard-ass commanding officer—a real stickler for going by the book—would approve his leave request. He hadn't, and Perry was still pissed off that he had missed seeing Janelle sworn in.

The memory of his own departure at Union Station slipped to mind: his mother's low sobbing, Aunt Dedee's choke-hold embrace, Janelle's barrage of encouraging words. At that moment, poised to begin his first separation from Janelle, he had unconsciously shifted their differences to the very back of his mind. He had left Columbus feeling calm, satisfied, as if he were turning one of those mysterious corners his father had spoken about.

Assigned to the 648th Army Signal Corps, Perry studied the radios and intercoms and telephone equipment that kept far-flung units of the Army in touch. Simulated maneuvers in installation, repair, and maintenance of battalion communication bridges occupied his days. He and the other members of his squadron hoped they'd be able to use their skills on the front lines, but so far there were no indications they'd be sent overseas.

Leaning back on his bed, Perry put one hand behind his head and watched three dull brown moths circling the light overhead.

"What'd you think, Roy?" the soldier on the bunk next to his abruptly asked.

Startled, Perry rose onto one elbow, blew smoke across the room, and turned toward Leroy Mather, a muscle-bound heavyweight from Biloxi, Mississippi.

"About what?" Perry asked, totally unaware of the conversation that had been swirling around him for the last ten minutes.

"Mess," Leroy spit out, propping thick, square hands on his thighs, tilting his bulging torso toward Perry. An amateur boxer with an impressive record, Leroy spent every spare minute lifting weights or jumping rope, determined to stay in shape and make it into the professional ring as soon as he completed his stint in the Army.

"Tonight?" Perry hadn't thought too much about it.

"Yeah, tonight! And last night and all the nights before that." Leroy's words were punishing, as if chastising Perry for not listening to him.

"Guess I've had better," Perry casually admitted, trying to remember just what he had eaten. Not a picky eater, Perry certainly missed his mother's cooking, but as long as his meals were filling and hot and not too visually unappealing, he never spent much time thinking about food.

"I think it was coon," Leroy said in disgust.

"Bet it was rabbit," Private Joe McGinnis threw out, pushing his glasses up farther on the bridge of his nose. The squirrely-looking young man with pinched tight lips had glasses much too large for his face.

"Naw," said Heywood Hodges, a private from Texas, who spoke with authority. "There is no way you can make a rabbit taste that bad. I know because my father is a butcher, and I've eaten close to every animal that's edible." He got up from his bunk and moved into the small circle of soldiers gathered at the foot of Perry's bed. Heywood plopped down on Perry's footlocker and drew himself up as if he were about to deliver a sermon. "I've eaten alligator, rattlesnake, pig brains, and armadillo, and I've never had indigestion the likes of what I've had since I got here. I don't know what they're giving us, but it sure isn't coon or rabbit."

"Well, whatever it is, I'm damn sure sick of it. Every goddamn night the same stringy stuff." Private Mather stuck out his tongue as if he were gagging. Flexing his biceps, he said, "I'd like to meet that cook in a dark field one night and let him know what I think of his slop."

"Yeah," McGinnis piped up, running magnified eyes over Leroy's hulking frame. "He'd probably listen to you."

Perry leaned down and stubbed out his cigarette, then picked up the last copy of the Columbus *Sentinel* his mother had sent. Absently flipping through the pages, he dismissed the nightly debate that always ran in circles and never solved a thing.

Isolated in the center of Rapides Parish, Perry and the men in his unit tried to keep up their morale but had no outlet for their frustrations other than their heated discussions. Perry saw their bellyaching as entertainment, something to do to pass time.

"What's the big deal?" Perry finally said, disgusted to be sitting in the barracks talking about food on a Saturday night. "Let's go into town."

"Yeah, *sure*," Private Hodges muttered sarcastically, checking his watch. "The colored bus left at six while that asshole noncom kept lecturing us till nearly seven. Probably on purpose. We'd have to walk."

Mather's mouth drew down at the corners as he raised his thick, flat hands and turned them, palms up, in Perry's face. "You guys walk it if you want to. I ain't going." He pressed his corded arms across his chest. "Ain't no pussy over there in Alexandria worth hoofing five miles to get." He flipped over onto his back, face shining under the bare bulb hanging above his bunk.

"Ha!" Heywood snorted. "Believe that if you want to! I'm game! I saw a pretty little thang at the Tiki Lounge last Saturday that I wouldn't mind running into again."

"Who's coming?" Perry demanded, shoving his newspaper under his pillow. "I've gotta get out of here. But I ain't walking alone."

"You got that," Heywood said. "The KKK got a branch in town. Buddy, I wouldn't *let* you walk that road alone." Heywood started pulling on his shoes and socks. "Wait up, I'm coming. Ain't nothing to do here."

Perry stuck his silver lighter in his shirt pocket and splashed a handful of cologne across his neck, anxious for action, any kind of action to liven things up a bit. After his picketing and protesting in the streets of Columbus, Army life seemed pretty tame.

"Come on. Let's shake this place," he said, looking pointedly at Mather, who usually went along. McGinnis and Heywood grabbed their hats. Then the three banged out of the barracks, leaving Leroy Mather behind.

After an hour and fifteen minutes on the road to Alexandria the third whites-only bus passed them by. Perry cursed the dust it kicked up in his face and was picking up a rock to throw after it when a black farmer careened around the curve, stopped, and offered to give the guys a lift.

As soon as Perry got to the Tiki Lounge, he went straight to the bar, ordered a beer, and scanned the room for Sadie Harris. There she was, at a table in the rear, her rhinestone earrings sparkling in the dark.

Perry went over and pulled a chair from the shaky card table near the jukebox, glancing up at the whirring ceiling fan above him, wishing it did a better job of cooling the stuffy room. He'd worked up a sweat on the walk into town and hated the dark wet circles staining his khaki shirt. He looked down at his shoes, scowled, then rubbed each toe on the backs of his pants to bring back the spit shine he'd lost.

This Army life ain't worth shit, he thought, resentment churning his stomach. *I didn't put up with crap like this in Columbus. Why the hell they think I'm going to down here?*

Throwing one leg over the chair, he eased himself down and rested his forearms on its back, then turned to lock eyes with the somber young woman who sat alone at the table, sipping a glass of beer.

"Have a seat, why don't you?" A thick, arched eyebrow lifted in question as Sadie Harris raked Perry with mock offense. The rose-colored lamp on the wall behind their table glowed pink, softening Sadie's broad, flat face.

"Don't mind if I do." Perry smiled, glad to see Sadie,

trying to read her expression, trying to gauge her mood to-night.

For the past three weeks—every Saturday night he could get off base—he'd met Sadie at the Tiki Lounge, and each time he saw her she was in a different state of mind, always keeping him guessing. Sometimes she'd be gay, bubbling, telling dirty jokes, and laughing with the guys. Other times she'd be calm, almost insolent, exuding a kind of nervous energy that made him edgy. Perry wondered if Sadie Harris did more than drink whiskey sours in the cozy little room she maintained upstairs above the bar. But whatever Sadie did was really none of his business. All he wanted was escape from the barracks, some decent music to listen to, and, if possible, a few hours between the perfumed sheets on Sadie Harris's bed.

"I should have known you'd show up." Sadie's haughty attitude was more seductive than critical.

"Why you gotta say it like that?" Perry asked, warming to the repartee she initiated.

"Well ... it's payday. Saturday night. I could hear the change rattling in you guys' pockets from the base clear into town."

Perry laughed and put his cheek near Sadie's. "You saying you're not glad I came?"

She nudged closer, licked her full lips, then ran her tongue over Perry's smooth cheek. "I didn't say that," she murmured. "But all you soldier boys strut your stuff around here on Saturday nights, then go away and forget about us town girls completely."

Perry squirmed, unwilling to rise to her bait. It was obvious she was testing him, and he'd have to tread very carefully if he intended to get her upstairs without making any kind of commitment. "Aw, don't say that. You gotta remember we have jobs to do. We're in the Army. Our time is not ours to give."

Sadie twirled the cheap charm bracelet around her thin wrist, attention riveted on her half-filled glass.

"Let's not get moody," Perry said. "You're here. I'm here. Have another drink. Okay?"

Sadie tilted her glass, drained it, then pushed it across the table. "Sure, as long as you're buying."

Perry got up and threaded through the crush of people toward the bar. As he passed the pool table, McGinnis reached out and tugged at his shirtsleeve.

"Perry, get me a Jack Daniel's on the rocks while you're at the bar."

"Sure," Perry said, noticing a bleary, unfocused veil was already clouding his buddy's eyes.

Poor Joe, Perry thought, as he laid a five on the bar and picked up the cool glasses. He always drank too much, too fast, and got pissass drunk. Unless they managed to snag a ride, he and Heywood would probably have to *carry* Joe back to the base, and this time he'd better not throw up. Last time he'd ruined Heywood's pinks, the only Class A dress pants he had.

Straightening up from the green felt surface, Joe took the amber drink from Perry, grinning as he cocked his head toward the door.

"See who just straggled in?" He tilted the glass and drained half the whiskey.

Perry swung his eyes to the front of the lounge. "Mather? I thought he was staying in."

"Yeah," Joe said, leaning back down to sight his next shot. He ran the pool cue through his fingers, biting down hard on his bottom lip. "But you know Mather. Afraid he'll miss out on something. Musta caught a ride 'cause he was already in here when we arrived. Just standing over there watching everybody."

Perry shouldered his way through the crowd, starting back to his table, when suddenly Mather appeared at his side.

"Hey." The would-be boxer made his presence known.

Perry assumed a blank, uninterested look. "Hey, yourself. See you decided to join the party, huh?"

"Yeah," Mather said, reproachful eyes on Sadie. "Thought I'd better not make myself too scarce."

Perry kept walking, but Mather stepped into his path. "Don't be getting too comfortable over there with Sadie," he said. "She might have come in here alone, but she'll be leaving with me."

Heat flared inside Perry at those words. He usually steered clear of Mather, not trusting a man who liked to bully and push his way around. He was angling for a promotion to sergeant so he could move out of barracks 37 and have an official reason to boss soldiers around. Tonight Perry wasn't about to let the thick-necked brute horn in on his plans with Sadie. "Mather, just 'cause you're about to make sergeant don't mean you got dibs on anybody you choose. Sadie asked me to sit with her."

Perry flinched as Mather slammed down his bottle of beer, breaking it into slivers of brown glass. The guys huddling over the billiard table began easing back, cutting their eyes from one to another.

"You got one thing right, Private," Mather growled. "You're talking to a man who will soon be an officer. So don't do anything foolish. I can make your life miserable."

"This has nothing to do with rank," Perry calmly insisted. "Sadie wants me to sit with her."

"That's *my* seat you put your black ass in, and I don't want to see you back in it." Mather gritted his teeth and made a fist, watching, waiting for Perry to say something.

"Hey," Perry snapped, "don't you threaten me. If the lady knew it was your seat, why she didn't say something about it to me." Perry tried to push through the crowd, muttering, "Better clue Sadie in on who she's to sit with." Then he made the mistake of laughing aloud.

Mather's hand shot out and wrapped around Perry's neck, encasing it like a hard brown vise. The soldiers nearby shouted and drew back, making a clearing to watch the fight.

Perry reached up, trying to pry off Mather's deadly grip, but the soldier roared only more loudly, clamped his beefy lips shut, and squeezed tighter. "You go find a seat some-where else, pretty boy."

Fumbling blindly, Perry felt McGinnis shove a pool stick into his hand. He clutched it, swiftly raised it in a sure, even swing, then brought it down on the top of Mather's head.

"God damn you!" Mather growled, letting go, pressing his palms to his head. "Who the hell you think you are?" He lunged toward Perry, who stepped back suddenly, caus-ing the raging private to miscalculate his assault and fall forward. Going down, he struck his forehead on the edge of the pool table.

Perry stood above the injured man, chest heaving, strug-gling to breathe, desperate to gain control. He wanted to shout his triumph, but when he saw a trickle of blood drip down Mather's nose, he shuddered instead, knowing his troubles were just beginning.

From the floor Mather stirred, then croaked, "You-all see what he did? He started this. He attacked me!" After touching the side of his nose, he stared in astonishment at the blood on his fingers. "Shit! Outside. Somebody go outside. Across the street. Somebody get the MPs in here. Now!"

A clamor of excited voices shrilled through the bar, ris-ing in pitch to drown out the song still drifting from the jukebox. From the corner of his eye Perry saw a blur of khaki as several frightened privates hurried out the front door. He also saw Sadie Harris calmly get up from the ta-ble and slip out behind them, followed closely by the other girls who roomed upstairs.

Perry shouted at McGinnis, "Let's get out of here."

Heywood grabbed a bottle of vodka off the bar and put a strong elbow hold around Joe's neck. "You heard the man, McGinnis. Let's blow this joint before we all of us wind up in the slammer."

Perry, McGinnis, and Heywood pushed through the crush of soldiers and headed through the kitchen, into the alley behind the bar. Once outside, they slipped down to the end of the street and sank down in the entryway of an abandoned cotton warehouse.

"Shit!" Perry cursed. "Mather should have kept his stupid black ass on the post."

"Hell, let it go," Heywood said, twisting open the bottle of vodka. "Here, take a drink. Let the MPs cool down. We got plenty of time to get back."

From where they hid, Perry could see the front of the Tiki Lounge, bright lights shining on the dirty pavement. He saw Sadie Harris, standing right in the door, one leg to one side, arms crossed on her luscious bosom, no emotion whatsoever on her face.

The three sat in silence for about thirty minutes, passing the vodka bottle back and forth. By the time Perry thought it safe enough to venture out, the bottle was empty and Joe McGinnis had passed out.

"How the hell we gonna get *him* back to the base?" Heywood wondered aloud, barely able to stand himself.

Perry got up, wiped his handkerchief over his face, and belched, feeling as if he were going to throw up. "Lemme think" was all he could say. Then he nudged a numb McGinnis with his boot. "Goddamn, the boy's really gone!"

"We can't leave him here." Heywood was starting to panic. "No way we can carry him, and I ain't gonna pull KP again for getting back late."

Perry stumbled into the street, looked it up and down, noticing all the white soldiers still parading between the juke joints and crawfish shacks lining the district. He watched them laugh as they lurched drunkenly from club to club, not a care in the world, because buses stood waiting to take them back.

"Hell," Perry said, reaching down to grab McGinnis by the shoulders. "Get his feet, Heywood."

Heywood did as he was told. "Where we gonna stash him?"

"On that bus over there," Perry said, starting across the street, Joe's shoulders under his palms.

Heywood struggled along behind him. "That bus? Perry, that's the white bus."

"A bus is a fucking bus," Perry shot back, beginning to move faster across the street, tugging Heywood along in his anger.

"This is crazy, Perry. They ain't gonna let us on."

"It's a government-contracted bus. I'm a citizen. I'm not walking back to the post!"

After carrying Joe across the street, Perry tapped on the glass door of one of the waiting buses. It quickly flew open with a whoosh. Without a word Perry began backing up the steps, pulling Joe and Heywood with him.

"Hey! You!" The bus driver shot to his feet. "You can't get on this bus!"

Perry clamped his jaw shut, shoved past the driver, and plopped Joe McGinnis on the very first seat.

"Well, I *am* on it, and I'm not getting off." He settled in next to Joe.

"Listen, you niggers, you ride on a colored bus."

"There are no more colored buses running tonight, and you know it."

"Get offa here! Now!"

Perry glared. Heywood started toward the rear.

"Heywood! You get back up here and sit down," Perry shouted. "We're going back to the base."

"Not on this bus you're not," the driver said, and descended the steps to the street.

Perry resolutely folded his arms, crossed his legs, and looked out the window as if he were about to be given a tour of the city.

Heywood sank into the seat behind Perry, leaned up to his ear, and whispered, "You gonna get us killed, Perry. *Killed.*"

"This bus is supposed to transport U.S. soldiers between the post and the town. What do I look like, a fucking gypsy? I got every right to be here!"

"God Almighty," Heywood muttered. But he sat back, anxious to see what would happen.

Two white MPs boarded the bus. "You boys gotta get off," said one of them.

"We can't," Perry replied, his voice surprisingly polite. "My buddy here is sick. We got no other way to get back to the base."

One of the MPs stepped closer to Joe, leaned down, sniffed loudly, then leveled a grave eye to Perry. "Too bad, boy. But y'all shoulda thought about how you'd get back to camp before you got so damn pissing drunk."

Perry stonily refused to comment.

"Get off. Now," the MP at the door ordered, slapping his billy club against his palm.

Perry didn't budge. "I got rights. I know what my civil rights are," he finally said.

"Then write a letter to your congressman, buddy, 'cause you're in Louisiana now, and you're gonna follow the local rules."

When Perry grunted loudly, the MP standing by Joe reached over and grabbed him by the collar. Furious, Perry leaped up and pushed the soldier to the floor, jumped astride him, and reared back to strike.

Heywood bolted forward and grabbed Perry's hand. "Don't hit him. For Christ's sake, Perry. Let's get off."

Distracted, Perry relaxed, allowing the MP to flip upright and drive his fist straight into Perry's left jaw.

"Oh, hell!" Heywood screamed. "You busted his face."

"That's right, boy. You want the same?"

Heywood dropped down and began to pull Perry by the shirt. "Come on! Come on! Let's get out of here!"

But Perry shook Heywood off and struck the MP across the mouth with the back of his hand, grinning to feel the smack of his white flesh against his knuckles. It was too late to salvage the situation. At least he had got in a lick.

Now the MP at the doorway lunged up the steps and cracked Perry on the head with his thick billy club.

Perry felt a searing pain shoot through his head, and everything before him flashed red, then black.

When Perry regained consciousness, he was back on the post, flat on his back, strapped to a cot in the stockade.

CHAPTER SIXTEEN

Dalton sniffed the delicate fragrance of grated coconut, savoring its tropical perfume. As he paused, wooden spoon in midair, a drift of memories surfaced from the shadows of his past. The sticky white fruit dripped stringy and thick, while Tahti Lantina's lyrical voice invaded his bachelor's kitchen, whirling him back two years.

"Peel the coconut first, then the sweet potato, then the cassava. The success of the pudding is in keeping all the steps straight!"

He could see Tahti now, reaching across mounds of papayas, bananas, guava fruit, and coconuts, her long red-enameled fingernails wagging in mock lecture, her velvet bronze cheeks round and beaming, ripe and sweet as the perfectly polished mangoes she sold in her narrow stall.

Rushing through the Columbus Central Market, he had heard her voice before he saw her: a chiming singsong lure that stopped him in his tracks. Then he turned around, and there she was: a winsome riot of yellow and orange and red and blue, full, laughing lips, the swell of curving breasts and hips draped in sun-splashed madras.

Over the next two months Dalton had made it a point to cut through the bustling market on his way to court. He'd buy an apple, an orange, an overripe banana and make nervous, almost embarrassing small talk about his genuine interest in cooking.

Soon Tahti opened up, steering him toward exotic fruits

and vegetables, encouraging him to try her favorite Brazilian recipes.

Captivated, he had impulsively asked if she would come to his place and show him how to make the cassava pudding she referred to as sugar-spun-from-heaven. When she agreed, he was almost too excited to go through with the date. But he did.

Tahti had swirled into his west side apartment carrying cloth bags bulging with coconuts, sweet potatoes, and starchy white cassava roots. They had laughed and teased and conversed with an ease that seduced them both that evening. His home had vibrated with the tinkling chime of her musical words, which rang through his kitchen like a sprinkling of golden glitter, sticking to everything: the countertops, the pots and pans, the sensitive surface of his heart.

After devouring the heavenly dessert, they had gone out on his moonlit balcony. There she had let him kiss her on the lips, caress her pliant, full-curved hips, and murmur endearments into her gold-ringed ears.

The sheen of joy in her eyes, the way her skin, flawless and velvety, had felt beneath his hands, the memory of all the nights they huddled together by the fire, eating her tropical concoctions from a single bowl with two spoons now invaded Dalton with punishing clarity.

He cringed, wishing he hadn't gone through the market this afternoon and bought all this stuff. Regret knotted his stomach, and he laid the spoon aside.

Give it up, Dalton, he told himself, knowing the telephone call from Janelle that morning had pushed him to cook the sticky Bahamian pudding, had forced him to confront the aching loneliness he had convinced himself was normal.

Janelle had gotten herself accepted into the Army Nurse Corps. Though he was happy for her and proud that she'd made the cut, the news had left him numb, and nothing he did seemed to dampen the flame she had ignited in him.

Blood pulsed through him at near-boiling point, making him light-headed, unfocused.

At the office he drank cup after cup of bitter strong coffee. Unable to concentrate on the files on his desk, he spent the afternoons staring out his dirty window, looking down into the street, imagining he saw her standing on every corner. And whenever Norma buzzed him with a call, he had jumped, praying Janelle was calling back to tell him she had changed her mind.

He had wanted to drive straight to her house, gather her into his arms, confess his feelings, beg her not to leave. Instead he had wandered gloomily through the Central Market, buying food he knew now he'd never eat.

If only he could have abandoned himself to the promise of Janelle's warm embrace instead of stubbornly allowing pragmatism to rule his heart.

Compressing his lips, Dalton picked up the spoon, stirring again, beating cinnamon, milk, and eggs with frenzied strokes.

Beautiful, pride-filled, ambitious, and direct, Janelle had mysteriously beguiled him with her forward flirtation. She charged through his veins, pricking at his heart with a needlelike sharpness that he could not ignore.

Now, too late, Dalton confessed to himself that Janelle was the woman he longed for. And what price might he pay if he dared reach out to draw her into the bigoted world he sometimes felt he roamed alone?

During a ninety-minute delay at the Birmingham station, throngs of resolute passengers pressed their way into the already overstuffed colored passenger car to poke and prod and scour it for any unoccupied space. An unhappy baby shrieked its discomfort at the top of its lungs, an old woman complained loudly about pains in her back, and an obviously distraught young wife sat in a corner miserably sobbing into her lace handkerchief.

Uniformed soldiers squatted in the aisles on their Army-issue duffel bags while harried civilians stowed their battered suitcases, settling down next to strangers. Oblivious of the clamor going on around her, Janelle quietly leafed through the papers in her lap, carefully rereading her orders.

She went over the personal belongings list again, hoping she had packed in her single suitcase no more or less than the Army had said she could bring. With a grimy hand, suddenly sick to death of the outfit that used to be her favorite, she tried to smooth an ugly network of wrinkles from the front of her blue and white suit. For two days now she'd sat in it, slept in it, used the jacket as a pillow under her head. As soon as she got her official Army uniforms, she would put the suit at the bottom of her trunk or maybe even give it away.

The train lurched off again, continuing its southerly route across the Alabama countryside—oddly green and vibrant in February—barely touched by the cold hand of winter.

Turning from the window, Janelle looked over at Emma. who was sleeping soundly in the seat next to hers. Emma's breathing was even and steady, but her head lolled back and forth with the sway of the train, and a damp layer of perspiration shone on her forehead and cheeks. She had complained of feeling headachy and too warm. Janelle reached over and touched her friend's cheek, then drew back, alarmed by the heat that met her fingers.

Pulling a bottle of aspirin from her purse, Janelle started to shake Emma awake, then changed her mind and leaned back. It was probably best to leave her alone, she decided, relieved one of them was finally getting some decent rest.

Janelle stretched both arms above her head, then rubbed the muscles cramping in her shoulders, remembering how badly she had slept the night before. Trapped in the pint-size, claustrophobic lower berth with Emma, she had awakened in the middle of the night, then lain staring into darkness for hours, listening to the clack-clack of the heavy train, absorbing the fact that she was officially in the Army.

A clean slate, that's what I'll have, Janelle told herself, folding her orders, slipping them back into her purse. She hoped the long delay in Birmingham would not cause problems with the tight connection between Montgomery and Chehaw—the tiny pit stop of a station in the middle of Macon County where everyone headed for Tuskegee got off.

Janelle snuggled down in her seat, cradling her head against folded hands. Tension eased from her neck and shoulders.

Images of her swearing in at Fort Hayes appeared. Facing the American flag, eyes brimming with tears, she had raised her right hand and made her pledge of service. She was glad her mother had been there to watch, though Janelle knew Alice considered entering the service an act of desperation, a commitment hastily made.

Dad would never have viewed it that way, she thought, still struggling to absorb the story her mother had told. So maybe he *had* been unfaithful. Lots of men were. That didn't make him a monster. She and Perry had doted on their father, had been lucky enough to be loved. Completely loved. By a man she refused to think badly of. The revelation hurt—there was no way to deny that—but Janelle pushed it away whenever it surfaced, determined no good could come by lingering on the issue.

In her opinion, Garrett Roy's love had helped prepare her for the challenge facing her now. True, military nursing would be demanding, structured, and not so easy to adjust to after private-duty work, but Janelle was anxious to join the colored military personnel who—in spite of the swirl of political criticism and local hatred that plagued the segregated airfield—remained totally committed to serving their country.

Exhausted, Janelle sighed, letting a newfound inner peace anchor her to the moment. For the first time in her adult life she felt free—released of responsibility for anyone other than herself, finally liberated from the pressure of her family. No longer driven to pry her way into the segregated circles of wealth and social status—a world that had cruelly turned against her—she now looked forward to practicing her profession in an arena where she was valued, needed, and wanted.

As the train rattled over an old trestle bridge, Emma stirred, then opened her eyes. "Where are we?" she managed to say, her voice hoarse. She sounded as if she were trying to swallow a piece of dry, burned toast.

"Somewhere between Birmingham and Montgomery," Janelle answered. She leaned back to see Emma better. "You don't look so good."

Emma forced a smile. "I don't feel so good either." She ran her fingers through her tangled black curls, then touched her forehead. "My head is splitting, and my throat is on fire." She licked her parched lips. "I've got to get some water." When she started to rise, Janelle stopped her.

"Here." She handed Emma her bottle of aspirin. "Better take a few of these. I think you've got a fever."

"Thanks, I sure feel like hell." Emma took the bottle, poured two tablets into the palm of her hand, and struggled up out of her seat. "Be right back."

That's all we need, Janelle thought dispiritedly, hoping Emma was not coming down with the flu or, God forbid, something more serious. At least the trip was nearly over. If the connection to Chehaw didn't cause a long delay, they'd be at the airfield before dark.

From her window seat in the middle of the car, Janelle looked around the train. A trim, uniformed man stepped into the aisle, giving up his berth turned passenger seat to an elderly gentleman who had been squeezed between two frustrated young mothers whose babies had been fussing and squalling nonstop since the train pulled out of Birmingham.

The old man clutched a floppy black hat in big, gnarled hands. His heavy wool suit was cut like a preacher's frock. Even from a distance, through a veil of low-hanging cigarette smoke, Janelle could tell the aging man's white shirt was starched as stiff as the side of a pasteboard box and his red bow tie, anchored at the base of a dark, wrinkled throat, was so frayed and softened from years of wear it no longer turned up at the corners.

As the fragile man haltingly lowered his frame into the soldier's place, Janelle watched him mouth words of gratitude, though the noise of the fast-moving train and the crowded car made it impossible to make out exactly what was said.

The smiling soldier made a gesture with his hands to put the man at ease. Then, steadying himself by grabbing the upholstered backs of the seats, he worked his way down the aisle.

Impressed by his first lieutenant's stripes, the shiny pilot's wings on his chest, Janelle openly assessed him. His confident military strut drew attention away from a youthful round face that on any other man would have stripped him of authority.

Moving with the agility of an athlete, the good-looking pilot searched the car for a place to sit down. Janelle could not take her eyes off him. He reminded her of the larger-than-life images that beamed out from Army recruitment posters plastered on walls all across the nation. The only difference: This handsome GI was not white.

What a polite thing to do, she thought, impressed by the soldier's readiness to give up his seat. As he neared, she did not lower her eyes but caught his attention as he slowed his pace. He came to a halt in front of her.

"This seat taken?" His low, pleasant voice touched Janelle like a sweet embrace. He was taller than she had first imagined, and his physical presence now overwhelmed her. Her lips curved upward in greeting.

"Yes. I'm sorry it's taken," she replied, relieved that she could speak normally.

The skin at the corners of his eyes crinkled when he smiled, spurring her heart to pump even faster.

"Just my luck," the pilot replied, removing his brimmed flight cap. "I should have known you wouldn't be traveling alone."

Janelle studied him, intrigued by his subtle flirtation, flattered. What harm could come from chatting? She straightened her navy blue skirt and ran a hand over the front of her hair. "My *girl*friend went to get some water," she told him.

"Oh." He accepted the statement with the beginning of a smile.

The encouragement in his voice was not lost on Janelle, who sat composed, letting his inquisitive eyes roam from her face to her waist and back up. In a fluid motion the pilot lowered himself into Emma's empty seat.

Struck by his bold move, Janelle decided he had finessed his way around quite a few women and knew exactly what effect he was having on her.

"Where you headed?" he asked.

"Montgomery . . . Tuskegee, really." Both grateful and annoyed that he had assumed she wanted him sitting beside her, engaging her in conversation, Janelle lowered her eyes to half lids.

"You a student at the institute?"

"No. I'm a nurse. So is my friend," she said. "We're supposed to report to Tuskegee Airfield tonight."

"I'm Lance Fuller, a pilot at the base. That's where I'm headed, too." His boyish grin, complete with irresistible dimples, started a slow burn somewhere in Janelle's middle.

Accepting his outstretched hand, she introduced herself. "Janelle Roy, Columbus, Ohio."

"A long way from home, huh?" He gazed at her, in no hurry to let her hand go. "The connections from Montgomery to Tuskegee can be pretty tricky. If you haven't made other arrangements, I'll be glad to take you and your friend out to the base."

Janelle eased her hand from his, keeping her lips slightly parted in as nonchalant a half smile as she could manage, praying she didn't look like a wide-eyed puppy. That was pretty darn close to how she felt.

"Well, I have been worried that the delay in Birmingham might make us miss our connection."

"Happens all the time." He chuckled. "I go up to Birmingham to visit my great-aunt whenever I get a little time. She's ninety-two, still pretty lively, but I don't know when I might get shipped out, so I wanted to see her one more time."

"You really care about old people, don't you?"

He put a finger to the side of his face, perplexed. "Oh, the old man up there? Yeah, he kind of reminded me of my grandfather. Hey, I don't mind giving up my seat for someone who needs it more than I do." He treated her to another cocky, adorable grin. "How about it? Will you let me drive you out to the base?"

"Oh . . . if it's no trouble. I mean, if you don't mind—" She stopped, hoping she wasn't being foolish.

"Good. I'll look for you and your friend at the front entrance to the station." He started to rise.

"Sorry, you don't have a seat," Janelle said, wishing he'd stay, flustered but not angry that the young lieutenant had so easily and successfully unnerved her.

"Hey, that's okay," he said, shrugging, comically turning both palms upward in exaggerated resignation. "Guess I'll see what I can find in the back."

"Good luck," Janelle said, meaning it.

"Thanks." Lance nodded, then gave her a brash, sexy wink.

Janelle froze and held her breath, silently counting to ten. Then she leaned over the empty seat and peered down the aisle to see where he went. A trip-hammer started pounding far down inside her chest as she saw him pull the door open and disappear into the tangle of colored military personnel filling the adjoining car.

Slowly sinking back in her seat, Janelle let the encounter sink in. If this soldier's behavior was typical of what she would find at Tuskegee, life certainly would not be dull on the base.

Holding a paper cup of water, Emma emerged from the rear of the car. She slipped into her seat.

"Did you see that soldier?" Janelle asked.

"What soldier?" She twisted around.

"You must have passed him coming back up the aisle. The cute one. Tall. A pilot." Both palms flat, Janelle pushed herself up, craning to look over the back of her seat.

"Sorry I missed him," Emma said, sipping her water. "My head is aching so bad I did good to find my seat." She flopped back and closed her eyes. "But if *you* are interested, he must have made quite an impression." She smiled, amused, then murmured with eyes still shut, "Good for you, Janelle. I think you're beginning to come around, old girl. You'll see. Life at Tuskegee is going to be good for you. You'll recover from Dalton Graham real fast."

Janelle waved a hand of dismissal at Emma. "I haven't thought about him in weeks."

"Good. I'm happy to hear that." She squeezed Janelle's arm. "Things can only go up, you know?"

Janelle grinned and turned her face to the window, knowing Emma was right. Change was coming, and it felt good to face each day with excitement. She watched the huge orange-red sun ease toward the horizon. The train slowed. A uniformed attendant came through the car to announce their arrival at Montgomery.

CHAPTER
SEVENTEEN

"All right. Let's get moving," Janelle said to Emma, who attempted to rise, then fell back with a groan. "You okay?" Janelle asked, now worried that Emma was really sick.

With difficulty Emma swallowed, then placed her hand beneath her chin. "I feel like the devil is tap-dancing on top of my head." She shuddered, forcing her eyes open. "Whew! I'm tired." Grabbing the seat back in front of her, she stood, steadied by Janelle's arm around her waist. "God, I'm not sure I can make it off this train."

Alarmed, Janelle put her hand to Emma's brow. "You're burning up with fever."

Emma lowered her head into her hands. "I think I'm going to be sick."

"Oh, no." Janelle scanned the departing crowd as passengers emptied their berths, gathered their belongings, and exited the train. She saw no one she could ask for help.

"Sit still, try to relax. Concentrate on something other than your stomach." Slipping past Emma, she stepped into the aisle. "I'll go see if I can find an attendant to help us get out of here."

After waiting until a passenger had moved out of her way, Janelle headed toward the rear of the car. There she saw an attendant checking seats, looking for items people usually left behind. He moved with practiced steps through the train.

"Porter! Up here!" Janelle called out. "Can you help us?"

"Yes, ma'am." He followed Janelle back to Emma.

"My friend doesn't feel very good. I think I can get her off the train if you could see to our bags."

"Yes, ma'am. Most surely," he said, stepping back as Janelle guided Emma toward the exit. "What's the name on your bags?"

"Janelle Roy and Emma Brown."

"Where you headed?"

"Tuskegee. The airfield."

"Oh, you's military?" He gave the two a respectful nod.

"Yes," Janelle answered, placing an arm about Emma's waist, letting her lean on her shoulder. "Just not in uniform yet."

"Well, don't you worry 'bout a thing. You just leave it to me. Go on into the station. I'll be sure your bags catch up with you."

Janelle and Emma managed to get across the platform inside the station and found their way to the colored rest room. Emma was violently ill, vomiting until Janelle was convinced the poor girl's stomach was going to split.

"Emma, you're not pregnant, are you?" Janelle asked, handing her friend a wet paper towel, watching closely for her reaction as she dabbed at her temples.

"Heavens, no!" Emma's reply was adamant and swift. "Don't even think a thing like that."

"Oops! Just asking." Janelle grimaced, thinking how awful it would be if Emma were dropped from the corps now. The nursing recruiters at the Red Cross had been very clear: No married women or anyone with a less than spotless reputation could serve in the Army Nurse Corps. Of course, that was a special colored requirement; lots of white nurses were married. Softly Janelle probed. "Is it a possibility at all?"

"No. Really, no. You devil! Are you implying that I've

been unfaithful to Kenneth?" Even in her agony Emma's words were touched with humor. "Nothing quite that dramatic going on here. Probably picked up some bug on the train. Oh!" Gripping the washbowl, she gagged again, then stared morosely into the sink.

"Want me to get you something? A Coke. A Bromo?"

Emma turned on the faucet and ran water over her wrists, then splashed some on her face. "No. I think the worst is over." After drying her hands on a paper towel, she said tentatively, "Let's go on, or we'll miss the connection to Tuskegee."

"Don't worry about that." Janelle's expression turned a little sheepish. "I didn't tell you, but the pilot I met on the train—well, he said he could drive us out to the base."

"Oh?" Emma's brows inched higher, animating her drawn face. "You think we should?"

"Well, I know his name. Lance Fuller. Lieutenant Fuller. He's stationed at Tuskegee. I feel okay about it."

"All right, let's do it," Emma said. "I'm so sick he may be sorry he's letting me in his car." Exhaling a shaky breath, Emma glanced into the mirror, fluffed her bangs with two fingers, then pressed her lips together. "Not a pretty sight, eh?"

Janelle's chuckle was sympathetic. "Forget about that. You're in the Army now. I have a feeling appearances won't be that important."

"I don't know," Emma said, following Janelle through the door. "Remember, the men outnumber the women four to one at Tuskegee. I think we are going to be very much on display."

Reentering the large open area, they were greeted by the familiar clamor of a busy railway station. In the small waiting area set aside for Negroes, the porter stood guarding their two lonely suitcases. Next to him, in the center of a cluster of laughter and animated conversation was Lance Fuller. He was leaning against the wall, relaxed, smiling and chatting with two other soldiers and a pretty, curvaceous young woman. She tugged at her too-tight pale purple skirt, then placed her arm possessively around Lance's trimly belted waist.

Tightening her grip on Emma's shoulder, Janelle averted her eyes and headed away from the group, feeling an odd sense of betrayal. It was obvious Lieutenant Fuller had other obligations.

Emma collapsed on a scarred wooden bench and pressed a cool wet paper towel on her brow.

"Stay here, relax. I'll get our bags." Janelle strode at a no-nonsense clip across the waiting area, thanked the redcap, and pressed a quarter into his palm.

"Where do I make the connection to Chehaw?" she asked.

"Chehaw?" The redcap twisted his lips in thought, shaking his head. "Don't reckon there's gonna be another trip out that way till morning. You missed the last regular run."

Gulping dryly, she asked, "You mean we have to spend the night here? In this station?"

The redcap's blank expression held her answer.

"My friend is sick. We can't stay here. And we have orders to report to the air base by twenty-four hundred hours tonight. Army orders. Is there no other way to get out there?" It was hard to remain calm and not raise her voice, though she knew it wasn't the redcap's fault. "What about a taxi? A bus?" she pressed.

"Well." The redcap scratched his chin in thought.

"I was wondering where you went." Lance Fuller's voice burned the back of Janelle's neck. She jerked around so quickly her purse slipped from her hand and fell to the floor with an embarrassing thud.

Lance removed his cap, stooped down, and retrieved Janelle's bag. Luckily nothing had spilled.

"Lieutenant Lance Fuller at your service." He grinned, flashing his dimples, and immediately dispersed Janelle's fear that he had not meant his offer of a ride.

Hand visibly trembling, she took her clutch bag, feeling a flush inch from the soles of her feet to her cheeks.

"Thank you," she managed to say in a fairly cool tone, tugged toward him by the captivating pull of his eyes.

He turned and tipped his hat to the redcap. "Thanks for your help, buddy. I can take it from here."

Janelle let her uneasiness fall away as she led him back to Emma and made the introductions.

When Lance bowed slightly, sweeping the air with his flight cap, the courtly gesture was not lost on Janelle. She wondered if Lance Fuller might be a little too smooth, too absolutely gorgeous, too cocksure confident about himself to be for real. An inner voice cautioned her not to let herself get carried away.

"I've got a car outside." He nodded toward the group he had been standing with. "My buddies and I share a well-used Ford. It belongs to my grandfather, but he doesn't drive anymore. The guys came in to pick me up, but I can use the car to run you out to the base."

"Oh, if you have other plans," Janelle said, noticing the girl approaching, hands on hips, painted lips pressed into a pout.

"Lance, we're gonna be late!" the girl said, hooking her fingers through the belt loops on his khakis. "The band starts at seven, and you know if we don't get there early, we're gonna lose our table."

"Christine, this is Janelle Roy and her friend Emma. They're on their way to the base."

With a swift glance, Janelle appraised the girl, who seemed to be about twenty. Up close Janelle noticed that she wore too much makeup, and silver barrettes pinned back her coarse black hair. Long red earrings brushed the sides of her neck as she impatiently tugged Lance's arm. The pungent scent of her dime-store perfume breezed over to Janelle in sickening waves.

"Come on. Let's go." Christine raked Janelle from head to toe, sniffed loudly, then complained, "Gladys and Maggie are waiting at the club."

"Please don't change your plans for us," Janelle insisted, sensing an argument about to ensue. Why the devil had Lance offered to drive her to the base when his evening was obviously taken? She questioned Emma silently, who fluttered her fingers as if to say, "Don't worry, that's his problem. We need a ride." Then she lifted her chin toward the ceiling, waiting.

"It's no trouble," Lance said, giving Christine a look that Janelle knew would have sent *her* on her way. Untangling himself from Christine's clutch, he told her, "The Propeller Club doesn't close until twelve. I've got plenty of time to run them to the base."

"We'll miss the show," Christine whined. "You promised we'd go tonight. I gave Jimmy two dollars to hold the table." Her hands swung to her hips. "I've been waiting three months to hear the Five Flames."

"I know. I know. But hold on, Christine." Lance stepped away from Janelle to guide Christine a few feet to the side, though his whispers still rose above the din in the station. "I've got a couple of stranded Army nurses here."

"So who appointed you knight in shining armor? Call the base. They'll send out a jeep. You promised we'd see the Five Flames tonight."

"Why don't you guys take a taxi, go on over? I'll meet you later."

Janelle watched Lance bite his bottom lip impatiently, jaws tensed as he waited for a response.

"You promised you'd take me to the Propeller Club *tonight*," Christine muttered between clenched teeth. "You're the one who told me to get Gladys and Maggie for your buddies over there." She jerked her head toward the two soldiers, who were watching in amusement.

"All right. Calm down!" Lance pleaded, now visibly embarrassed by her pressure. "I'll get there before the show starts." His tone was softer, placating. "You know I won't let you down. I'll be there. Here." He opened his billfold and pulled out a five-dollar bill. "You guys take a cab and go ahead. I'll take the car, straight-line it out to the base, drop off these stranded gals, and be at the club before you have time to miss me."

Christine's answer was a stony, skeptical stare.

"I will. I promise." Lance held up his hand like a Boy Scout taking a pledge.

Christine snatched the money from Lance and stuffed it into her purse. "You already stood me up one time too many. You better not do it tonight!"

Ignoring her, Lance jerked his head toward the door, signaling the two soldiers to get going.

Christine gave Janelle a look that could have melted ice, pushed her shoulder bag up higher on her arm, and stalked off. Lance's buddies lifted their hands in a gesture of resignation and started off after her.

"Let me take your bags, ladies," Lance announced a little too loudly. His words dissolved the tension that had crackled like an exposed electrical wire, and Janelle accepted his grin as his apology for the embarrassing encounter.

"Just a friend from town," he said. "A little high-strung, but she'll settle down. . . . You two ready to report for duty?" He changed the subject.

"Very much so," Janelle replied, dismissing Christine from her thoughts, falling into step at Lance's side.

As they left the bustling depot, Janelle let Lance hold on to her arm and guide her through the crowd. Emma trailed behind.

"I feel better already." Emma sighed, taking her first whiff of the cool Alabama night air.

"Good," Janelle replied, following Lance toward a travel-worn '35 Ford sedan parked between two towering magnolias at the edge of the road. One of the running boards was missing, and a dent the size of a football decorated the right front fender, just behind the headlamp. The paint job was still in pretty good shape, though the windshield contained a long crack.

"Looks like hell but runs like a charm," Lance said, helping Emma into the backseat so she could lie down during the forty-minute ride. Then he ushered Janelle into the front seat, where she sat flush against the passenger door, waiting as Lance put their bags in the trunk. When he slid behind the wheel, she glanced over to see his eyes appraising her—seriously, as if he were contemplating making a confession. For the first time she noticed the hint of a cleft in his chin and wondered if it might be a trick of the shadows.

An ache, some kind of yearning that she'd never felt before, eased into the base of her throat. Waiting for him to start the car, she pressed her tongue against the backs of her teeth, a habit her mother had always said would ruin her smile. Aunt Dedee assured her it hadn't.

Lance turned the key in the ignition. While they waited for the engine to warm, Janelle boldly edged closer toward the center of the seat.

"All the way from Ohio, huh?" He pulled the gearstick down, and they entered the pitch-black highway.

"Yeah," she answered. "My first time in the South."

"Well, I guess I don't need to tell you, things are quite different down here. Might take some getting used to."

"I can imagine," Janelle replied. "I've read and heard a lot. Guess I'll find out soon enough how much of it is true."

"I'm a native son of Alabama," Lance said proudly. "So were my father and his father, too."

"Really?" Janelle tried to see him in the darkness. "Where were you born. Birmingham?"

"Naw." Lance hugged the steering wheel, focusing on the road. "I'm from Congregation Hills. Ever heard of it?"

Janelle let out a short chuckle. "Surprisingly, I have."

"Yeah?"

"A woman at the Red Cross recruiting station was telling me about Alabama. She said Congregation Hills is known as a center for the manufacture of railway cars and military uniforms."

"Well, well. The Yankees have us on the map, huh?"

"The Red Cross does anyway. How far is Congregation Hills from Montgomery?"

"Not far. Over that ridge to the left, five miles west. My grandfather is the mayor."

"The mayor? I'm impressed," Janelle said, intrigued by the prospect of getting to know Lance better. "You must be proud of him."

Lance shrugged but didn't answer.

"Well"—she straightened up—"my father held an important position with the city, too. He and the mayor of Columbus were very close friends."

"Oh, yeah? What does he think about you joining the Army?"

"He's dead," Janelle said flatly yet respectfully, hating having to say it at all. "He died a little over a year ago."

"I'm sorry," Lance said. A short silence filled in for additional words.

"But if he were alive," Janelle continued, "I know he'd be happy that I'm serving my country. My dad was very political and patriotic, too. He was decorated in World War One."

"So, you're the daughter of a war hero, huh?"

"You might say that," Janelle replied, hoping Lance was impressed so far. "As soon as the War Department issued its call for colored nurses, I went immediately to the Red Cross and signed up. There was never any question in my mind that I'd serve, just as my father had done."

"Can't say I was quite that anxious. But being a student at Tuskegee did give me an edge on getting into the aviation program. I've always wanted to fly. This opportunity was heaven-sent. I was in the right place at the right time, that's for sure. I couldn't pass up trying to get in. And I've made it so far. A lot of guys washed out on the first cut."

"Is your father alive?" She thought it odd he had only spoken of his grandfather.

"No." Lance paused. "At least I don't think so. He disappeared when I was a little boy."

"Disappeared?"

"Yeah ... more like ran away. But that's a long story that takes some time to tell."

Sensing the subject was closed, Janelle said lightly, "If I ever get stranded in a train station again, maybe then you'll have time to tell me."

Lance laughed, shifted in his seat, then pressed his hand against her thigh. "I'm hoping that opportunity won't be too long in coming."

Janelle flinched but did not move, ecstatic to hear him admit his interest.

When Lance rolled his window halfway down, crisp night air drifted over them. Speeding along beneath the star-filled sky, he never moved his hand. It pulsed warmly against her thigh, and she kept her eyes glued on the bright yellow stripe in the center of the road, though she yearned to look at his ebony profile.

As the perfumed night-blooming jasmine whirled its scent from the tangled vines along the road, it began: a tumultuous sweep of elation, a joyful new awakening, a rapture that stilled the unfulfilled yearning that had plagued Janelle so long. The wondrous discovery of Lieutenant Lance Fuller held her with a tender caress, nudging her gently into the future.

CHAPTER EIGHTEEN

It was pitch-black outside when reveille sounded, jolting Janelle from the first real sleep she had had in three days. She lay still, adjusting to the manner in which she had been thrust into her day, gradually realizing where she was: the nurses' quarters at Tuskegee Army Airfield.

Janelle blinked as lights came on throughout the barracks. Groaning under her breath, she lifted herself onto her elbows and looked around the room.

One by one, the thirteen other nurses who shared the boxlike structure that was so recently built it still reeked of pine tossed back their green Army blankets and stiff white sheets, cursing the ungodly hour, heading toward the communal lavatory at the far end of the building.

"How'd you sleep?"

Janelle rolled over, glad to see the familiar face of Lillian Dorsey in the bunk next to hers. She was the nurse in charge of the quarters who had welcomed her and Emma last night.

"Like a log," Janelle said, squeezing her eyes shut, then forcing them open again. "Guess I really collapsed, huh?"

"I'd say so." Lillian lowered her feet to the floor. "Don't feel too bad. I was the first to arrive, and every nurse who has come in after me has entered in a similar state of confused exhaustion."

Janelle looked around the room. "Where is Emma?"

"She's down there on the right, the last bed," Lillian answered, running a hand over her halo of light brown hair, which rose in a frizzy explosion at the top of her head.

"She got very sick on the train," Janelle said.

"Yeah. Lieutenant Raney managed to rustle up a cup of tea for her last night. It seemed to help. Then she collapsed too."

"What now?" Janelle asked, wanting to learn the routine.

"Just follow me," Lillian said. "Won't take long to get the hang of things around here. Not long at all." She opened the locker at the head of her bed and pulled out a towel and washcloth. "There's clean linen in your locker. Get yours and hit the shower."

In the white-tiled common stall Janelle got her first dose of life in the Army. Relaxing as a flood of water pummeled her aching shoulders, she knew modesty was out—privacy a thing of the past—except for some lucky nurses, who had friends or relatives in town and were permitted to live off base, commuting to the hospital for duty.

Upon their arrival she and Emma had been allowed to put their names down for a room in a boardinghouse for nurses not far from the base, but the waiting list was discouragingly long. Janelle expected to complete her tour of duty right there in the overcrowded barracks.

Through the rising clouds of steam she saw Emma humming to herself, lathering her arms, and was relieved to see her friend looking a great deal better than she had when they'd stepped off the train.

Now, as Janelle enjoyed the splash of warm water over her body, she thought of Lance Fuller. *I wonder what he's doing right now.* The thought of him standing naked in the shower, slick with soap, initiated a hot sensation between her thighs. The rosy full tips of her breasts stiffened as she recalled his voice, the easy way he had talked and joked with her, the dark hulk of his shadow at her side.

He had really been very helpful, telling her and Emma what to do, where to go, what to expect when they reported to the commander. And he had been charming, exuding a brash confidence that Janelle found powerfully appealing. Sitting in the car, Janelle had tingled with a vibrant sense of adventure, and she liked the feeling of starting over, in a place where no one knew her, in a place where she could set aside the unhappy events of the past year.

Had Lance kept his promise and met Christine at the Propeller Club? Janelle wondered. Had he danced and laughed and flirted with the girl only minutes after dropping Janelle off at the post? She hoped not.

As she leaned back, streams of soothing water fell deliciously over Janelle's face. She could still feel the intimate squeeze of Lance's handshake and was convinced he wanted to see her again.

Yes, Lieutenant Fuller, I want to see you, too, she told herself as water sluiced over her full breasts. Rivulets of soap foamed across her taut, flat stomach, down between her legs. She wondered where Lance Fuller's quarters were and if he was thinking of her.

After toweling off, Janelle took her cue from the way Lillian was dressed and pulled on her stockings, shook out the wrinkles in a white cotton blouse, and slipped it on with a gray flannel skirt—the only skirt she had brought. Then she stuck her feet into a pair of brown penny loafers.

"The commander is supposed to be coming in this morning to welcome us to the base," Lillian said, smoothing the scratchy drab blanket over white sheets. Lillian's frizz of light brown curls made her appear much taller than the five feet two she was, a head shorter than Janelle.

"Would that be Colonel Kimble?" Janelle asked.

"Yes. Wait till you meet him."

"I've already heard a few things. Lieutenant Fuller gave me a pretty good rundown," Janelle replied, remembering that Lance had told her the base commander rigidly enforced Jim Crow laws by ensuring that signs designating "white" or "colored" were properly placed over every latrine, barracks, recreation, and eating area on the base.

"Lance Fuller?" Lillian stopped in mid-tug, letting the blanket fall from her hands.

"Yes. He drove me and Emma out to the base last night."

"A lieutenant in the Ninety-ninth? Good-looking? Rather pushy?"

"Well . . . I wouldn't call him pushy." Janelle wondered where this was leading. "He was very helpful to us."

"Hmm." Lillian's expression was puzzled. "I thought he was in Birmingham last night."

"You know him?" Janelle held her breath.

"Oh, yeah." Lillian grabbed her pillow and gave it a vigorous shake. "I met him the first day I got here. He took me on a tour of the institute. We went out to the lake. Had coffee, that's about it." She squinted at Janelle. "How'd you happen to hook up with him?"

Janelle paused. Obviously Lillian didn't know that not only was Lance in Montgomery last night, but he was with a girl named Christine.

"We met on the train from Birmingham. Then, when Emma and I missed the connection to Chehaw, he offered to drive us out."

"Oh. Yeah. Well, let me give you some advice." Lillian leaned conspiratorially toward Janelle. "He's really full of himself. Tries to spread his charm around. There're a medical student at Tuskegee and two other nurses on this base that I know of who find the lieutenant irresistible." She plopped the pillow down on the bed and gave it a punch. "All these pilots are alike. Put 'em in uniforms, pin wings on their chests, and they think they're God's gift to every woman on base and off." She let out a curt, nervous laugh, waving her hand. She went over to the mirror and began combing her tangled hair.

Janelle stood looking after Lillian, not sure if what she felt was anger, relief, or a challenge. After putting her nightgown into her locker, she finished making her bed, tucking the blanket snugly under the mattress in military style.

Her face began to burn. How foolish to get all stirred up over a man she knew close to nothing about. How could she have been so vulnerable as to believe that Lance Fuller's behavior yesterday had been anything more than plain military courtesy?

Janelle glanced over her shoulder at Lillian. Lance Fuller might be a skirt chaser right now, she thought, but she had a feeling he wouldn't be one very long.

In a sudden flurry of movement the nurses quickly snapped to attention, standing in front of their metal footlockers. Janelle hurried to take her place.

Eyes front, shoulders back, they waited as Colonel Frederick Kimble surveyed the Spartan quarters. Chief Nurse Lieutenant Della Raney introduced the commander to the group.

"Welcome to Tuskegee," the colonel said, directing his stern gaze down the center of the room, over the tops of the nurses' heads. "On behalf of the United States Army, and in particular the men at this base, I want to express my appreciation that you have offered your services to the war effort. The colored squadrons stationed here have great need of your services, and I want to assure you that everything is being done to provide you with first-class medical facilities and the best environment in which to carry out your duties. As you can see, construction continues here at Tuskegee, and we ask for your patience and understanding as supplies and equipment are still arriving. When completed, this base will shine as an example of what can be accomplished when everyone works together for the good of the country."

He stepped back slightly and indicated the chief nurse. "Lieutenant Raney is in charge of this unit. She will assist you in getting outfitted and assigned to your various service duties." He hesitated, then looked at each nurse individually and directly. "Things here at Tuskegee may seem very different for some of you who have never lived in the South. I must impress upon each of you the importance of following the local customs and ways of doing things that have been in place for many, many years. To do otherwise will only bring a great deal of trouble and unnecessary complications—not only to you but to your fellow service-men and women." He drew himself up even taller. "Do you understand?"

"Yes, sir," the entire group responded.

"Good. Now, don't hesitate to speak with your chief of-ficer if you encounter any difficulties or have any ques-tions. We want your tour of duty here to be a positive experience." He pressed his lips together firmly for a mo-ment, then abruptly closed. "Good luck to each of you as you move through your training and get settled into life here at Tuskegee Army Airfield." Then he saluted sharply, turned on his heel, and left the barracks.

Chief Nurse Raney stepped into Colonel Kimble's place. "At ease, ladies." She waited until the tension brought about by the commander's presence abated. "I second the commander's welcome. You are sorely needed at this post, and I'm sure I don't have to remind you girls that you must be sensitive to the close scrutiny and pres-sure from outsiders, especially the colored press, that is constantly going on. A great deal of controversy has been generated by the creation of this training facility, but we must carry on with our duties without getting involved in the political debate about whether or not we should be here. We *are* here, and there is work to do."

The chief nurse surveyed the women with a critical eye. "You have been selected from hundreds of qualified appli-cants who wanted the chance to become members of the Army Nurse Corps," Lieutenant Raney went on. "Your presence here bespeaks your dedication and your willing-ness to assist in the success of this 'experiment.' I have been told, and do believe, that President Roosevelt himself keeps a keen eye on us here at Tuskegee. Our men deserve and need your support to help make sure they are physi-cally and mentally prepared to do the job when they are called. The morale of our aviators will greatly influence the success or failure of their missions, so do your part and keep a positive attitude both on and off the base."

A charged silence settled over the room. Janelle focused on the windows in front of her, watching the first light of day begin to push its way through the darkened shadows at the bases of the small glass squares lining the barracks walls. Her first day in the Army. She knew a lot was riding on the success of the 99th Fighter Squadron—Lance's unit—the first group of commissioned Negro pilots in the United States Army Air Force. And when she thought about Lance, she could not picture him failing . . . at anything.

"Welcome to Janelle Roy and Emma Brown from Columbus, Ohio. And now that the last two nurses assigned to our unit have joined us we will proceed with the assignment of uniforms and supplies immediately after morning mess."

Janelle could not help smiling over at Emma at the mention of finally getting properly outfitted in Army clothing. The reality of her new role was closing in.

From the barracks the nurses were marched by twos across the post into the mess hall. They were directed right up to a series of steam tables that held standard hearty breakfast fare. Following Lieutenant Raney's direction, they served themselves, ate self-consciously in silence, and were soon marched out of the mess hall, across the post to a clothing warehouse for fittings.

There the nurses were measured for white indoor working uniforms and olive drab outdoor uniforms with matching caps. They got stockings and shoes and shoulder bags and khaki-colored skirts, shirts, and jackets. They were issued raincoats, and overcoats, and all-purpose coveralls that resembled the jumpsuits that parachutists wore. They got sturdy brown oxfords and equally sturdy white nursing shoes, and mufflers, and ties, and even bras, panties, and girdles.

Their attempts to fit into Army-issue clothing struck the nurses as riotously funny. They rolled their eyes, holding back muffled laughter as one by one they discovered that some part of their anatomy staunchly refused to conform to the standard sizes the Army said they should be wearing. In an attempt to accommodate everyone, many alterations would have to be made.

With their fittings behind them, the nurses piled into jeeps for a brief tour of the sixteen-hundred-acre military base where they would be carrying out their duties.

The compound was made up of the headquarters, classrooms, barracks, mess halls, infirmary, and surgical units, post officers' clubs, recreational and training facilities, and a variety of special buildings for various activities. Constructed of fresh yellow pine cut from nearby forests, the structures were one- and two-story box-frame buildings painted white and raised two feet off the ground. Though still under construction and plagued with muddy half-finished roadways, the air base was bustling with activity. The personable noncoms driving the jeeps managed to get around the sprawling facility without any problems, joking, chatting with the ladies.

Janelle held on to a strap at the side of her door and tried to keep from bouncing around in her seat.

"Do you think we'll ever get used to all this noise?" she called over to Emma, her words nearly swept away by the loud buzz of a low-flying plane.

"That's a BT-thirteen," the driver of their jeep told them, pointing toward the sky.

"I can't tell one plane from another," Emma said.

The driver turned in his seat. "Don't worry, won't be long before you know the planes on sight. Believe me, ladies, while you're here at Tuskegee, you're gonna learn more about planes and flying than you ever wanted to know."

"I guess we'll have to go up in those things," Emma shouted to Janelle, shading her eyes with one hand as another plane lifted from the distant runway, circled overhead, then roared away.

"It might be more pleasant than riding in [...]
Janelle replied, gripping the strap to keep upright[...]

The low-flying BT-13 buzzed the nurses, creati[...]
flurry of waves and shouts from the ground. Janelle imagined it was Lance strapped in the cockpit, grinning down
at her, observing her from his seat in the clouds. When the
aviator banked his plane and rocketed off toward the east,
Janelle's heart soared with the dazzling speck of metal as
it climbed higher and higher into the sky. She listened to
the unsettling drone of its engine until the small plane disappeared into a bank of clouds.

Janelle vowed to find Lance Fuller and decide for herself just what his intentions were. She had an odd
sensation—like a premonition—that very soon the handsome lieutenant would become as familiar and predictable
a part of her life as the sound of reveille in the morning.

Once the small cadre of fourteen nurses had been properly inoculated, oriented, and outfitted, they were assigned
their schedules and began ward duty at once. For Janelle,
the ensuing days became a blur of activity as she adjusted
to the routine of her new Army life.

Cheerfully carrying out her duties, she annotated medical charts, made rounds with the doctors, gave medication
and treatment ordered by the medical officers, and completed the stacks of government paperwork required on
each patient. In addition to her nursing duties, she drilled
and paraded and studied with the other nurses, attending
classes on X rays, physical therapy, aeromedicine, and
chemical warfare.

On a rainy morning two weeks after her arrival, Janelle
scraped mud from her rubber boots, kicked them off near
the door, then entered the hospital and reported for duty as
usual. After checking in, she pulled the charts of the patients in her ward and began her morning rounds. She had
twenty-two men to check on before the chief medical officer arrived for sick call.

Walking through the ward, she observed each patient's
condition, making notations on the chart which she left at

the foot of each bed so that everything would be ready for the doctor's examination and prescription of treatment for the day.

She stopped to check on Thomas Painter, a ground crewman who had suffered first-degree burns three days ago when a can of gasoline exploded in his hands. The flaming liquid had seared the skin on his hands and forearms, but the injury was more painful than serious. Luckily all indications were that the burns would not blister and should not keep the mechanic away from the hangars and runways too long.

As Janelle approached, she saw Painter staring at the ceiling, his lips pressed grimly together.

"Good morning," Janelle smiled, greeting her patient as she came to the side of his bed. "How are you feeling this morning, Thomas?" She reached to take his pulse.

"Oh, all right, I guess," he mumbled. "Slept okay for the first time since the accident. Guess the pain's not nearly so bad."

"Good," Janelle said. She made a note of his pulse on his chart.

"Just still trying to figger out what went wrong," Painter said. "Musta been vapors built up in the shop. Wasn't no fires or cigarettes burning . . . nothing like that." He frowned, shaking his head. "Just my luck. Laid up like this."

Janelle put down the chart and inspected the tannic acid jelly dressing covering his arms. "Things are looking better already, soldier. You're progressing just fine."

"I sure hope I get out of here soon." He glanced up at Janelle. "Not that I don't like it . . . you taking care of me, I mean." He grinned sheepishly, lowering his eyes. "Just wanna get back to the squad. The crew can't manage so well shorthanded."

"My job is to help you get out of here as fast as possible. Yours right now is to rest and let those burns heal up. You can't leave until you can take care of yourself," she told him, slipping a thermometer under Painter's tongue. "All in good time."

At nine-thirty the doctor arrived, and Janelle accompanied him on his rounds. Just as they were finishing up, a ward attendant brought her an admission card.

"There's a soldier here who needs to be checked," she told Janelle. "He ran a piece of metal through the center of his hand."

"Oh, my," she said, accepting the admission card, clipping it onto her board. "I won't be but a minute. Have him wait in the admitting area. I'll be right there."

With sick call completed, she made out her ward report in duplicate, had the doctor sign it, then hurried to the area where several soldiers sat waiting. Two had their backs to her; one sat facing her, head down staring at his hand.

"Over there," the attendant indicated.

As the soldier looked up, Janelle found herself staring into Lance Fuller's dark brown eyes. The magnetic pull started up again, as if the tide were drawing her out to sea, though beneath the tremor of seeing him again ran a deep current of relief.

Looking down at the admission card, she bit her lip. "Lieutenant Lance Fuller." Somehow she managed to say his name.

In a sleek, fluid movement he rose, consuming the space in front of her while everything else in the room slanted away and disappeared.

"That's me," he said.

"Good morning, Lieutenant. I understand you hurt your hand?" Janelle worked to keep her voice and manner strictly professional.

"Sure did." His even tone propelled her careening heart.

"Come with me, please." Janelle walked in front of Lance, her back flaming from the physical nearness of the man she had been praying she would see once more.

Inside the examination room Janelle casually indicated with one trembling hand that he sit atop the white draped table. She turned to the washbasin and began scrubbing her hands.

"Too bad I had to run a nail through the center of my hand just to get to see you again." Janelle jerked around to see the coy little-boy grin she had memorized ease itself over his lips.

"Very funny," she said lightly, drying her hands on a sterile cloth.

"Scout's honor." Lance held up his good hand, three middle fingers pointed up. "I did it on purpose. No other way I knew of to get a medical pass."

She ignored his comment but silently wished it were true. Taking his injured hand in hers, she pulled it closer, leaning so near she could feel the heat rising from his body. She turned the hand over, observing two small puncture wounds on either side. "When and how did this happen?"

"You don't buy my story that this wound was intentionally inflicted in order to see you?" His lopsided grin became an expansive, heart-melting smile.

God, you're a charmer, she thought, realizing how easily and swiftly he had pulled her in. "No, I don't," she said. It was useless to summon up a stern voice, but she tried. "I'm serious, Lieutenant. I'll need to write up a report on this." Janelle let go of his hand. "What happened?" She went to the supply cabinet and took down a bottle of iodine and sterile cotton swabs.

"Guess I gotta come clean, huh?"

"Army regulations, Lieutenant Fuller," she said briskly. "No way to get around it."

"Well, I was coming into the mess hall and reached up to grab the door. It had a big old rusty nail where the handle should have been. Some brute before me probably tore it off. There's a lot of raw construction around here, coulda happened to anybody, I guess."

Janelle nodded as she placed a towel under Lance's injured hand and began to apply iodine to the puncture. He winced, grimacing when the red-brown liquid dribbled into the fresh wound.

As she worked on his hand, she felt him staring at the top of her head, and she steeled herself to keep her hands from shaking. The sound of a squadron going through parade drills outside filtered into the room.

"How's it going?" Lance finally said, the banter gone out of his voice.

Janelle raised her head and let his dark eyes capture hers. "All right."

"You like it in the quarters? You learning the ropes? Can you tell a captain from a sergeant yet?"

"Whoa!" Janelle laughed, capping the iodine bottle, pulling out a dry sterile dressing. "Yes. Yes. And no." She smiled, her heart soaring. "I still haven't gotten all the stripes and buttons and badges straight."

He gently closed his fingers over her hand. "I can help you with all of that."

"I'll bet you can," she replied, easing her hand from his.

He wouldn't let her get away so easily and reached out with his good hand, taking her wrist. Like a hot branding iron, his fingers seared her flesh.

"I'm serious." He gave her a level, dead-on stare. "I can help you find your way around. On and off the base."

Suddenly Janelle remembered Lillian Dorsey's warning, but just as quickly dismissed it. "What do you want to show me?" The words leaped from her throat. She hoped she didn't sound too anxious, but she'd been praying for just this moment.

"The campus . . . the Booker T. Washington Monument, for one. The Alabama countryside. It's beautiful, even in winter. I'll take you to my hometown, if you'd like to see it."

"Congregation Hills?"

"You remembered," he said, clearly impressed and pleased.

"Um-hmm," Janelle murmured, busying herself by applying a sterile bandage to his wound. This was exactly the invitation she'd hoped would come. "And your grand-father is the mayor, right?"

Lance slipped down from the table. "Would you let me show you around?"

"I don't even know how to contact you."

"All you have to do is call barracks number fifty-four and ask for me." He started toward the door. "Let me know when you can get a pass. There's a whole lot more to Tuskegee than this ugly airfield, and I'd love to show it to you. Is it a deal?" he asked.

Janelle let a soft, easy smile curve her lips.

"It's a deal," she answered firmly, her mind whirling with the prospect of being alone with Lance Fuller, off the base.

CHAPTER
NINETEEN

"I'm not sure there is anything I can do to help you, Perry." Dalton gripped the telephone, feeling at a loss. What did Perry expect him to do?

"Well, the NAACP needs to know how we're being treated down here." Perry's voice cracked with indignation. "The white officers treat us like shit. I served fifteen days in the stockade because there's no transportation in and out of town."

"Hold up, Perry. It was my understanding that you got yourself in the slammer because you socked an MP in the jaw."

"He had it coming," Perry said tersely. "That's not all. . . . The colored lodge is a deplorable excuse for a recreation hall. You should see it—nothing in it but a few pieces of broken furniture and a radio that won't even pick up New Orleans. The white soldiers have a bar and billiard tables. We've got nothing! Can't you guys at the NAACP put some pressure on somebody down here?"

Dalton wished it were a simple matter of making a few telephone calls, talking tough about equality and decency and the need to keep up morale. But things were much more complicated than that. Any challenge to the War Department's policy of segregation had to be carefully and cautiously thought out.

"All we do is parade around the grounds, then go

through practice drills, usually loading and unloading supplies."

"You attend radio repair classes, don't you?"

"Yeah, but what good is training in communications if all I'm gonna do is stick around Louisiana and tear radios apart and put them back together?"

"I hear what you're saying, Perry," Dalton said. It was true that Perry's squadron would probably never see action. As long as the War Department persisted in training colored troops as labor units, they'd never be qualified to enter combat. "I know you're frustrated," Dalton went on, "but you've been there—how long now?"

"Exactly seventy-two days."

"Well, you're going to have to go along with things as they are. Have faith, we're working on change."

"Working on change? The war will be over before the government will admit that colored soldiers can handle guns as well as the white boys. Humph! The only talk I hear about going overseas is having us shipped back to Africa."

"I'm afraid I've heard that, too," Dalton replied. A story in the *Sentinel* had mentioned that the War Department considered Negroes unsuited to European climates, and if they were to be used in combat, it would be only in the North African theater. Dalton sighed, turning Perry's bitter words over in his mind.

"Can you imagine," Perry continued, "how hard it is to stay pumped up about being in the Army when day after day we gotta take this bullshit from white officers who treat us like animals . . . *dumb* animals. You'd think we didn't have a brain in our heads the way they push us around. I'm sick of it."

Dalton knew he could do little to appease Perry's rage. "Hang in there" was all he could say. "I'll see what I can do."

"That's easy for you to say. We get nothing but service details. Why can't we learn about artillery and combat tactics? Why do we have to content ourselves with cleaning up the rear? I don't know how long I can take this."

"What does that mean?" Dalton tensed, remembering Perry's initial desire to file as a conscientious objector.

"Just what I said, Dalton. Morale around here is at rock bottom. The colored units are grumbling about something all the time, and the white officers just play deaf. If all I'm gonna be is a white man's lackey, I may not stick this out."

"Don't do anything foolish, Perry. The consequences could be devastating."

Perry gave Dalton a curt, nervous laugh. "Don't worry, Counselor. When I get to the point where I've had it with this pitiful bunch down here, you'll be the first to know."

After hanging up, Dalton remained rigid at his desk, hoping Perry was only blowing off steam. Maybe he should have helped him go for an exemption after all.

Glancing at the clock above the door, Dalton picked up his notepad and a brief he'd been working on and started down the hall, hoping the emergency meeting with the regional director wouldn't last too long. He was due in court in half an hour.

Gerry Thackery's stuffy cubicle was not much bigger than Dalton's, but at least the local director's office had pictures on the walls, a colorful rug on the floor.

Dalton slipped into a chair at the table where Thackery and another gentleman sat, leaned back, thought about Perry's phone call, and wondered how the government could afford to waste so much manpower. *When the going gets tough and the body count mounts, they'll be happy to call in the colored troops,* he predicted, scooting his chair aside to let Oscar Green squeeze in next to him.

"What's this all about?" Oscar asked, propping his elbows on the wide mahogany table.

"Your guess is as good as mine." Dalton surveyed the two men on the opposite side of the table.

Gerry Thackery started right in. "Dalton. Oscar. Thanks for coming. I know you two are on a tight schedule with your own projects and cases, so I won't keep you long. There are a couple of situations that I've been asked to help move toward a peaceful resolution. Dalton, I'm going to need your help." He paused and looked directly at the young attorney. "In Newport News, Virginia, there's a union in a shipbuilding plant that is about to stage a walkout. The whites are refusing to work with the Negroes who have recently been hired. And our help is needed in Alabama at a factory where the manager has bid on an important defense contract but refuses to hire a single colored person. We've got to convince him otherwise. He's also suspected of submitting falsified documents in order to acquire this contract. A hell of a mess, I assure you."

A shadow passed over Oscar's face. This was really not news to him; he'd handled a similar case last month.

Thackery continued. "I've brought Bob Morris in from national headquarters to explain the seriousness of these situations and how we can assist his efforts. I'll let him explain it to you. Bob, you can take it from here."

Bob Morris, the overweight, red-faced representative from national headquarters in Washington, D.C., scratched the side of his cheek and spoke in a strong voice. "Dalton. Oscar. Right now the War Department needs more tents, more blankets, more ships, and more railcars to carry supplies to ports across the country. The threatened union walkout at the Burrnow Shipyards cannot happen. We've got to get all parties to the negotiating table and work something out. Soon. Twenty-five highly skilled welders, who happen to be Negroes, have been put on the production line, and by God, they're going to stay there."

The scenario sounded all too familiar to Dalton. His desk was covered with similar complaints.

"Down in Alabama, near Tuskegee," Morris continued, "there's a factory owned by the Keystone Company that manufactures tents, uniforms, and turns out railcars, too. John Gray, the president, is anxious to get another government contract to increase his output tenfold. And he can do it. He's got the raw materials and the labor ... only problem is he refuses to integrate his plant."

Dalton nodded in understanding.

"The contract that Keystone has bid on is lucrative. Very lucrative," Morris said. "John Gray is chomping at the bit to snag it, and the War Department wants him to get it."

"Why?" Dalton interjected. "If Gray's facility isn't integrated, why doesn't the government stick to its guns and award the contract to some other plant?"

"Because if Keystone gets the contract, the railcars can be delivered in a matter of months. Any other plant would need a year just to gear up for the project. What we've got to do is get someone down there to convince Mr. Gray that it would be in his best interest to hire qualified people from the local area regardless of color. He's been a stubborn ass about it so far. At least two hundred new jobs will be created, and Macon County residents, especially the Negroes, have every right to get their share."

Dalton's heart raced. Macon County. The Tuskegee airfield. If he took the assignment, he could see Janelle again. Dalton signaled to Bob. "If you're asking me to volunteer to go over to Newport News, then down to Macon County to try to talk some sense into Mr. Gray, I'd be willing to give it a shot."

"I was hoping you'd feel that way, Graham. You'll probably be on the road for a while—from now right through late spring. And if something else breaks that we ought to investigate, your assignment might change ... on little notice."

"If it's okay with Thackery, it's fine with me," Dalton said.

"Fine with me," Dalton's boss told the regional director.

Morris made a tent with his fingers, pressed it to his lips, and peered over his hands at Dalton. "Another thing: You might be in danger—at the shipyards and at Keystone.

Rocking the boat in the heart of Jim Crow is not often done."

"I've been in touchy situations before." Dalton uncrossed his legs, placing his hands flat on the table. "I've been known to ruffle a few feathers and still manage to come out on top."

"Amen to that," Oscar said, nudging Dalton in the side.

"Good." Morris turned his attention to Oscar. "Graham's going to need help gathering background information on Burrnow Shipyards and the Keystone Company. He'll need summaries of Labor Department and War Manpower surveys and every applicable regulation at his fingertips. The NAACP can't sit down to discuss anything without hard facts and a thorough understanding of the law behind us. You willing to help?"

Oscar Green tipped his head. "No problem here. I can get on that right away."

Morris's belly shook with his vigorous nod. "Great. Let's put everything we've got behind this and get John Gray to reconsider his position. I feel certain we can."

Late that evening, as Dalton packed his bag, he tried to still the anticipation that had been building since the meeting. He wanted to go to Janelle. Maybe, just maybe, he'd be able to convince her they should try to be more than friends. Things *had* changed. She was in the Army now, not under her mother's roof. He only hoped she'd be willing to hear him out.

Since her departure he had not stopped thinking of her and had seriously examined his feelings. Weary of his bachelor's life, he felt ready to love just one woman, and the woman he wanted was Janelle—if she'd have him.

After absently folding and unfolding his pajamas, his shirts, his underwear, unable to decide what to pack, he stopped, went to his desk, and pulled out the only letter he had received from her. His hands began to sweat as he read the single page again.

Tuskegee Airfield
February 20, 1943

Dear Dalton,

I know it's been weeks since I called you and told you
good-bye, but I just had to drop you a note to let you
know I've arrived safely and am adjusting to military life
much more easily than I had expected. It's really not too
bad, but I'm dreading going up in those teeny-weeny
planes.

I've thought about you many times and your request
that we remain friends. I think I'd like that very much. As
I told you on the phone, I hold no hard feelings about the
way we parted in Columbus. I understand now, as I
couldn't before, the wisdom of your decision. You knew
what was best for both of us and were right to pull away
as you did. You are a very wise man who deserves great
happiness.

I'm including my address. Please write. I hope we can
stay in touch because I'd like to count you as a friend forever.

Fondly,
Janelle

Dalton scanned the creamy white paper one more time.
Suddenly filled with good humor, he grinned, tossing the
letter inside his suitcase. *She has been thinking of me! She
wants me in her life! When I get my arms around Janelle
Roy this time, nothing is going to make me let her go.*

Inside the nurses' quarters, Janelle faced Emma, the letter
from Kenneth lying on the bed between them like the lifeless message from hell it was. Janelle placed the palms of
both hands flat on her knees and pressed down hard, silently willing Emma's tears to stop, wishing she knew
what to say. The other nurses had discreetly slipped out of
the barracks, leaving Janelle alone to console the distraught Emma.

"How *could* he?" Emma chewed her lips, glancing distractedly about the room, her hard dark eyes flitting from

bed to bed, doorway to doorway, from the floor to the ceiling and back down again. "Janelle! How could he do this to me?"

"Such a coward," Janelle said. "Breaking it off by mail. At least he could have telephoned. My God, the only reason you came down here was to wait for him." She dug her fingernails into her gray flannel skirt, observing Emma with a cautious eye. She'd been crying for close to an hour, and Janelle was fearful she would make herself sick.

"Right!" Emma wiped her eyes, crushing the handkerchief to her flaming cheeks. "And he'd better not show his face around here too soon. I might do something I'd regret."

"Oh, Emma," Janelle murmured. "I'm shocked. I really am. I can't imagine what's going on with Kenneth." She reached over and picked up the letter and read it a second time. " '. . . breaking off now is the only solution.' " She threw the letter back on the bed. "Solution to what?"

"I wish I knew." Emma's voice broke with the strain of the news. "Whatever it is, he's decided not to tell me."

"But it's so sudden. Did he ever give you the impression that he would end it like this?" Janelle asked, unable to bring herself to admit to Emma that she had always feared Kenneth might hurt her this way.

"Never." Emma fingered the letter as if it were contaminated, then angrily shoved it back into the envelope, staring at the hated paper. "I talked to him a week ago—last Saturday, remember? He said he loved me, and as soon as the last round of examinations were over, he would get his new assignment." She shielded her pain from Janelle's sympathetic eyes by covering her face with her palms. "He was positive he'd be sent to Tuskegee," she mumbled through her fingers. "Something must have happened."

"Call him. Find out."

"Hell, no." Emma jerked her head up, eyes fiercely determined. "If he's too cowardly to tell me exactly what's going on, why should I bother to track him down?"

"I don't know. Maybe he failed his exams and is too embarrassed to tell you."

"If that's the case, he ought to love me enough to let me share his disappointment."

"Yeah," Janelle said, not wanting to bring up the possibility that Kenneth had found someone else. She glanced down at her watch. "I wish I had some answers for you, Emma. You want me to call him? I will. I've got nothing to lose."

"No, thanks. I don't want you in the middle."

"I will, if you want," Janelle insisted.

"No, better stay out of it. . . . If he doesn't have the guts to tell me the truth, I don't want him sending messages through you."

"Okay, you're right." Janelle checked her watch again. "You're late, aren't you?"

Janelle nodded. "Yes, but I don't want to leave you alone like this."

"It's all right. You're meeting Lance?"

"Yeah. In ten minutes. At the front gate. We seldom can get the same leave times, so . . ."

"Please, go. And have a good time. I'm so happy for you, Janelle. Lance seems like quite the gentleman."

Beaming at Emma's approval, Janelle took her friend's hands and held them fast. "He's wonderful, Emma. Perfect."

"Seems so, but . . . be careful, Janelle. Don't give your heart away too fast." She wiped her face and smiled. "Make him wait and worry a little. Maybe I was the one who moved too fast."

"Oh, Emma, who knows what's going to happen? How could you have guessed that Kenneth would do a thing like this? Don't go blaming yourself. You hear?"

Emma's features softened, losing their bitter cast.

Repeating Emma's own advice of just weeks ago, Janelle said, "The men at Tuskegee outnumber the women four to one, remember? You just find yourself a nice colored boy here on base."

Laughter bubbled unexpectedly from Emma's lips. "All right, you got me. But—" She stopped, the pain of her bad news resurfacing in her face. "I hope you never suffer a blow like this. I feel as if there's been an explosion in the center of my chest." She sniffled, heaving her narrow shoulders. "Men. Sometimes they're a pain in the butt, that's for sure."

"Yeah, take two aspirin, Emma. You'll be fine." That raised a bit of a smile, and they giggled, holding hands.

"Janelle, I wouldn't be able to stay in the service if it weren't for you," Emma said in a low voice. "This is so awful. You really didn't want to come down here, and I pressured you to come with me so I could try to meet up with Kenneth. Don't hate me."

"Hate you! Emma, don't you see what has happened? I was on a real downward spiral at home. By convincing me to join the Army and come to Tuskegee, you actually saved my life. I'm not the same person I was in Columbus, thank God! And face it, you aren't either."

"No, I'm not, especially now. But go on, you're making a pretty good case for me not to feel guilty."

"Well, think of it this way," Janelle said, giving Emma a parting hug. "When we're old and fat, spending our days wiping snot off our grandkids' faces, we'll have a hell of a lot of good stories to tell."

CHAPTER
TWENTY

"Give me a big smile," Lance said, backing up, his camera trained on Janelle.

"How's this?" She lifted her chin, looked at Lance through half-closed eyes, and bared her teeth in the sunlight. The surprisingly warm March breeze ruffled her wavy, loose hair, lifting it from her shoulders. At least the Alabama weather was a vast improvement over what she would have been enduring back in Ohio.

"Great shot! Don't move." Lance snapped the picture, then changed positions, squatting down to capture Janelle from a different angle.

"These are going to be great!" Lance peeked up over the lens at her, his brows rising as he spoke. "With such a beautiful subject, how can I miss?" He winked seductively at her.

At that moment Janelle thought of pulling him close, putting her hands behind his neck, lifting her lips to his. With the sunshine bathing him in gold, he radiated sexual promise. Exhilarated at the sight of him, she felt herself blushing. "You'll have to give me a copy to send to my mother."

Just yesterday Janelle had received the first letter from her mother since she moved to California. She'd begged for pictures of Janelle, and she could sense her mother was lonely.

Lance eased himself upright and strode toward Janelle.

She watched his hardened muscles rippling in his thighs beneath his khakis.

"Sure," he said. "We can drop the film off at the PX on the base."

"You know, my mother has always wanted to see this campus, especially Booker T. Washington's home."

Lance clicked a button, turned the handle to advance the film, then gazed up at the three-story redbrick house nestled among budding dogwoods. "Maybe she'll get to Tuskegee for a visit while you're still here."

"I doubt it," Janelle said, knowing her mother was scraping by with help from Aunt Dedee and had no money to splurge on a trip. Preferring not to go into a long explanation about the loss of the house, the embarrassing destruction of the only place Janelle had called home, she decided to disguise her mother's current situation. In her opinion, living with Aunt Dedee in California was just a temporary situation. After the war things would get back to normal. Somehow.

"My mother is very busy this time of year," Janelle improvised. "Preparing the house and her students for spring recitals."

"She teaches piano?" Lance asked.

"Um-hmm," Janelle murmured, falling into step beside Lance's long stride as they made their way across the campus. "Every March my mother holds recitals at our home for her students."

Under the low-hanging branches of lacy willow trees, sunlight dotted the sidewalk, warming Janelle's cheeks. It felt good to be off the base and out of uniform, though she was glad Lance had dressed in his short Eisenhower jacket complete with wings and stripes. Every girl who strolled past looked him over twice.

"You must live in a pretty nice house," Lance said.

Memories surged back to Janelle. On the first Sunday in March for as long as she could remember, the three or four students under Alice Roy's tutelage had been permitted to invite their parents into her home. The recitals in

Oakwood Alley had been performed in the tiny front room, everyone gathered excitedly around the old Hackley upright.

"Very nice," Janelle heard herself say. "Sometimes we'd have as many as fifty people in attendance."

"Gee." Lance whistled. "Fifty people? Your place sounds more like a mansion than a house."

"Oh, no." Janelle fluttered her fingers. "Eight rooms. That's all. And a furnished attic . . . I used to play up there when I was little." She tried to sneak a peek at Lance's face, hoping her background was coming closer to his. If his grandfather was the mayor of Congregation Hills, he must have grown up in very good circumstances.

Lance stepped forward, holding her elbow to guide her across a broken walkway. "Be careful. It's pretty muddy right there." She leaned slightly toward him, the brush of his arm against her breast sending slow shivers down her side.

As they neared the raised concrete base of the Booker T. Washington Monument, he asked, "Did you live in the heart of Columbus?"

"Not really. Our house is on the far east side, near a beautiful area called Alum Creek. The creek runs through a ravine behind our house. A great place to watch birds and squirrels and all kinds of wildlife." As Janelle went on to give a detailed description of the Werner property, she was pricked by Dalton Graham's stern warning to be truthful.

But if she had to bend the truth just a little bit to get Lance interested in her, what harm could it possibly do? Unashamed, she went on. "The place is so lonely now that my brother and I are in the service my aunt decided to move in to keep my mother company."

"That's nice." Lance sounded as if he didn't know what to say. He pulled his camera to his face again. "Go sit on the bench under the statue. Let me get another shot of you."

Janelle assessed the towering monument dwarfing them.

The bronzed rendition of the founder of Tuskegee held a piece of cloth above the head of a kneeling man. "What does the inscription say?" Stepping closer, her shadow fell over the words.

Lance came up behind her, bent down, and read, " 'Booker T. Washington 1856–1915. He lifted the veil of ignorance from his people and pointed the way to progress through education and industry.' "

"How moving." Janelle ran her index finger over the smoothly carved words. "I've read a lot about this place and heard my parents talk about it, but it sure has more meaning to stand here, actually on the spot where so much happened so long ago."

She reverently mounted the white granite base and sat on the circular bench beneath the statue.

Lance quickly snapped two pictures, then snagged a passing student and asked him to take their picture together.

"You'll give me copies as soon as they're developed?" Janelle asked, straightening her skirt, adjusting the sleeves of her sweater.

"You bet I will," Lance replied, draping his arm loosely over her shoulders.

An electric current passed between them, and Janelle relaxed, allowing her body to fit more snugly against his.

As soon as the student snapped the photo, Lance jumped up, ducking playfully, swinging away from Janelle. He took back his camera, thanked the student, and turned back, graceful in his movements.

Taking Janelle by the hand, he held it firmly in his. "How about a drive into town? Then I want to take you to Congregation Hills."

"Sounds fine to me." Janelle flushed with excitement. He was taking her to meet his grandfather!

Driving through the Lincoln Memorial Gates, they left the campus and headed east. The Gothic spires of Tuskegee Methodist Church rose above the city in the distance.

She was finally beginning to get the lay of the land. There was Tuskegee Army Airfield, where the colored military personnel lived. Then there was Tuskegee Institute—the historic campus and the neatly trimmed, tree-lined streets where professors and employees of the university resided. And finally there was the town of Tuskegee itself, a sleepy little cluster of one- and two-story buildings centered in the southern tradition around a grassy square. At its heart stood a statue honoring the Confederate soldiers of Macon County.

This was the hub of white power—shopkeepers, bankers, and local businessmen who controlled the political, economic, and social pulse of the county, whose population was close to 85 percent black.

"If it weren't Saturday, we wouldn't be coming down here," Lance said matter-of-factly as he drove past the shops, circling the square.

"Why?" Janelle asked.

"Because it's the only day colored are allowed to shop on the square."

"Allowed?" She looked closer and saw that each store had a sign above the entrances marked COLORED or WHITE ONLY. Jim Crow was firmly and clearly in place.

"During the week this place is like a ghost town." Lance pulled the car into a space in front of the orange brick courthouse and turned off the engine. "The guys from the base steer clear of it. The locals were dead set against the colored division being based at Tuskegee, and they keep everybody on edge. Some folks say that the whites have an arsenal of shotguns and ammunition to defend themselves in case the black soldiers attack."

"That's wild!" Janelle glanced around, beginning to feel uneasy, surrounded by people obviously filled with hatred.

"Hey, about a year ago there was almost a riot," Lance said. "The Tuskegee police arrested a colored soldier because he was drunk. Of course, we have our own military police—MPs, you know?"

"Yeah, I'm learning the language, Lance." She playfully wrinkled her nose.

"Well, the MPs from the base are always on the watch for things like that, and when they saw what was going on, a terrible incident occurred right here."

"What happened?"

"The drunken soldier got caught in the middle of a tug-of-war between the white police, who said they had custody, and the black MPs, who refused to let him go. It went back and forth like that until the news reached the base. A bunch of the airmen got their guns and started marching toward town to save the guy."

"Did they?"

"Well, somebody called Colonel Parrish, the director of training at the base, and he intercepted the airmen and got everyone calmed down."

"What happened to the soldier?"

"Wound up in the hospital, nearly beaten to death."

"Oh, my. I can see what you mean about everybody being on edge around here."

Lance put the car keys into his pocket. "Enough of that," he said, dismissing the topic. "Anyway, this place is dry—no liquor allowed. Not much reason to come to town. Nothing to do, nothing to buy. I get what I need on the base or drive into Montgomery, where colored have their shops."

"This is all so strange." Janelle watched Negroes complacently going in and out of their separate entrances.

"Well, I don't know about strange," Lance said, giving Janelle the first hint of his bitterness. "It's just the way things are done." He rolled up his window and put his hand on the door handle. "Let's get out and stretch our legs."

They strolled past the Alabama Exchange Bank, the Tuskegee *News*, an assortment of hardware and dry goods stores. Lance bought two bars of chocolate from a street vendor, and they sat under a big elm tree to eat them.

"You said your brother is in the Army?"

"Yeah. His name's Perry."

"You don't talk about him very much, do you?"

Lance's question caught Janelle off guard. She munched on her Hershey bar before answering. "We've had our differences, that's true. But now that he's in the Army, all that old mess we used to argue about seems so unimportant."

"Where's he stationed?"

"Camp Livingston."

"How does he like it there?"

"He doesn't." Janelle's reply was unhesitating. "He's already served fifteen days in the stockade."

"Wow. Sounds like he's on a downhill ride. What happened? Or do you want to talk about it?"

"I didn't find out until after he'd served his time. He wrote me that he'd been beaten up." She finished her chocolate, twisting the wrapper as she spoke. "In Columbus he was very active with an organization called Jobs for Progress, arranging desegregation activities to open defense plants to colored. Seems his reputation preceded him into the service, and his CO considers him an agitator, an instigator of sorts."

"But he isn't?"

"I don't think so. Perry just has a hard time with people telling him what to do." She looked out over the street. "And Camp Livingston is so isolated. He's used to being in the center of all kinds of protest activities. It'll take him some time to adjust, and I really hope he does before it gets worse."

"Well, he's in for a miserable two years if he doesn't settle down." Lance shook his head slowly. "If he's smart, he'll keep his mouth shut and just go along with the program. He's not gonna change the Army single-handedly."

"Yeah, that's what I wrote him, but I doubt he'll take

my advice. Perry always pushes the system as far and as hard as he can." Janelle hoped that would close the subject. She didn't want unpleasant thoughts of her brother to ruin her precious time alone with Lance.

CHAPTER
TWENTY-ONE

The late-afternoon sun beamed steadily down, bronzing the red dirt surface of Notasulga Road. On either side of the deserted strip, tall pines soared up from dense wild sumac, and yaupon bushes hugged thick craggy trunks. A lush stand of ostrich ferns waved their curled fronds while feathery branches of wild azalea flagged so far into the road they brushed the sides of the car.

Lance thundered along, a great puffy cloud of burnished dust streaming southward behind him. He propped his arm in the open window, calmed by the familiar smells of the damp forest that hung thickly in the air. A gorgeous day, a beautiful woman at his side—he should have felt utterly at peace. But the closer he got to the site of his birth, the more unsure he became about his mission.

How could a sophisticated, cultured woman like Janelle appreciate his simple country upbringing? From the little she'd told him about her family, it was obvious she came from the black upper middle class, wealthy Negroes with political power and economic status who generally stayed to themselves. Janelle had grown up in a big northern city, in the kind of house he used to tiptoe past when he was a boy because making the slightest noise in those neighborhoods might cause the white owners to run him off the street. Surely Janelle would find his hometown quaint, but hopelessly backward and boring.

Lance managed to sneak a glance at Janelle without

turning his head, capturing a portion of her profile, a glimpse of her wavy hair. Proud, beautiful, she was fascinating.

Of all the women he'd been with—and he had to admit there were many—this one intrigued him like no other. He wasn't quite sure just what it was about her, but Janelle Roy had, in the short time since he met her, completely seduced him with her unusual blend of innocence and passion.

At times she seemed intensely sure of herself—focused on her profession and her desire to serve her country. But at other times Lance got the distinct impression that Janelle would not survive her stint in the Army without someone to protect and guide her. She seemed, to Lance at least, more suited for the private-duty work she told him she had done before entering the Army. Yet Lance found this contradiction attractive, compelling him to draw closer, to learn more. He hoped he wasn't moving too fast.

After juggling three or four relationships at one time for so long, he had almost convinced himself that brief, superficial affairs made him happy. But at twenty-four Lance thought perhaps he'd had enough of playing the field, was tired of the footloose reputation he had garnered. It was exhausting, really. And Lance wondered if Janelle Roy could be that special woman he needed in his life right now. Could he embrace her with a commitment that would not waver? More important, was she truly the generous, open-minded woman she seemed to be, or would she turn out to be too spoiled by her fancy upbringing to adjust to his simpler way of life?

The car bounced over a jagged rut and veered to the side of the road, jolting Lance from his thoughts. Holding the steering wheel firmly, he turned it quickly to the left, calling out, "Wow, sorry about that. This road is in terrible shape."

"I see." Janelle turned in her seat, feeling so much at ease with Lance she now dreaded meeting his grandfather. After such a perfect afternoon she was suddenly unwilling to allow a stranger to break the intimate bond they had created. "How much farther to Congregation Hills?"

"Almost there. Just over the hill up ahead."

The minutes ticked by in silence until they crested a hill blanketed with budding spring trees, bringing into view a picturesque gathering of white frame houses nestled in the distance. The rolling hills swept with grass, the bright green roofs and gleaming red barns took Janelle's breath away.

"Congregation Hills." She read the chalk white sign at the side of the road.

"Yep. This is it," Lance said.

"Everything is so green. All the trees have buds. At home there's probably still snow on the ground."

"We had a very mild winter this year. That makes the seasons kind of all run together. Bad thing is that usually means we're in for a scorcher of a summer."

Lance whizzed down the slope, racing along the single-lane road, passing neatly kept houses, square and raised from the ground on concrete blocks. A little blond boy played tag with his dog in a field blooming yellow with wildflowers.

Janelle sat smiling, charmed by the scene that could have been a model for a Norman Rockwell painting. When they came into the town proper, they passed a long row of shops connected by a wooden boardwalk, protected from the sun by bright blue awnings. The stained glass windows in the church on the corner appeared to have been set in gemstones. The high school, comparatively sleek and modern in design, had a full-size stadium complete with covered bleachers.

As the manicured lawns and ruffled lace curtains drifted from view, Janelle congratulated herself for embellishing her past; Lance Fuller's hometown was the picture of rural American prosperity.

They curved off to the west and left the main road, entering a newly paved strip of black asphalt that threaded away from the heart of town until it circled a sprawling industrial complex.

"Where are we going? You left the town."

"No, just detouring. To get to the other side, you have to pass by this plant."

Beyond a line of low brick buildings was an open railway yard filled with freight cars in various stages of construction. Welders, faces masked with protective goggles, stood atop gleaming metal boxcars, sparks radiating like fireworks from their torches. On the other side of the expansive yard, taller buildings stretched out in a series of concrete clusters so far into the distance Janelle could not see the northernmost boundary of the facility. Chain-link fencing surrounded everything in sight, and uniformed guards, holding rifles, stood stiffly at the main gate.

"What's that? A part of the air base?" Janelle asked, knowing they'd just passed the turnoff to Tuskegee Field.

Lance laughed aloud. "John Gray would like to think Keystone Company is as important as a United States government post."

"What do they make?"

"Keystone manufactures refrigerated boxcars, prefabricated aluminum buildings, tents, uniforms—lots of things the government needs to keep the war effort going."

"It sure is big."

"It'd be a lot bigger if Gray could get the folks living to his north to sell their land to him," Lance commented.

"I take it they haven't been offered a decent price."

"Folks in the northern part of the town don't put a price on their land. It was hard won and is not for sale."

Lance slowed, pointedly observing the guards, then stepped on the accelerator and sped up the road. "You want to know about this place? I've got a story to tell you . . . about my mom and dad. I told you they disappeared, remember?"

"Yes, you mentioned something about it," Janelle said, thankful that Lance felt comfortable enough to let her into his past.

"The Keystone Company covers close to a thousand acres. What you see here is just the front of the complex. If we'd come up the eastern edge of the county, we'd have passed the monstrous woodframe warehouses where hundreds of women sit behind sewing machines for ten and twelve hours a day, making tents and blankets and uniforms by the thousands. There's even a hospital on the premises for the employees; most of them live in those company-owned houses we just passed."

"Keystone owns Congregation Hills?" How in the world had Lance's grandfather become the mayor of such a place?

"Yeah. The southern side belongs to Keystone. It even has its own police force. Big business, let me tell you."

"Is the plant government-controlled?" Janelle asked.

"Well, I'll put it to you this way. Since the Civil War the Gray family has been a major civilian supplier of military necessities not only to the United States but to Mexico and many other Latin American countries."

"Really? Well, I guess that's good; they must employ quite a few people."

"Thousands. But the Keystone Company is about ninety years old and to this day has never hired a colored person. Not even to sweep the floors. You know, Macon County is eighty-five percent colored, but not one Negro resident has ever walked through the doors of Keystone. Not to go to work anyway."

"How disgusting." Janelle turned in her seat to get a better view of the factory as it dissolved into the dusty swirl behind them. "No one's ever challenged this man John Gray? If he gets government contracts, I think it's illegal to discriminate like that." Janelle spoke with authority. "Back home my brother picketed places like Keystone." A touch of pride came with her words.

"Oh, yeah, there have been challenges—without happy endings. That's where my family comes in. You see, Calvin Gray, the founder of Keystone, was a ruthless, vicious man. In 1869, after the Civil War, he decided he needed more than his two-hundred-acre family plot to expand his company, so he regularly burned homes on the north side and terrorized the blacks who had settled there after the war."

"So the north side of Congregation Hills is colored, the south side white?" It was beginning to become clearer to Janelle just how Lance's grandfather fitted in.

"Yep. That's it exactly." Lance shifted gears, speeding down the road. "Some colored had been deeded their land by whites who fled North during the war. Some sharecropped until they scraped up the money to pay off delinquent taxes and claim a few acres. Gray didn't care how they got their land, he just wanted it, and any Negroes who got in his way were killed or run out of the county. He threatened and beat people until they signed over their farms. Sometimes he just plain drew up a bill of sale and lied about what it was and got people to sign; many freedmen back then could not read or write and believed anything they were told."

Janelle shuddered, thinking herself fortunate to have escaped such injustice by growing up in Ohio.

"Well, according to my grandfather," Lance continued, heading onto a dirt road, "John Gray, the founder's son, tried the same tactic to expand the plant after World War One. I was just a baby then, and apparently my father, who could read and write and understood his rights, refused to sign papers giving up our land. Father took the documents into Montgomery and got himself a liberal, northern-educated white lawyer. When he brought this young, smart-talking Yankee back to Macon County to confront John Gray, all hell broke loose. An investigation was started, and in the end Gray had to give up about three hundred acres he had falsely acquired."

"I'm sure that was a bitter pill for Gray to swallow. Bet it wasn't the end of things, was it?" Janelle was aware of the grave change in Lance's mood.

"Not by a long shot. Two days after the court case was settled and the colored got back their land, my father and my mother were found—" Lance stopped, cleared his throat, and glared into the distance.

"It's all right," Janelle said, alarmed by the tortured expression on Lance's face. "If you don't want to talk about it . . ."

"No, that's not it." He slowed the car to a crawl. "Look through that ridge over there."

Janelle rolled the window fully down and peered beyond the tangle of laurel and hawthorn that covered the land.

"You see where those two rows of oaks separate? You see that big tree set apart from the others? Well, that's where my parents were found. Tied with leather straps to the trunk. Beaten unconscious. People said my mother . . . had been violated. My daddy had two broken legs." His hoarse voice cracked.

"Oh, Lance, how horrible." Janelle shifted closer and put her hand on his shoulder. "Did they recover?"

"I don't know. Lady Skyhawk, a Creek Indian woman who lived back behind those trees, cut them loose and took them in. It's said she spirited them away in the night. No one ever heard from my parents again. The shock of it killed my grandmother. She had been ill; she died three days after the incident." Lance ran his tongue over his lips, frowning. "All kinds of tales circulated about where they might have been taken, but one thing I know for sure: John Gray robbed me of my parents. My childhood. And he got away with it, too."

"Did your grandfather try to find them?"

"Naw, and he never mentioned their names outside the house again. But when we were alone, he'd tell me stories. He said some white ladies from the local church came around after the news had spread about my parents' disappearing. They wanted to take me to an orphanage in Montgomery. He pulled a gun on them. Can you imagine a black man holding a gun on two white ladies? Well, he raised such a fuss he scared them off. So he got to keep me. It was just me and him. You know, there are times when I still have horrible nightmares of being sent to that colored orphanage in Montgomery. Crazy, isn't it?"

"No, I don't think so." Janelle's heart went out to the hurt little boy in Lance. She remembered the look on his face the first time she met him—on the train—and knew this was the vulnerable side to him she had clearly seen. "I'd think any child who lost his parents like you did would naturally be traumatized."

"Back then the state orphanage for colored children was called the Dungeon—a dark hole where little black boys and girls who had no one to support them were sent to starve to death." He shook his head and snorted a curt laugh. "I doubt it's changed in twenty years."

"I can see why you and your grandfather are so close. Is that why you stayed around here and went to school in Tuskegee? You didn't want to leave your grandfather?"

Lance took one hand off the steering wheel and placed it over Janelle's. He glanced momentarily from the road. "You understand exactly." He faced her with a swell of pain and pride pressing inside his chest. "Janelle, I've never told this story to anyone before, and I'm still not sure what's happening here."

"What do you mean?" Janelle said, pushing Lance to be more specific, wanting to know his feelings.

"I guess I've never felt as close to a woman . . . so quickly. I'm still wondering how it happened. . . ." Lance's words trailed off.

"Why don't we just enjoy it and see where it takes us, because I feel the same way, too?" Then, in a bold move, Janelle reached up and ran her index finger lightly along the jut of Lance's jaw.

At a fork in the road Lance turned left and crossed a bumpy railroad track. A stained sign, CONGREGATION HILLS NORTH. POP. 306 was tacked to a telephone pole. Old, dilapidated houses with sagging porches and screenless windows came into view. Boarded-up, abandoned frame dwellings faced the street. Some had gaping holes in their roofs; others were surrounded by splintered stick fences and tangled, unkempt foliage. A few stray dogs and cats roamed the dirt roads.

At the corner they slowed near a square log structure that looked as if it had been plucked from the hills of Appalachia and plopped down right there on Main Street. A sign told Janelle the rustic place was the local general store.

A spotted hound sniffed at garbage cans stacked at the curb where barefoot children sat playing in the dirt. Janelle felt as if she had stepped back in time fifty years. There was nothing modern or gleaming or even decent about the place; it was downright depressing and sad.

"Hi, Mr. Lance." One of the children looked up at him and waved.

"Hello, Cindy." Lance leaned out the window. "How's your daddy doing?"

"He's fine. He's sitting on the porch over there." She pointed across the street with a mud-caked hand.

"You tell him I'm gonna be coming around to see about that hunting gun he's got for sale." Lance grinned at the children and drove on slowly down the street.

Afraid to say a word, Janelle bit the inside of her cheek, but her fury at Lance for not telling her the truth flared so intensely she thought she might be sick. *How dare he spout off half-truths for my amusement and misrepresent himself to me? His grandfather, the mayor. Indeed!* Janelle stiffened, seething, looking at the dreary neighborhood. What a mess! She was so angry at Lance she could hardly keep her mouth shut.

A grove of cypress trees shading the far end of the street created a feathered shadow curtain in front of a clearing. Lance swung to the right, then took a grassy path among the trees, winding past tin and cardboard shanties the likes of which Janelle had never seen. Women squatted on the ground, cooking over open, sooty fires, while their children walked around barefoot. Even the most neglected, destitute areas of Columbus, Ohio, had nothing to compare with what she now saw.

The horrifying poverty astonished Janelle. She had to close her soul to the desperation in the eyes of the children who ran, yelling, begging, alongside the car.

Within seconds Lance left the shouting children at the end of the lane and pulled into a smooth red-dirt yard that fronted a boxlike bungalow. It sat gray and squat, raw and splintering, in the midst of flowering peach trees that lined a rock pathway up to the porch. Compared with the shantytown they'd just passed through, this shabby little house looked royal, but even her house in Oakwood Alley would have been considered palatial compared with this.

"My home," Lance declared as he turned off the engine and waited for the dust to settle.

Janelle stared at the tiny house, her mouth slightly agape.

Lance tilted back his head, anxiously cutting his eyes toward her.

"Is this where your grandfather lives?" Janelle broke the awkward silence, trying to keep an even tone to her words.

"This is it." Lance took Janelle's hand and squeezed it hard, as if he feared she might run away. "I know this is a shock. Most people don't even know this place exists. When I was young, I thought I lived at the edge of the world—where no one would ever find me or rescue me. I was isolated, poor. It was very discouraging. I used to dream of escaping, of somehow being accepted on the other side of town . . . living the kind of life you had. Rather silly, but as you can see, Congregation Hills has two very different lives."

"Well . . . yes. I thought it would be different." Janelle's mumbled reply faded in her throat along with her anger. So he had misled her about his background. Hadn't she done the same thing? And now he trusted her enough to come clean, more than she could do.

"I know you've probably never seen a place like this, and I can't make any excuses for not being more honest." Lance reached over, placed both hands on Janelle's shoulders, and pulled her around to face him. "I never lied," he said. "I just wanted a chance to get to know you, and I was afraid—"

"Afraid I was too good for you?" she said, hating the lies *she*'d told. "Lance Fuller! Did you really think I would be so shallow as to judge you by where you grew up?"

Lance lowered his eyes. "It crossed my mind."

Janelle put her hand under his chin and lifted his lips toward hers. "It doesn't matter to me what kind of house you grew up in or what part of town you come from." Leaning closer, she felt the tug of his dark, somber eyes, then the press of his soft, warm mouth over hers.

Lance's feathery kiss soon blossomed into a heated, hungry melding of his lips to hers. When the tickle of his tongue flicked over hers, Janelle felt herself melting with a heart-stopping draining that transported her beyond the junk-filled yard, beyond the pitiful, shabby pocket of mud and sticks and smoky fires that existed outside the car.

Lance ran his hands through the thick, soft waves in Janelle's free-flowing hair. He explored her face with kisses, searching her cheeks, lids, brows, and forehead for a spot to caress.

Janelle arched forward, thrusting her breasts against the silver wings on Lance's chest in a blinding desire to get closer. Thrilling to the flurry of his kisses, she closed her eyes, trying to imagine his naked body against hers. Flushed with passion, she held him tightly when he began to ease away gently.

"Just give me a chance, Janelle," Lance murmured. "That's all I'm asking. You may not think I'm good enough for you, but let me prove you wrong. Please. I might come from humble beginnings, but I'm not ashamed of who I am. Congregation Hills will always be my home, but you may be sure I've got big plans for my future."

They may not include me once you learn how I've deceived you, Janelle thought glumly, embarrassed by the honesty in Lance's confession.

Tensing as he reached for her, she forced a smile, then

relaxed and set her troubling thoughts aside. When he wrapped his arms around her, she laid her head on his shoulder, inhaling the comforting scent of him, wondering how and when she would find the nerve to tell him the truth about herself.

CHAPTER
TWENTY-TWO

"My, my, my. Who's this at my door?" Deacon Fuller pulled back the sagging screen door, its hinges wailing at his tug. "Y'all come on in here. My, my, my. I was just thinking about you, boy." His pudgy, worn hands flew up in welcome.

Lance preceded Janelle into the little house, stopping just inside the door to embrace his grandfather firmly.

"And who's this angel you done brought with you?" Deacon moved right up to Janelle and clasped both her hands in his. "Child," he said, "don't make me no difference if my boy just met you this morning or been knowing you forever, I'm gonna give you a kiss hello."

Puckering lips that protruded from a wiry white mustache, he pecked Janelle on the cheek. He stepped back and looked her up and down and back up again. "You the prettiest woman ever come through this front door."

Janelle smiled under Deacon Fuller's scrutiny, feeling heat rise to her cheeks as he patted her hands between his.

"You just come over here and sit down, child, and let me look at you." With surprising agility, the rotund man ushered Janelle to a ladder-backed chair pulled up to a square table at the edge of the room.

She stared at Lance's grandfather. With his riot of cottony white hair fluffing out about his face, and his long, flowing beard resting on his chest, he looked a lot like

Santa Claus—a chocolate brown Santa Claus—like the one her father had sworn brought her gifts at Christmas.

"Grandfather, this is Janelle Roy, a nurse at the base."

Janelle smiled, nodding her greeting. "It's a pleasure to meet you, Mr. Fuller."

"No. No. The pleasure is all mine. You hear me? All mine. I ain't had a pretty girl grace this poor old place since my Mary went off to heaven."

Lance slipped down into the chair across from Janelle.

"How're things going, Pop?" Lance took off his cap, twirling it in both hands, wondering what Janelle was thinking. Did the unfinished walls and bare wooden floors shock her? Did the damp, moldy smell that he had grown accustomed to nauseate her? And what would he do if she needed to use the bathroom, show her outside and point down the path to the lean-to stuck behind Pop's toolshed? He kept his face turned toward his grandfather.

"Doing pretty regular," Deacon Fuller replied, settling down in a hand-carved rocking chair that had wide, flat arms and a surprisingly elegant slatted back that rose above his head. Tilting back and forth, he told Janelle, "You know, nothing much changes in Congregation Hills."

"Lance told me you're the mayor," Janelle said.

Lance could tell from the rapid-fire run of her words that she was trying to ease his discomfort.

"Mayor? Well, yeah. But with so many boys going off to join the Army, ain't nobody much left here to 'mayor' over!" Deacon lifted his bearded jaw, his loud guffaw bouncing off the walls. "Don't nobody want the job of fooling around with the problems we got here. Somehow I got elected to try. Don't exactly remember how long it's been, but I been doing the best I can for our poor little community for quite a spell now. It'll soon be time for somebody else to take over." He looked pointedly at Lance.

"Don't be giving me that look," Lance quickly said, a hint of amusement in his voice. "I have no interest in tangling with the county, the state, or the federal government to keep this place on the map. Sorry, Pop. Much as I love you and my sorry little hometown, I don't plan to stay around here forever."

"I know. I know," Deacon said, waving his thick hands in the air. Turning conspiratorially to Janelle, he said though his laughter, "Lance been threatening to run off and leave me here since he was no more than a sprout playing in the fields behind the house. You see how far he's gone, don't you?" Deacon chuckled lovingly under his breath. "Thank God he got on at that school for colored pilots. All he ever wanted to do was fly airplanes."

"That's what he told me," Janelle said, glancing over at Lance. "It must be great to have him so close by."

"Aw, yes," Deacon said. "That airfield's been a blessing. A bunch of folks from around here been getting good jobs over there." He tugged his beard, then leaned forward. "But the big stir is over at Keystone."

"What's going on there?" Lance asked.

"Heard the NAACP is just about to step in and put some pressure on John Gray. Something needs to be done about that place. I ain't got all the particulars, but I heard there's some big government contract in the works. You know that devil Gray is gonna be doing some mighty fast talking to get his way. Colored folks need work, and something's gotta break or there's gonna be trouble. Wait and see."

"See what I mean?" Lance said to Janelle. The painful memories of his lost parents flickered to the surface and burned. Telling his story to Janelle had ignited scenes in his mind he had buried long ago; now they were fresh and clear. "I told you change comes hard down here."

"Is the NAACP very active in these parts?" Janelle asked, somehow unable to imagine a picket line in front of the Keystone Company.

Deacon's bushy white eyebrows wiggled as he spoke. "Talk is negotiators from Washington gonna be coming. Got the blessing of the government. If Gray don't integrate Keystone, he ain't gonna get any war contracts, and you can bet that old devil ain't gonna let that happen. That family done made a fortune off making war supplies since way before slavery ended. No black man ever passed through those gates 'cept the chauffeur what picks up John Gray every evening and brings him back in the mornin'."

Lance shook his head skeptically. "Do you think people coming down from Washington are going to change what's been going on for generations?"

"I don't rightly know," Deacon said, "but it sure can't hurt to try."

"I agree," Janelle said boldly. "The NAACP in Columbus once helped me out of a jam." She fleetingly thought of Dalton Graham, then added, "The fact that people continue to make such a big deal about color absolutely infuriates me."

Lance cocked his head to one side. "I'm surprised to hear you say that. All this talk about integration. Well, the NAACP ought to take a good look at Tuskegee Airfield. In the morning the white officers drive to the base in their big black cars, and they leave every night before sundown. Just like overseers riding out to the fields to be sure the darkies do their chores. It's disgusting." Lance tilted his chair back on two legs. "It'd suit me fine if all white people disappeared completely from the face of the earth. Smiling in your face one minute. Calling you a nigger the next. They can't change. They won't change, believe me. I can get along fine without them."

Lance's bitter tone shocked Janelle. He might just as well have slapped her in the face. "I wouldn't say that!" Her words flew like sparks from a blacksmith's anvil. "That's terrible. You can't lump all white people together like that."

"They do it to us." Lance spoke with conviction.

"I don't think so. Maybe some but not all white people do that." Janelle began to tremble, frightened by the dark frown souring Lance's usually gentle features. "I've known quite a few white people who willingly put their lives on the line for integration. Picketing, protesting.

There are white lawyers who work for justice, too. I've known plenty of white people who want everyone to get along; they are not prejudiced at all." She looked from Lance to his grandfather. "And ... I've had my share of problems with some very mean colored people, too."

Suddenly she floundered, grasping for the right way to say it. Her mother may not have wanted her involved romantically with a white man, but she had never been encouraged to hate white people. "I mean ... it's not fair to judge everyone by your experiences." Again she fell silent, deciding to tread carefully, not wanting to cause a big stir. After all, she was on foreign soil in Alabama.

Without a word Deacon Fuller got up from the table and went into the next room. He came back with a heavy rosewood picture frame in his hand.

"Little lady, I know you speak from your heart." He placed the picture on the table between Lance and her. "This here's my boy, Thomas. Lance's pa. Standing beside him is Katy. Lance's ma. On the other side of the yard there, with the broom in her hand, is my beautiful Mary, my wife." Deacon's voice began to quaver. "They all gone. John Gray drove my family away, left me only Lance." He turned the photo toward himself, staring at it with watery eyes. "So—you gotta understand why some of us don't have real good feelings about white folks."

"I do," Janelle murmured, momentarily lowering her lashes against his terrible pain. "Lance told me what happened to his parents. I understand. I do. It's just that my experiences have been so different."

Lance reached across the table and took Janelle's hand. "It's hard for people around here to shake feelings and attitudes that they've lived with all their lives."

"Doesn't that go for both colored and white?"

Lance nodded. "Yes, it does. And I didn't mean to start a fuss. You come from a world very different from mine." He could imagine her as a child sitting on the veranda of her eight-room house, unaware of the grinding poverty and blatant racism that he had endured every day. "If I sounded angry, I'm sorry." He nervously fidgeted with his cap. "I shouldn't have shot off my mouth like that." Running his thumb over the stiff brim, he asked, "Let's drop it, okay?" His tension eased as he saw the unflattering wrinkles on Janelle's brow begin to fade. Damn, he'd better be more careful. He'd come close to spoiling his chances with her.

Lance stretched his arms out above his head, inhaled deeply, then stood. "Pop, what do you think? Should I drive Janelle out to Lake Eden? Show her a prettier side of Congregation Hills?" He was purposefully speaking in a much lighter manner.

Deacon grinned broadly, stroking his protruding stomach. "Now that's a good idea. Show Janelle the roots of our town. Laurel's near to blooming. The dogwoods is full of buds. Gonna be a real early spring 'round here. Yes, yes. Enjoy the rest of the day. You young folks don't need to be spending the little free time you got sitting with this old man talking race. Nothing's gonna be solved this afternoon."

Janelle took her lead from Lance and got up, taking care not to scrape her chair on the bare wooden floor. "It was very nice visiting with you, Mr. Fuller."

"Child, just call me Deacon." He shifted nearer and gave Janelle a bear hug and another quick peck on the cheek. "And you make my boy bring you back." He turned to Lance. "Now don't you do nothing foolish like running this pretty gal off."

Lance clasped his grandfather by the shoulder and slipped one arm around Janelle's slender waist. "Aw, Pop, don't worry." His features folded into a little-boy grin. "If I can work it out, we'll be back next Sunday."

"No word yet about when you boys gonna ship out?" Deacon had to steady himself with both hands on the wide, flat arms of his chair to push his heavy body upright. He laced his fat fingers together, propping them atop his stomach.

"No. But I think things are finally moving in that direction. Stimson's coming down to inspect the squadron, and Colonel Davis has been pumping up the guys—feels pretty sure we'll be getting orders to shove out soon."

Janelle gave Lance a questioning look. "The secretary of war? He's coming to Tuskegee?"

"Yep," Lance answered proudly. "Everybody seems to think that means the Ninety-ninth will enter combat soon."

All three fell silent, standing awkwardly for a second, not wanting to interpret what that meant.

Finally Lance broke the invisible fear. "Hey! You ready to see Lake Eden?"

"Yes," she said, centering her gaze on his face. "I'd like that very much."

On the way to the lake Lance detoured back toward town and pulled to a stop in front of the general store.

"Thirsty?" he asked Janelle, one hand already on the door handle. "I think I could use a soda."

"Me, too," Janelle replied, realizing she'd eaten only a candy bar since breakfast.

As she watched Lance stride up the wobbly steps and pull the door open, her heart nearly leaped from her chest. Sunlight caught the wings and brass buttons on his jacket, reflecting their brilliance toward her. How absolutely gorgeous he was! And gentle. And easy to be with. She didn't ever want the day to end.

From the corner of her eye Janelle noticed a slow-moving figure advancing on her right. Turning in her seat, she saw a young woman carrying a cloth shopping bag, making her way toward the store. Though the cut of her dress was youthful, almost stylish, she looked worn out, much older than she probably was, and Janelle thought her cheeks were too heavily powdered and definitely over-rouged.

At the foot of the steps the woman halted, holding the railing to get her balance, signaling for help from a tattered little boy at her side. Janelle watched curiously as he dutifully took hold of the woman's arm and helped her up the rickety stairs, where she paused, took a deep breath, lifted her chin, then entered the store.

The child, whose gaunt face had the hollow look of persistent hunger, and whose arms looked scarred and pocked from years of insect bites, appeared to be about seven years old. He remained outside, sitting atop a tall staved barrel, dangling his skinny brown legs over the edge, banging his scuffed high-top shoes against the side as he whistled a tune to himself.

Tall, narrow pines filtered shadows over the porch of the flat-roofed structure, darkening its splintered, uneven floor. Janelle's eyes traveled over the deeply shaded area. The store might have been called quaint up North, but down here it represented no more than a place to get supplies to survive.

White stone jugs, enameled pans, metal dishes, chairs and lamps and odd pieces of furniture were crammed into piles in the front of the store. A black potbellied stove and a blackened kerosene lamp took up space at the far end of the porch. A three-legged icebox tilted against a stack of galvanized washtubs that looked nearly rusted through and useless. A huge pile of broken wooden crates and tattered baskets created a mountain of tinder at the side of the door.

Janelle thought of Lance's childhood in this isolated town that looked as if the twentieth century had not yet arrived. There were so many differences between them. He had lost his parents while still a baby; she had been blessed with both mother and father while she was growing up. He'd attended school in rural, segregated Alabama while she had been educated in an integrated public school. He'd been raised in a two-room shack in the middle of Macon County; she'd grown up in a five-room house in the center of a big city. Janelle was certainly no stranger to hard times, but the dank, little town of Congregation Hills struck her as being in another league altogether.

It was obvious to Janelle that Lance's love for his

grandfather and pride in his family had helped him rise above the poverty and discrimination in Congregation Hills, but her lies stabbed her conscience. Janelle had to face the blunt truth. She had no home to return to. Whom was she trying to fool?

How in the world can I tell him the truth now? She worried, clenching her fingers into a hard fist. She set the problem aside when Lance burst out of the store, and she relaxed as she watched him cross the porch.

As he passed the whistling boy sitting atop the barrel, Lance stopped, looked oddly at the child—as if annoyed by his presence—then walked right past him, headed down the stairs.

The woman who had come with the boy was right behind. She followed Lance to the foot of the steps and grabbed him rudely by the arm. Janelle was shocked by the grim set to her face. What was going on?

Rolling down the window, she strained to hear what was being said but could not understand the rapid exchange of words. Janelle flinched when the angry woman shook her long finger in Lance's face, scowling and hissing abuse between her teeth.

Lance shrugged, dismissing her, then walked briskly across the loose dirt yard, leaving her frowning after him.

"What was that all about?" Janelle asked, her heart pounding. How could anyone be so angry at easygoing Lance?

"Aw, that's Minnie Easter. She does my grandfather's laundry and cooks for him now and then." Lance popped the cap from a bottle of Coke and handed it to Janelle. "I owe her some money . . . for two weeks of laundry, to be exact."

"She certainly seems upset."

Lance took a long swallow from his drink. "I'm gonna pay her. She'll just have to wait. A pest, that's all she is. If I could find somebody else to help Pop out, I would."

"Is that her child?"

"I don't know ... maybe ... some relative or other. Why are you so interested anyway?"

Janelle nonchalantly lifted one shoulder, realizing her questions were disturbing to Lance. "No reason in particular. Just asking."

"Forget it. Minnie is a pain in the ass." He started the car. "Everybody around here knows that. I'll settle with her next week."

As they headed away from town, Janelle glanced back and murmured, "Oh, my!" when she saw the woman cuff the boy roughly on the back of his head and push him ahead of her across the yard.

Lance didn't even look in the rearview mirror.

The road they took wound eastward out of Congregation Hills for about three miles, then veered north until it split at a grove of pecan trees.

"If I were to go right," Lance said, "we'd be headed back to the base. It's just above the hill—maybe two miles."

Janelle tried to get her bearings. She peered down a narrow, dusty red dirt lane that cut through dense foliage to the left. Bees buzzed loudly above a carpet of goldenrod, and a covey of yellow-hammers squawked overhead.

"And down there?" she asked, wondering if the lane was wide enough for the car to get through.

"Lake Eden," Lance replied, easing off the asphalt highway. At a slow crawl he inched forward, the lane narrowing as he went. When branches of mulberry and holly raked the side of the car, Lance still did not stop. He pressed forward until the car broke through a tangle of vines and shrubs and entered a spacious green clearing.

Janelle gasped aloud. Before her, glittering under the descending sun, was a lake the color of a dazzling emerald. Low sloping hills, terraced in the distance, created a hazy green backdrop for the calm, mirrorlike water. Crowded with water lilies, it shimmered coolly, reflecting the dense gathering of magnolias, pines, cypresses, and gum trees that spread from the edge of the lake straight up into the hills. Two white-tailed deer stood drinking from the sun-drenched pool.

Mounds of crumbling stone, scattered beneath the trees, gave Janelle the eerie sensation that she'd stumbled on to ancient ruins no one had ever seen before.

"This place is beautiful." Unable to wait for Lance to open her door, Janelle jumped out, taking it all in. Against a backdrop of blue sky fading to purple, elongated fingers of steel gray clouds drifted lazily toward the rapidly setting sun. She could almost taste the honeysuckle and jasmine that trailed thickly along the edge of the lake.

Lance came to stand beside Janelle, slipping his hand around her waist, caressing the soft, fuzzy back of her angora sweater.

"This is the origin of Congregation Hills North." Pride tinged with melancholy colored his words.

Easing his hand up to Janelle's shoulder, Lance guided her away from the car. "Let's go down to the water."

Janelle relaxed, loving the protective feel of Lance's body next to hers, feeling as if she had stumbled upon an enchanted, magical world. Isolated deep in the woods, with all thoughts of race, politics, and war set aside, Janelle allowed herself to hope she'd finally found the man who would bring her the kind of happiness she desperately wanted.

Approaching quietly, they startled the deer, which looked straight at them, then scampered soundlessly away.

Lance pulled Janelle closer, then turned her slightly. "See that log cabin up there—on the right?"

"Yes. It looks very old," she said, delighted to see violet plants clustered at the foot of the whitewashed stoop. Her home in Oakwood Alley had had a lush violet patch along the back fence. She and Perry used to cut the flowers, tie them with any ribbon they could find, and present the nosegays to their mother. "Does anybody live there?"

"Not now, but that little cabin is where my grandfather was born."

"Gosh, how old is he?"

"Sixty-seven next month."

"Who keeps the place up?"

"He did . . . for a long time. Now he's too stiff and old to get out here and do much anymore. Whenever I get the chance, I come and clean things up, patch the broken logs, and try to secure it . . . keep stray animals out."

Janelle fell back into step with Lance at her side.

"Pop hates to admit he can't do much anymore, so I usually just come out here alone and do a little work without making a big fuss. He gets all teared up when I talk about the cabin at Lake Eden. I've spent a lot of time working here alone, taking care of this place for Pop."

"So he still owns it?"

"Yeah. This area was settled by slaves from nearby plantations at the end of the Civil War. My great-grandfather paid forty dollars for his little half acre plot of ground where he could build a cabin and live peacefully. Other families followed and lived happily, until the Grays decided to run everybody off. At one time there were close to forty cabins on Lake Eden—all grouped together like a big family compound. My dad was born here, too, and most of the people in town have their roots at Lake Eden."

Janelle looked closer to discover the meager remains of other cabins that had long since rotted away. At the far end of the lake a broken mud-brick chimney jutted skeletally into the air, its ancient stone fireplace still partially intact. The only cabin that remained whole was the one Lance had pointed out, nestled ahead among a stand of wood fern four feet high.

"There was a raging fire here a long time ago," Lance said as they walked along the lake. "It started over there." He pointed across the water toward a flat, grassy area at the foot of a low, vine-covered hill. "According to Pop, the wind whipped the fire into a ball of flames that scorched everything in its path. Everything was ashes in a matter of minutes. Old folks say women and children burned to death in their beds; the smell of charred flesh hung in the air for weeks. That's what I was told. Wild sparks leaped from one cabin to another until everything standing was burned to the ground—everything except this cabin. The back caught fire, but Pop and my dad managed to put it out and eventually rebuilt the ruined walls. After that people drifted away, and my dad began calling his place Wild Embers."

Janelle slowed her pace, murmuring, "Wild Embers, that's nice." She stopped to observe the cabin, absorbing Lance's story. "It's so quiet here, so peaceful."

"Yeah, but can you imagine the horror of that night? Sometimes I come out here to fish, but nobody cares about this place anymore. Tales were told that white folks believed Pop's cabin was cursed, or haunted, or something like that because it was the only one to survive the fire."

"And what do you think?" Janelle asked.

Lance chuckled. "Well, I'd rather say it's blessed. But then again I wouldn't spend the night out here alone. Could be ghosts haunt the lake at night."

"Don't try to scare me," Janelle said lightly, noticing dark shadows beginning to creep over the front of the cabin. "Can we go in?" Curiosity and the chill that came with sunset made her anxious to go inside.

"Sure." Lance stepped in front of Janelle. "Can't promise what you'll find inside, it's been awhile since I was here."

Gravel crunched under their feet as they came up the path. Lance pushed the squeaky door open.

"Wait here," he said, entering to light an oil lamp.

When it sputtered into life, a square room dominated by a huge gray stone fireplace sprang into view. In front of the hearth sat a low wooden bench that was nicked with scars of wear. Under the slanted eaves, a narrow trundle bed was tucked in the alcove next to a big old humpbacked trunk. Above the bed, hanging askew, was a faded rendition of Rebecca at the well.

Janelle went over and straightened the picture, then looked across the room at Lance. "This place is charming."

Lance scratched his chin. "Charming? I don't know if I'd use that word."

"Well." Janelle blushed, but pushed on. "It *could* be charming—with a little work."

Lance smiled. "Are you saying it could use a woman's touch?"

Janelle was ready with her reply: "Definitely."

Lance hesitated. "Maybe, but right now it's just a musty old cabin that I hope I can hold on to. The taxes go up every year. But I won't let it slip away. This little scrap of land means a hell of a lot to me."

At the fireplace he pulled out a few small logs and some kindling from the nearby stack and laid them in the hearth. With his back to Janelle, he struggled to still the rapid beating of his heart. The day had been perfect, just as he had imagined, and now he prayed he wouldn't scare Janelle off by telling her what was on his mind. He'd waited for a woman like her for so long, a woman to trust with his past and his future. Now he'd have to take the chance of being brutally honest if he hoped to keep her in his life.

"Would you ever live here?" Janelle asked.

Lance kept his back to her. "Oh, I don't think so. It's just that Pop will never leave Congregation Hills. It may sound morbid, but when he dies, I'd like to bury him out here." Then he faced her, his voice dropping to a halting murmur. "And if I ever found out that my dad and mom were dead and buried in some strange place, I'd bring them back here, too."

"That doesn't sound morbid to me," she replied. "I think it would be a lovely thing to do."

"I want Pop to know that his birthplace, the place he fought and struggled to hang on to, the land that cost him his son, will remain in the family after he's gone."

"And you? What does the cabin mean to you?"

"I—I think a lot about my father and mother when I come out here. I get a kind of lost feeling that takes two or three days to shake."

Lance returned to building the fire, striking a match on the small stack of kindling. The wood crackled into life, flooding the corners of the room with a soft yellow glow.

Knowing the emotional toll this was taking, Janelle had to find out where she fitted in. "If it's so painful for you to come here, why did you bring me?"

Lance crossed the room. "Because I want you to know exactly who I am. Where I come from. What's important to me."

"And what's that?" Janelle could not resist the opening to push for more. She had to know how Lance really felt, and she had to know tonight. The thought of returning to the base, their attraction still undefined, was not what she wanted at all.

"What do I want?" Lance repeated, stopping before her. "A family." He frowned when he said those words, a perplexed look as if he'd gotten ahead of himself. "I want a woman in my life to build my future with." He eased nearer, opening his arms, sighing when Janelle allowed herself to be drawn to his chest. He placed his chin atop her soft brown hair. "Janelle, I think I'm falling in love with you."

An explosion of nervous joy shot through Janelle. She pulled away slightly, gazing into the depths of Lance's dark brown eyes.

"I know, Lance. This feels so right. I—I feel as if I've finally found the answers to so many questions."

Emma was right, Janelle silently admitted. Loving a man of her own race did make a difference. It brought a sense of unity, satisfaction, a completeness she would never have found with Dalton Graham, as handsome and kind as he had been. Her misguided, desperate attempt to seduce him had been a mistake all right, and thank God he had been brave enough to end the relationship before it ever really began.

"I feel the same way," Lance murmured, his shoulders rising and falling with each ragged breath. "I know exactly what you mean."

"Do you?" Janelle placed the palm of one hand on his chest and splayed her fingers over the sharp crease of his khaki tie, wishing she could feel the warmth of his smooth, muscled chest under her fingers.

Lance lowered his chin, his face coming closer, inviting Janelle to tilt hers up toward him.

"My life has had its share of twists and turns," he said, a flicker of anguish dimming his joy. "I haven't always been the gentleman my grandfather raised me to be ... and I'm afraid I've deluded myself about facing certain responsibilities, and now it's time to—"

"Don't." Janelle placed her fingertips on his lips, not wanting to hear him confess his affairs with all the women he'd been chasing on the base. If half of what Lillian Dorsey had told her about Lance Fuller was true, she'd be in for some unpleasant revelations. "You don't have to tell me anything you'd rather not."

Playful now, Lance asked, "Are you certain you don't want to know my deepest, darkest secrets? All my regrets?"

Janelle smiled generously, removing her fingertips from his lips. "I'm certain," she said with conviction. "Very certain."

Maybe it was the knowledge that he could be shipped off to foreign soil at any time. Maybe it was her fear of hearing hurtful truths that might shatter the magic of the moment. Or maybe, now that she thought she'd found the right man for her, she would not let anything come to light that might prevent her from loving Lance Fuller.

"Let's begin on a clean white page," she said, inhaling the masculine scent of him, trembling inside. What good would it do to have visions of his past affairs tumbling through her head all night? And if he poured out his heart and soul to her now, she'd have to clear up her own pretentious lies. Now was definitely not the time to do it. "Just hold me, Lance. No confessions, please. All I want is to feel your arms around me. The past is just that: the past."

When Lance's lips descended over hers, Janelle moaned lowly, hungrily accepting the urgent press of his fingers on her arms, her shoulders, down her back. Intoxicated by his sheer physical presence, she floated on the blissful current of desire that coursed from him through her.

Running her hands along his spine, Janelle kissed Lance with a sureness and passion that surged forth from an untapped wellspring she didn't know she possessed. She captured his lips between her teeth, rejoicing in the taste of him, the feel of his body pressed to hers, the flaming touch of his cheek to hers. Behind them the fire blazing in the hearth created a golden glow of intimacy.

Lance gathered Janelle so close she could feel the rapid beating of his heart, pounding rhythmically beneath his jacket, straining against her breasts. A responsive quiver surged, then settled back between her thighs to linger in delicate promise. When they sank onto the low trundle bed under the eaves, she folded in surrender, his caresses like commands. She had no will to pull away.

"Lance," she murmured, her pulse racing, "don't ever let me go."

He eased her down beside him, ever so gently, tucking her head beneath his chin, rubbing his cheek against her hair. "I don't plan to," he whispered. "Not now. Not ever, and I hope you want me as much as I want you."

"I do, Lance. I do." Nothing else needed to be said.

Lance unbuttoned his jacket, peeled off his shirt, and slipped down, bare-chested, next to her.

Janelle shifted slightly, trying to look up at him, giggling as he captured her lips with his, thrilled by the unexpected gesture. She dissolved, blinded to everything except the invisible web that threaded them together. At that moment no one existed in the world but the two of them, and nothing mattered but the love of the man next to her.

Lying in Lance's arms, Janelle wished she could shimmer and melt and transform herself to be one with him, never to leave his side. Pressing closer to the heat of his bronze, silky chest, she urged him to devour her with all the love he had to give. Tonight she craved him, had waited too long to feel him stretched full length against her.

Lance nestled Janelle deeper into the center of the lumpy straw mattress, but she was unmindful of the musty odor rising from the ancient quilt, smelling only the scent of the man in her arms.

Surprised—yet not—that she would be crying silently in joy, Janelle felt the salty wetness of tears on her lips. She shuddered in anticipation as Lance moved his hands lightly over the tiny pearl buttons on her blouse.

Soon Lance's hard, naked body rippled beautifully above the pliant nakedness she surrendered to him. Their ascent consumed them, burned them, molded them into an intricate assemblage of limbs and torsos, silken and locked in passion.

Crushing her with driven hunger, Lance somehow held back enough to enter Janelle with nearly unbearable tenderness. Feeling him deep inside her, she tossed her free-flowing hair from her eyes and cried aloud when the rapturous release of their union swept over her in unrelenting waves.

Deep in the woods of Macon County, in a deserted cabin no one visited or wanted, Janelle lost herself to the world as she knew it and embraced the promise of the future.

CHAPTER
TWENTY-THREE

Dalton Graham wiped his forehead with his handkerchief, dusted a fine mist of gray dirt from his trousers, then shaded his eyes against the sun. He'd never seen a battleship up close and could scarcely believe that the monstrously bulky vessel rising up in front of him would not sink as soon as it was launched.

The thirty-five thousand tons of gray steel that rocked silently on the water had a beam of 110 feet and would carry more than twenty-five hundred officers and enlisted men into dangerous, watery battlegrounds halfway around the world. The chief engineer on this job, who had been gracious enough to let Dalton aboard, had told him that once the ship was fully loaded and geared up for battle conditions, it would weigh in at more than forty-two thousand tons. Massive, not only in size but in dignity, the newly constructed battleship represented the pride and strength of the nation.

Turning his back on the awesome man-of-war, Dalton headed back toward Andrew Burrnow's office, hating to admit that his efforts so far had not been as productive as he had hoped. And now, in the wake of the mysterious, brutal beating of a Negro engineer who had insistently protested at Burrnow's guarded gates, the FBI would most likely get involved in the nasty situation. If his round of talks with union leaders stalled again this morning, Dalton feared he might have to refer the case directly to the President.

Six tense days of argumentative meetings with management, the all-white union, the colored welders who feared for their lives, and the local NAACP officials had not brought compromise. Sadly Dalton's presence at the shipyard had inflamed its undercurrent of hatred, exposing a seething zone of hostility, which he knew was close to erupting.

Removing his hat, Dalton opened the heavy glass door and spoke to the receptionist. "I'm here to see Mr. Burrnow."

"Oh, yes. Mr. Graham. He's waiting for you. Go right on in."

Dalton turned the knob to the president's office, determined to reach some conclusion today.

Andrew Burrnow did not stand when Dalton entered. Waving his hand to a chair at the conference table, the haggard-looking man sat silently, his face pinched in irritation. Three other men—the union boss, a Negro representing the welders, and the president of the local NAACP—sat at the table. No one offered a murmur of greeting.

"Good morning, gentlemen." Dalton attempted to warm the atmosphere.

Only Burrnow inclined his head slightly, then picked up a sheet of paper. The others remained distrustfully immobile.

"Mr. Graham, I told you when you first arrived that I personally have no qualms whatsoever about putting Negroes on the welding line. It's the union that has balked my efforts."

Mr. James, the union president, glared icily at Andrew Burrnow. "The union here has excluded Negroes from membership since the beginning. I had nothing to do with that decision."

"I am aware of your predicament," Dalton said.

Burrnow cleared his throat. "I don't want a riot. I don't

want any more violence. There's work to be done, and we're losing too much production time fooling around with this issue."

"Then let's get it settled," Dalton said, a streak of impatience rising. "You know what you've got to do."

"Yes. I do." Burrnow handed the piece of paper to Dalton. "Mr. James and I have been in serious discussions since late last night. It wasn't easy to come to an agreement, but I think I've convinced him that the federal government will not back down and we'd better settle this among ourselves. Neither James nor I want to stand by while federal troops storm in here, causing more trouble than we've already got. So here you are—a copy of my letter to the Office of Production Management, just as you requested."

Dalton took the paper and quickly read it.

"Does that cover everything?" Burrnow pursed thin lips together and waited.

"This letter to the FEPC states that you will abide by Executive Order number Eight-eight-oh-two. A smart move, Burrnow. This will be taken in good faith that you do not and will not have any discriminatory practices or policies at your shipyard. This will suffice—for now." Dalton laid the page aside, turning his attention to the union president, who was scratching the side of his neck, looking very uncomfortable with the discussion.

"However," Dalton went on, "the FEPC will be following up on your promise. If violations are found, you'll be fined. Heavily. Possibly shut down. Those federal troops will be down here so fast you won't know what hit you. You do understand that, don't you? It's up to you to enforce the President's directive."

"Yes," Burrnow said, adding, "The union is in complete agreement. Negroes will be allowed to join, and there will be no more threats or violence on the premises. As a matter of fact, I plan personally to escort the colored personnel to their workstations this morning, and I promise to relieve any protestors of their duties immediately. Decent people only want to keep their jobs, Mr. Graham. These are hardworking people who have been asked to adjust to radical changes in our way of doing things."

"That may be true," Dalton said, relief starting to ease through him. "But violent behavior and blatant disregard for federal law can't and won't be tolerated."

Andrew Burrnow turned to the Negro welder and spoke as if he were making a vow. "I plan to keep the shipyard at full production as long as this war goes on." Then he tilted his jaw toward the union boss. "James? This has passed the vote, hasn't it? The colored will be allowed to join the union?"

James assented with a curt nod of his large blond head, a blink of his small green eyes.

"Good." Dalton stood, extending his hand to Andrew Burrnow. "I'm counting on you to make it happen."

By nightfall Dalton had concluded his business at Burrnow, telephoned his report back to Thackery in Columbus, and was settled into a private berth on the Seaboard Coastline Limited, speeding west toward Macon County, Alabama.

Too weary to read, he set his newspaper aside and closed his eyes. *One down and one to go,* he mused, feeling a little smug that he'd been able to diffuse the potentially volatile situation at Burrnow without calling headquarters for help.

Dalton knew he ought to be studying the background reports on the Keystone Company that Oscar had meticulously prepared, but all he wanted to do right now was relax and think about seeing Janelle again—visualize the bronze glow of her skin, the thick, feathery lashes defining her beautiful, doelike eyes, the cascade of her perfumed hair.

He'd been on the road for weeks. Not a day had passed that he hadn't thought of Janelle, imagined the taste of her lips upon his. Dalton's mind was firmly made up. He had no doubt that Janelle *could* fit into his world without compromise, and he knew he could live in hers.

Being on the road, living out of suitcases, he had seen everything fall into perspective.

I was a coward once and let Tahti slip away. Janelle has come to me as another chance at happiness, and this time I'm going to grab it.

The higher Lance climbed into the quiet blue sky, the more lightheaded with exhilaration he became. The hum of the engine, the sensation of floating: these were what he loved about flying. Flushed with joy, he soared upward, slicing through banks of dense white clouds that gathered him into their feathery nest. His thoughts turned to Janelle.

Over the past ten days they had managed to slip back to Wild Embers three more times, each encounter more impassioned than the last. Abandoning themselves to the tumultuous discovery of love, they had melted into the beauty of their union, making love from sunset to dawn.

When not at Wild Embers, they met on the post: under the shady oak trees outside the nurses' quarters, behind the infirmary after her shift, between the vacant training buildings that stood still and black after all the cadets had left—anyplace where they could be alone. Remembering the blissful taste of her lips, the unrestrained press of her breasts to his chest, Lance had to blink back unexpected tears of elation in his eyes.

Pushing his droning P-40 even higher, Lance savored the awakening that now consumed him, glad to have Janelle on his mind. Her presence in his life, his persistent thoughts of her helped crowd out the uneasiness, the destructive sense of gloom that hung over every member of his squad.

The 99th was ready for combat. The secretary of war's optimistic words bolstered Lance's belief that the squadron would soon see action. But two weeks after his historic visit no combat orders had come through.

The pilots, the instructors, the ground crews, and most of the civilian and enlisted men on the air base were becoming frustrated and irritable, complaining about the condescending reporters who intimated in their articles that the colored pilots were destined to be mothballed at Tuskegee for the duration.

Luckily for Lance, his love for Janelle so consumed his thoughts he could push the possibility of not fighting out of his mind, for a little while at least. Shutting out his disappointment that newspapers would print such demoralizing rumors was much more difficult to do.

Breaking out of the clouds, Lance swung to the right, into a sunny patch of blue. Beaming, he recalled his last visit to Congregation Hills. Janelle had charmed his grandfather with a tin of hard candy and several back copies of the *Negro Digest* and *Life* magazine, which she had pried from the nurses in her quarters. Lena Horne's visit to Tuskegee had been in one; a story about Josephine Baker's efforts to sell war bonds, in another. Now his grandfather was completely smitten with Janelle, inviting her to come visit anytime she wanted, with or without Lance. For the first time in Lance's life everything seemed perfectly in order.

But for how long? he had to ask himself, banking the plane to the left, sweeping into a low pass over a fallow cornfield. When combat orders finally came through, how in the world could he possibly leave?

Last night he had seriously considered asking Janelle to run off with him to Montgomery and get married before he left. But what if he didn't make it back from combat? Or God forbid, what if she met someone else while he was gone and wrote him one of those dreadful letters every soldier lived in fear of getting?

Pulling up out of his low-altitude sweep, Lance entered an abrupt chandelle, gritting his teeth as a familiar sensation gnawed in the pit of his stomach. He had not felt it for years. The harder Lance pushed his tight little plane, the harder he tried to clear his mind of the shameful guilt he knew he had to face. The time had come to reckon with it, yet he remained stymied about what he ought to do.

Lance moaned lowly, wishing he had been able to tell

Janelle the secret he couldn't shake. He *had* tried that first night at Wild Embers, but she had stopped him, and he had let her. To dredge up and expose her to the kind of shame he struggled every day to keep hidden from himself? Impossible! Janelle was upper-crust; he couldn't expect her to understand. The shock would drive her away.

But he should have spoken the whole painful truth, then let her help him decide what to do. Isn't that what people in love usually did with their fears, their dreams, their disappointments?

Well, the time was not right, Lance convinced himself. Too much was at stake. How fair would it be anyway? To leave Janelle stunned and angry and disappointed with him as he boarded a ship to sail out of her life to a war halfway around the world?

CHAPTER
TWENTY-FOUR

"I hate to say it, but you look terrible, Janelle," Emma said.

"Oh, I'll be all right," Janelle answered, more brusquely than she intended. She was not in the mood for Emma's sisterly concern. "I am a little tired. These double shifts are hell."

"You're dead on your feet, and you know it." Emma pushed the night duty roster across the counter to their harried supervisor, who was talking on the phone while trying to sign them out. Emma put her hand on Janelle's arm, bit her lip, then said, "You might consider getting to bed at a decent hour." She signed her name with a flourish, then handed the pen to Janelle.

"Does it show that much?" Janelle asked, scribbling her signature on the last line of the roster, replacing her charts on the rack behind the desk.

"Yes," Emma said truthfully. "It shows. I know you had only three hours of sleep yesterday. Then to take on night duty, too. You can't keep it up."

"I know. I'm going to go back to the barracks and get some rest while I can. Things are only going to get more hectic around here."

Emma pulled her starched white cap back and tucked a flyaway curl beneath it. "Did you read the notice that was posted in the quarters last night?"

"What notice?" Janelle had barely made it in before lights out and had gone directly to bed.

"A special nursing unit is being put together to go to Africa. Liberia. There are thirty-seven spaces to be filled."

"Liberia! Why? That's miles from the front."

"No one knows how the tide will turn over there. The nursing station might serve as a backup to accept the wounded who can't be cared for farther north." Emma walked to the door and held it open. "I've been thinking of signing up."

Janelle passed in front of her into the morning sunlight. "You serious? I thought you said you'd never leave me here."

"That promise was made when I was at a very low point, remember?" Emma let the door bang shut behind them.

Janelle pulled her sweater from her shoulders, enjoying the sunlight on her back. "Africa, huh? Gosh, that sounds so far away!"

"It is," Emma said, starting down the cement walkway. "I know some of the girls are pretty reluctant to sign on, but I really do want to go. I'm ready for a change. Besides, I might be able to do more good there than here."

Janelle didn't respond, not knowing quite what to say, understanding why Emma might want to go, but *she* had no desire to leave Tuskegee—at least not as long as Lance was still there.

"Oh, Emma. What is happening? We came into this together. I hate to think of you going off to Africa." A frightful sense of impending separation clutched Janelle. "Everything is changing too fast."

"I know. There are rumors circulating all over the base that the Ninety-ninth might ship out any day. Chief Raney already warned us. We have to assist with packing medical supplies; some pilots need updated physicals, shots, tests. The pressure's just starting to build."

Janelle was only half listening to Emma, her mind filled with thoughts of Lance's flying combat missions overseas.

She awkwardly cleared her throat. "I feel it" was all she could manage to say.

"In light of all that's going on, Janelle, you'd better be careful. Dorsey told the chief about you and Lance, so I'm sure she's watching."

"What'd Dorsey tell Raney?" Janelle panicked. That gossipy Lillian Dorsey *would* be the one to take it upon herself to sabotage Janelle's relationship with Lance.

"I'm not getting in it," Emma said. "But I must say— and don't get all huffy—your evening trips to the infirmary to check on sick patients is a pretty weak excuse to get out of the barracks after hours."

"I'll bet Dorsey has been following me. Spying."

"I don't know about that," Emma said. "I wasn't there, but I heard Raney got hopping mad and all of a sudden began yelling a blue streak, reading all the nurses the riot act about *fraternizing* with the pilots."

Janelle frowned, adjusting her purse strap more securely on her shoulder. "Damn that bitch Dorsey. I'll straighten her out."

"Be careful, Janelle. She tells everyone that you took Lance from her."

"Please. He told me he took her out once, to a dance over on campus." Janelle breathed a nervous laugh. "And you know they enforce the three-foot rule at those dances. He couldn't have gotten very close."

They turned to the right, their barracks in sight. Three nurses on their way to duty saluted as they passed.

The sun was full up now, casting its bright yellow rays across the bustling post. Planes buzzed and streaked above them, blanketing the air base with their never-ending drone. They walked in silence until they reached the nurses' quarters. Janelle stopped under a leafy oak and stood with her back against the trunk, feeling the beginnings of a migraine headache prick at the base of her skull.

"Please, Emma, don't be mad." She glanced toward the quarters, then back at her friend. "I know my behavior has not been exemplary, but I can't help it. Lance could be called up any day, any moment. Every minute we can be together counts for so much." Biting her lip, she looked down to hide brimming tears.

"Oh, Janelle, you think I can't see that you're hopelessly and crazy in love with that guy? I've been there, remember?" Emma said. "But slipping out of the quarters, staying away so late. You might be moving too fast; you could get hurt. Lance does have a reputation, you know."

"But there's so little time," Janelle said despairingly.

"Time for what, Janelle? What is it you expect to happen?" Emma raised her hands in question. "Don't you see how dangerous your behavior is?"

Janelle stood silent. Planes roared and swooped overhead.

"I don't care, Emma. I'm scared. I refuse to lose Lance to this crazy war, let it destroy the happiness I've finally found."

She thought about how far she'd come since leaving Columbus, realizing that the selfish, material woman doing private-duty nursing was now buried beneath her determination to serve her country and nurture her love for Lance. This time she'd get it right. Marrying Lance, having his children, settling into the life she knew they could create together were the only issues crowding her mind. "What will I do when Lance leaves?" Janelle sank down on a bench under the tree. "Emma, it's not fair. None of this is fair!"

"Nobody said it was going to be fair." Emma stood looking down at Janelle. "But you have to think beyond yourself. You're not the first woman in love who has had to watch her sweetheart go off to war. You're Army! You're a part of this great big machine, so pull yourself together, okay?"

Janelle shifted to the end of the bench to make room for Emma to sit beside her. "I don't want trouble, Emma. And I want to stay in the service."

"Then take my advice, hon, and ease up with the night visits to Lance. We all have a lot of work facing us. Pilots are going to revolve through this base like visitors going through a hotel lobby. We've got to take care of the guys. Help keep up their morale. Treat them and make them well ... ready to do their part. Some will return; some won't. You know that, Janelle." Emma's words were nearly lost to the din of a fleet of P-40's churning above their heads.

"Lance wants to get married. He hasn't said anything, but I can tell."

"Is that what you want?"

"Yes," Janelle murmured.

"Are you ready to put yourself through the emotional wringer you'd be caught in when he leaves?" Emma tried to see into Janelle's eyes, but she turned her face away. "Janelle, I love you like a sister, and I'd hate to see you hurt if things don't work out as you hope. You always have such high ideals. . . ."

"I don't care! I love Lance! And if he asks me to marry him, I *will*!" Janelle rose abruptly and ran up the path, leaving Emma staring helplessly.

When Janelle entered the nurses' quarters, she slammed the door so hard one of the windows in the front of the barracks popped out. Emma was wise enough not to go in right after her.

After splashing her face with cold water, Janelle lay down on her bed. Most of the other nurses were still on duty or in classes, and the place was quiet and calm.

Janelle pressed her shoulders to the mattress to relieve the cramping below her neck. *Let her go off to Liberia if she wants to. I'm staying here with Lance, and I'll see him every chance I get. How dare Lillian Dorsey discuss me with Chief Raney? I'm going to put that meddlesome girl in her place.* Closing her eyes, Janelle lay very still, praying sleep would ease her troubled mind.

Lance assumed a resolute stance, pushing out his chest, expressing his displeasure. "You get away from here and leave me alone."

Minnie Easter sniffed, her nostrils distended on her once-pretty face. "All I'm asking for is a little help. Not much. A few dollars."

"I told you the last time I saw you to leave me alone. I'm not giving you a dime."

"The floor's rotted through in my place. Gotta move out. We ain't got a thing to eat."

"Well, I have nothing to give you. And what's put it in your head after all this time that you're entitled to anything from me?"

"Things are real tight. I can't even get enough ration stamps to get a pound of sugar, a little lard. You Army boys got it easy over here. You ain't got to worry about a thing. You could help. Times is hard. Harder than ever before."

Appalled that she had dared come out to the base to confront him, Lance inched away, as if separating himself from her unwanted presence might make her disappear.

Undaunted, Minnie stepped nearer. "I'm not here to hurt you or ask for myself. It's Al, the boy. He needs things, you know? Shoes, clothes, decent food."

Lance drew a ragged breath at the innocent child's name. Alabama Easter, the boy everyone in Congregation Hills knew to be his son. When Lance had seen him sitting on the high barrel outside the general store, he had been shocked. When had Minnie returned to town?

"I've given you money too many times, Minnie. And why is it that every time I do, you disappear. When you come back, the boy's appearance is only worse. I won't let you use me again." Lance was determined this time not to let her pile on more guilt. Didn't he have enough? Hadn't he carried this burden every day for seven years, since the afternoon Minnie had brazenly mounted the steps to Pop's house with that squirming bundle clutched to her bosom?

"Why won't you help us? You know Al is your child."

"I've never denied the possibility," Lance said, remembering how he, at the age of sixteen, had entered Minnie's cheap room. His buddies had dared him to do it. And how could he back down? So he had crawled into her much-used bed, surrendered himself to her patient, experienced hands, which had guided many of the boys of Congregation Hills into manhood. But unlike those who had come before and those who slipped in after, Lance had been the only one to father a child while nearly a child himself.

"Just because I'm in the Army now, don't figure me for a soft touch. Nothing has changed, Minnie. I will not give you money to use for gin and your partying trips over to Montgomery."

"Your grampa used to give me money when I asked," she slyly said.

"Because he knew Al *could* very well be mine."

"Wasn't nothing but the truth making him guilty," she said.

Lance snorted. "Yeah? Then why did you run away when Pop finally offered to take the child into our house? Why did you refuse Pop's offer to let us raise the boy as our kin?"

"Al is my flesh, too. What mother's gonna just let her child go?"

"A mother who has no means of support. No legal, decent means, I should add."

"That's not necessary, Lance. I never set out to hurt you."

"No? Then why did you come back to Congregation Hills, and why are you parading around Tuskegee now?"

" 'Cause I ain't got nobody else to turn to."

Lance had had it. He threw up a hand in dismissal. "Well, you'd better get down on your knees and pray to the Lord for some money, 'cause you're not getting another penny from me."

"Deacon wouldn't treat me like this."

"Don't go bothering Pop," Lance warned. "Leave him alone, you crazy woman."

"You can't tell me what to do."

Incensed, Lance raised a finger in Minnie's face. "Oh,

yes, I can. And if you don't quit harassing me and clear out of here, I'll get that MP over there to throw you out."

Minnie narrowed her eyes, scowling. "You ought to be ashamed. A fine young man like you, not willing to support his own flesh and blood." Shoving her ashen hands into a pair of black cotton gloves, she clucked her tongue. "There'll come a time when you'll change your mind. When you're old and broken and got nobody to love, you gonna remember how you tossed your only child away." She left him there, wretched, wishing there was something he could do, but knowing his money would never reach the boy. Maybe he ought to look into some legal means of gaining custody—but what would he tell Janelle?

"Lieutenant Roy?" A voice from the front of the barracks woke her.

Rubbing her eyes, Janelle sat up, immediately feeling the intensity of the headache throbbing in her temples. Working two shifts had drained her completely.

"Yes?" Janelle said to the civilian woman standing at the door.

"You've got a visitor up at communications," the messenger said matter-of-factly. Without waiting for any reply, the woman turned away, leaving to deliver the next message on her list.

After dressing quickly, Janelle hurried across the post to the huge building designated as the place where servicemen and women could greet family and friends. The banks of telephones lining the walls always had long lines of patient soldiers standing in front of them. Communications headquarters reminded Janelle of the train station in Montgomery. People hugging and kissing. Joy and sorrow. Laughter rising to the high pine rafters. Arrivals and departures all day long.

As Janelle rounded a corner, approaching the entrance to the barnlike building, she was surprised to see the same weary soul she'd seen in Congregation Hills, making her way toward the road. The little boy hustled along beside her, tugging urgently on her arm. Janelle was annoyed by the way the woman brushed and swatted at the boy as if he were no more than a buzzing, pesky mosquito she wanted out of her way.

She must have relatives working on the base, Janelle thought, remembering Deacon Fuller's comment about the number of folks from his town who now had jobs at Tuskegee.

A top-heavy old bus lumbered up to the curb, creating a huge cloud of dust. The woman and the boy got on.

Janelle shrugged, rushing through the heavy doors, entering the clamorous din that was the heart of the base. Filled with people, thick with smoke, the room vibrated with conversations and ringing telephones. At the information desk Janelle gave the attending cadet her name, then was directed to a table at the back of the room.

Before she had walked two steps, Dalton Graham's coal black hair and white skin caught her eye. In the sea of dark faces, his stood out like a blooming magnolia in a forest of pines. Elbowing her way through the crowd, knees weak with surprise, she advanced closer.

"Dalton!"

He stood, smiling, waving his hand above the crowd, a flush of excitement coloring his face.

Janelle's pounding heart drummed against her ribs. No wonder she had tried to seduce him. She could not deny it: he was one of the most handsome men she had ever encountered. But what on earth had brought him to Tuskegee? Surely he had not come this far just to see her?

"Janelle!" Dalton extended both hands. She took them. He pulled her to his chest, wrapping both arms around her waist. Impulsively he kissed her fully on the lips. The passionate kiss took Janelle completely and alarmingly by surprise.

From the other side of the bustling room Lance Fuller stared in horror. Who in the world was this white man kissing Janelle, and why would she allow him to paw her as if he had some rights? Through a haze of blue smoke,

Lance watched the embracing couple, his lips parted in disbelief.

So, that's the real deal, he thought glumly. *That's why she's always so fast to come to the defense of white people. She's got herself an ofay boyfriend in the closet and plays both sides of the game.*

Despair swept through Lance as he concluded that Janelle had been lying to him. There *was* another man in her life. He watched the two settle down on the bench, side by side, knees touching, eyes locked, still holding hands. Disgusted, Lance quickly stepped back into the shadows of an arched doorway and flattened himself against the wall. How could she have led him on? Acting so innocent. And he had been thinking of asking her to marry him. Now this?

Shame rose bitterly at the back of his throat. Sweat beaded and dripped from his temples. Closing his eyes, Lance tilted his head back, pressing it to the rough pine wall to keep from slipping to his knees. *At least I found out the truth about her before I made a damn fool of myself,* he thought, cursing himself for being so naïve.

When the churning in his stomach began to lessen, he slipped out a side door and took long, angry strides toward his barracks.

Damn her! Damn her to hell! Lance raged to himself, fighting the tears he felt pooling at the rims of his eyes. His emotions propelled him into a heated sprint, and he began running across the base, putting distance between him and the ugly sight of Janelle in that white man's arms.

Choking with exhaustion and disappointment, Lance cut between two deserted classroom buildings, then stopped, wondering when she had planned to tell him about her relationship with her white lover. Well, he wasn't going to wait around to give her the chance. He'd make a clean break with her.

He hoped the 99th got activated tonight! He was ready to go, and he never wanted to lay eyes on Janelle Roy again.

* * *

"The Keystone Company?" Janelle shrank away from Dalton, but he put a restraining hand on her arm.

"What's wrong?" His voice was surprised, concerned. "Do you know something about it?"

"Well, it's just that . . . yes, as a matter of fact, I have heard of it." Tilting her head to one side, she watched Dalton, feeling his hand pressed warmly on her wrist. How odd that he would be the one sent to challenge the man who had shattered Lance's childhood.

"An old company. Never have hired Negroes," Dalton said. "But times have changed. If John Gray expects to profit from this war, he's going to have to abide by the law."

"It might not be easy to change things around here, Dalton," Janelle cautioned.

"Settling the dispute at Burrnow Shipyards wasn't easy either, but it's amazing what can be accomplished when the threat of losing money enters the picture."

"Yeah," Janelle said. "Money. It's at the bottom of a lot of sticky issues."

"Since we're on the subject of money," Dalton said, pulling his heavy briefcase onto his lap, "there is something I've brought for you." He unbuckled the worn leather case. "The money due you from the Werner estate finally came through." He pulled out a pale blue envelope and proffered it to Janelle.

"What's this?" She was almost afraid to touch it.

"A check made out to you . . . for three thousand dollars." He grinned, pushing the envelope toward her. "Take it. It's yours."

Carefully Janelle accepted the check, staring at it as if it were a live snake wriggling in her hand. "Gosh, I had put this completely out of my mind."

"I hadn't," Dalton said. "I told you I'd stay on top of things and make sure Sara Johnson honored her sister's wishes." Closing his attaché case, he waited for Janelle's response.

"Cordelia Werner really left me all this money," Janelle murmured, turning the check over, examining it closely.

"And there's more to come," Dalton reminded her.

"I swear I had convinced myself that I'd never see a penny." Janelle shook her head in amazement. "She really was a nice old lady, you know? I used to feel sorry for her. She was in so much pain, so alone . . . bullied and dominated by Sara Johnson. It seems like a million years ago, working in that house."

"A lot has happened to you since that morning, huh?"

"Really." Janelle absently ran her index finger over the check. "But joining the Army was, without a doubt, the smartest thing I have ever done."

"I'm glad to hear you say that, Janelle. I worried about you after you left."

"Worried? About me? Why? Did you think I couldn't take care of myself?"

"No," Dalton replied with a grin. "Not at all. I just worried that you'd find life in the South . . . in an isolated place like this, pretty hard to take."

"It *was* difficult at first," Janelle said. "Adjusting to the military way of doing things, the long hours in class. Flight training was the worst! I was scared to death to go up in the plane. Only one of the nurses here had ever flown before. It's been quite an experience, believe me."

"So now you're an old pro?"

"I wouldn't say that, but I'm definitely over my fear of heights."

"Do you like military nursing?"

"Yes. The guys on the base are so appreciative; they're genuinely glad we're here. It's been an eye-opener for me because I've never felt needed, wanted, so vital to my patients. Before this nursing was just a job, a way to make money." Pride enriched her voice. "I've grown up a lot in the short time I've been here, Dalton. Now I think I understand why you do the work you do."

"Good for you." Dalton blushed pink, seemingly embarrassed by Janelle's praise. Clearing his throat, he abruptly changed the subject. "Better put that money in the bank."

"Oh, I plan to," she said. "I'll get into Montgomery and open an account as soon as possible."

"Please do. It took too much work to get my hands on it. Don't let anything happen."

Janelle gave him an indulgent smile. "Don't worry. As soon as I can get away, I'll go straight to the bank and deposit it." She folded the check in half and slipped it into the breast pocket of her uniform.

"What have you heard from Perry?" Dalton asked.

"Not much," Janelle replied, wishing she could shake the feeling that something was terribly wrong.

"He's called me twice," Dalton said.

"Then you know more than I do. I've received only one letter not too long after I got here." Janelle felt a familiar loneliness begin to settle in. She missed Perry, wished he would stay in touch, but knew they still had a long way to go to bring their relationship back to the way it used to be. If only they hadn't allowed their own stubborn ways to create such an emotional gulf.

"He did tell me about the stint in the stockade," Janelle said. "What a mess! Do you think he's settled down?"

Dalton thought for a moment before answering. "That's hard to say. I know he has a change of assignment. He's out of the Signal Corps, pulling guard duty."

"Guard duty? What is he guarding?"

"German prisoners of war," Dalton said.

"At Camp Livingston?"

"Yeah. Like a lot of the camps in the South. No place to hold the Jerries overseas, and according to Perry, they don't seem unhappy at all. In fact, they are delighted to be in the United States. They're being treated royally: good food, new clothes, decent housing. Even working for wages. Eighty cents a day."

"Really? That's hard to believe."

"Right. A lot of people don't like it, including your brother."

"I can imagine." Janelle began to worry in earnest. Perry guarding white men? The enemy? Sounded like a powder keg of a situation to her. "I don't think Perry's cut out for an assignment like that. He's got the temperament of a fast-burning firecracker. Why in the world would he be put in charge of German prisoners?"

"From what I understand, POW guard duty is pretty grim. Those who get it are not exactly the best men the Army has to offer. Usually the guards are men who have been in some kind of trouble or have a reason not to be going into combat. I doubt the intellectual types are put in charge. If Perry keeps his mouth shut and follows orders, he'll make out okay. All the government wants to do is honor the Geneva Convention, hold on to the Germans until this mess is over, then ship 'em back home as soon as possible."

"We'll see," Janelle murmured, still uneasy about this development. Why hadn't Perry written to her? Why did she have to get such news secondhand? She'd write him tonight, let him know she was concerned, and try to do a better job of staying in touch. "Enough about Perry!" She abruptly closed the subject, putting her brother's problems to the back of her mind.

Dalton turned his attention more fully on Janelle. "Yes. Tell me what's going on with you? Perry said your mother left Columbus?"

"Yes. She's in California with my aunt. Happy, it seems. We manage to stay in touch. I'd love to get out there if I could get a furlough."

"You must be happy," Dalton said. "You look great. As beautiful as ever."

Shaking her head, she wondered how to take the compliment. "I'm very busy working. If you'd seen me a few hours ago, I'm not sure you'd have called me beautiful. I just came off a double shift. The Ninety-ninth is about to be activated. They're headed to North Africa. Things are pretty tense around here."

Dalton took off his trench coat, draping it over the back

of the bench. "The Ninety-ninth is finally going to enter combat? Good. There will be colored pilots in the fight now. These guys have damn near trained themselves to death. It's about time something gave. They've been under a microscope since the day the base opened. I'm glad they're finally going to see some action. Just wait. The Ninety-ninth will prove all the critics wrong."

Janelle could not help laughing. "I see you're still the eternal optimist."

"You bet. It's a habit that's hard to kick. Picked it up when I was a boy." He reached out to finger a stray wisp of Janelle's dark brown hair. "There's so much I want to talk to you about." His voice became serious, intimate.

A wave of uncertainty charged through Janelle. What was Dalton doing, touching her as if he still had romantic feelings? Kissing her with such inappropriate passion? Surely he didn't expect her just to pick up where they'd left off. Puzzled, Janelle drew back her shoulders, gathering her courage. "Yes, there is a lot to talk about. Let me go first."

"Shoot."

"I'm in love!" she blurted in a joyful rush, carefully watching the flicker of surprise that darted over Dalton's face.

"In love?" He sounded slightly hoarse, uncertain.

"Yes! Aren't you happy for me?"

Dalton slowly nodded, shock draining the color from his face.

"Dalton, you were absolutely right. But you always seem to be right! I've met the most wonderful man. A pilot. First Lieutenant Lance Fuller. He's gentle and handsome and smart and talented."

"Whoa." Dalton laughed nervously. "Sounds like just the type of man I would have ordered up for you."

"He is. Oh, Dalton, he really is. But I'm scared to death the war is going to take him. He flies with the Ninety-ninth Squadron."

Dalton willed his disappointment into submission. He

had waited too long. Now he'd lost her. Just as he'd lost Tahti.

Cautiously inhaling to garner control, he felt himself suffocating. Janelle was in love. She was happy! And he had been the one to drive her away.

"Remember what I told you in Columbus, Janelle." His voice was thin. "Stay positive, believe in your own strength, and everything will work out as it's supposed to." Looking at her, he noticed a sadness playing around the corners of her eyes, a worry line creasing her forehead. "Don't waste time getting caught up in trying to predict the future. If you've found someone to love, make the most of the time you've got."

Janelle crossed, then uncrossed her ankles, shifting back and forth on the bench. "That's hard to do around here. Regulations, extra duty, pressure from all sides." She put both hands on her knees, leaning forward as she gazed across the room. "Why now, Dalton? Why did I have to meet the man I want to share my life with just when he's about to be sent halfway around the world . . . to dodge bullets and bombs from enemy planes?" She swung around to face him. "I can't lose Lance, Dalton. I don't think I'd survive it. He is everything to me. Everything!"

The fear in her voice pained Dalton. "Don't worry, Janelle," he said. "You'll survive. He'll return. Trust me. Your sweetheart *will* come back to you." Letting his voice trail off, he brushed her cheek with one finger. "Your pilot would be a fool to do something stupid like get himself killed and leave you behind for some other man to love. Believe me, he'll make it back."

A forced smile came to her lips. "I'm so glad you're going to be around here for a while." Dalton's unsettling blue-gray eyes tugged at her. "You always know the right thing to say and how to say it. Thank you for being such a good friend."

The noise in the room swelled, filling an edgy silence. "I wish I could get away and take you into town, but

Chief Raney has called an emergency meeting at sixteen hundred hours. All the nurses are required to be there."

"That's okay. Don't worry." He seemed relieved she couldn't make it. "I think I can find the Atlas Hotel. On the square, right?"

Janelle laughed. "You can't miss it. The town of Tuskegee is really very small. Everything centers on the square. The hotel is across the street from the courthouse."

"Any idea where I might get access to a car?"

"Afraid not. You're on your own on that one."

She walked with him until they reached the front gates, where several buses idled, spewing exhaust fumes at the curb. When the bus driver shifted into gear and gunned the engine, Dalton hurried forward.

"I've got to go!" He turned back and hugged Janelle, smothering her against his shoulder. Placing one hand atop her soft, coiffed hair, he murmured, "Remember, I'm only a few miles away. Keep in touch. Let me know what's going on."

"I will," she said, letting him go, stepping back from the curb to watch him board the crowded bus. She remained staring after Dalton, already missing him, feeling oddly as if she had hurt him. Janelle didn't move until the top-heavy vehicle disappeared through the guarded gates of the base.

Exhaustion pulled at her shoulders. Her mind went foggy with worry. She needed to talk to Lance.

Making her way across the base toward the barracks, Janelle began calculating how long the meeting might last. Despite Emma's stern warning, she would be at the airfield to meet Lance at eighteen hundred hours in the grove of weeping willows that bordered the edge of the eastern runway.

CHAPTER
TWENTY-FIVE

The fact that the meeting was held in the nurses' day-room instead of the barracks meant something official was about to be announced. When Janelle entered, she saw all the nurses sitting solemnly in thought, yet no one seemed to be frightened or worried. The women appeared preoccupied, as if great decisions had to be made.

Raney is going to tell us about the task force to Liberia, Janelle surmised, wondering how many of her unit would be going.

Slipping down into a chair next to Emma, Janelle felt the sense of foreboding that hung in the room like layers of thick smoke.

The grim silence persisted until Chief Nurse Raney entered and put them all at ease. "Ladies, I come to you with an opportunity for you to serve your country on foreign soil. This is a rare opportunity for colored military personnel, and I am honored to let you know our government is asking us to take on this difficult assignment."

Clearing her throat, Lieutenant Raney swept the group with pride-filled eyes. "For several months now the Second Cavalry Division—a unit of Negro engineers and service troops—has been working in Liberia to establish air bases. They also patrol the coastal areas for signs of Axis activities. They are building roads, creating sanitary facilities, preparing for the eventual arrival of more support for the North African campaign. The Liberian government has signed agreements giving us control over its air bases and all military installations. As you can imagine, our boys in Monrovia are coming down with malaria and typhoid. Many are seriously ill from the assault of driver ants, which have been known to kill men and animals in very little time. There are a variety of other tropical infirmities our boys have to deal with that require immediate care. Quinine is now more valuable than gold."

Janelle stole a glance at Emma. What was going through her mind? Would she really go to Africa? She remembered the night she'd made Emma promise she'd never desert her if she agreed to join up.

Lieutenant Raney continued. "I've just received official notice that the War Department is recruiting colored medical personnel to serve in Monrovia, to support the Liberia task force."

Lillian Dorsey motioned to the chief.

"Nurse Dorsey? You have a question?"

"Yes. What would the tour of duty be? How long will the nurses be in Africa?"

"Indefinitely. Until we're no longer needed or the war ends."

Emma was next. "Yes, Lieutenant Brown?"

"How many will be going?"

"Only thirty nurses, nine doctors. This recruitment is going on at each Negro Army nursing unit in the States."

"How soon would the nurses embark?" Jane Miller, a nurse from West Virginia, wanted to know.

"Immediately," Chief Raney said. "As soon as the unit is fully staffed and outfitted for tropical service."

"Will you be in command of the unit?" Emma asked.

Now Chief Raney softened. "No. First Lieutenant Susan Freeman, of Fort Huachuca, Arizona, will lead this overseas unit of colored nurses. This is a historic move. Never before have Negro nurses served on foreign soil. And I must tell you, those who go will be serving under one of the best military nurses in the United States Army."

Janelle pulled in her bottom lip and bit down hard.

Maybe it would be the patriotic thing to do, volunteer for service in Africa, but she couldn't imagine leaving now. Lance might ship out any day. And if the 99th didn't sail, they could be together until the end of the war. No, it was better if she stayed put. There were plenty of soldiers at the air base who needed her, too.

"Sign me up!" Lillian Dorsey called out, obviously ready to pack her bags. "I'll go!"

Great, Janelle thought. *At least she'll be out of my hair.*

"Thanks, Lieutenant Dorsey. Any others who are interested must let me know within forty-eight hours. Tomorrow I will begin personally to interview and recommend the nurses I deem suitable for this assignment. Service records and medical histories will also be checked. Remember, there are only thirty openings for this unit, and I want some of my girls from Tuskegee to be on that ship when it sails."

The meeting broke up quickly after Chief Raney left the room. Everyone began talking at once.

"I'll go. Anything's better than sticking around this Jim Crow place. At least in Africa I'll be in the majority."

"Not me. I have no desire to step off U.S. soil. Not unless I have to, that is."

"Sounds exotic to me. Exciting! Can you imagine sailing all the way to Africa?"

"Yeah. Just like going home."

"Maybe *your* home, not mine. I was born and raised in Brooklyn, New York, and I plan to get back there when all this is over."

"Well, I can just imagine the size of the mosquitoes that will greet you guys as soon as you set foot onshore."

"I hope I get chosen."

"I do, too. 'Cause if they don't get enough volunteers, we may get drafted."

Janelle pulled Emma aside. "Are you going to sign up?"

Rubbing her hands together, Emma answered lowly, "Yes. I want to go."

"Oh, Emma. Please—"

"Don't, Janelle." Emma let out an exasperated sigh. "I think it would be the best thing for me to do. I would like to serve the troops in Africa."

"The guys here need you, too."

"Yeah, but I can easily be replaced. Chief Raney told me there are more than one hundred fifty colored nurses now commissioned in the Army. The waiting list of those who want to serve here is probably longer than my arm. If I go, I'll create an opening for some other nurse."

"Maybe," Janelle conceded. "But when I joined the Army Nurse Corps, I did it to serve our boys here at home. Going off to Africa is not what I had planned to do."

"So it's not for you. Okay. But it may be exactly what I need to get Kenneth out of my system. Out of my mind."

Touched by the anguish on Emma's face, Janelle held her breath. "You can get over Kenneth without going so far away."

"Maybe so." Emma sounded miserable. "It's been weeks. And what do I know? Nothing more than I did the day I opened his letter. He won't accept my calls. It's as if he dropped into a crevice and disappeared. I want to get away from here. I came to be near Kenneth. Well, he's not coming. And now that you're so involved with Lance . . . What do I have to lose?"

"So go," Janelle said softly, who was frightened at the prospect of Emma's disappearance from her life.

The war had pushed everything familiar into hopeless disarray. Her mother now lived in California. Perry was suffering in Louisiana. Dalton was about to go up against one of the most blatant racists in Macon County. And what about Lance? His days at Tuskegee were counting down. In a panic she wondered why Emma had to leave her, too.

After gathering up her purse, Janelle went to the door, leaving Emma standing in the center of the room. She had to get out of the dayroom, away from all the chatter about shipping out, leaving town. Without saying good-bye,

Janelle left the building. It was too painfully difficult to try to sort out now.

Shadows had already begun to settle over the sprawling, restless base. Janelle checked her watch. There was not much time to meet Lance at the willow grove beside the bomber runway and still make it back to the barracks before lights out.

Lieutenant Colonel Benjamin O. Davis, Jr., assumed his most official West Point posture and leveled his high-bridged nose above his squadron. One of the original thirteen cadets in Tuskegee's first preflight class, the son of Brigadier General B. O. David, Sr., he had moved so quickly from student officer to captain to lieutenant colonel he had skipped the honor of wearing his major's oak leaves. Now he and his father bore the honorable distinction of being the only Negro line officers in the United States Army.

"Men," Colonel Davis said, "the waiting game is just about over. I know you feel as if you've trained and retrained in every phase of combat tactics and are getting pretty damn sick of all this waiting. Many of you finished your training in July and are anxious to move on. Tonight I can say that the time of departure is drawing very near."

The cheer that rose up was loud, spirited, echoing relief. The 99th would enter the fight!

Colonel Davis continued. "As we await final embarkation orders, you will be expected to absorb every bit of knowledge there is left for you to grasp about aerial combat, formation flying, night flying, radio communication, and radar. Where you are going you will need every one of these skills."

Lance could barely keep from screaming aloud. Soon he'd be right in the thick of it, just as the white boys had been for months. Within weeks he'd have his chance to shoot down a Focke-Wulf or two, and nothing would make him happier. Grinning at Colonel Davis, thankful his prayers had been answered, Lance pressed his perspiring, fidgety fingers together. Getting out of Tuskegee as soon as possible was exactly what he wanted to do.

Colonel Davis's words faded as Lance thought of his disastrous morning. Minnie Easter would not stop pressuring him for money. If he had thought she would use the money to improve Al's life, he'd have gladly given her all he could. But he knew she wanted money to support that filthy cathouse she stayed in most of the time. He ought to place an anonymous call to the sheriff and get that hellhole shut down.

Poor Alabama! Who was he really? A pitiful child with no future, no roots. Lance doubted Al had ever lived in a real house—with furniture and running water and curtains at the windows. He'd probably never eaten a meal at a dining room table or entered a schoolhouse door. Any child deserved better than that.

And Janelle! His heart contracted. What God-awful demon had entered his head and made him think she would love him? He should have known it would blow up in his face. He'd really set himself up for this one!

A white lover! Lance fumed, his flesh shrinking tighter around his jaw as visions of Janelle in the other man's arms mocked him unmercifully. A groan escaped his lips, and he ground his teeth together. He'd break off with her before she did it to him, because as far as he was concerned, Janelle was dead. Gone. Out of his life.

In fact, it felt good not to have to concern himself with leaving her behind. The future stretched out: a great black slate. Who knew what might be written on it? All he wanted to do was climb into his plane, soar off into the sky, knock off a bunch of Germans, and be finished with this war.

Like an echo, the colonel's remarks continued. "The reporters won't be calling you the lonely eagles anymore. You are not destined to fly alone. We're entering the fight, boys, and we're ready. Really ready! I know you are going to do a fine job. . . . You've been preparing for too damn long not to!"

A wave of optimism undulated through the group. Leaning forward, hanging on the precious words that testified to their readiness, their manhood, their usefulness in this fight, the men of the 99th Fighter Squadron waited to hear exactly where they were headed.

Lance tensed when he heard "New York." If they were headed to New York, it would be to board a troop transport ship. This was really happening!

Lance could not concentrate on the colonel's words. He might never see Janelle again. Was that really what he wanted? Could he leave Tuskegee and not tell her goodbye?

The colonel went on, but his words no longer reached Lance, who was thinking of Janelle waiting for him at the grove of weeping willows. She was there, he knew; she was always on time. What use was there in going to meet her? The squadron had its destination. They were finally shipping out!

Colonel Parrish, who had been in charge of training the 99th from the beginning, added his words of support. "You are fighting men now. You have made the team. Your future is now being handed into your own hands. No one knows what you will do with it; you yourself do not know. Your performance, good or bad, will depend largely on how determined you are not to give satisfaction to those who would like to see you fail."

Colonel Davis concluded: "The information about our move should be kept confidential for now. The communication has come through, but not the official word to ship out. So keep a lid on it, men. As soon as I get orders, you'll know."

"It's about time! Let's get on with it."

"All right, men. Another thing: All furloughs are canceled. One-day passes will be granted at a minimum and can be pulled at any time. I know that's difficult for those of you who have families far from here. But those are the orders. From now on we stand ready to leave on a moment's notice. Understood?"

All the men responded, "Yes, sir!"

"Good. Dismissed."

The excited pilots stood stiffly at attention until their leader left. Then all hell broke loose in the barracks.

"Who's got a car?"

"Let's go to the Propeller Club and celebrate!"

"Yeah, you heard the colonel, furloughs are out. Better grab tonight to tie one on."

Lance glanced at his watch. Janelle was waiting for him. Maybe he should go meet her, confront her, let her know how much he detested the way she'd two-timed him.

"Fuller! You still got access to that big old clunker you been driving 'round the countryside?"

Jolted from his thoughts, Lance jerked up. "Yeah. I can get it. Why?"

" 'Cause you're gonna drive us into Montgomery and we're gonna raise the roof."

Lance hesitated for a second, then snatched his cap from the top shelf above his bunk and pulled it down rakishly over one eye. "You've got it. Let's go. I'm driving, but I'm not buying," he said jokingly, his words coming out much louder than he'd expected. "Who's got enough cash to set up the bar?"

"Hell, when Jimmy hears the Ninety-ninth is about to ship out, he ain't gonna charge us nothing. Wait and see if the house don't pay for this send-off."

Grabbing his Eisenhower jacket, Lance slapped the pilot standing next to him on the back. "All right, you slobs. This is it! Let's get the hell out of here!"

Pacing back and forth beneath the weeping willows, Janelle frantically checked her watch. Seven-thirty. This morning on the phone they had agreed to meet at seven, as soon as the squadron flyby was over.

Funny, she thought, eyeing the sheet of black sky spreading out overhead, there hadn't been a plane up there all evening. The atmosphere was eerily calm. Usually pilots were swooping and darting at all hours, preparing for night flights overseas.

A bunch of bats fluttered up from the trees. Startled, Janelle lifted her eyes, half expecting to see the pinpoint dot of a P-40 overhead. But the sky above the runway stretched out in a silent canopy draped in rolling dark clouds.

Why had night-flying maneuvers come to an end? How odd, Janelle thought. What was going on? The bright flare of the huge biscuit guns that usually flashed signals to the pilots was dark.

Something had changed. Janelle paced the grove, her eyes straining into the shadows surrounding the runway. Suddenly, a jeep pulled alongside the deserted runway. Its headlights cut through the black air, illuminating the trunks of the tall, graceful trees. Janelle shielded her face, clenched her hand into a fist, and tried to think. Were the pilots getting their orders to ship out? Racing from beneath the low-hanging branches, Janelle cut out across an open field, heading straight for barracks 54.

At the path curving off toward the men's quarters, Janelle was met by a burly military policeman. He saluted, then said, "This area's been closed for the rest of the night, Lieutenant."

"Why? What's going on?" Something *had* happened!

"Well, it ain't exactly official yet, but the scoop is our boys are getting ready to ship out, that's what." He grinned widely, his big white teeth illuminated by the moonlight.

"When?" she asked weakly, her voice a whisper.

"Well, not tonight exactly—but soon. Colonel Davis put the squad on alert." He seemed proud to be privy to such confidential information.

"I need to get a message to barracks fifty-four. Please. I've got to talk to Lieutenant Fuller."

The MP curled back his lips. "Lieutenant Fuller, you say?"

She nodded. "Can you give a message to the lieutenant? It's very important I speak with him."

"I'll bet it is . . . but you just missed him, Lieutenant. He and almost all of the squad went over to Montgomery. The Propeller Club, I'm sure. Probably be late getting back. Real late. You'd better head on back to your quarters."

Far into the night, when the only sound in the barracks was the familiar snarl of Wilma Harris's snoring, Janelle lay awake wondering what had happened.

How could Lance take off for Montgomery to get drunk with the guys and leave her waiting for him? Such nerve! How dare he treat her like all the other girls he had romanced, then shoved aside?

Janelle jerked her scratchy Army blanket over her shoulder and flipped onto her side. Partying in Montgomery while she was left to worry and wait! Maybe Lillian Dorsey had pegged Lance Fuller right! His behavior was unforgivable.

Blinking back tears, Janelle tried to muffle her sobs against the backs of her hands, tried to quiet the small voice that persisted in her mind. Lance Fuller had deliberately dazzled her with his charm. She had set her expectations entirely too high. After all, how much could a man who was raised in a shanty in the backwoods of Alabama really know about how to treat a lady?

CHAPTER
TWENTY-SIX

The train began to slow, gliding toward the brightly lit station before abruptly jolting to a stop. With a deafening screech of grinding wheels and straining brakes, the lumbering iron beast announced its arrival at Alexandria.

Clutching his Garand rifle to his side, Perry Roy looked around the crowded coach, resentfully assessing the prisoners under his guard. Sitting smugly in their passenger seats, the Germans marveled that the Americans would transport them in such luxury.

While riding the trains, the Germans appeared docile, harmless, just like ordinary men, but Perry never forgot they were the enemy—a cog displaced from the grinding Axis machine that was gnawing a path across North Africa and Europe. He wasn't about to forget why they were now on American soil.

Though the Allies had successfully pushed Rommel back to the sea, the victory had saddled them with thousands of enemy soldiers. The British prison camps were already overloaded. American soldiers were needed at the front. So Churchill and Roosevelt had struck an agreement: The captured Jerries would be shipped to America on troopships that otherwise would have made the return crossing with empty berths. Camps to hold the POWs were quickly constructed across the nation.

Now we've got to feed and house and take care of the lousy bastards, Perry thought, letting his eyes flit over the sixty-eight German prisoners of war in his charge. In their U.S. military-issue clothing, they almost looked human again—a dramatic change from the skeletal, ragtag, vermin-infested lot that had first arrived at Camp Livingston.

Perry had been assigned to the prisoner processing center, searching the POWs for knives, guns, and any potentially dangerous objects that might be used to attack the guards.

Working the shower detail had been the worst—herding frightened naked men under disinfectant hoses. Then he had to prod them through fingerprinting, photographing, and an attempt to set up records.

Now Perry fumed, wishing Captain Lord hadn't decided to stop and feed the prisoners tonight. After an exhausting day guarding the timber-cutting detail, Perry wanted to get back to camp.

Perry made his way toward the exit at the back of the car. As soon as the doors opened, he jumped to the ground, circled the train, and scaled the sooty, grimy side until he reached the top. There he anchored his long-barreled rifle on his hip, aiming it down over the stream of German prisoners spilling out of the passenger cars.

"Single file!" he ordered, knowing they knew what that meant. He'd been herding this same work detail up and down the track between Camp Livingston and Camp Beauregard for twelve days now, and every time the men got off the train, they obstinately gathered into groups, feigning confusion.

"Single file! Break it up!" he yelled at a cluster of men standing on a grassy area near the depot entrance. Carefully scanning the sea of blue denim, he searched for signs of weapons. This week he'd uncovered two knives, a handful of homemade metal files, and five crudely fashioned billy sticks whittled from wood found along the road. Anything could happen at any time.

Several days before, a prisoner had slugged a guard and fled into the woods, where he got mired down in a bog.

The man was easily captured and returned to the camp. The stupid fool! Thinking of it now, Perry smirked with disgust. All this damn trouble and expense to take care of the enemy. If he'd been on duty, he'd have left the Jerry in the murky water for the alligators to feed on.

Captain Richey Lord, the commander of the wood-cutting crew, barked orders as he swaggered along the platform. The prisoners hurried from the train, up a patterned brick walkway, passing beneath a sign that said WHITES ONLY as they entered the tiny depot. Most of them were smiling, anticipating the hot food they would be served at the dime-size café tucked into a corner of the railway station.

As soon as the train was empty, Captain Lord and the white guards followed the prisoners inside. The three colored guards, including Perry, would have to dine outside, on C rations—canned meat and biscuits—if they ate anything at all.

Perry hated this layover on the way back to Camp Livingston. He hated it most when the Germans got back on the train, laughing, belching, praising American food. They found it fitting and proper that the blacks were kept outside while they dined on beef and apple pie. After all, they were white, weren't they?

Perry and the other colored guards had to stand by in silence, playing deaf, letting the Germans' taunts wash over them, as if they didn't know what was said, as if they didn't care. Just thinking about it now made Perry burn with rage that such injustice could be flaunted in his face—by the enemy! *A hell of a way for the United States government to treat its own,* he thought.

"Hey. You. Get inside!" Perry hollered down at one prisoner who had hung back from the group. Perry recognized him as a troublemaker who insisted on making pro-Nazi speeches despite the fact that such actions were strictly prohibited. He'd gotten four days in the guardhouse for it, but the punishment had not broken his vocal loyalty to the Reich.

Lowering his gun on the prisoner, Perry shouted one more time. "You. Move on! Get inside."

The German looked up, raised a fist in Perry's direction and yelled back, *"Nein! Neger!"*

Under his breath Perry muttered, "You rotten bastard kraut, don't you give me any trouble. I'd like to splatter your brains all over this train station." He waved his gun in the direction of the depot and yelled, "Inside!"

The prisoner spit on the ground and shook his fist at Perry, who stiffened, raising his rifle. Training the barrel on the defiant German, he threatened, "Get going! Now!"

When the prisoner shouted, *"Nein! Neger! Schmutziger Neger!"* Perry fired.

The exploding round seemed to echo from afar, as if the shot had not come from his rifle but had burst from the thick, lush interior of the forest like a startled covey of geese. As the hollow roar faded out over the land, Perry stiffened.

The prisoner collapsed on the ground. Perry stood locked in firing position, eye still trained through the sight.

What's he doing? Playing dead? Perry thought, waiting for the heap of crumpled blue denim to get up and laugh in his face.

"Get up, you crazy kraut!" Perry yelled at the man. When nothing happened, he knew it was no joke. How could he have hit him? He'd aimed above the man's head. He'd meant only to scare the sucker. *Get up, you lousy bastard. Get up!*

Captain Lord burst out of the depot, his Colt .45 in his hand. "What the hell is going on out here?" He stopped at the bleeding form at his feet, squinting up at Perry.

"Private Roy! How did this happen?" he shouted above the clatter of an oncoming train.

My God, I've killed him! Perry took in the grim scene spread out on the ground. A stream of perspiration dripped between his shoulder blades, fusing his stiff khaki shirt to his back. Before his eyes, an ugly dark red pool of blood slowly expanded beneath the prisoner's head. Perry eased in a deep, controlled breath, trying not to panic.

Oh, shit! I've killed a German prisoner of war! What the hell? He tossed his Garand to the ground as if he were surrendering. The heavy weapon thudded to the red clay clearing, inches from Captain Lord's boots.

"Private Roy! You get down here! Now!"

The train vibrated as an oncoming locomotive raced toward the Alexandria depot.

"You get down off that train. Now!" Captain Lord screamed above the tinny whistle shrilling in the distance. "That's an order, Private Roy! Do you understand?"

Perry remained gaping, terrified, as more guards rushed outside to see what was going on. Through a tight, clammy throat, he hoarsely screamed at Captain Lord, "All right. I'm coming down!" But his words were lost to the noise of the train streaking behind him into the station. He knew it would be the Crescent Coast Express. It always sped through Alexandria at this time, but it wouldn't stop, not until it reached Natchez, Mississippi.

Stepping back from the edge, Perry moved his head up and down in a jerky nod, indicating he understood the captain's orders. But as soon as the passing train pulled alongside, Perry turned his back on the stunned captain and leaped across the narrow strip of black space that separated one train from the other.

With a flat, dull thud, he landed on his side, and the excruciating pain that flashed up his leg, across his groin, into his chest seemed to slice his body in half.

Slumping onto his back, Perry vowed, *I can't go back to the stockade. Not for this. If I have to leave this country to be treated like a man, I will. But I won't face a firing squad for killing a kraut.*

The telephone rang at five forty-five, interrupting the restless stream of disjointed thoughts that had plagued Janelle for hours. She lay still, praying the call would be from Lance.

"Roy! Telephone." Jane Miller set the handpiece down on the table and jumped back into her bed, snuggling down under the covers to savor the fifteen minutes before reveille.

Oh, please, God. It must be Lance! Janelle grabbed her robe and hurried to the far end of the barracks. She snatched up the phone and pressed it to her ear.

"Yes?"

"Is this Lieutenant Janelle Roy?"

"Yes, this is she." Well, it certainly wasn't Lance. Spiraling panic began its awful coil.

"This is Commander Herbert Young, Camp Livingston, Louisiana."

"Yes?" She forced herself to remain calm. Surely this call had to do with Perry.

"Have you heard from your brother, Private Perry Roy?"

"No—not for several weeks. Is anything wrong?"

"Yes." There was a pause. "Private Roy went AWOL last night."

"AWOL? What do you mean?"

"You're in the United States Army, Lieutenant," Commander Young said gruffly. "I'm certain you know what AWOL means. Your brother is in a great deal of trouble."

Closing her eyes, Janelle slumped down on a nearby chair. He'd run away?

"Please tell me what happened."

"He shot a German prisoner under his protection. Witnesses say he was not provoked and was not in any danger. He hopped a train headed east. We thought he might be going to see you."

"Oh, I—I don't think he'd come to me."

"No? Why not?"

"We haven't been very close . . . lately, I mean." She struggled to put it in the right words. "I doubt Perry would even want me to know what he's done." How awful that sounded, having to admit that her brother, her flesh and blood, did not trust her enough to confide in her at a desperate time like this.

"A search is under way for Private Roy. We will find him, I assure you."

Janelle listened, unable to say a word.

"If he contacts you, Lieutenant Roy, I expect you to let the authorities know. Immediately."

"Yes," she murmured, knowing the seriousness of the situation. "Yes. I understand, Commander."

"Good. I was unable to reach your mother. Can you tell me where she is? Private Roy may contact her."

"My mother is in transit to California," she lied, not wanting her mother to get news of this catastrophe from some stranger calling her in the middle of the night. "I don't have an address for her now."

"Well, when you get it, call me. Camp Livingston, CL-eight-eight-zero-zero."

"Yes. Of course. I'll do whatever I can to help."

"I would expect so, Lieutenant. Your brother is wanted for murder. It's tense enough around here without something like this to contend with. I'm going to clear this damn mess up in record time. Don't try to protect Private Roy if he comes to you. It's gone too far."

"Yes, sir," Janelle said lowly, feeling slightly sick as the telephone line went dead in her hand.

By midday Janelle was a bundle of raw nerves. Emma, who was undergoing her interview for the Africa unit, was not around to confide in. Janelle suffered in silence, her misery gnawing away at her resolve to stay strong, hold herself together until she finished her shift. As she moved through the crowded ward, it was difficult to concentrate on her patients. Perry had killed a German prisoner of war! Why? And where was he now?

Perhaps she could have been more help to Perry. If she had written him more faithfully, called him now and then, shown more interest in his military life, could she have helped him accept his lot? Guilt eased its heavy yoke onto

Janelle's slender shoulders, pressing her close to tears off and on throughout the day.

By the end of her shift Janelle had come to one conclusion: Perry's predicament was out of her hands, but as soon as she got back to her quarters, she would telephone Lance and have it out with him.

If he wants to call off our relationship, he has every right to do so, but I'll be damned if he unloads me the way Kenneth dumped Emma. Lance Fuller is going to have to tell me himself that he no longer wants me in his life.

Back in the nurses' quarters, Janelle dialed the number to barracks 54. She asked for Lieutenant Fuller.

Lance came to the phone, his heart thumping against his chest.

"Lance. It's Janelle."

"Hello." He heard his own voice, flat and toneless like the response of an uninterested stranger.

"I—I waited for you at the willow grove last night."

"Oh, yeah." He hesitated, tortured by the unnerving image of Janelle in that white man's arms. Oh, God, why did she have to call? He didn't want to discuss it. "Sorry about last night. I got a little tied up."

"So I heard." Janelle's voice was flinty.

"What did you hear?"

"That you're shipping out, that you went out to celebrate." She ran the words together.

"Where'd you hear that? It's supposed to be confidential. Anyway, no orders have come through," he said crisply, letting her know he didn't want to talk.

"Well, everyone in Tuskegee knows what's happening."

"Yeah? Good. It's time the Ninety-ninth got into this fight."

Janelle plunged ahead. "How soon do you think you will leave?"

"I don't know. Tomorrow. The day after. We're on alert. No furloughs. Final overnight passes were granted today." What he really wanted to tell her was to meet him at Wild Embers one last time, but he didn't have the guts.

"Lance?" Janelle said.

"Yes?" He was holding the telephone so fiercely his fingers began to go numb.

"Is it over? Is that what's going on?"

"What are you getting at?" he asked, dreading a confrontation.

"Don't be cruel, Lance. Just tell me what's going on."

He heard a quaver threading her voice.

"All right." He readied himself to be done with it. "I was surprised to learn you crossed over."

"Crossed over. What's that mean?"

"I know about your white boyfriend. I saw you two together in the communications room yesterday."

"Oh."

She sounded amused. He couldn't believe it.

"You mean Dalton. He's nothing to me."

Now Lance was really annoyed. "Several of the guys in the squad saw you, too."

"Oh, so you had me to bat around at your drunken party last night?"

Lance felt more wretched with each word. "No, I'd never let that happen, but I can't keep people from saying what they want ... sure made me feel like ... I'd better not say what's on my mind."

"Maybe you'd better!"

"All right. I don't like being two-timed and especially with a white boy. You could have been honest about it. We still could have had a good time."

"That's what I've been to you? A good time?"

"You know what I mean," he said.

"No, I don't." The line hummed with silence. "Dalton Graham is the attorney from Columbus who helped me out of a jam. He's a friend. I told you about him ... that situation with my patient who died."

"Yeah, you did. But I don't remember you telling me that you and your lawyer were that personal. Shit, Janelle. I saw the way he kissed you. You kissed him back. That was a hell of a lot more than a friendly hello."

"Oh, Lance, listen to me. Everything is so crazy. Let me explain."

"I gotta go. I don't want to talk about this."

"We have to talk!"

"You take care of yourself. Okay? It's not a good idea for us to see each other again. Let's say good-bye now. Let everything drop, all right?"

"No! It's not all right!" she cried, her voice breaking with tears. "I love you. You love me. I know you do. Why are you throwing away everything we have? What about the future we talked about? Loving each other forever. What happened to your promises, Lance? What has happened to you?"

"Don't ask. Please, Janelle. And don't cry. Please. I'm leaving."

"Maybe not. The Ninety-ninth has been put on alert before. Nothing happened."

"I don't think this is a false alert. We're packing gear." He shuddered, his tangled emotions unraveling.

"This is an awful way to say good-bye, Lance. You'll come back. *You will!* And what then? Don't you want me here waiting for you?"

"No. That wouldn't be fair. Go on with your life and take care of yourself. Forget about me. I'll be fine."

"Maybe you will! But I won't!" Furious, she hurled the words at him.

"I didn't mean it that way." The less he said, the better, he decided. This was too damn hard to keep up.

"Well, what in God's name *do* you mean? You make love to me one night, ignore me the next. Then you accuse me of stringing you along? That's a hell of a way to treat a woman you pledged your undying love to just a few days ago. Or have you already forgotten what you said?"

"No. I said I loved you ... and I do. But I'm sorry, Janelle. It's not going to work out."

"Why?"

"Janelle, the way things are right now ... I can't offer you anything."

"Is that what this is about? You think I want more than your love?"

He did not answer.

"Material things mean nothing to me, Lance. I admit . . . at one time . . . I was consumed with thoughts of money, pretty clothes, social status. No more. Not since I came to Tuskegee. Not since I met you. Believe me, Lance, all I want is your love."

"We're worlds apart, Janelle. I was fooling myself. It won't work." He felt as if she had stabbed him with the same hand that had stroked his arms and smoothed the hollow of his back only two days ago.

"Are you sure?"

"Yes, I'm sure," Lance said, wishing he sounded more confident, wishing his hunger for her would dissipate. "I gotta go, Janelle. I've got to finish packing, then I'm going home, to Congregation Hills. I want to tell my grandfather good-bye."

Janelle said nothing.

Raw grief clawed at Lance. He started to speak but changed his mind and let the void between them linger. Shading his eyes, he stared at the floor and, for the second time that day, found himself with tears running down his cheeks.

"If you will excuse me now, Mr. Graham, I've got a factory to run." John Gray's sugary southern drawl did not soften his terse dismissal. Putting his stub of a cigar between bright pink lips, he sniffed loudly, waiting for Dalton to leave.

"It's hard to believe that in more than ninety years not one qualified Negro has ever made an application for work at Keystone," Dalton remarked, not rising.

"May be hard for you to believe, but that's the truth." Gray puffed on his cigar while drumming his desk with pudgy fingers, flashing a diamond the size of a pea. "The God's truth," he added. "Feel free to check around. Ask all the questions you want to. Anybody working here will tell you the blacks just don't come here looking for work. I'd hire 'em if they were qualified."

"What are the qualifications? For a woman to work on the sewing line, for example?"

"Well, making tents ain't all that easy. The ladies gotta be strong. Lifting canvas is hard work. They gotta be able to read and understand directions, too. You know? There's safety warnings and machine shop directions posted all over the plant. I can't take on anybody who can't follow written instructions."

"There must be plenty of colored women in Macon County who meet those qualifications."

"I haven't seen 'em flocking over here for jobs. That's for sure."

Dalton thought for a minute. "What about welders? Have you advertised?"

"I post notices of job openings at the front gate. Word circulates when Keystone's hiring. Not my fault no colored show up."

"So, you've never advertised in the Montgomery paper? Put notices up at the institute?"

"Naw. For what? I figure if people want a job, they'll find me. I ain't got money to be wasting on placing ads in the papers."

"All I'm saying, Mr. Gray, is that if you want the government contract, you will have to do a better job of attracting Negroes to your plant."

"You're damned right I want that contract. Keystone deserves it. There's not another plant in the United States that can meet the production quotas as fast as we can. I assure you, Mr. Graham, I have never discriminated against colored. Never."

"But you've done very little to seek out Negro applicants, Mr. Gray."

"And I don't plan to do more." John Gray stood, snuffing out his cigar. "You can send all the colored you want to over here for an interview. I'll let 'em make out applications. Got no problem with that. But they gotta be qualified. Ready to go to work." Laying his hands over his stomach, he grinned slyly at Dalton. "I ain't about to pick a bone with the federal regulators. You send me some blacks who can run an industrial sewing machine or a welding torch, and I'll take 'em on. If they can read and write."

Dalton picked up his trench coat and folded it over one arm. "I'll do that, Mr. Gray." He leaned over and shook the big man's hand. "You'll be hearing from me. Soon. And thanks for your time."

In the empty hallway outside John Gray's office, Dalton set down his attaché case and shook out his coat. Through the glass-paneled door he heard Gray bark at his secretary. "Louise! You get them files from out that cabinet in the closet and get rid of 'em. You hear?"

"The ones in the blue folders, sir?"

"Yeah. We got an NAACP official snooping around. No use in having those papers where he can get his hands on 'em."

Dalton pushed open the tall front door of Keystone and walked toward the car he had rented from a mechanics' garage near the hotel. Unlocking the car door, he thought about his conversation with John Gray, wondering what tactics the man had used over the years to keep colored applicants away so effectively.

CHAPTER
TWENTY-SEVEN

Janelle pushed through the doors of the Atlas Hotel and approached the registration desk. "Please ring Mr. Dalton Graham's room." Unflinching, she stared at the astonished woman behind the counter.

"I can't do that." Nervously turning a pencil around in her hand, the clerk glanced across the empty lobby. "You'll have to leave."

"Leave?"

"Colored use the back door." Pursing her lips, she shifted to one side and peeked around the corner. "There's a phone just outside the kitchen. You can use it to call the desk. If Mr. Graham is in, I'll connect you."

"That's ridiculous! I am Lieutenant Janelle Roy, United States Army. And I have business with Mr. Graham."

Not impressed, the woman went blank with uninterest.

"Mr. Graham is my attorney."

"Doesn't matter," the clerk said tersely. "You can't stay here in the lobby."

Janelle remained firmly planted at the desk.

"If you don't leave, I'll have to summon the manager."

"I guess you'd better call him," Janelle calmly advised, "because I'm not going around to the back to telephone from the kitchen."

"Don't you go causing a fuss around here!" The woman slammed the pencil down and started around the counter.

"Janelle!"

Turning, she saw Dalton Graham, unbuttoned coat hanging loosely from his shoulders, hat in hand, crossing the lobby toward her.

"Dalton. Thank God you're here." She met him in the middle of the carpeted area. "I got a phone call from Camp Livingston this morning. Perry's in serious trouble."

"What?" Taking Janelle by the arm, he guided her to a sofa at the side of the room. "Sit down." He removed his coat as he spoke. "Tell me what happened?"

"Excuse me, Mr. Graham." Mr. Frank, the manager of the Atlas Hotel, cleared his throat loudly and folded his arms. "I am sorry, but you cannot entertain your 'friend' in the lobby of this hotel."

"I am not entertaining the lieutenant, Mr. Frank. This is official business."

"Humph. I'm very sorry, but still, no colored are permitted in the lobby. Military or not." His eyes raked Janelle's uniform with distaste. "It's the law, you understand?"

"No, I really don't," Dalton replied as he got up, extending his hand to Janelle. "My room is paid up . . . two weeks in advance. I think I have the right to talk to whomever I please. Come with me, Janelle. Tell me what's happened to Perry."

Leaving the hotel manager staring after them, Dalton and Janelle climbed the wide marble staircase to the second floor and entered his room at the end of the hall.

Pale green, smelling of bleached cotton and Old Golds, Dalton's room faced the tiny town square. Furnished only with a bed, a chair, and a scarred mahogany table supporting a top-heavy lamp, the narrow cubicle had the appearance of a cell. Dalton hung his coat in the closet, then opened the venetian blinds.

"Who called you?"

Janelle sat on the edge of the vinyl-covered steel-frame chair. "The camp commander."

"And what did he say?"

"Perry shot and killed a German prisoner under his guard."

"Oh, hell! When? Why?"

"All I know is that it happened last night. Then Perry hopped a train headed east and hasn't been seen since."

Sitting on the foot of the bed, Dalton gave Janelle his full attention.

"The commander said that according to witnesses, Perry was not provoked, but I find that hard to believe." Pressing her fingertips together, Janelle paused. "Perry is not a violent person. If he's killed someone, he must have had a very good reason. Something happened. Something the commander is not telling me."

"Probably so," Dalton said.

"Where do you think Perry would go, Dalton? I don't think he's coming to see me."

"I think he'd leave the country," Dalton said bluntly, remembering Perry's raging phone call.

"Canada?"

"Yeah. If he's on the run, he's not going to stop until he's out of the States." Rubbing his chin, Dalton went on. "When Perry got his draft notice, he asked me to help him get out of serving."

"He was that unhappy about being called up?" An odd sort of jealousy surfaced. Why was she just now learning the extent of Perry's fears?

"Yeah, but after we talked, he resigned himself to doing his duty, and I hoped everything would work itself out. Guess it didn't."

"Apparently not."

"Janelle, if Perry does contact you, call me first. Let me make any arrangements to turn him in. This could be tricky. Damn tricky."

"I doubt he'll try to see me. He's got to be frightened. And he's not going to walk into a bunch of military here at Tuskegee. I can imagine how awful he feels." Janelle got up and walked to the window, keeping her back to Dalton. "I wish I'd written him more often. Called him."

She turned. "He *must* have been provoked. Perry wouldn't kill a man in cold blood for no reason. Do you think he'd do that, Dalton?"

Dalton shook his head no. "Sounds strange to me. I'm going to make a few calls, see what I can find out. In the meantime, Janelle, please don't let yourself get implicated. Call me if you hear from Perry."

Tilting her head back, Janelle let it rest against the window frame. "So much is happening. So fast."

"Yeah. The town's been buzzing with talk about the Ninety-ninth shipping out." Dalton forced himself to bring up the subject. "I guess saying good-bye to your pilot is going to be hard, huh?"

Janelle smiled weakly. "We've already said our good-byes."

"Oh, yeah? You doing all right?"

"We've broken up."

Dalton eyed Janelle curiously. "Whose idea was that?"

"Lance's."

"He broke off with you? Out of the blue?"

"Yeah, he delivered a sort of Dear John letter . . . over the phone." She felt tears gathering. "Better now than later, I guess. A letter from Europe would have been more distressing than facing the truth of it now."

Dalton wanted to hold her in his arms and confess his own feelings, but he held back, knowing Janelle's heart belonged to someone else. "What went wrong?"

"Oh, I don't know if anything went wrong." Stepping from the window, she moved closer to Dalton. She was determined not to make him feel responsible for the breakup. "Our timing was off. Under different circumstances, if he were not a pilot, if the country were not at war . . ."

"You never would have met Lance Fuller." Dalton finished her sentence.

Janelle smiled ruefully. "You're right. And I never would have fallen in love."

"Vicious cycle, huh? Please tell me, Janelle. What happened? Yesterday morning you were in a very different mood."

"Lance is shipping out. That's it. He doesn't want me waiting around for him. You know, the old I-may-not-return cop-out."

Dalton shrugged. "It's true he might get killed in action. Or wounded seriously. Anything could happen. You understand his apprehension, don't you?"

"No," Janelle said. "He's not the only one who is afraid. I think he's being selfish. I'm scared. The entire country is scared. So what's wrong with my waiting for him, loving him, praying for him while he's gone? Tell me, what's wrong with that? Wives, girlfriends, sisters, mothers— thousands of them are waiting for men in every city in the nation. Why should I be protected from such pain?"

Dalton suppressed an urge to reach out and touch her. "Where is Lance now?"

"Probably at Congregation Hills, telling his grandfather goodbye."

"Go to him, Janelle," Dalton said, wishing he were the one she wanted. "Don't let him go away like this. Not if you really love him."

"I do, but he knows how I feel. And I don't doubt his love for me, but he refuses to make a commitment."

"Hogwash," Dalton remarked. "Lance knows what he's done, and he is probably miserable about it. You two need to take the time to set this thing straight, and there is not a hell of a lot of it left."

"I know. And I'm exhausted."

Dalton could not resist covering Janelle's hand with his. "How did you get here? How much time do you have?"

"I was in such a panic to tell you about Perry I pried an overnight pass from the chief. I showed her the check you brought me and told her I wanted to go into town and put it in the bank. Luckily she agreed. So one of the nurses who lives off base dropped me here. She said to give her a call when I was ready to go back."

Dalton reached into the pocket of his jacket. "Here.

Take the car I rented. You go find your pilot and tell him exactly how you feel. Don't let him get away before you see him once more."

Janelle hesitated. "I don't know. Lance was adamant on the phone. Dead set on ending our relationship."

"Trust me. If he loves you, he'll be happy to see you and he won't turn you away."

"What makes you so sure?"

Dalton smiled. "Call it male intuition. . . . Lance Fuller is just confused." He laughed, pushing an unruly shock of dark hair from his forehead. "Men have a way of miscalculating some of the most important moments in their lives."

Hugging Dalton, Janelle silently gave thanks for his friendship. She accepted the car keys he placed in her hand.

"Don't give up so easily, Janelle. You two settle everything tonight. If you really love Lieutenant Fuller and he truly loves you, your love won't get lost in this chaos of war." Dalton's tone softened as he went to the door and held it open. "I'll worry about Perry. You go on and find your lieutenant and give him the good-bye he deserves."

Janelle fumbled with the buttons on the dashboard, her fingers clumsily groping over knobs and switches and levers until she hit the right one and illuminated the road. Settling back against the gray plush upholstery, she clutched the huge steering wheel with both hands. As the afternoon light dissolved into shadows, she guided the car up Notasulga Road, carefully following the rutted pathway, tracing its red clay soil.

She'd traveled this path so many times with Lance, anticipating their time together at Wild Embers. Now her fear of losing him, of arriving too late to salvage their relationship overshadowed the possibility that he still might reject her.

This is the right thing to do, she told herself reassuringly. *Even if Lance pushes me away, I have to see him*

*this last time. He has to tell me to my face that our love
is not strong enough to survive this war.*

Glancing over at the gate to the Keystone Company, she
wondered if Dalton was making any progress in his nego-
tiations with John Gray. Being so caught up in her own
crisis, she hadn't even asked him about it.

At the turnoff to Congregation Hills, Janelle pulled off
to the side of the road, her confidence shaken, her heart
thumping in her chest. Shifting the car into park, she hesitated. Did she really want to swoop in unannounced, in-
truding on the last moments Lance and his grandfather had
together? What right did she have to spoil their good-bye?

Janelle lowered her head to the steering wheel, rested it
there, closing her eyes, aching for Lance. Soon the 99th
would board a train headed north, then be loaded onto
troopships for the crossing, and finally they'd be up in
their planes, fighting the enemy. Sadness colored her
pride. It was all closing in too fast.

Through a shimmer of tears Janelle peered down the
road into the crumbling little village. Knowing she could
not go to Lance, she whipped the steering wheel with a
firm turn and swung to the left, entering the overgrown
trail she knew would take her to Wild Embers.

The soil, spongy and marshlike, gave way beneath the
car, but Janelle pressed forward through the thick under-
brush spreading into the road. Finally she rolled to a stop
below the squat deserted cabin. When she emerged, slamming the car door, all anxiety melted away. The glassy surface of Lake Eden glowed peacefully dark green against
the hills. As she approached the log structure, memories of
loving Lance calmed her, releasing the last threads of her
anger.

Janelle pushed open the mud-caked door and entered the
musty room. A thick stub of candle on the table caught her
eye. Folds of yellow wax had dripped in smooth strips
down its length, settling on the glass dish beneath it. The
sight jarred Janelle back to the last time she had been

there, when she and Lance had abandoned themselves to the moment, even making plans for their future.

She struck a match to the stub, and a dull amber light filtered out, caressing the craggy bark walls that had stood watching for generations. At the hearth Janelle sat on a low bench fronting the cold, banked ashes, thinking about those who had been there before her: Lance's grandparents, his parents. On their last visit she and Lance had lain together, snuggled under the thick feather quilt, discussing ways to restore the little cabin after the war.

Running a hand through her disheveled hair, Janelle sighed, wishing circumstances were different.

She went to the pine trundle bed tucked under the eaves and laid her palm on the quilt. Lance said his mother had made it and it was the only thing of hers he had. Still neatly folded, just as she'd left it, it seemed waiting for her return. Janelle pressed it to her cheek, certain she could smell the scent of Lance, the scent of their love, the perfume of the life she had hoped they would share.

The light from the candle flickered and sputtered as Janelle wrapped the quilt around her shoulders and lay down on the bed. Staring at the ceiling, she let herself relax, wondering how Lance and his grandfather were bearing up under what had to be the most emotional moment of their lives.

CHAPTER TWENTY-EIGHT

The sound of an approaching car woke Janelle from a half sleep. Moonlight had entered the curtainless window and silvered the shadowed room. The candle had completely burned out. Sitting up, Janelle looked out the window and saw Lance, duffel bag on his shoulder, walking toward the unfamiliar car parked in front of the cabin. He looked around, then cautiously came up the walkway.

"Who's here?" he called out, easing the door open. "You are trespassing on private property!"

Janelle slipped off the bed and stepped into the moonlight. "It's me, Lance. Janelle."

He stood with silver light behind his head, one hand still holding the latch. Perplexed, he asked, "Janelle? Whose car is that?"

"Aren't you going to ask me why I came?"

Lance pushed the door shut and walked past her to toss his heavy bag on the floor at the hearth.

"Why the bag?" She closed her eyes, waiting for his answer.

"We pull out in the morning," Lance said stiffly. "I've got to be back on base at oh-five-hundred hours." He reached up to the mantel, took down a hurricane lamp, turned up the wick, and lit it. "I have a pretty good idea why you're here." His voice was not angry but filled with apprehension.

"Then tell me, Lance." Janelle moved toward him, entering the bright yellow circle of light that flared from the lamp in his hand. "You tell me why I would risk reprimand to get an overnight pass and come all the way out here with no assurance that I'd see you."

Lance set the lamp down slowly, then straightened up to face her. "Please don't, Janelle. Why *did* you come? Why are you making this so damn unbearable?"

"Because I love you too much to make it easy." Tensing, terrified that he might leave, Janelle halted a few feet from Lance. "I want you to tell me to my face, Lance. Tell me again what you said on the phone: that you never want to see me again."

He turned his back to her and held on to the rough pine ledge above the fireplace, gazing down at the leaf-strewn floor. "You should not have come out here."

"It's too late. I'm here. And I don't plan on leaving until you've convinced me you no longer care."

Lance sighed but did not face her. "Care, you say?" His voice was hoarse and strained. "No, it's a lot more than that, Janelle. I love you. Is that what you came to hear me say? All right. I told you on the phone, and I'm telling you again. I love you. All right? Are you satisfied?"

"No. That is not what I came to hear. Tell me you never want to see me again. Tell me that, Lance." She went over and pulled gently on his arm. He turned. "Convince me you are glad to leave me behind."

Lance anxiously rubbed his hand across the stubble of a beard that had begun to show on his face. "There are too many danger zones in this relationship for it to survive."

"Danger zones?" Janelle waited for an explanation, dreading what she feared he might say. "What have I done other than confess my love for you? Ask you to listen to me?"

Bereft of an answer, Lance stood trapped.

Janelle's mind raced. Had her lies caught up with her? Was that what had happened? Surely Lance wasn't still jealous of Dalton. She'd better clear up the mess she'd so thoughtlessly created, end all her pretense and salvage their love. "You've learned the truth about me, haven't you?"

Lance blew out a harsh breath, a gleam of wary interest in his eyes. "I was wondering when you'd come clean."

"I made a big mistake, Lance," she said. "And when I realized how stupid I'd been, I was so ashamed—and afraid the truth might make you turn away."

"Go on," he urged in a whisper.

"Much of what I told you about myself was not true. Not exactly . . . I only wanted to impress you."

"Finally. Let's hear it, Janelle. Tell me everything." He was not sarcastic, just curious.

Locking her fingers together, Janelle sat down at the table. "I was born and raised in a small house in one of the poorest areas of Columbus. We had little money. And now there's no home. Literally no home. It was condemned and razed before I left Columbus."

"Why are you here? At Tuskegee, I mean?"

The genuine interest in his question spurred her on. "My father did serve in France," Janelle said, "but he was not a war hero, not by a long shot. He did his duty and came home. And I am not the patriotic, socially conscious woman I led you to believe I am. I joined the Army to salvage what was left of my ruined nursing career."

"The blackballing by the rich white lady?" Lance asked bluntly.

"Yes. It was a damaging turn of events. Dalton Graham helped me clear my name and get the inheritance that was willed to me."

Lance stared oddly at her, shaking his head as he circled the table. "Well, well, well." Standing above her, he looked down. "Now you have an inheritance? I guess I am not nearly good enough for you now."

"Don't say that, Lance. Please."

"I'm sorry. But what am I supposed to believe?" A flicker of disgust passed over his face.

"You have every right to be disappointed," Janelle replied.

Lance let his face soften. "You know, Janelle, I think we're not so different after all. Now that the falsehoods have been stripped away, very little separates us."

"That's right." Thankful he had not yelled at her or berated her or made her feel like the fraud she had been, Janelle rose to stand close to him. "I was wrong. I misjudged you and thought you wouldn't have anything to do with me unless I was better than the others."

"What others?"

"Oh, you know ... the nurses talk."

"So I have been the subject of discussions at the nurses' quarters?"

Janelle clenched her jaw and said nothing.

"What else, Janelle?" Lance pressed her. "Isn't there another rather important detail you left out?"

"What are you talking about."

"Tell me more about the white man who seems to enjoy kissing you so much."

Her inner torment easing, she lifted her chin. "Dalton Graham was my attorney. Nothing more."

"You never had an affair with him?"

"No, believe me. We didn't."

Suddenly Lance's anger flared out of control. "Why did you have to let him put his hands all over you! Kiss you like that in public? You were laughing, smiling, touching. I was mortified to see you like that!"

Janelle cringed, turning aside. "He's just an expressive person. He's flirtatious. Don't misread what you saw. He's a very nice person." She flung out her arms as if begging Lance to come to her, forgive her for not being more concerned with appearances.

"What's he doing in Macon County?" The question sounded like an accusation.

"He's here on NAACP business—trying to integrate Keystone."

Lance put his hand on Janelle's shoulder, forcing her to look at him. "Integrate Keystone?"

"Yes," she said. "He travels around the country, checking defense plants, seeing if they comply with federal regulations."

"So this is the man Pop was talking about? The one who's supposed to get jobs for the colored folks of Congregation Hills?"

Janelle nodded.

"Well, you better stay out of it. John Gray is a dangerous man who can make your life hell."

Janelle shrugged. Lance held her more firmly.

"I mean it, Janelle, don't get involved in this integration mess. You have not lived in Macon County all your life. Your friend Mr. Graham is in for a fight. He can't come down here with the blessing of the government and change things overnight."

"I have nothing to do with any of it, Lance. Dalton helped me clear my name of false accusations. That's all. I owe him nothing, but I do consider him a friend."

"Suit yourself," Lance said, pacing to the far side of the room. "So you are asking me to believe that nothing has ever happened between the two of you?"

"Yes. Nothing." Janelle stood. "That's his car outside. He lent it to me so that I could come to you. He *sent* me here! Don't you see, Lance? Dalton wants me to be happy—happy with you."

"Maybe, but the man is in love with you; anybody can see that. If he's helping you, it's because he loves you, whether he says so or not."

A hint of a smile came over Janelle's face. "You're jealous." Then she rose on tiptoes and boldly laced her arms around Lance's neck. "Forget about Dalton Graham, please. Forget about everything. Hold me, Lance. There is not much time, and I don't want to talk about or think about anything but us."

Lance swallowed.

She saw the misery rising on his face and grew frightened at the prospect of his leaving. As he acquiesced and bent to embrace her, she savored the familiar clean smell of Army soap that drifted to her. Then he covered her mouth with his, removing all inner torment. His kisses, hungrily and fiercely coming one after another, plunged them back to the source of their love.

Against her hair Lance whispered, "Yes, I am jealous. You have become the most important person in my life, Janelle. I couldn't accept losing you ... not to any man. I didn't know what to do but cut you off."

"It was my fault," Janelle replied, hearing her own heartbeat in her ears. "The time we've had together has been so precious I was concerned only with myself." Contrite, Janelle snuggled her forehead beneath Lance's chin.

"When I told Pop good-bye," Lance said, "it was awful. How can I possibly go through it again with you?"

"Our good-bye will be different," she said, teasing the back of his neck with her thumb. "I want to fill it with memories for you to carry with you into war."

Lance threaded his fingers through her loose brown hair and held her at a distance to gaze upon her face. "Pop cried. . . . I'd never seen him cry before." Lance tilted his chin toward the ceiling, then sighed. "But you know the last thing he said to me?"

"What?" Janelle asked, her mind spinning, as she leaned over to lay her cheek against his shoulder.

He said against her hair, " 'Before you leave Tuskegee, you tell that pretty gal of yours that I expect to see her real regular.' "

"Oh, yeah? He wants me to visit?"

"Yes. And I do, too. He's old. Lonely. He looks better than he feels, but he'd never admit to anyone that his circulation is so poor he can hardly make it to the mailbox and back."

"Don't worry. I'll check on him by phone, and every chance I get I'll go see him," Janelle told him. "But, Lance, what do *you* want?"

He put his hand under her chin and kissed her long and hard before he answered. Giving her that little-boy grin, he relaxed, putting one finger to her cheek. "I want you to write to me every day. Send me cookies and fruitcake or whatever it is that all soldiers over there want to get. Most of all, I want you and Pop to be right here in Congregation Hills, waiting for me when I get back."

Janelle smiled as he lazily traced the swell of her cheek with a light touch. "And," he added, "I want you to wear this locket while I'm away."

Janelle leaned back as Lance put his hand in his breast pocket and pulled out a small gold locket dangling from a delicate chain.

"It was my grandmother's. Pop gave it to me tonight and told me to go find you . . . put it around your neck before I left." Lance seemed amused. "I came out here to think about that. I've never seen the old coot so deadly serious about anything, and he forced me to rethink the way I'd treated you. Will you wear it? For me?"

Janelle didn't hesitate. "I'd be honored."

Lance slipped the locket around Janelle's neck and fastened it, kissing her gently at the base of her throat. "This feels right, doesn't it?"

"I know," Janelle said, relieved that her lies were now behind her. She didn't realize until now how heavily they'd weighed on her conscience.

"I'm glad Pop likes you so much, Janelle." His hands roamed over her back as he spoke. "And I'm sorry I got hotheaded and jumped to the wrong conclusion." He grimaced. "It's just that . . . I couldn't bear waiting around for you to tell me that you were involved with that man. Don't you see? I had to break off first. If—"

"Shh." Janelle placed a finger to his lips, then took his hand and led him to the bed, where she slipped down and gathered him into her arms.

Touching the cool gold heart, Janelle said lowly, "I will be right here when you return, and I will never take this off."

Lance chuckled softly. "At least not until I can give you a wedding ring. How would that be, Janelle?"

The kiss she placed on his lips was her answer. As silver moonlight filtered through the window and the cracks in the walls, and the hoot owls in the forest called back and forth across Lake Eden, Janelle and Lance dissolved into one.

Throughout the night, entwined in an effort to blot out the reality of their impending separation, they fulfilled their promise of love, though behind every kiss and every embrace lay the cruel specter of the lonely lives they would face in the long months ahead.

Without their speaking, their lovemaking shifted from tender, searching caresses to fierce, desperate need, coming close to erasing all thoughts of war.

Lance nuzzled the warm spot between Janelle's shoulders, fighting to clear his mind of nagging, pricking guilt. Janelle had the guts to tell him the truth. Why couldn't he come clean about Al? She had the right to know he existed and should not hear about him from someone else, especially not Minnie Easter.

But when Janelle placed her smooth, long legs over his, urging her warm flesh against his, Lance knew he could not bring up the disturbing subject of the illegitimate child that he'd tried so long to forget. Not on their last night together.

Toward morning, as the mist began to rise on the lake, Janelle felt Lance slip from beneath the flame-stitched quilt. Through half-closed eyes she watched him dress and shove his gear into his bag.

With a tender touch he stirred her. Janelle leaned up on her elbows, and he sank down beside her, kissing her gently on the forehead.

"Don't get up," he said, his voice rough. "I don't want you to go to the station." He enveloped her in his arms and ran his hands down to the warm, silken spot at the flare of her hips, then splayed his hands around her waist.

Janelle refused to be put off. "But, Lance, what kind of send-off would that be? Me not going to the station to wave good-bye?"

Lance brushed his lips across her forehead, down the

side of her face and captured her lips for a moment. "Don't wave good-bye, Janelle. My grandmother always said that people who waved good-bye never returned. She said it was a gesture that meant a permanent separation. When slaves were sold off to other plantations, they'd wave and wave until they disappeared out of sight. She'd seen it too many times." Stroking her shoulder, he added, "I want to remember you like this. Right here."

Janelle forced her sobs down into her heart, praying she could hold them at bay until he left. Clinging desperately to Lance, their hearts pounding in tandem, neither daring to speak, both unwilling to cry, she tried to memorize the feel of his body pressed to hers.

Finally, Lance guided Janelle back onto the pillow, drinking in her presence with a long, hungry gaze. Then he let her go and rose to pick up his bulky duffel bag.

Clutching the quilt to her breast, Janelle watched from the bed as he disappeared through the door. She listened to his footsteps on the rough broken path. A rush of tears stung her, taking her breath away. The raw edge of her longing began to dull as the mournful sound of loons on the lake echoed her grief through the morning.

He's gone, she realized, a sense of panic rising at the sound of his car churning onto the road. *Within hours he'll be out of Alabama, headed to New York, on his way to the other side of the world to help end this God-awful war.*

Snuggling down into their warm nest, inhaling traces of Lance's presence, Janelle pulled the quilt fully over her naked shoulders and squeezed her eyes shut tight.

I'm glad we were able to say good-bye this way. She consoled herself, groping for a way to ease the pain. *And I'm glad Lance left with his last memories of me here, in this cabin, on the land where everyone who ever loved him was born.*

CHAPTER
TWENTY-NINE

The mottled hound stopped gnawing on the bloody rabbit clamped beneath its mud-covered paws, warily assessed the unwelcome intruder, then resumed its ravenous attack. Thankful for the foggy mist swirling over the field, Perry skirted the skeletal dog and hunched down in the field of tall cockspur grass to make his way toward a splintered shack in the distance.

After an agonizing night ride into Natchez, Perry had managed to elude authorities at the bustling train station and wrangle a pair of pants and a plaid flannel shirt at the thrift store on the edge of town. Now, as he crept toward the hut to change clothes, he realized the white-hot pain in his right side had finally subsided to a dull but constant throb.

Stopping at the edge of a clearing, Perry cautiously surveyed the campsite, sensing the weathered lean-to tacked to the base of a towering pine was not abandoned. In fact, signs of life were everywhere. A cold ten-gallon steel drum that had been used as a stove sat next to a pile of yellowing newspapers. Old chicken bones not yet bleached by the sun lay scattered at the edge of the woods, and a piece of mirror was propped against a tree, where someone had left an old shaving mug and razor.

Remaining at a respectable distance, Perry called out, "Anybody here?" When no one answered, he crept forward. "Anybody here?"

The door creaked open, and a tall, grizzled man in oil-stained coveralls stuck out his brown, leathery face. "Who's there?"

"I've been hurt. I just need a place to rest. Some water. I'll be on my way."

Stepping outside, the lanky hermit lowered the hunting rifle he held loosely in one hand. "You in da Army?" He came out onto his junk-filled porch. "What you doing way out here?"

"I was on my way back to—uh, Tuskegee," Perry said quickly. "Had a little trouble. Think I busted a rib."

"You rowdy Army boys." The man clucked his tongue against yellowed teeth. "Tuskegee, you say? That's a ways from here. Where you come from?"

Perry backed up slightly, leaning against the trunk of a tree. "Uh, Texas. I been home to see my folks. Got off at Natchez and got turned around. Missed my train."

"Well"—the old man stepped down into the clearing—"I ain't got no car or no way to help you. Might wanna head on down the road a piece, somebody passing north probably pick you up."

Perry just stood there, clutching the bundle of clothes under his arm, leaning on the tree.

"What you want?" Irritated, the man squinted.

"Like I said, a place to rest, a little water."

The man shook his head. "I don't want no trouble."

"I'm not going to hurt you. I'm just tired. Been on the train all night." *Flat on my back with wind and rain and dirt in my face,* he thought, feeling a little faint. If only he could change his clothes and stay put long enough to get a few hours' sleep, he'd be on his way: across Mississippi, through Tennessee, Kentucky, and Ohio. Once he got to Cleveland, he'd find a way to cross into Canada.

"All right," the man relented, "I can see you ain't in no hurry to get back to the Army. Can't say as I blame you. I heard how they treating you boys. Come on over here. You can sit on my porch. I'll make you a cup of coffee."

By midmorning Perry had drunk three cups of the old

man's bitter coffee and eaten a plate of squirrel stew. As he polished off the gritty brown meal, he thought of the food at the camp—of Joe McGinnis and Heywood Hodges, the only men in his barracks he cared about.

What were they saying about him now? he wondered, knowing there was no way he could possibly go back. Surely the military police were not far behind, and a long prison term for killing a German prisoner was a destiny Perry could not bear.

If he took his time and was very careful, Perry believed he could make it out of the States. It could be done. Heywood had told him of the enclave of colored Americans, a first cousin from Georgia included, who had chosen to flee their hometowns and settle in Toronto rather than serve in a segregated Army.

The faint perfume of water lilies drifted up from Lake Eden. Janelle drew in their scent, listlessly baring her face to the pale sun, allowing its early-morning rays to dry her tears. She'd been crying for what seemed an eternity, unwilling to rise from the craggy log, head back to the base, and resume a routine that she refused to call normal.

From a distance she heard the chilling wail of another train whistle, its shrill echo causing her heart to thunder. Tensed, she sat listening—as she had been doing since daybreak—while every half hour one train or another pulled into or out of the tiny Chehaw station. With a shrug she exhaled, her shoulders slumping as the wail ended. She wondered which blast had come from the train that was taking Lance to war.

He was gone. The very thought clawed her insides raw, but oddly she did not feel angry. Unable to resist a smile, she recalled him as he'd stood at her bedside, handsome in the faint morning light. Class A dress. Looking proud and scared and vulnerable and strong. Her lonely eagle was finally getting his chance to prove himself and would make history by flying in integrated skies.

He'll do fine, Janelle mused, standing, brushing off her

skirt, already thinking about the letter she'd write tonight. If only she knew his final destination, she'd post it first thing tomorrow morning.

Bumping over the back road, trying to remember the shortcut to the base, Janelle found herself at the turnoff to Congregation Hills North. She checked her watch. There was time to visit Deacon Fuller before reporting for duty.

With cool fingers, she touched the gold locket at her throat, and Lance's husky request that she wear it reverberated in her ears. She had to thank Deacon this morning for the wisdom of his welcome interference.

Janelle turned left and headed down the hill, through the village, past the general store to the Fuller house at the end of the lane. Nothing had changed. If anything, the grimy little village looked more pitiful than she remembered.

Janelle got out of the car, slammed the door, started across the yard. A black and white puppy bounded to her, sniffed her shoes, then bolted onto the porch to settle in the lap of a young boy who sat with a comic book up to his face. Janelle recognized him at once as the laundress's boy, the one she had seen at the store and at the base.

When she mounted the steps, the boy got up, clutching his well-worn comic in one hand.

"Hello," Janelle said, glad to see him in neatly pressed clothes. His curious eyes lifted to hers, oddly stirring her to want to reach out and hold him. There was definitely something sad behind the shy grin he offered so tentatively, as if he weren't sure what might happen.

"Hi," he said lightly, rolling the comic into a tube.

"That your puppy?" Janelle asked, trying to put the child at ease.

"Yeah. Cute, ain't he?"

"Sure is." Janelle stooped down to pet the soft, furry bundle, then glanced up at the boy. From his body size she judged him to be about seven years old, but he carried an expression that made him seem older, less innocent.

"Is your mother in the house?" Janelle asked, remembering Lance had said that she cooked and ironed for his grandfather.

"Nope," the child replied as he tickled the puppy's soft underbelly.

"What about Mr. Fuller? Is he home?"

"Oh, sure. He's around back. Fooling around with some old rabbit skins. Trying to tan 'em or something."

Janelle leaned over the porch railing. Seeing Deacon squatted down on the ground at the back of the lot, she went into the yard, then circled the house.

"Good morning," she called out.

"Well, Lawd, look who's here. Musta been reading my mind."

Janelle crossed the loose red dirt, stopping at the pile of hides at Deacon's feet. Wrinkling her nose, she moved to stand beside a flowering gooseberry bush.

A faraway whistle blast came to them. "You can hear the trains out here," she commented, unreasonably irritated.

Deacon continued massaging and stretching a glossy brown fur. "Yep. Been listening to 'em all morning." He straightened up, propping his hands on his hips. "Reckon he's out of the state by now?"

"Maybe," Janelle said. "If he was on one of the first trains out."

Deacon tossed the piece of fur on a pile and picked up another one.

"I miss my boy already." He paused, craning his neck toward Janelle. "Lance found you okay last night?"

"Yes, at the lake."

"And you wearing my Mary's locket?"

Janelle smiled, holding the small piece of gold out for him to see. "It was a very sweet gesture, Mr. Fuller. It means a lot to me. To Lance. I miss him terribly, too. But you know what? It may sound strange, but really, in a way, I'm glad he's gone."

Deacon gave a throaty chuckle. "I know just how you

feel. It's a relief. Them white boys ain't gonna do it alone. I'm so proud of Lance I ain't got time to feel scared."

Janelle nodded, savoring the kinship they'd so quickly established, thankful that Dalton had urged her to find Lance, that Deacon had sent Lance to find her. These men loved her, wanted the best for her, and without them things could have ended much differently.

"Strange, isn't it? Feeling happy and sad at the same time. I wish Lance were here, but flying is what he has been trained to do. Now he can do his job and hurry back home."

"Ain't got no doubts about that. Before you know it, he'll be right back here, fussing over me again." Deacon beamed. "Now maybe I can get a little rest."

"Don't be too sure." Janelle cautioned him with a grin. "He put me in charge in his absence."

They eyed each other at the same moment, then laughed, their voices rippling out in unison over the yard.

"I see you have a visitor," Janelle said.

Deacon wiped a hand on the leg of his overalls. "Yep. That's my great-grandson. Alabama. He hates his name. Better call him Al."

Janelle ran her tongue over dry lips. Her chest tightened. "Your great-grandson?" Lance had told her he was Deacon Fuller's only grandchild. What did his grandfather mean? In a light tone she said, "So, with Lance gone, you've already adopted a replacement, huh?" A nervous giggle escaped.

Deacon picked up a rag and rubbed it over a pelt. "Adopted? No," he said, keeping his head bent to his chore. "He ain't adopted." Deacon vigorously massaged oil into the taut cracked skin. "You mean, Lance never told you about Al?" His words plunged straight into the ground.

Told me what? Janelle agonized silently, beginning to feel faint. "No," she whispered, "I know nothing about the child."

"Oh, my. My." Deacon put down the pelt and pushed

himself up from his knees, centering his face in front of hers. "Guess he's left it to me to tell."

"Please. Tell me." Janelle urged him evenly, her eyes not leaving Deacon's face.

Glancing toward the house, he said, "That's Lance's boy on the porch."

"Lance has a son?" Janelle was horrified. "How old is he?"

"About seven, I reckon," Deacon answered.

How could that be? Janelle quickly calculated, knowing Lance was only a few months older than she. "Lance was married?"

"Naw. Lance ain't never been married. Never even brought any woman but you out to the house to meet me." Deacon reached out as if to touch Janelle, looked down at his dirty hands, then drew his fingers back. "You come sit down on the bench over here, outa the sun. This ain't nothing to discuss standing up."

Janelle followed him to a crudely carved settee that tilted at an angle; its thick, rough legs had sunk halfway into the spongy red soil.

"You wearin' my Mary's locket, and I know my Lance is right serious about you." He paused as if thinking things over. Shaking his head, he said, "The way I see it, you got every right to know exactly what happened. Too bad I gotta be the one to tell it."

As Deacon Fuller began his story about Alabama's origin, Janelle drew her lips into a thin line, resolved to keep her wits about her no matter what was said. Fighting hard to keep her mind from shutting down in denial, she listened as Deacon described the complicated situation.

"When Minnie marched up to this very door and put that baby up against the screen, liked to scared Lance to death. Wasn't nothing but seventeen then. Now I ain't condoning none of what he done, but nature kinda tricked him up. Well, I figgered wasn't no way to disown the child," Deacon explained. "Just one look and I knew the boy was kin. Lance got mad as the devil with me. Tried to deny it, but I stood by my feelings. Minnie's boy is a Fuller all right. I felt it ... way down deep ... the first time I laid my eyes on the chil'. Ain't no way to get around it."

"Does Lance believe Al is his son?"

"You mean has he accepted the chil'? Put his name to the boy?"

"Yes."

"Aw, as much as he can. Ain't no papers been drawn. He was embarrassed at first. Turned mean, too! And Lawd, was he mad at me! We had a row that lasted most all that afternoon. Then he stomped off into the woods. Stayed away two days. When he come on back home, we never really talked about it again. We kinda recognized the boy as ours without really saying it, you know? Then Minnie disappeared. We just let it drop through the cracks, let the problem settle down on its own."

Janelle felt frozen, not knowing what to say.

Deacon scratched the side of his face. "All I ever wanted was to take the boy, raise him up right. Give him some kind of a home."

Janelle found her voice. "Why didn't you?"

"Minnie Easter, that's why. All she ever wanted was money." Deacon threw back his head and frowned at the sky. "Money! From me! She's a hustler. Selfish, too. Don't care about nothing but a good time."

"Minnie Easter never did your laundry? Cooked for you?"

"Minnie?" He lifted his white-bearded chin and roared. "From what I know, that lazy heifer don't do nothing but play cards most all night and sleep all day. A shame, too, 'cause she used to be a right pretty gal."

Lance lied to me. Janelle fumed silently. *And he let me give my horrible confession while holding on to his own dirty little secret.*

"Where is Minnie?" she wanted to know. "Why is the boy sitting on your porch?"

"Minnie got herself beat up in a ruckus last night. Got took over to the county hospital. Nothin' serious. She's been through worse, I reckon. One of the gals at the place where Minnie lives brought Al out here to stay till she gets back on her feet."

"So you and the boy are close?" Janelle pulled the question from the pit of her stomach, wishing she could flee from the answer. "Do you see him often? Does Lance?" How could he have left without telling her this?

"No. Like I said, Minnie roams in and out of Congregation Hills. Last time she came back Lance was studying over at the institute, so I convinced Minnie to let the boy stay with me a spell. Got close to the little tyke then. Guess Alabama musta been about three years old. Minnie let me have him for ten days. Kinda got attached to him."

Janelle began to tremble.

"Too bad that woman ain't much of a mother. She traipses up and down the state, letting Al see all sorts of things. He's so young. He don't need to be learning what goes on in the places his mother frequents."

Janelle swallowed hard, then asked, "How long will he be here?"

"I'm gonna take care of Al till his momma gets well. Where else he gonna go? If the gal from the house where Minnie was living didn't bring Al out here to me, the state woulda sent him down to Montgomery, to the colored orphanage over there. Any abandoned black child gets sent there. Ain't no question I gotta keep him. Don't you think so?"

My God, what have I gotten myself into? Janelle thought, but she was unable to give herself any reply. Growing more miserable by the second, she stood up, gripping the settee to keep steady.

"With Lance gone," Deacon continued pleasantly, "I think I'm gonna like having Al here with me."

Perspiration beaded on Janelle's temples, and she felt as if she were slipping into a bottomless, spiraling whirlpool. Lance was the father of a seven-year-old boy, and he hadn't bothered to mention it to her! He had dared talk of a future but had conveniently forgotten to tell her of a child he had fathered while still a child himself?

Janelle swayed slightly, then placed a closed fist to her chest.

"You all right?" Deacon hurried to her side.

"I—I have to admit I am shocked," she stammered.

"Well, Lance shoulda told you. But don't fault the child," Deacon pleaded.

"Oh, no," Janelle replied, knowing the child was a victim of adult stupidity. "But I do wish Lance had been truthful about this. I'm sorry he felt he couldn't tell me."

"Sometimes it's hard for a man to admit his mistakes."

"He was young when it happened," Janelle said. "But the real mistake he made was hiding it."

"Um-m," Deacon murmured, "you right about that." He stood watching as Janelle started across the yard.

"I've got to get back to the base," she said, walking faster, carefully pronouncing each word.

"You look a little peaked. I've upset you, haven't I?"

Turning around, Janelle said to Deacon, "Don't worry about me. I understand what happened. And thank you for telling me the truth."

He started toward her. "I didn't mean to cause no trouble. I just ain't one to lie."

"I told you—I understand, Mr. Fuller." Janelle lifted her chin, her voice hoarse with forced control. "You did the right thing. Now, do me a favor, please."

"Anything." Misery drifted over his face.

"When you write to Lance, don't tell him that you told me about Alabama."

"If that's what you want."

"It is," Janelle said, making up her mind to wait for Lance to tell her the truth—if and when he decided to. This was one issue he'd have to divulge on his own, and she had no plans to make it easy.

As she drove back to the base, Janelle felt as if she were going to faint. Her mouth grew bitter, she had trouble focusing on the road, and a tremor coursed through her chest gathering strength until it turned into a throbbing that would not go away.

Light-headed, soaked with perspiration, Janelle wanted to pull off the road, surrender herself to the bitter disappointment—but she knew she didn't dare. If she let her stifled sobs begin, she might keep crying forever.

Shoulders firmly pressed against the seat back, Janelle stared down the winding country road, then stepped down hard on the gas. Blinking away tears that scalded her eyes, she zoomed ahead, squinting against the late-morning sun that reflected brightly from the hood of Dalton's car. Recklessly careening into a deep curve, she held the wheel tightly, gritting her teeth, trying to push Al's trusting face into the remotest corners of her mind.

"Damn you, Lance! Damn you to hell!" she cried, still stunned by this turn of events. "Why did you leave this awful mess behind for me to struggle with alone?"

Dealing with the presence of the child was bad enough. But to put up with a meddlesome, money-hungry whore? A haunting specter that would plague them for the rest of their lives? How in God's name could she put up with that? Her suppressed tears dissolved into sobs, and it was all Janelle could do to hold the car on the road.

Emerging from the hilly countryside, the highway leveled out into a black ribbon of asphalt leading directly to the gated entrance of Tuskegee Army Airfield. A low-flying P-40 made a graceful pass overhead. Janelle thought of Lance, glanced up, and the car drifted across the double yellow stripe in the center of the road.

When Janelle lowered her eyes, she saw a huge Army transport truck bearing down on her like a thundering overloaded freight train.

Pulling to the left, Janelle spun off the road. She pressed down hard on the brakes, but the heavy car did not slow down. Cutting over the soft, rutted earth, it catapulted ahead and broke through a high slatted fence to slam into the side of a thick-trunked pin oak just outside the gates.

A low-hanging limb, torn from the tree, shattered the

front windshield and ran straight through the car. Black smoke billowed up, forcing out a hissing sound that mingled with the insistent blare of the horn.

The soldiers in the transport truck jumped down and raced across the field. "Hold on. Hold on, lady!"

Janelle tried to call out, but the tree limb pressed painfully against her throat. Opening her mouth wide to draw in air, she clawed at the rough bark jammed against her neck. Then everything went black.

PART III

We are beginning to find that there is no work dependent upon skill and dexterity that women cannot be taught to do very well.
    —Fairchild Aircraft Company official, 1943

CHAPTER
THIRTY

When Janelle opened her eyes, she saw the familiar face of Dr. Madden, chief of surgery, centered above her bed. As the blurred image gradually grew clearer, she distinctly heard him calling her name.

"Nurse Roy." The doctor's quiet voice drifted down and entered Janelle's consciousness, making her feel safe, comforted, in the presence of someone she could trust. She had assisted Dr. Madden with quite a few operations, and now, there he was, standing over her with his customary expression of calm reassurance.

Janelle tried to speak, but a terrible pain flashed through her neck, down her throat. Unable to make a sound, she blinked at the surgeon, then looked down the length of the bed. Her right leg, bound in a padded splint, was elevated high above her head.

"Nurse Roy?" Dr. Madden leaned closer, searching her face. "Nurse Roy?" he repeated.

Afraid to try to speak, Janelle fluttered her eyelids open and closed. A sharp pain flashed through her chest, then subsided to a dull ache that spread throughout her upper torso.

"Don't try to move," the doctor told her, placing a hand on her arm. "I'm glad you've come around. You've had a pretty bad time of it."

How bad? she wondered, remembering the awful drive back to the base, the huge transport truck in her path.

Licking parched lips, she lifted a hand and placed it at her throat, indicating she wanted a drink.

"Yes," Dr. Madden said. "I expect you want some water." Turning slightly, he spoke to the nurse behind him. "Lieutenant Brown, I need to go sign for the pain medication for Nurse Roy. I'll be right back. Will you help her with a little water?"

"Of course, Doctor," Emma said, stepping into the surgeon's place.

Janelle tried to summon a weak smile, but her tongue and lips were numb. She felt as if a plaster cast had been molded over her face.

"Just lie still," Emma said gently as she poured a small amount of water into a glass vial and held it to Janelle's cracked flesh. "Take your time now. Just a sip . . . and don't try to sit up. You've got an awful bruise on your neck."

A bruise on her neck? Janelle thought as the cool liquid dripped between her lips. That didn't sound too bad. But what about her leg? She forced a broken whisper. "Emma?"

"Don't talk," Emma said in her official nursing voice, the tone that Janelle was now glad to hear. "You crashed into a tree. Luckily the soldiers on the transport truck got to you right away. A limb broke through the window and lodged against your neck. Thank God it's only bruised, though badly. Another half inch and your neck could have been broken."

Relieved but weary, Janelle went limp. Then she pointed at her leg.

Picking up a towel, Emma acted as if she hadn't understood the implied question, calmly wiping beads of water from the corners of Janelle's mouth.

"The doctor will be right back," Emma finally said. "He'll explain everything." Folding the towel, she frowned. "I've been so worried about you. Where were you all night? I know you were not at Carole Stiler's place in town. Where did you go?"

Janelle closed her eyes for a moment. Wild Embers. Lance's sleek, hard body next to hers. His promise-filled good-bye. Deacon Fuller's disturbing revelation that had sent her on her reckless journey. Even if she were able to speak, she couldn't tell Emma about Lance's son. It was still too new a betrayal.

A pain suddenly ripped from her hip down the length of her right leg.

"Oh! Emma!" Janelle's eyes began to tear. "Emma!" she screamed again, clutching the sheet with one hand.

"I know." Emma rushed to hold Janelle by the shoulders. "I know it hurts, Janelle. Lean back, hon, don't move."

Emma moved to sit in the bedside chair. "I know you feel like hell. But really, Janelle, it could have been a lot worse." Her eyes studied the purple bruised flesh splayed out above the layers of gauze wound around Janelle's swollen neck.

"Dalton?" Janelle croaked, attempting to sit up.

"He hasn't called. Do you want me to get in touch with him?"

Janelle nodded, flinching with pain.

"The Atlas Hotel, right?"

"Yes," she breathed, then closed her eyes.

Emma said gently, "You *do* know the Ninety-ninth pulled out this morning, don't you?"

Janelle fluttered her eyelids in answer.

"Right, you should not be talking. Don't try." Emma picked up a tray of bandages from the bedside table and folded them as she talked. "It was a great send-off from what I heard. There was a band, people singing; the guys really looked sharp. I wish I had been there, but I couldn't get away."

Now Janelle felt envious of those who had gone to the station, those who had seen the unit off. *They* had got to see Lance one last time. She squeezed her eyes tighter shut, then turned her face to the wall.

"Janelle," Emma said, "I hate to leave you, but I've got

to report to Raney in ten minutes. It's about the Liberia unit."

"Were you accepted?" Janelle selfishly wished Emma would be passed over. They had been friends for fifteen years. How could she possibly be glad to hear that Emma was leaving? And under such frightening conditions, too.

"I don't know yet." Her words faltered. "I wish I didn't feel like a traitor for wanting to go."

"Oh, Emma." Janelle was struck by the torment lining Emma's face. "Don't feel like that." She stopped, unable to go on, a lump of emotion adding to the pain in her throat.

"Well, the final selections will be announced this afternoon. Lillian Dorsey already got the word. She's going."

Janelle raised her eyebrows.

"Yeah, Raney's thrilled that so far four in our unit made the cut."

Sinking back into the soft center of the bed, Janelle knew she would find a way to deal with Emma's absence, just as she would have to do with Lance. "Good luck," she murmured as Dr. Madden came back in and Emma stepped aside. "I'll go make that call for you," said Emma, and left.

Dr. Madden twirled his pen between his fingers. "Well, young lady, you are pretty well banged up. Your right leg was pinned between the dashboard and the seat. X rays show a fractured kneecap."

Janelle asked bluntly, "How bad is it really?"

"Will it heal? Will you walk again?" He nodded, patting her arm in a fatherly way. "Of course it will heal. The plaster cast will keep the patella together. Ligaments were repaired in surgery. What you must do now is lie still, rest, let your body begin to heal itself."

"How long?" Janelle asked, her voice raw and strained.

"Let's not talk about time." His tone was surprisingly brusque, and his face took on a grave expression, one Janelle interpreted as I've-got-bad-news-to-tell.

Suddenly the pain in her leg was almost unbearable.

"You're a nurse. You know, your complete recovery depends a lot on how well you follow orders, Lieutenant." Now he frowned, leaning back. "But this injury may be cause for your discharge from the Army."

Janelle's mind drifted back to the day of her arrival at Tuskegee. A discharge? Her tour of duty already over? After all she'd gone through to get this far? And she'd just come to understand and appreciate the full importance of her work.

"It can't," she muttered sternly.

"And it may not," Dr. Madden replied. "But I have to be fair and tell you that more than likely you won't be able to stand on your feet for long periods of time."

Closing her eyes, Janelle let the horrible news find a corner of her overburdened mind.

Dr. Madden cleared his throat. "Don't dwell on it, though. You'll only set your recovery back. Who knows? You're young. It may be that you'll heal much faster and more completely than I've estimated."

Janelle gave the doctor a sympathetic half smile. After all, he was only doing his job.

A nurse stuck her head into the cubicle. "Dr. Madden, you're needed at the nurses' station. Sergeant Harris. Something about his medication?"

"Oh, yes." He glanced down at Janelle. "Get some rest. The pain medication should help."

At the door he stopped to caution Janelle. "No visitors, no talking. Not for a while. Don't strain your esophagus." He took Janelle's chart from beneath his arm and made a notation. "I'll check on you during evening rounds."

Janelle lay completely exhausted. Lance was gone. Perry was a fugitive, hiding out somewhere on the road. Now Emma was about to leave her, too. How God-awful life had become.

She hoped Dalton would get the message and come. Quickly. Maybe he could help her think things through, help her handle the upsetting changes in her life. His uncanny way of putting problems in perspective made life seem more manageable, survivable at least. Besides, Janelle reasoned, Dalton might have news about Perry.

During the remainder of the afternoon, Janelle drifted into a numbing sleep, then awakened with a start, adjusting to her pain all over again. Though staff doctors checked on her twice, Emma did not come back.

Supper was liquid—clear broth and warm orange juice—excruciatingly sucked through a straw. Restless, unable to free her mind of the innocent face of Lance's child, she was lying alone with her thoughts when Dalton entered the ward.

"Hello there," he said.

"Hello," Janelle whispered.

"I spoke to the doctor. He told me everything. Don't try to talk, Janelle. Just relax."

"The car," she breathed, unwilling to remain silent.

"Shh. I know. I've seen it. Quite a crash you had. You're lucky to have gotten away with only a bruised neck and a busted knee." He grinned at her, then threw his trench coat over the chair. "Seriously, Janelle, you could have been killed. Thank God those soldiers were around to help."

Inching up higher on her pillow, Janelle tried to see Dalton better. "Perry?"

"Nothing. Not a word. I made some calls to railway depots and talked to stationmasters, ticket agents. Nobody's seen a thing. Nothing. Perry seems to have made it out of Louisiana. But I'm not finished. I plan to keep on checking."

"Oh," Janelle groaned. What did she expect? Would news of his capture make her feel better or worse?

"This is tough . . . not knowing where he is, what's happening," Dalton said. "But you can't help him, Janelle. If Perry has made up his mind to run, he'll have to live with that decision for the rest of his life or suffer the consequences if he's caught."

Sinking to his knees, Perry collapsed on the bank of the Homochitto River. Plunging both hands into the cool, shallow water, he lay there, the moldly smell of rotten wood strong in his nostrils, the scratchy serenade of crickets grating in his ears.

How the devil had he gotten so completely turned around? He'd headed east across Adams County, following the jagged swell of blue spruce that curved along the foothills, just as the old man had directed. But where was the road leading out of the forest that would set him on a northern route?

Perry scooped up water with both hands, splashed it over his face, then plunged his head down and took big, thirsty gulps. The water tasted awful, and he probably should not drink it, but after traveling all day on squirrel stew and coffee, he'd take his chances—anything to ease the gnawing hunger that had been cramping his stomach since late afternoon.

Dusk began its descent, cloaking his hot, perspiring flesh with chilly air that swept quickly through the trees. Hunkering down, Perry dug his hands into the soft, crumbly soil and flattened his back against a sheltering spruce. With a low groan, he let his head fall forward, weary to the point of passing out. He had no idea where he was, how far from Natchez he had traveled, or where he would get the strength to travel on until he reached the Canadian border.

Perry curled himself into a tight ball, hugging his arms around his body, alarmed by the unrelenting throb in his side. For the past two hours the pain had coiled tighter and tighter, slowing his pace, pushing him, unwillingly, to tears. His chest felt as if it were filled with hot coals, burning raw from his neck to his diaphragm. As each hour passed, it was becoming increasingly more difficult to draw a decent breath. For the first time he was beginning to doubt his plan.

Putting cold hands over his ears to blot out the unnerving chirp of the crickets, Perry thought of his mother, knowing she would be thoroughly disgusted with the way he had ended his brief stint in the Army.

Perry cringed, remembering how he had bragged about his new assignment in his last letter, making it sound more like an honor than the slap in the face it actually was. *She's going to hate me,* he thought, knowing he could never face her again. He'd disappointed his mother for the last time.

I tried to make the best of it, Mom, Perry lamented. *I did try! And I didn't aim to kill that man.* Or did he? he wondered, biting his lip. Only a fair marksman, he was still shocked that his bullet had struck the prisoner's head.

Now, cowering in the woods, a hunted fugitive, he shivered, unable to cast off the biting chill that invaded his body. Perry shoved his soggy boots down beneath a layer of dry leaves, settling in for the long night ahead, fearful he might not be able to continue his journey. If he could make it to Tuskegee, Janelle would help him. Wouldn't she? As he squeezed his eyes shut, he prayed that he was making the right decision.

CHAPTER
THIRTY-ONE

In New York, at the sprawling embarkation port of Camp Shanks, the members of the 99th, which had burgeoned to more than four hundred men, let go of their doubts and with great jubilation began preparations for the journey overseas.

For ten days the men endured inoculations, the tedious routine of filling out government forms, and the long lines where clothing and additional supplies were distributed. While some soldiers took advantage of the down time to rest—lounging on their bunks, playing cards, smoking cigarettes—others made tearful telephone calls, mourning the lack of time for one last visit, a final embrace for those they would soon be leaving behind.

Lance pulled his knees to his chest and propped the tablet against his thighs, trying to block out the activity all around him. The order to board ship had just come through, and pandemonium reigned in the barracks. Shouts, tears, and excited speculation swirled through the quarters, spilling out across the base.

Lance quickly finished his letter to Janelle and hurried to reread it, blotting out the nervous banter of several guys tossing wisecracks back and forth as they dressed and stuffed their heavy canvas bags with their Army-issue gear.

Camp Shanks, New York
April 15, 1943

Dear Janelle,

We just got orders to prepare to board ship, and my thoughts are not on our eventual destination, or the fight that lies ahead, but are consumed by memories of you—as I left you at Wild Embers only ten days ago. It seems so much longer. Perhaps that's because here at Camp Shanks we've had little to do but sit around and talk about all we're leaving behind: the people we love, our favorite foods, even the cities and towns we pray we'll return to.

I have to admit it is a little scary, knowing I am going so far away, but the challenge of entering combat, especially with all the criticism our squadron has had to endure, pushes fear and worry to the back of my mind.

Colonel Davis has been appointed senior officer on the transport ship. Can you believe it? Close to four thousand officers and enlisted men—colored and white—all under the command of a Negro officer! I never thought I'd see the day. Let's hope there is no trouble. I expect quite a few people are not pleased at all by this turn of events.

I love you so much, Janelle. For us to be parted so quickly after finding each other is not fair. But knowing you will be there at Tuskegee waiting helps anchor me and will give me the strength to push on with this fight and finish with it. Whipping the Jerries and getting home to you and Pop as soon as possible are all I want to do.

Please take care of yourself. And thanks for checking on Pop. He didn't seem his usual self when I last saw him. Maybe it was just that I was leaving. I've included the APO to write to me. Will you give it to Pop when you can? I don't have time to write him now. God only knows when I will.

I must go. Remember, having your love means everything. Everything. I cringe when I think that my childish jealousy almost drove you away. Thank you for not giving up on me. I'm the luckiest guy in the world. Take care of yourself, Janelle. I love you. You go with me on this journey.

Love forever,
Lance

Jumping down from the bed, he stuffed the envelope into his backpack and heaved the heavy satchel over his shoulder, knowing he could drop the letter in the bulging mailbag conveniently placed near the gateway at the dock.

Six hours later the USS *Mariposa,* weighted down with soldiers, slipped out of the pier and glided down New York Harbor. Thousands of men crowded onto the deck of the former luxury liner now pressed into troop transport service. Cloaked in darkness, unable to get a final glimpse of the country they were leaving, the soldiers huddled against the deck railings for hours, staring uneasily into the pitch-black night as it folded in silently behind them.

Lance staked out a spot with the guys from his squadron on the starboard side of the massive ship. There he made a hollow place between two duffel bags and sank down, promptly nodding off into an exhausted, dreamless sleep.

When the sun broke over the horizon the next morning, the ship was already far out to sea, but despite a hazy light fog, the solid, indomitable skyscrapers of New York City rose reassuringly in the distance. To Lance it caused a strange feeling, infusing him with courage to defend the country that had not always treated him fairly, that had doubted his ability to serve.

After watching the shoreline fade into gray mist, Lance turned his eyes to the teeming deck where soldiers had begun to stir and stretch their legs. Black, white, young, and anxious, helmeted against possible U-boat attacks, the men appeared strong, fit, and ready for war. As Lance's eyes flitted from one face to another, he solemnly guessed that fewer than half the men on board the *Mariposa* would make the return trip home.

* * *

"I wish you would consider it," Dalton urged, letting Janelle steady herself against his arm.

After easing herself down onto the bench, Janelle stretched her injured leg out straight.

"Chief Raney told me this morning my discharge will be final in thirty days. Let me get through that; then we'll see."

Still reeling from the Army's ruling that she would be medically discharged, Janelle felt off kilter, uneasy about her future, and couldn't seem to make a decision about anything.

She had even put off answering Lance's letter. He had asked her twice to take good care of herself; how could she not let him know what had happened? But each attempt to break the news of her accident invariably threaded its way back to Al—to Lance's child, whose presence she still struggled to accept.

After three miserable weeks in the hospital, the sting of betrayal had eased, but in the desperate hours, late at night, when its chilling weight pressed her to tears, she often considered writing Lance, telling him how deeply she had been hurt by his inability to share this piece of his past with her.

By daybreak her mind always cleared, and the shadowy confusion dispersed, leaving her longing to see him, hear his voice, stroke his back again. At times she conjured up a picture of them, together with Al, in the home they could make for the little boy.

"Give me a little time, Dalton," Janelle said.

"Sure. I don't mean to pressure you." Dalton sat down beside Janelle, gazing seriously out over the hospital grounds. He threaded his fingers together in contemplation. "Headquarters wants me to go out to the Vultee plant in Fort Worth, Texas. I'd like to get this situation with Keystone under control before I leave."

"I'm sorry things have not turned out as you had hoped. I'd like to help you but . . ." Janelle shrugged, unable to concentrate.

Leaves on the huge hickory trees fluttered in a gentle breeze. Across the lawn, patients and visitors sat on benches absorbing the warm April sun.

"I understand," Dalton said. "You've got enough to handle without my asking you for help." With Perry still AWOL and her long recovery ahead, he did feel a little guilty asking Janelle for help.

"You know I won't need to work for a while," Janelle said. "Remember, I have three thousand dollars in the bank, and eventually I'll get disability."

"You ought to hold on to that money you got from the Werner estate. You'll need it when you and Lance get married." How easily he had said that, yet how much he wished it were not true. "You can't support yourself on what the Army will pay. Believe me, it won't be much."

"I won't need much," Janelle replied. "Just enough for a room. Emma didn't get accepted to go to Africa and has been looking for a place that we can share. The veterans hospital is right here. All my therapy and medical treatment will be taken care of. I'll be fine."

"Is that enough for you?"

"Why shouldn't it be?"

"Living in a rented room, going to therapy twice a week, waiting for Lance to come home?" He tried to keep his dismay from showing.

Janelle thoroughly surveyed Dalton's handsome face, remembering the first time she had seen it. He'd changed since his arrival in Alabama. A little thinner, a little older, he carried a perpetual expression of worry.

"You've been great," Janelle said, meaning it. "I know how much work you have to do, and I want you to know that I appreciate your visits, your concern, and all you are doing to find Perry. But a job at Keystone? I don't know, Dalton. That might not be a wise thing for me to do."

"Because your lieutenant asked you not to get involved with my work for the NAACP?"

Without hesitation Janelle answered firmly, "Yes. That's one reason. I told you I gave Lance my promise to stay out of your political affairs." But she hadn't told Dalton about Al, the child whose face unexpectedly flashed into her mind. "Also, I'm not sure I want to sit in front of an industrial sewing machine for the rest of my life."

"I didn't expect you to make a career of it." Pushing his glasses up higher on his nose, Dalton added, "But it would allow you to do sedentary work until you are fully recovered, earn a little extra money. What's wrong with that?"

Janelle knew he had a point. Other than the air base there were not many places in Macon County to find work, and until she was able to stand on her feet for eight to ten hours a day, her nursing career would be kept on hold.

"There is nothing wrong with earning money, Dalton. I just don't think I want to work for John Gray. From what I have been told, he and his family have done some awfully despicable things to the colored in this county."

She thought about the fire that destroyed the cabins at Lake Eden, the beating Lance's parents had suffered, the reign of fear John Gray had been able to perpetuate for years.

Dalton continued his argument. "I need someone I can trust on the inside, Janelle. I've been putting pressure on Gray for weeks; nothing has happened. I've got to find out what's going on."

"You said you sent several applicants over there. Maybe they just didn't have the right qualifications."

"I don't believe that. And not one of the people who went to Keystone for an interview will talk to me now. They refuse to tell me what John Gray said."

"They're afraid of what he might do to them."

Dalton nodded. "Precisely. Gray is systematically shutting out all colored applicants and somehow managing to discourage them from making a complaint. I've seen his bid for the defense contract. In it he says the plant is fully integrated. It's a bald-faced lie, and I'm going to nail him for it." Dalton was fueled, ready for a fight. "You can help

me by going over there for an interview. You can run a
sewing machine, can't you?" he thought to ask.

Janelle's mouth curved into mock exasperation. "Of
course. But an industrial machine may be an entirely different matter."

"Well, you're smart, you can learn. If Gray refuses to
hire you, maybe together we can make a case." Dalton fell
silent, thinking. "You would help me make a case,
wouldn't you?"

Remembering her promise to Lance, she flinched,
though the vow had been made under compromising circumstances. Why should she be worried about going back
on her word, when he had gone his merry way, leaving her
in the dark about a part of his life that would have a mon-
umental effect on their future?

During her recovery she had had plenty of time to think
things through—while lying in bed, or sunning herself on
the hospital veranda, or urging her injured leg through
therapeutic exercises. If only Lance had told her the truth,
her loyalty would be unshakable.

"All right, Dalton." Janelle relented. "As soon as my
discharge is final, I'll put in an application for work at
Keystone."

"Good," he said, grinning, reaching for her hand.

Janelle immediately pulled it away.

"What's wrong?"

"Nothing," Janelle said, a subtle bite to her voice. "I
don't want anyone to get the wrong impression." Could
Lance have been right? Did Dalton still have romantic
feelings for her? Janelle folded her hands together in her
lap.

"You're worried about that?"

"Yes, I am." Janelle boldly took control. "There was a
time when I took such gestures too lightly. My naïve approach nearly ruined things with Lance. I want us to be
friends, Dalton, but I don't want any complications."

"I see," he said slowly, picking up his hat, pulling it on.
"When I came to see you in Columbus, I was desper-

ate." Janelle could tell Dalton was very uneasy. "You helped me through a very difficult time. I'm grateful for all you did."

"It wasn't that much, Janelle."

"To me it was. And you deserve the same from me."

Dalton restlessly ran his hands over his knees, still aching with disappointment over losing Janelle. "You don't owe me a thing. I'm a lawyer, remember? It's my job to help people."

"That's true," Janelle murmured. "I'm a nurse, remember? So is mine."

Clearing his throat, Dalton assumed a businesslike tone. "Okay. If you get on at Keystone and help me nail Gray, a lot of people will benefit. The NAACP can't accomplish much without assistance from people like you."

Flexing her injured leg, Janelle thought about Perry. A terrible sense of loss started to gather in her chest. How many times had she scoffed at her brother for thinking his activities could make a difference? Now here she was, agreeing to go undercover for the NAACP to try to bring one of the most powerful men in Macon County face-to-face with the law. Her mouth went bitter with guilt. What would Perry think of her now?

"Balek! Balek!" The lead driver of the convoy slowed to a crawl, waving his hands in frustration at the crush of Arabs in his path. "Make way," he called in English, trying to disperse the throngs of white-robed men and heavy-laden donkeys that refused to get out of the way.

Eight days after leaving Camp Shanks, four hours after entering the harbor at Casablanca, the 99th Fighter Squadron, in full battle dress, inched its way over bumpy, narrow cobblestone streets, moving deeper into the ancient city. From the wharves, to the sidewalk cafés, to the intricately tiled walls fronting dark passageways, swarms of little brown children and aggressive, ragged adults held out dirty hands, begging for American candy, coins, and cigarettes.

Lance wiped sweat from his brow with the back of one hand and stared curiously at a man in a flowing, hooded djellaba who was hawking pointed slippers he called babouches. The soldiers in the jeep in front of Lance laughed at the vendor's persistent, high-pitched call for trade and tossed him a handful of pennies. A cluster of black-veiled women, eyes downcast, scurried away from the rowdy Americans and entered a high-walled garden. Two blind almsmen, who looked as if they had sprung to life from the pages of the Bible, sat on square fringed rugs, shaking cupped hands in the faces of everyone who passed. Lance felt as if he had fallen asleep only to awaken ten centuries earlier.

As the African sun scorched the backs of their necks, the men in the convoy waved greetings to the Arabs lining the streets. The drab green trucks and camouflaged jeeps rumbled past whitewashed buildings, green tiled mosques, and open-air markets overflowing with exotic vegetables and fruits.

Too weary to think about food, Lance leaned back in his seat, propped his booted feet on the dashboard, and pulled his cap down over his eyes. He stayed that way for nearly an hour until the convoy came to a halt at their bivouac site in the desert outside Casablanca.

As soon as the sun disappeared, the temperature dropped sharply, and Lance spent the night fully clothed, wrapped in his Army blanket, trying to stay warm. Lying on his back in his tiny pup tent, Lance thought of how far he had come.

From a rural two-room schoolhouse, to the classrooms of Tuskegee Institute, to a lieutenant's commission in the United States Army. From the piney woods of Macon County, Alabama, to the shores of French Morocco. And now his thirst to enter combat was about to be quenched.

This is it, Lance concluded, a fearful quiver of relief rising inside. *I wanted my chance to get at the enemy. Now I've got it. There's no turning back.*

Closing his eyes, Lance let his mind carry him back to

the first time he had seen Janelle—on the train to Montgomery, in a wrinkled blue and white suit. *When I get back, I'll tell her about the boy. Together we'll decide what to do,* he silently pledged. She would understand. And if she was willing, he'd give Minnie money, whatever she wanted so he could get Al and give the child a decent home, the childhood he deserved.

Lance had suffered, not knowing his parents, and as wonderful as Pop had been, Lance knew how different his childhood would have been if he'd been able to look into his own father's face. What a joy it would have been to see his bloodline reflected in the plane of his father's forehead, in the spacing between his eyes, in the shape of his jaw.

That was what haunted Lance about his denial of Al. Though neglected and dressed in rags, the innocent boy was no more than an unfortunate portrait of himself in his youth. And the older Al got, the more the child would take on his father's features. It was scary to think about, but Pop had pegged it right from the beginning.

At the end of the week, when the squadron was adequately equipped for the next leg of its journey, Colonel Davis gave orders to break camp. The men boarded trains that looked nearly as ancient as the city of Casablanca and started off on a grueling, steamy seventeen-hour trek over 150 miles of desert.

Upon reaching their destination—the little town of Oued N'ja, just west of the medieval city of Fez—the men disembarked and set up camp once more. Late in the day they had a pleasant surprise; their mail from the States had actually caught up with them. Jubilant, the soldiers crowded up to the mail truck, groping for news from home.

Lance stood expectantly, hoping for word from Janelle, praying she had answered his letter. But when the last piece of mail had been passed out, he turned away, heading empty-handed toward his tent.

Sitting on the ground, his helmet and rifle propped against the closed flap, Lance lit a cigarette and took a long, hard drag. He blew smoke rings out into the dusty, still air. Through half-closed eyes, he enviously watched his buddies devour their letters, reassuring himself that nothing was wrong, he'd hear from Janelle very soon.

CHAPTER
THIRTY-TWO

Perry pulled the threadbare blanket over his shoulders and scooted away from the rain dripping above his head. Looking up at the cracks in the weathered, splintered wood, he worried that the roof of the abandoned watering shed would not hold up for the duration of the storm.

As water pooled on the hard dirt floor, a frenzied wind howled and pressed the ramshackle hut that still reeked of the bulls and cows and newborn calves that had trod through there for years.

Perry rested his chin on his knees, wrapping his arms about his legs, trying to ignore the pangs of hunger that had plagued him for close to thirty days.

By moving cautiously, he had been able to forage a little food from isolated farms, steal a few pieces of clothing—the blanket included—from the clotheslines of unsuspecting farmwives, the shelves of sleepy rural stores. Thank God he'd had the foresight to hold on to his Army knife; more than one jackrabbit had been skinned and roasted when nothing else could be found to eat.

With a thick, full beard—a curly mat of hair covering nearly half of his face—he believed no one would recognize him, at least not at first glance. He had probably lost over fifteen pounds, and in his stained flannel shirt and pants that, unfortunately, stopped right above the ankles, Perry looked no different from any other down-on-his-luck hobo out on the roads, asking for a handout.

The furtive journey to the Alabama border had not been easy, but Perry had to admit that it hadn't been that difficult—other than yesterday, when he had been chased by an angry farmer from whose weed-filled garden he'd stolen a cabbage.

Perry had bolted across the countryside, running as he had in Army field training—scaling fences, dodging tree stumps, heading through the woods—a rifle-waving redneck and a pack of ferocious hounds closing in. When he came to the murky, mosquito-infested swamp, he had plunged in, holding his breath for what seemed an eternity until the man and his dogs turned back.

The experience had really shaken Perry up, forcing him—for the first time—to face the reality that the punishment for stealing a cabbage from a white farmer in Mississippi might be a far sight worse than what the Army would do to him.

There, in the cold, dank glade, he had crouched among the wood ferns, watching the rippling currents for water moccasins and the stealthy approach of alligators. By nightfall, his clothes were sodden and cold. Rigid with fear, he had seriously considered giving up.

He'd failed everyone—himself, his family, his country—just as he had when he dropped out of school, refusing to listen to his mother or Janelle. Now he could see how wrong he had been—selfishly and arrogantly wallowing in his grief, while his mother and his sister had struggled to keep the family whole.

He had wasted two years—years when he could have finished his education by completing the drafting course his mother had spent her precious hard-earned money on. Years when he could have prepared himself to move forward with courage, as his father had constantly urged him to do.

Hiding in the swamp, Perry had examined his self-destructive behavior and for the first time, cursed his father for dying, for leaving him when he needed him most.

Toward dusk, when the determined farmer and his barking hounds gave up their search and left the area, Perry had pressed on, weaving his way through the snarl of vines and bushes until a slate-colored veil covered the sun and the clouds burst open with thick sheets of rain.

Now, huddling in the damp shack once used to water cattle, Perry assessed the place in more realistic terms. With a little effort he could repair the holes in the walls and the roof, shore up the sagging back wall, make a sapling door, cover the broken window. An abandoned well, still holding water, was no more than fifty feet away. Yes. He'd stay right where he was for a while, let things cool down. Maybe the Army would figure he had already left the country and ease up on its search. Anyway, if the farmer spread the word that a black man was wandering the countryside, raiding local farms, he'd better stay off the roads.

Yes. Lying low was the answer right now. Later, when he was stronger and ready to make his move, he'd head straight to Tuskegee and find Janelle.

Red dust swirled up behind the noisy gray bus as it pulled off the side of the road. Fanning dirt from her face as she checked her watch, Janelle stood watching until it lumbered around a curve. Only twenty minutes by bus from the apartment that she had recently moved into with Emma to the front gate of the Keystone Company. Not so bad.

At first being passed over for the Liberia unit had been very difficult for Emma to accept, but finding a place to live off base had eased her disappointment. The news had rolled over Janelle in a wave of relief, pushing her to tell Emma all she'd been holding back. In a torrent of painful words she had told Emma about Perry's disturbing, dangerous situation and the surprising existence of Lance's child.

As Janelle expected, Emma had started in with her I-told-you-so lecture about Lance, then had relented, admitting she was glad to be staying behind at Tuskegee and would do whatever she could to help.

Their dreary three-room suite on the second floor of a decaying Victorian house smelled of mothballs, damp plaster, and the lilac powder that Miss Grace, the soft-spoken widow who lived downstairs, insisted on sprinkling behind every door. In light of the acute housing shortage that plagued Tuskegee, Janelle and Emma were satisfied, feeling extremely lucky to have escaped their barren, communal quarters on the base.

Now, turning toward the shiny chain-link fence on the other side of the highway, Janelle thought of the pictures of the battlefields she had seen in the paper yesterday.

Shuddering, she wondered where Lance was at that very moment. Had he shot down any Germans? She wondered if her letter had reached him, the letter that had been so difficult to write.

Lance was engrossed in his job—flying combat missions—embroiled in the struggle for freedom. It hadn't seemed fair for her to burden him with the news of her accident, and her unfortunate discharge, but she had gone ahead and told him everything —everything except her knowledge of Al.

Since that day in early April when she'd learned of Al's existence, she had spent a lot of time thinking about the lost, lonely boy. After coming to accept the truth, Janelle was willing, even anxious to do what she could to help Deacon Fuller care for the child. As soon as the interview with John Gray was finished, she'd go over to Congregation Hills.

Warily assessing the uniformed man sitting in the cramped wooden booth, Janelle approached the main entrance to Keystone.

"I have an appointment with Mr. Gray," she told the curious guard, pleased with herself for walking without a cane. Her knee bothered her only when she had to stand for long periods of time, as she had done while waiting for the bus. Maybe working at Keystone would allow her to earn enough money to buy a car. But, if she got on, she reminded herself, she was going to stay only until Dalton made his case.

"You applying for work?" The guard sounded bored, uninterested, as if she were wasting his time.

"Yes. I was referred by Mr. Graham."

"Oh," he said flatly, turning up his lip as he reached under the table and pulled out a piece of paper. "I take it you can read and write?"

Drawing in a breath to stay calm, Janelle answered in a controlled voice, "Yes."

"Well, I gotta be sure. Read this." He shoved a page of tightly spaced words in her face. "No use in wasting Mr. Gray's time if you can't read this."

Determined to keep her promise to Dalton, Janelle tightened her jaw, took the page from the man, and began reading aloud: "The business of human living is enormous. It demands mental cooperation to be realized in full. No one alone can know what life means, but people in a group who belong together can pool their mental resources and see life in all its ramifications and possibilities."

Janelle handed the page back to the man, asking, "Would you like me to interpret it for you?" She was sure the passage had been copied from a freshman psychology textbook.

"Nope," he said shortly. "All I gotta do is hear you read it." He put an open register down in front of her. "Sign your name on line twenty-seven."

After signing in, she was directed into the building, where another guard met her and escorted her to John Gray's office on the second floor.

A worried-looking woman with a pinched face and the whitest complexion Janelle had ever seen greeted her, quite warmly, as soon as she entered the room.

"Miss Roy?" The woman blinked her pale blue eyes, as if trying to focus, then pulled a pencil from behind her ear. "I'm Louise Richards, Mr. Gray's assistant."

"Hello. I have an appointment for two o'clock."

"Correct. I see it here in Mr. Gray's book." Louise got

up from her desk and approached Janelle, an application blank in her hand. "I am so pleased that Mr. Graham sent you over."

She sure does sound sincere, Janelle thought. "Thank you. Mr. Graham told me that Keystone is hiring women for the production line . . . making uniforms, tents?"

"That's right. Business is booming. We're doing our part, you know?"

For some reason Janelle felt an immediate connection with the efficient, mature woman, convinced that Miss Richards wasn't forcing her small talk or her pleasant attitude but was genuinely trying to help.

"Please have a seat and fill this out. Do you need a pen?"

Janelle shook her head. "No, I have one."

"Good. When you are finished, Mr. Gray will see you."

Janelle wondered why Dalton had said such unpleasant things about Keystone. So far everyone had treated her decently, at least better than she had expected.

After jotting down standard, identifying information that was normally requested on an employment application, Janelle was surprised to see so many questions about her family: her mother's name and address, the same for any siblings. The form even asked about her family's religious preference. Janelle hesitated, unsure if she should mention Perry, then put down his name, followed by "U.S. Army," and let it go at that.

When Janelle finished, she handed the paper back to the secretary and waited until she was ushered into John Gray's dingy office.

Everything in the room was gray: the walls, the carpet, the upholstered furniture grouped at the far end of the office, the steel file cabinets stacked against the wall. A squat gray safe, raised from the floor on cinder blocks, dominated the space beneath the only window. Advertising posters with pictures of uniformed men from generations of wars standing at the front gates of Keystone hung on the wall behind the owner's massive desk.

Mr. Gray, a bulky mound of soft pink flesh squeezed into a wrinkled three-piece suit, waved a hand, indicating that Janelle should sit down. Leaning halfway across his desk, he wheezed loudly, rudely scrutinizing his visitor.

"Let's get one thing straight ... right up front, Miss Roy."

Janelle matched his stare.

"I am using valuable time to interview you for two reasons." His eyes narrowed into black slits embedded in a flushed, beefy face—a face that looked as if it had recorded every bourbon and soda the man ever drank.

"First, I want the goddamn NAACP off my back and out of my business. Second, I expect my bid for the government contract on railcars to go through without a hitch." He scowled at Janelle. "This company is close to one hundred years old. My family has produced railroad cars, uniforms, and tents for every war since Abe Lincoln was in office. I don't plan to get forced out of business. Not by a bunch of nigger-loving liberals sent down here from Washington to harass me."

Janelle kept her face perfectly still, unwilling to reveal the fear gripping her. Gray was dead serious about having things his way, and here she was, hoping to be his token offering to appease the federal government.

Gray's wiry eyebrows knitted together as he scanned her application. "Time is running out," he said gruffly. "And I don't plan for Keystone to get passed over. The only reason I'm willing to bring colored into my plant is because I have to." He glanced up. "You got that?"

"Yes," Janelle said as evenly as she could.

"You just got out of the Army, I see?"

"Yes. Unfortunately I injured my knee, had to have surgery on it. Of course, the Army couldn't let me continue as a nurse. Right now I need sedentary work."

"Um-hmm. You don't need crutches? A wheelchair? Nothing like that, do you?"

"No. I can manage quite well, as long as I don't have to stand."

"You got a brother in the Army, too, I see."

Janelle tensed. "Yes" was all she dared say.

"He over there at the colored flying school, too?" Gray made no attempt to hide his displeasure.

"No, he's not."

"Where's he stationed?"

"Camp Livingston," she said quickly, praying her voice had not trembled.

"Oh, yeah? I got a neighbor. His brother is a . . . lemme think, a captain or some kinda officer over there." A disapproving smirk came to his lips. "From what I hear, he's got his hands full, whipping those colored boys into shape."

Pulling her shoulders back, raising her chin, Janelle fixed John Gray with a look of contempt. Now she understood what Dalton had been talking about. This man was a brute. No humanity whatsoever.

"Says here you can run a sewing machine. Doubt you know a thing about the kind of machines we use here."

"I can learn," Janelle said, unwilling to let Gray denigrate her.

He nodded. "Probably." Then he set her application down. "At least you're good-looking. And you've got some education. Guess I can't ask for more, now can I?"

"What does that mean?" Janelle bristled at his comment.

"It means I'm gonna take you on." He folded his thick fingers around the butt of a cigar and shoved it into his mouth. "Be here tomorrow. Seven o'clock sharp. My secretary, Miss Richards, will show you where to go."

Janelle stood, relieved that the interview was over.

"And, Miss Roy?" Gray said, striking a match to his unlit cigar, squinting one eye against the rising smoke.

"Yes?"

"Use the back entrance. The government might make me hire you, but they can't force me to let you come through my front door."

As soon as Janelle had disappeared through the door,

Gray burst into the outer office. "Louise!" he hollered. "Get Crowley Hibbs on the line."

"Right away, sir." Louise jumped to pick up the phone.

"Crowley's got ways to dig up the dirt I'm gonna need to make sure that gal don't get too big for her panties."

Louise fumbled with the dial.

"May be I gotta hire *this* one, but I damn sure ain't gonna let my plant fill up with darkies! Tell Crowley to get his ass over here. We got plans to make."

For some reason Janelle had expected to see Al sitting on the front porch of Deacon Fuller's house, the comic book still clutched in his hand, the puppy playfully licking his face—the image of happy innocence she had carried in her mind for the past six weeks. But the porch was empty, no puppy ran to greet her, and as she approached the teetering clapboard structure, she found it too quiet. Even the chickens that Deacon always let run loose, to cluck and scratch and flutter around the place, were not there.

Janelle stepped onto the porch and knocked. When no one answered, she tried to see through the grimy front window. It was too dark inside to see much except the shadowy outlines of the table and chairs and the tall glass-fronted curio cabinet that held a few precious cups and saucers that had belonged to Lance's mother.

Concerned, Janelle went around to the back. The house only had three rooms and three windows, and she thought she'd better check each one before she left. At the back door she peered in again and saw a pile of dirty dishes on the sideboard, pots on the stove, and a quarter loaf of moldy bread sitting out. Remembering her promise to Lance, Janelle tried the door. It was open.

Cautiously entering the dim, silent house, she called out, "Mr. Fuller? Mr. Fuller? Are you home?" After passing through the dirty kitchen, where the smell of soured milk burned her nostrils, she went into the front room, scanned it quickly, then poked her head into Deacon Fuller's bedroom. There he was, lying flat on his back, a sheet draped across his chest.

"Mr. Fuller!" Janelle rushed to the bedside.

He gave her a weak, tired smile. "Miss Janelle."

"What's wrong? Are you sick?"

"I was thinking about you," he wheezed. "No more than ten minutes ago." Closing his eyes, he coughed roughly, then ran his tongue over his lips.

"What is it?" Janelle placed her fingertips on Deacon's wrist, feeling for a pulse. His skin was warm but not feverish.

"Just plumb tired out, that's all," he murmured.

Janelle frowned as Deacon's slow, irregular heartbeat pulsed beneath her fingers. "How long have you been feeling like this?"

Letting out a breath of exhaustion, he thought for a moment. "Too long, Miss Janelle. Seems I started going down right after you was last here. I was hoping everything worked out for you. I got a message you'd had a little accident."

"Yes," Janelle said, glad her note had reached him. "I didn't want you to think I'd forgotten you, but I had some recovering to do." She checked Deacon's pupils, wishing she had her nursing bag; a thermometer and a stethoscope would have been helpful. "Don't worry about me, I'm fine, but I am concerned about you."

"I've had spells like this before. I'll be all right, Miss Janelle. Just gotta get my rest."

"Where is Al?" Janelle asked.

Deacon's body shuddered, the sheets trembling jerkily. "Is Al here?"

A scowl descended over Deacon's features. "No, I had to let him go."

Janelle watched the scowl turn to grief. Something awful had happened. "Let him go? Where? With whom?"

Now Deacon rolled his white, wiry-haired head back to face Janelle. "Minnie didn't make it, poor soul. And the woman what brought Al over came out to break the bad news. I was down flat on my back. Just about like I am right now."

Janelle felt no sadness for Minnie's death but was worried about what might have happened to Al. "Who was this woman? Where can I find her?"

"Her name was Ruby, I think. Yeah, Ruby. Never did tell me more than that."

"And she took Al away?"

"Yeah. She could see I was in no shape to care for him." Deacon reached toward Janelle with an unsteady hand. "She seemed real happy to help, but I don't like it. I want Al here with me. When I'm back on my feet, she'll bring the boy back."

Unable to mask her concern, Janelle said, "Mr. Fuller, you need to be in a hospital. Your heart is not strong. You can't stay here alone."

He sighed in dismissal. "Don't go making a fuss now. These spells pass. This one's just seemed to hang on."

Janelle went into the kitchen and grimaced at the mess as she drew a basin of water from the indoor pump. In the bedroom she wet a towel and gently cleansed Deacon's face. It was obvious he had been trying to feed himself; there were biscuit crumbs and pieces of dry ham stuck in his beard.

"Where can I find Ruby?"

"I never been to her place," Deacon said apologetically.

"She stays in town? Here in Congregation Hills?"

"Far as I know. Just ask Bert at the general store. He'll know."

Janelle turned to a heavy oak chest, opened it, and took out a clean but wrinkled shirt. As she eased the tired man's arms out of his dirty flannels she asked him, "Is there a phone at the store?"

"Yep. One of two in the whole town."

Glancing out the window, she saw the battered Ford she and Lance had spent so many hours in. It was parked in the yard under a tree. "I came out here on the bus. I'll need to use the car. I'm taking you to the hospital in town.

"The Macon County Hospital?" he said. "I don't think—"

"Sh," Janelle said, easing Deacon back on his pillow. "It's where you need to be."

In town Janelle stopped to use the phone at the general store. Emma answered on the first ring. "How sick is he? Really?" Emma asked after hearing Janelle's observations.

"Sick enough to have lain in bed alone for what looks like several days. His pulse is irregular, he's not complaining of pain, but I want him checked out to be sure."

"Probably the best thing to do," Emma said, then asked, "And you said the boy is gone?"

"Yes, but the man here at the store says the woman who is caring for Al lives right around the corner. I'm going to stop by. And, Emma, if Al is there, would you be upset if I brought him home with me?"

"Upset? Janelle, of course not. But are you sure you want to get this involved?"

"Yes. I'm sure. What else can I do, Emma? I feel so bad for him. None of this is the boy's fault."

"I know. But what will Lance say when he learns you've gotten involved in affairs he thinks you know nothing about?"

"I'll take my chances. He's the one who left this mess behind. I promised him I'd watch out for his grandfather. I am. I'm doing what I think is best."

"Okay. I'll have some decent food waiting for you and Al."

"Thanks, Emma. I'll call you from the hospital."

The woman who cracked her front door looked as if she'd just gotten out of bed. As she pulled her robe closed at the neck, Janelle asked, "Are you Ruby?"

"Yes?" she answered with a question in her voice.

"I'm a friend of Deacon Fuller. He's not well."

"I know." She nodded sympathetically. "I told him he ought to see a doctor."

"I'm taking him over to Macon County Hospital now."

"Um-hmm," Ruby murmured. "That's good."

"Is his great-grandson, Al, here with you?"

Now Ruby frowned, pulling her lips up in a pucker, as if concentrating on what to say. "I had him for a while, but he ain't here now."

"Where is he?"

Ruby pulled the door open more fully but did not invite Janelle in. "Had to send him over to Montgomery. I couldn't afford to keep him any longer. The ladies at the colored orphanage said they'd take real good care of him and when Deacon got better, he could come get the boy."

Janelle's mouth opened slightly as she stared at Ruby. "You sent him to the orphanage in Montgomery?"

Ruby nodded.

"How could you do that?" Janelle began to feel ill.

"Hey, lady, the boy wasn't my responsibility. When Minnie died, I did right by picking him up. Ain't my fault the old man is sick and can't care for his kin." She sniffed loudly and squinted at Janelle. "You go on over to Montgomery and get him if you want to. Ain't nothing keeping you from doing that."

"I will," Janelle shot back, disgusted with the woman's nonchalant attitude.

Back at the car she told Deacon not to worry, that she'd go over to the orphanage in the morning and straighten the whole mess out. But as Janelle headed toward the hospital on the bank of Lake Tuskegee, she worried about frail little Al.

He had seen his mother knifed in a cathouse brawl and watched his great-grandfather fall ill and take to his bed. Now he was alone in a dreary county orphanage. What must be going through the poor child's head?

In an attempt to get her mind off Al, Janelle switched on the radio. The announcer's words did little to calm her nerves.

"At ten o'clock last night the Germans were finally routed from Tunis. Both Tunis and Bizerte were captured by the American Second Corps and the British First Army.

Allied armies hammered at retreating Axis forces and rounded up thousands of prisoners. The beleaguered residents welcomed the Allies with songs and shouts of greeting as Germans fled. It is believed they are fleeing up the Cap Bon Peninsula for a final stand in North Africa."

Looking over at Deacon, she caught his eye, then asked gravely, "What do you think?"

"Humph," Deacon snorted, holding a hand to his chest. "I think it's about time those Jerries turned tail. We got 'em where we can whip 'em now. Don't start frettin' about Lance, Miss Janelle. He's gonna come through all this just fine."

CHAPTER
THIRTY-THREE

Thirty days after arriving at Fordjouna, the final training phase for the 99th was considered complete. Attached to the 33d Fighter Group, the all-Negro squadron had finally been included in the great Allied fleet that was going up against the enemy in unending waves.

At their base on the Cap Bon Peninsula, the men of the 99th honed their fighting skills under the capable instruction of Lieutenant Colonel Phil Cochran, whom the men quickly nicknamed Mr. P-40. For weeks Lance and the members of his squadron had been put through rigorous dive-bombing practice and tactical maneuvers for desert warfare in brand new P-40 Warhawks ferried over from Casablanca. For the first time since entering flight training, as far back as those early days under Chief Anderson, Lance was experiencing the thrill of flying a shiny new plane.

Now, as the briefing session for their first assignment came to an end, Lance looked at his buddies: Herbert Carter, Charles Hall, William Campbell, Clarence Jamison, and James Wiley, all nearly giddy with nervous anticipation. Tomorrow morning at six hundred hours they would be up in the sky, prepared to meet the enemy, making their mark on history.

Walking across the base, Lance thought about the responsibility he and his fellow pilots would be carrying into battle. Blacks and whites in all parts of the country would be following their every move.

In his tent Lance found that someone had stuck a letter from his grandfather into the side of his bedroll. Eager for news from home, Lance squatted down on the floor, ripped open the envelope, and held the letter close to the light to make out Deacon Fuller's uneven, shaky handwriting. He noticed the letter had been written close to two weeks ago.

May 15, 1943

Dear Lance,

Your letter was like sweet music. I could just about hear you talking to me as I read it. Son, sounds like Africa ain't a place I'd wanna be. All that heat and dust, but seeing Josephine Baker in person! Bet she put on some kinda show—you boys being treated right, far as I can tell!

Miss Janelle brought your letter to me here at the county hospital. No reason to worry. I just need rest, the doctor says. I got real tired, had a few pains in my chest. Nothing serious. Gonna be good as new real soon. Don't worry, Miss Janelle checks up on me every day or so. She's been a real help, Lance. You are lucky to have a woman like her waiting for you here at home.

I was happy to hear that you are well and the white boys you flying with are treating you just fine. It's been all in the papers over here, about the 99th hooking up with the 33d. Well, sir, now you got yourself in the thick of things all right. Give 'em hell, son. Give 'em hell.

Wish I didn't have to send you bad news, but I guess life ain't supposed to be rosy all the time. A few things happened since you left, and I think you need to know that Minnie Easter got herself killed in a ruckus in town. Can't say that was a surprise to anybody. A lady friend of Minnie's—name was Ruby—brought the boy to me. I cared for him best I could till I fell sick. Then, when Ruby came back to bring Al a pair of shoes, she took him. Give him over to the colored orphanage in Montgomery. I hated that happening, but maybe it's best. When I get strong enough to go back home, I'm gonna see about getting Al back.

Don't go getting mad at me for this. I know you never claimed the boy, but I guess I'm too old and soft to let a little boy grow up without a family. Not when there's a chance he's kin. Al's a nice child. No trouble. If I don't claim him, who will? You write to me, you hear? And don't go getting yourself in a hissy over this. You just finish off those Jerries and get on home.

> Much love,
> Pop

Lance crushed the letter in one hand. How could Pop do such a thing? What right did he have to put his nose into an affair that was complicated and absolutely none of his business? One good thing, he thought coldly: Minnie was dead. Out of his life. For good. But it was too bad that the boy had been sent to the orphanage. Hell, there was nothing anyone could do about that.

And what about Janelle? Did she know that he had a son? The thought made Lance nervous. He would write Pop tomorrow, when he got back to base, and tell him to leave everything just as it was until he got home.

Surely, if Janelle knew about Al, she would have mentioned it in her last letter. All she had told him was that she was looking for work, though why she bothered, Lance still didn't understand. She ought to take it easy, live off her disability. When he got home, they were going to get married; then she'd have to quit working anyway.

After an uneasy night Lance woke to the blare of reveille and went immediately into another briefing session. There the pilots were given their orders: They'd be flying wing for the 33d on a strafing mission to the Italian-held island of Pantelleria. Now that Tunis had fallen to the Allies, the press toward Sicily was on; the invasion of southern Europe, imminent. Colonel Davis continued his briefing while Lance focused intently on his leader's words, all thoughts of home banished.

* * *

"Why are you so certain that Deacon Fuller hasn't written to Lance and told him you know about the boy?" Emma plunged another dirty plate into the sudsy water, swishing it around.

"Because he gave me his word he wouldn't," Janelle replied, taking the clean plate from Emma, rinsing it, rubbing it dry with a towel. "I have to believe he'd keep his word."

"Kind of chancy, isn't it?" Emma glanced over her shoulder at Janelle. "You need to sit down right now and write a letter to Lance. Tell him you know everything."

Janelle rolled her eyes as she reached up to put the clean plates in the cabinet. "I don't think so, Emma. Lance is busy fighting a war. What good would it do to tell him I know about Al? We can't solve a thing through the mail. I'm sure Lance is planning to share this unfortunate part of his past with me. I'm going to wait for him to bring it up."

"Then you ought to drop this idea of getting Al out of the orphanage. Deacon Fuller is sick, and you're not related to the child. Would the authorities even release him to you?"

"I don't know," Janelle admitted. "But I think getting him out of that place would do a lot toward helping Deacon get better. He's pining away. Having Al around might make up for Lance's absence. Every time I see him all he does is talk about the things he'd like to do for the boy."

"Well, I can understand that, but my God, Janelle, you're taking on a big responsibility. This may be morally right and all that, but legally I don't think you can do it."

"Dalton should be back from Texas tomorrow. I'm going to ask him what to do." Janelle closed the cabinets and turned to lean against the counter, facing Emma.

"I hope you don't let him convince you to do something else you're going to regret," Emma said bluntly, then muttered under her breath, "He might be a good attorney, but, Janelle, I'm worried he's using you." She loved Janelle like a sister and dreaded the possibility that Dalton might hurt her again.

"Remember," Janelle said, tossing the striped dish towel on the kitchen table, "I willingly took the job at Keystone." Since moving into the new apartment, they'd avoided any real discussion of that touchy subject.

"I firmly believe there's going to be trouble over there," Emma said. "Those whites who are picketing and threatening to walk off their jobs are going to wear Gray down. You've been there two weeks. Dalton is nowhere in sight. What help is he going to be if this thing flares into a riot?"

"He'll be here tomorrow. He'll tell me what he wants me to do."

Emma sighed. "Well, for someone who used to go out of her way to avoid any involvement with activists and protests, you sure have walked in a circle."

Janelle clenched her teeth, but she had to admit the truth. "You're right, Emma. Before you convinced me to come to Tuskegee, I never concerned myself with anyone but me. Me and my career. I was selfish. I was wrong to scold Perry like I did, wrong to turn away when he needed me. Perry was the one who was doing the right thing, and now I don't even know where he is." Janelle's voice cracked. Tears came to her eyes. She buried her face in her hands.

Emma wrung out her dishrag and draped it over the faucet. She went over and hugged Janelle. "Don't cry. I know it's tough. Yeah, Perry was always right there—in the heat of the action. I wonder where he is."

"Me, too," Janelle said softly, wiping her cheeks. "But I can't sit around and go crazy thinking about it. I have to help Dalton out."

"Maybe you're right," Emma conceded, "but after two weeks don't you think it's strange that no other colored employees have been hired? And that woman Louise? Didn't you say she's been hanging around the workroom, chatting with you, trying to be real friendly?"

Janelle folded her arms across her stomach and sat

down at the kitchen table. "She seems lonely. I can tell she's unusually liberal. Her son is in the service . . . married to an Oriental woman. Japanese or Filipino, I don't remember which. Louise is very supportive of integrating Keystone."

"You are not stupid, Janelle," Emma said. "Watch out. Something is going on. In less time than it takes to pronounce her name, Louise Richards can turn on you and make your life more miserable than it already is." Emma lifted an eyebrow. "You haven't forgotten Sara Johnson, have you?"

"Louise Richards is not like that. She's the only person at that place who even says hello."

"Right. Why?" Emma sat down across from Janelle. "Why is that woman, the *boss's secretary,* always coming into the plant to speak to you?"

"She wants to help me adjust. I'm the token darky, you know. She's watching out for Gray's investment."

"That's really degrading!"

"It's the truth! And I don't like it, but I'm doing this to help Dalton make a case. He'll force Keystone to open its doors more fully. If he can prove that Gray falsified his contract bid and that hundreds of colored people have been wrongfully denied jobs, the pressure for full integration will be on. Dalton showed me a copy of the paperwork. John Gray wrote down that he had fifty-seven Negroes employed at Keystone. Fifty-seven! He can't even claim that I was working there at the time he submitted that bid."

"I'll bet he has paid somebody off to fix everything," Emma said lightly, waving a hand. "That's the way they get away with their evil schemes."

"But Gray can't shut me up."

"If you live to tell your side of the story."

"Don't be dramatic, Emma," Janelle said. "Now that I'm in the plant, at least the color bar has been broken. Others will soon follow."

"Don't count on it. Gray will find a way to keep us out."

"Not if he plans to get a defense contract from the U.S. government. One colored woman sitting at a sewing machine all day does not equal full integration."

The next evening Janelle sat at her workstation, looking down at her chapped, raw hands long after the shift whistle had signaled it was time to head home. Rubbing her fingers together, she shuddered at the rough, scratchy feel of her skin, the sight of black grime under her nails. Pushing heavy tough canvas under a needle all day was certainly much harder than she had thought. Some of the women wore gloves, and Janelle had tried but had not been able to manage very well. Afraid she might get fired for doing sloppy work, she had given up on the gloves and gone on with her work bare-handed.

After gathering up her lunch box and her sweater, Janelle headed across the empty workroom toward the back door. Of the seventy-five women on the tent production line, she was the only one who entered and left the plant through the rubbish-filled alleyway that wound like a dark snake along the rear of the Keystone building.

"Janelle!" Louise Richards appeared at the front of the room. Letting the door swing shut behind her, she made her way over the cement floor, her footsteps echoing in the hollow space.

Janelle turned and waited, not really surprised to see Louise but very surprised by the expression on her face. The closer she got, the more evident it became that Louise Richards had been crying.

"Janelle!" Louise came to a halt in front of Janelle, a handkerchief balled up in one hand. "I'm glad I caught you before you left."

"What's wrong? Have you been crying?" Janelle was genuinely concerned. Louise had been nothing but polite and friendly since the first day she met her. She hated to see her so upset.

Louise dabbed at her eyes, then wiped her nose. "Yes. I have been crying. And I need to talk to you."

Perplexed, Janelle hesitated. "Here? Now?" They had never talked together after hours.

"Not here," Louise said quickly. "Did you take the bus to work today?"

"Yes," Janelle said.

"Then let me drive you home."

Janelle stepped back, appraising Louise carefully. It was obvious the woman was in great distress, and a ride home would cut Janelle's commuting time in half.

"It's out of your way, Louise. I couldn't let you do that."

"Don't worry about me. I have to talk to you." Louise looked around the dusty workroom as if she feared someone was listening.

"All right," Janelle said.

"Thank you," Louise said, obviously relieved. "I'll bring my car around to the back."

They drove along in uneasy silence until Keystone faded into the bushy forest behind them. Then Louise switched off the radio. Her Plymouth rolled smoothly along over the darkening road.

"Janelle," she started, "I've been fired."

Oh, Lord, Janelle thought, *Emma was right. This woman is going to blame me.* "Fired? Today?"

"Yes." The color had left Louise's face, her cheeks now chalky white. "Right after lunch Mr. Gray called me into his office and told me to clean out my desk."

"Why?" Janelle already knew the answer.

"He doesn't think it's a good idea for his secretary to support integrating the plant. He says I am becoming an embarrassment, and I'm setting a bad example by spending time with you."

"I was afraid this would happen," Janelle said. "You've been great—helping me get settled and learn my way around the plant—but you shouldn't have jeopardized your job."

Louise laughed under her breath, a soft knowing chuckle. "Don't blame yourself, Janelle. Keeping a picture of my Filipino daughter-in-law on my desk didn't help much either." She turned right and proceeded down the road until she came to the four-way stop at the intersection that would have led to the air base. "I think those protesters at the front gates are getting to Mr. Gray."

"I am sorry, Louise. I know you meant to be helpful, but I can't say that I'm surprised to learn Mr. Gray would be so despicable. It's really unfair to you."

Louise shrugged. "Oh, I always struggled to keep our relationship professional. It wasn't easy to get along with him. When I first started there, he made passes at me. When he learned I was not going to let him have his way, he kind of stepped back and gave me a little respect. I needed the job so bad. God knows I put up with a lot."

Janelle said nothing. She wondered what Louise really wanted. As she stared straight ahead, a misty rain began to cover the windshield.

"Gray knew I would close my eyes to the nasty things he did to keep the colored people out of the plant," Louise continued. "For thirty years, Janelle, I've watched him ruin lives and helped cover up his dirty little business."

"Don't feel too bad, Louise. There are men like John Gray everywhere."

"True," Louise said. "But, Janelle—" she said, then stopped.

"What?"

"I know so much about him . . . and that plant."

"What are you saying?" Janelle asked.

"There's a box of papers on the floor . . . at your feet." Janelle looked down.

"Don't pick it up. Not now. But when I drop you off, take it with you. I think Mr. Graham will be very interested in the documents I managed to get out of the safe before I left."

"Louise, I don't know." Janelle cautiously moved her foot until it pressed against the hard side of a box. "Taking these files. Are you in any danger?"

"Probably. But I have nothing to lose." She checked

the rearview mirror, then pulled onto Calloway Street. She came to a stop in front of the house where Janelle lived.

"Is this it? Thirty-four twenty-one?"

"Yes." Janelle was surprised they'd gotten there so fast.

Louise put the car into park and turned in her seat. Facing Janelle, she told her, "Tonight I'm cleaning out my apartment. Tomorrow morning I'm catching a plane to the West Coast."

"Are you going to California?" Janelle thought of Aunt Dedee and her mother; she owed them both letters.

"Yes, until my son is discharged. And"—she smiled broadly, the crow's-feet at the corners of her eyes gathering into soft white folds—"I am happy to tell you that I am going to be a grandmother. It will be heavenly not having to get up every morning and face John Gray. That man nearly drove me crazy. Every day I was in that office, I had to cover up for some evil thing he'd done."

"Well, I hope everything works out for you, Louise," Janelle said.

"Take the files," Louise said, reaching down to pick up a flat black box. Handing it to Janelle, she added, "I think you will be shocked by what you read. Gray and all his ancestors took great pride in preserving every scrap of paper generated at the plant. There are records in the safe dating back to the Civil War. He asked me to destroy these, but I couldn't. Now I know why."

Janelle took the heavy box. "Thank you," she said, realizing she really was saddened that Louise had been treated so badly. "Not only for the records but for being so kind to me."

"I was born and raised right here in Macon County. I've come a long way myself, Janelle. I'll tell you the truth, when my son wrote me that he'd married a Filipino girl, I was outraged, sick to my stomach for weeks. It wasn't what I had planned for him. Then it dawned on me how little control I have. It's his life, not mine. Now I'm just glad he's alive and happy. You deserve to be happy, Janelle. Don't all people? So give the records to Mr. Graham. Maybe he and the NAACP can bring an end to all this hatred and injustice here at home."

CHAPTER THIRTY-FOUR

Janelle entered the apartment and immediately slipped the safety chain on the door. Hugging the files to her chest, she leaned back, breathing shallowly, relieved to be at home. She looked around the dimly lit room, eyes darting from the curtained bedroom entryway to the greenish glow in the kitchen, Louise Richards's words pounding in her mind. Janelle half expected John Gray to jump out from behind the floral-patterned drapes, his beefy face purple with rage, desperate to reclaim his files.

Anxious to see exactly what was in the box, Janelle kicked off her shoes at the doorway and headed directly into the kitchen. There on the table was a note from Emma.

Janelle—Dalton Graham called. He's back. Wants you to telephone him at the Atlas Hotel as soon as you get in. Double shift, remember? I may stay on base. Dinner's on the stove. See you—Emma

Janelle picked up the phone to call Dalton but stopped, her finger stuck in the dial. She'd better wait until she had looked the files over. Maybe the papers were worthless.

After an hour of sifting through the documents, Janelle pushed the box to the center of the table and lowered her chin to folded hands. Around her sat stacks of original applications for employment with the word "Colored" written in blue ink at the top of each page. Applications executed by blacks who had been definitely qualified for the jobs they sought: students from Tuskegee Institute, experienced welders with impeccable references, scores of women with years of experience in industrial sewing who had worked in factories all over the country.

Attached to each application was a rejection letter from John Gray, or whichever Gray had been in charge, turning the applicant down for being illiterate or not meeting basic job requirements. Shockingly, most of the letters also contained not-so-subtle threats of injury, loss of property, and even character assassination if the rejected party dared make a fuss.

There were brittle copies of Keystone bids for federal contracts, dating back over the years, filled with statistics boasting that Keystone was a progressive, fair-minded, fully integrated company. At the same time Janelle found boldly worded communications between John Gray and local businessmen, assuring them he had no plans whatsoever to bring Negroes into his plant.

What a sham, Janelle thought, wondering why the government had never investigated any of this before. But who really cared about a family-owned plant stuck in the woods of Macon County, Alabama? Saddened by the glaring truth of the consistent, blatant discrimination threaded through Keystone's records, Janelle understood more fully why Louise Richards was leaving town.

Well, it's a new day, Mr. Gray, Janelle thought, picking up the phone, dialing the Atlas Hotel. *I think the floodgates have opened, and there's not much you can do to stop the trouble that's coming your way.*

When Dalton arrived, he buried himself in the mound of records, carefully examining each piece of paper.

"This is exactly what we need to move forward with a court case," he concluded, fingering the documents as if they were pieces of delicate silk. "I had a gut feeling you'd be able to get to the source of the cover-up over there. My gut feelings usually pay off."

"Pretty grim records, aren't they?" Janelle said.

"Yeah, but I've seen worse. The eeriest thing about all of this is how carefully all these papers have been maintained."

"Yeah," Janelle said. "You can tell the Gray family is proud of their ability to keep the company lily white."

"I'm sure they are." Dalton put the lid on the box. "Getting you in there was our only chance. Janelle, these documents will give us a case that has teeth. Are you absolutely certain you want to go through with this?"

Janelle knew what he wanted to know: Was she ready to face John Gray's wrath, the outrage of the white citizens who liked things just as they were?

"It could be dangerous, couldn't it?"

"Extremely," Dalton said. "I'll need you to testify before the judge about how you got the records and the absence of other black employees at the plant."

"I've come this far, Dalton. Of course, I'll do all that I can to help you."

"You realize that when the NAACP finishes with Keystone, it will be fully integrated or out of business; without government contracts the company can't survive."

Dalton gazed at Janelle, and she remembered with a jolt the first time she had seen him in his office in Columbus. How patient and understanding he had been. They had come a long way together since then, and it was comforting to know he was still her friend, a friend she hoped to have forever.

"I'm glad your plan worked," Janelle said and smiled. "Now, where do we go from here? Do I return to Keystone tomorrow? Act as if nothing has happened? When will the court papers be filed?"

"Definitely don't go back to Keystone. Your job is finished. We have what we need."

"Don't show up?" It wasn't that she wanted to go back, but she didn't want to arouse any suspicion that she had helped Louise steal those files.

"Well, call over there. Tell the shift supervisor you're

ill. Unless Gray comes down to the production line looking for you, I doubt he'll know you're not there."

"I don't know, Dalton." Janelle could see trouble ahead.

Dalton reassured her. "Just stay away from Keystone.
I'll need a day or two to put all this in order. I've got to
contact headquarters, let them know how this case is progressing. I hope Gray doesn't connect you to the missing
files too soon."

"Of course, he will. I told you, Louise Richards was
openly kind and helpful to me. Gray will make the connection."

"You know nothing, okay? If he calls you or starts asking questions, lie. Tell him you have no idea what he's
talking about." Dalton put the box under his arm and
stood. Though he was trying to remain calm, deep inside
he knew Janelle could be in danger. John Gray was a powerful man.

Janelle walked Dalton to the door.

"Thanks again," he said a bit wistfully. "I really appreciate what you've done."

Janelle laughed softly, realizing Lance had been right:
Dalton still had feelings for her.

"Remember when I told you I wanted to join the Army
to keep my nursing career from falling apart, to serve the
colored troops, do my part . . . ?" She faltered, gathering
courage to explain what had been on her mind for weeks.
"I truly didn't understand what that meant, Dalton. I was
just doing my job as a nurse. Nothing more, really. The accident, the medical discharge caught me by surprise, kind
of stripped away this grand idea I had that I was helping
win the war. But you've opened my eyes: There is more
than one war that needs to be fought, and if I have helped
you in yours, I know I've served my country."

Dalton said nothing, bending slightly to place a light
kiss on Janelle's cheek. Straightening up, he winked at her,
opened the door, then left.

Janelle stood staring after him, one hand on the doorknob, the other to the side of her face.

* * *

Dinner was meat loaf, peas and carrots, mashed potatoes—the meal Emma always prepared on Wednesdays. They managed pretty well, with Emma doing the cooking and Janelle shopping for food. Everything was much more expensive and scarce now that rationing was on. She'd had to go into her little nest egg of savings to put curtains at the windows and pots and pans in the kitchen, and if her disability check didn't start soon, she'd have to dig back in to get her half of the rent.

Now Janelle sat at the table eating, thinking about Lance as she listened to the news on the radio:

"Pantelleria, Lampedusa, and Linosa are now securely in Allied hands. It is clear the invasion of southern Europe will soon begin."

The space in her soul opened up, and a frightful shiver slid over her heart. Lance was out there in the middle of it all, and there was nothing she could do to keep him safe.

Later, while soaking in a tub of warm water laced with perfumed bath salts, Janelle realized that in the midst of all the excitement over the Keystone files, she hadn't told Dalton about Al—a subject that would need his attention. But he had his hands full preparing the court case, she reminded herself. She'd wait a few days, then get his advice, when the issue with Keystone had settled down.

After drying off, Janelle put on her white cotton robe, the lightest, thinnest one she had. Though it was close to midnight, the heavy air of midafternoon still pervaded the stuffy apartment. Janelle lifted her long hair from her neck and twisted it into a neat French roll. As she slipped hairpins into place, she had a feeling that her first summer in the South was going to be a scorcher. Settling down in her bed, Janelle took out her box of stationery and began a letter to Lance.

June 12, 1943

My dearest Lance,

I ache to see you. Your last letter left me so worried. I just heard on the radio tonight that Pantelleria was taken by Allied forces and the fight for Sicily has begun. I try to imagine where you are, what you are doing whenever I hear news of the Allied movements or read anything in the paper about the push into southern Italy. Knowing you are somewhere out there, playing a part in all of it, makes me proud but frightened.

Good news. Your grandfather was released from the hospital yesterday. I drove him out to the house and left him under the care of his neighbor Miss Pinny. She was very nice to agree to check on him and be sure he takes his medicine and has enough to eat. As I am sure you know, he wants no help and is determined to manage alone. Quite a trooper, he is.

No news about Perry. I think he has disappeared from my life forever. I feel so hopeless, so lonely, not knowing what happened to him. Sometimes I wonder if he is dead. I know that is an awful thought, but anything could have happened.

I have left Keystone, but it won't be easy finding another job where I don't have to stand on my feet. I hope something turns up quickly. Living off base is very expensive.

Emma and I are settled into the apartment. It's spacious, and we are trying to make it as homey as we can. She's been working extra shifts at the base and sometimes stays over there, so I find myself alone quite a bit. I don't mind. It gives me quiet time to think of you and plan for the day when you will return.

Wherever you are, darling, remember I am with you. I love you and pray for the day when this war is over.

Love forever,
Janelle

As soon as he entered the lobby of the Atlas Hotel, Dalton Graham was rudely accosted by a man in a black-and-white-striped seersucker suit with a pad and pencil in his hand.

"You Dalton Graham?" he asked, blocking Dalton's path.

"Yes. Why?" Dalton guessed the man was a reporter.

"You the NAACP lawyer who represented those colored protesters at the Vultee plant in Texas?"

Dalton stopped at the foot of the aging hotel staircase, glanced around the empty lobby, then folded his arms across his chest. "Yes, I am." He wasn't about to volunteer more information.

"Can you give the *Tribune* a statement?"

"On what?"

"The Keystone Company, of course. The talk around here is that you are about to start up the same thing you did with Vultee and the Burrnow Shipyards here in Macon County."

Dalton's lips curved down in disgust. "I don't have anything to say to you." He started to push past the man but was stopped.

"Let me give you some advice, Mr. Graham." The reporter assumed a stance of authority. "Folks 'round here don't take kindly to Yankees coming in, trying to tell us what to do."

"My job is to help enforce federal regulations by bringing violators to the attention of the Federal Employment Practices Committee—or the President of the United States, if necessary."

"So you're saying that Keystone is in violation of Executive Order eight-eight-oh-two?"

"It's a possibility," Dalton said. "It's being looked at very closely."

"And if it is? What do you plan to do about it?"

"Mr. . . . ?"

"Jock Taylor."

"Mr. Taylor, the colored people of Macon County have just as much right to work at facilities that have federal defense contracts as white people do. The War Department is not going to allow those who violate the law to profit. Draw your own conclusions."

"You mean a court case is on the horizon?"

"I'd much prefer to see Keystone integrate voluntarily."

Taylor let out a loud guffaw. "Guess I got my answer."

"I guess you have," Dalton said, pushing past the man. He headed up the stairs, strode down the hallway, and entered his room.

Once the door was safely shut, he let himself go limp. Not a good sign, bumping into that reporter. If the press was already nosing around, John Gray was not far behind.

As moonlight shone through the slats in his blinds, Dalton sat under a green-shaded lamp on the table leafing through the Keystone records, planning his case, worrying about Janelle. If she became the target of Gray's fury, she'd be the one to bear the brunt of his anger. A cowardly bastard like Gray would have no problem going after a woman. He didn't have the guts to take the government on.

If this investigation ends up hurting Janelle, he thought, *I'll regret it for the rest of my life.*

Emma untied her nursing shoes, slipped them off, and rubbed the soles of her feet.

"I never thought I'd be so glad to see an Army bunk," she said, pushing herself back on Patricia Williams's bed.

"Hey, relax, take a nap. You've got a few hours until you have to go back," Patricia said. "I'm going over to the PX. Need anything?"

Emma leaned against the back wall, her feet tucked beneath her hips. "Just about twelve hours' sleep. Listen, Pat, are you coming right back?"

"Yeah, I won't be long."

"Good. Wake me up at ten hundred hours. Don't let me lie here and sleep through my next shift."

Patricia gave Emma a mock salute, then started down the narrow row of beds. "You got it. Have a good rest."

Before Patricia got to the door, the telephone rang. She picked it up, saying lightly, "Nurses' quarters, number four."

Emma closed her eyes against the glare of morning sun that streamed through the high rectangular windows.

Pressing her tired limbs into the familiar rough blanket, she tried to clear her mind. Still unused to working the night shift, she hoped she could fall asleep.

"Janelle Roy?" Patricia raised an eyebrow, glancing back at Emma. "Uh, she's not here. Who's calling?"

Emma sat up.

"What? Hey, wait a minute." Patricia put her hand over the mouthpiece of the phone and motioned to Emma. "A call for Janelle. What's your number at the apartment?"

"Who is it?"

Patricia grinned. "Some guy. I can hardly hear him. Do you think it's Lance?"

Emma got up and grabbed the phone. "Hello. Who is this?" The line was silent. "Is this long distance? Lance? Is it you?"

"No, it's not," a voice rumbled lowly. "I want to speak to Janelle Roy."

Emma had known Perry Roy as long as she had known Janelle, and there was no mistaking his deep baritone voice. Anxious, she turned to Patricia. "It's okay. This is her uncle from Ohio. I'll take the call."

"Sure," Patricia said, waving, going out the door.

Emma turned her back to the few other nurses in the barracks, facing the wall. "Perry? This is Emma. Talk to me. Please."

No response.

"I know it's you," Emma whispered into the mouthpiece. "It's you, Perry, isn't it?"

A mumbled response came through the line, "Yeah, Emma, it's me."

"Where are you?" she managed to ask as casually as possible.

"It doesn't matter."

"Yes," she hissed. "It does. Janelle is sick with worry."

"Let me talk to her."

"Uh . . ." Emma's mind raced. She couldn't let him hang up without getting more information. "Are you in Alabama? Nearby?"

"Emma, please. I've got to talk to Janelle."

"She's not here, but call this number. She'll answer. She's alone. RE seven-eight-nine-three."

There was a pause.

"Call her," Emma pleaded, hoping Janelle could convince Perry to turn himself in. "She's desperate to know—" Before she could finish her sentence, there was a click, then a loud, flat buzz.

CHAPTER
THIRTY-FIVE

It was a relief not to have to report to Keystone. Janelle called in, then slept until nine o'clock. Later, while sipping a cup of coffee she read the morning paper. Sugar allotments for industry had been cut 37 percent. As Janelle swallowed, she was glad that both she and Emma liked their coffee unsweetened; their ration stamps for sugar had been used up long ago when Emma got a sudden urge to bake apple pies for the nurses on base.

The local tin can drive was in full swing, and all residents were encouraged to drop off their cans at the Folder Grocery Store before noon. She and Emma had a sackful to donate; she'd go over there as soon as she dressed.

There was also an urgent, boldly lettered appeal for waste fat to be used in the manufacture of explosives. As Janelle turned the page, she wondered how that was done.

On the next page, along with guidelines for writing to American prisoners of war, there was a detailed story about the race riots in Detroit that had flared over the heated issue of integrated housing. Competition between blacks and whites for jobs and decent places to live had polarized the city to such an extent, Major Jeffries had organized a biracial peace board to make long-range plans for healing the community.

Folding the paper, Janelle thought of the Keystone documents, the case Dalton was about to file. She shuddered. Both whites and blacks in Macon County were already tense and edgy, openly expressing their support of or displeasure at the actions of the NAACP. Once the judge ruled, no matter which way the case turned, Janelle feared rioting could easily erupt in Tuskegee.

The quiet morning was suddenly shattered by someone pounding on the front door. Startled, Janelle checked the kitchen clock. Not yet ten. The landlady was not back from her daily trip to the market, so Janelle hurried down the stairs and opened the front door.

John Gray, his face set in a mask of purple contempt, stood glaring at her in the doorway.

Janelle's mouth opened slightly. Fearful of the bulky man standing on her porch, she eyed him cautiously, dreading the confrontation that seemed imminent. She had to admit she had halfway expected this to happen; the surprise was that he had come so soon.

Gray rudely pushed past her, slamming the door shut with such force the white lace curtains quivered on their rods.

"Mr. Gray!" Janelle stepped back into the parlor. He followed.

"I want my files. Now!"

Gripping the belt to her robe, Janelle made a knot, yanking it tightly around her waist. "What files?"

Gray shook his head, denying her denial as he said menacingly, "My first stop was Louise Richards's place. Seems she didn't understand the law. Now, Miss Roy, I'm sure your lawyer friend Mr. Graham has told you that breaking into a private safe and stealing documents is a crime. Don't stall and don't be stupid. Give me the documents. Now!"

Janelle's breath caught at the back of her throat. "I don't have them." Pulling herself up to her full height, she assumed a posture of indifference.

Gray took hold of her arm. "Where are they? You give 'em to that nigger-loving lawyer?"

Too frightened to speak, Janelle yanked her arm away, rubbing the spot where his fingers had bruised her skin.

A sly smile spread over Gray's pink, mottled face. "Listen, missy, if you're counting on the NAACP to get you outa the mess you're in, you're a lot dumber than I thought you were."

Janelle raised her eyebrows in apprehension.

Gray smirked. "Your brother is a fugitive . . . AWOL, isn't he?"

Janelle just stared.

"Isn't he?" Gray growled insistently.

Janelle defiantly refused to answer.

"And he's in the area. I know exactly where he's hiding." Gray stepped closer. "The Army wants him for murder. You stupid little bitch. I should slap your face." He raised his hand as if to strike her.

Janelle shied back, raising her arm to block his assault.

As he slowly brought down his hand, Gray smirked in perverse satisfaction while telling Janelle, "I could get my hands on Private Perry Roy in just a matter of minutes." He watched for Janelle's reaction. "That surprise you, huh?"

"Where is he?" *Oh, God,* Janelle thought, *what is happening?*

"Not far, really. He's hanging around the back alleys in town, living like a rat, eating garbage right from the cans, sleeping on the ground like the filthy dog he is. Guess he's trying to get up the courage to come see you." Gray's eyes furtively scanned the neat parlor until he saw the telephone atop a small Victorian table. "I can save your brother, Miss Roy. And you can get out of this nasty mess you've gotten yourself in."

"What do you want?" Janelle compressed her lips, waiting. Surely he wouldn't rape her or hurt her, not here.

"Right now Private Roy is safe. The Army has no idea where he is."

"Is he hurt?"

"Oh, no. He's fine. A strapping young buck like him . . . he's made it on foot all the way from the Louisiana border.

No, Miss Roy, he's not hurt. Not yet. Tell you what I'm willing to do. . . ." He dangled the offer like a threat.

"What?" Her voice was no more than a whisper.

"I'll arrange for you to meet your brother, give him a real goodbye. Then I'll get a friend of mine to drive your brother safely into Canada out of danger."

"Why would you do that?"

"Because you're going to call that nigger-loving lawyer and tell him to give me back my papers and clear out of Macon County. There will not be a court case involving Keystone, you understand? If you don't stop this, Perry Roy is dead . . . and it won't be the Army finishing him off."

Gray crossed the room, picked up the phone, and dialed. "Mr. Dalton Graham, please," he said in a businesslike voice. Covering the mouthpiece, he said to Janelle, "Now you tell Mr. Graham that you are not going to testify or support his case, so he better give me back my papers and forget about pushing niggers into my company."

Perry's face rose before Janelle's eyes: unhappy, confused, filled with grief over their father's death. He hadn't had a chance to grow up fully—grow beyond the loss that had trapped him.

"If you don't cooperate, missy, you'll never see your brother again. Not alive anyway, that's for sure." Gray cleared his throat and spoke into the phone. "Hello, Mr. Graham? Hold on." Holding the phone out to Janelle, he growled, "The choice is yours."

Tentatively she took the phone from Gray. The memory of Perry's voice echoed in her ears. The picture of him and Frank and Aunt Dedee that had sat on the piano since their childhood flashed clearly into her mind. She strained to remember how he had looked the last time she had seen him at Union Station—sharp, uniformed, ready to start a new life. Now it had come down to this?

"Dalton? . . . Yes, Janelle." She covered her face with one hand, looking down at the floor. "I've been thinking about everything you said last night." Her heart thundered under her robe. Appalled by the ghastly options given her, she hesitated, pressing the phone flat against her ear.

Gray stood nearby, wheezing loudly, his belly quivering with each breath. Janelle sensed the cruel power seeping from beneath his overtight vest, from the pores of his smug pink face. He tapped a foot impatiently as he waited for her to say what she knew in her heart she couldn't.

In a rush of words she confirmed her decision. "No, Dalton, I haven't changed my mind. I called to tell you to hurry and file the papers. Get this case into court as quickly as you can."

Gray snatched the phone from Janelle and slapped her across the cheek with it. Stumbling backward, she struck the wall, flattened, holding her face, eyes watering with pain and anger and guilt. Gray threw the phone across the room and smashed a cluster of silver-framed pictures crowded atop Miss Grace's oak sideboard. The tinkle of broken glass falling to the floor was lost beneath the crash of the door slamming shut as John Gray left the house.

Oh, Perry forgive me. Please, Janelle prayed, dropping to her knees. *I didn't have a choice. You know I didn't.*

After flying missions at Pantelleria for seven days straight without sighting a single enemy plane, the men of the 99th were on tenterhooks to engage the Germans in aerial combat. They had broken away from their role as wingmen to the 33rd and were flying independently with the group. On June 9 the first enemy sighting finally occurred when Lieutenant Charles Dryden and his flight group were attacked by twelve Focke-Wulfs and Messerschmitts that, out of nowhere, zeroed in on them.

The German warplanes, flying cover to eighteen bombers headed to attack the Allied invasion, dived through the P-40 Warhawks in loose formations of twos, hitting one of Dryden's fighters. Lieutenant Spann Watson managed to get in a few rounds before the Germans broke away, soaring off toward Sicily. Until enemy ground fire forced them back, the 99th remained in hot pursuit but lost the opportunity to score a hit.

By the time Pantelleria was in the hands of the Allies, the 99th had completed a grueling schedule of sixteen sorties a day. During the assault Lieutenant William Campbell earned the distinction of being the first Negro to drop a bomb on an enemy of the United States.

With the fight for Pantelleria behind them, the 99th soon merged with the 324th Fighter Group at El Haouria on the Cap Bon Peninsula. The Negro pilots, who knew the Germans referred to them as *schwartzer Vogelmenschen,* or black birdmen, were assigned to escort sixteen B-25 bombers to the western sector of Sicily to bomb the Castelvetrano Airfield. It was July 2, 1943.

Before heading to the briefing room in preparation for his sixth mission, Lance reread Janelle's letter, then folded it into a tiny square, pushing it inside his brown bomber jacket. He had to smile; it was damn hard to be mad at her. She had this innocent way of telling all, baring her soul like a child asking for forgiveness.

Sure, he'd been upset when she admitted embellishing her past to impress him. But could he really fault her for that? If anything, he ought to be flattered. He had to give her credit; her heart had been in the right place.

But what about Alabama? Still no indication that she knew of his existence. Lance zipped up his leather jacket and headed across the base. As soon as he returned from this mission, he was going take the time to write to her and get it off his chest. He'd better come clean if he wanted a future with the woman he loved.

Lance took his seat in the briefing room beside Lieutenant Hall. The intelligence officer began his briefing, revealing the target, how many of the enemy they could expect to encounter and from what position. The report from the weather officer was encouraging: They could expect clear blue skies above the equally blue Mediterranean.

After synchronizing their watches, the pilots got into

jeeps for the short ride to the dispersal area where their planes sat warming, ready for takeoff.

Lance jumped from the jeep and hurried to his plane, bolstered by the sight of the bright blue letters, JANELLE, he had painted in fancy, scrolled lettering on its side. Then he climbed into the cockpit and, with the aid of his crew chief, checked the equipment. Everything was okay.

Lance fastened his goggles securely over his eyes, thinking maybe this time he'd get close enough to the enemy to be able to score a hit. Though his job was to keep enemy fighters away from the bombers, it was time for an aerial victory.

Lance clenched his jaw. He and all the members of the squad had heard the rumors: The 99th was weak; it had not seen as much action as other units; the Tuskegee experiment had failed. The press seemed to take special satisfaction in reporting that some pilots in the squadron had already returned to the States, their allotted missions completed without their firing a single shot.

"Well, let 'em say what they want," Lance muttered under his breath, looking over to give the thumbs-up to wingman James Knighten in the plane next to his. "We're as competent as any white pilots out there racking up victories every day," Lance told himself. Killing a Jerry would be easy; all he needed was the opportunity to come his way.

Six P-40's had been assigned to the mission. Lance was third in line to take off. He made a smooth departure from the runway, assembling with the other pilots into their escort formation. Then they pointed their planes toward the coast to rendezvous with the bombers.

Up in the air it was calm and clear, though down toward the sea Lance saw a slight haze spreading out like a great gray blanket, shielding the enemy guns. Cruising along, the men tested their guns, adding a sharp rat-a-tat to the noisy drone of their engines.

Without incident the squad soon met the B-25's and fell into place, covering the bombers as they unloaded their deadly cargo. Upon impact, the bombs exploded in huge billowing clouds of black smoke that mushroomed sinisterly beneath the planes. Simultaneously ground fire erupted in a volley of black flak, and enemy fighters swarmed up for an attack.

Tensing against the pull of his engine, Lance saw two Fw-190's swing in behind them, following closely.

Breaking formation, the squad started its attack. Charles Hall pulled away and headed for the space between the fighters and the bombers. Lance soared high to cover him. Hall fired a long burst. Lance watched the tracers penetrate one of the Fw's. Hall had scored a hit! With a smile on his face, Lance watched the German swing to the left, then plunge to the ground and crash. A black cloud of dust whooshed up, marking the 99th's first victory.

"All right!" Lance yelled as he reefed his plane and climbed higher, trying to position himself above Dryden and Knighten, who were engaged with four enemy aircraft. Lance circled once, assessed the situation, then dived straight toward a Focke-Wulf. From out of nowhere, it seemed, a Messerschmitt appeared on his right and opened fire.

The impact of the gunfire threw Lance back in his seat and tore the goggles from his face. Shattered glass rained down, a deafening roar filled his ears, and for a split second Lance froze, expecting the plane to burst into flames.

It didn't, but the trickle of blood that rolled down his forehead into his eyes confirmed he'd been hit.

Pulling into a series of tight turns, Lance broke away and then climbed again, able to see the Germans being pressed far from their territory. Apparently realizing how far they were being led from their base, the Germans abruptly broke off the attack.

Wiping blood from his face, hardly able to see, Lance pulled in behind Hall and followed him back to base. Once on the ground he slumped in the cockpit, thankful to have made it back. Tentatively he pressed his fingertips to his forehead. There were bits of glass embedded just above his eyebrow. It hurt, but the pain was bearable. It was his right eye—clouded over and burning unrelentingly—that gave him the greatest concern.

Within minutes Lance found himself under the exacting scrutiny of a medical officer, who carefully cleaned the shards of glass from his wounds with a boric acid solution. After examining the eye, the doctor told him that the injury was superficial, away from the cornea and should not affect his vision. That was heartening news, but the fact that the injured eye had to be covered with a patch to heal completely—and that could take up to eight weeks—was shattering. Lance would be returned to the States for recovery. If his eyesight tested out, he'd be back in the cockpit. If it didn't, he'd probably wind up finishing out the war instructing cadets at Tuskegee.

During the next twenty-four hours Lance's jubilation about the success of the 99th's mission slipped away, leaving him in a despondent, foul temper. As he lay on his cot with his hands behind his head, awaiting the first signs of dawn, he dreaded the flight to Casablanca, the long ocean voyage back home.

It would be great to see Janelle, Pop, the buddies he'd left behind, but now was not the time to be going home. His combat stint wasn't supposed to end this way. With difficulty, he struggled to reconcile the disappointment, anger, joy, pride, and shame that alternately gripped him as he thought about the mission.

Could he have avoided being strafed by that Messerschmitt? Had he been so dead set on scoring his own victory that he'd let down his guard? Put himself and the others in the enemy's path? Had he permitted the exhilaration of watching Hall drop that Jerry skew his focus, push him into an uncovered, vulnerable position? He hated the fact that he would miss the recap of the mission, be left out of the detailed examination he knew Colonel Davis and the intelligence officers would give their victory flight.

I just hope this thing heals up fast, so I can get back into action, he thought, remembering the medical officer's words. His wounds should heal, his vision would be fine, but to go home with one eye patched and no score under his belt. This was not what he had expected.

As he turned onto his side and closed his eyes, a great booming sound exploded over the base. Tensing to a half-sitting position, Lance held his breath, waiting. Were air strikes getting that close to the base?

Silence followed the jarring noise, then the scream of sirens and yells for help reverberated across the base. Lance lay back down, worried, frustrated. Why the hell was he flat on his back when the squadron needed him most? What could he do? Nothing. Nothing but lie there, wondering what was going on.

Just when he drifted into a hazy sleep, Lieutenant Hall slipped in and gently stirred him. "Hey, buddy."

Lance opened his eyes and looked up. The African sunrise was pinking the desert behind Hall.

"Hey, Charles." Lance pushed himself up on his elbows. Hall lit a cigarette and handed it to Lance.

"Bad break, Fuller," he said. "But you'll be back. We'll keep your engines warm."

Lance grinned. "You'd better. This ain't nothing but a scratch. By the time I get to Tuskegee, it'll be healed."

"Moving out this morning?"

"Yeah. By air to Casablanca, transport ship to New York."

Hall took the cigarette back from Lance and took a deep pull. "I hate to send you off with news like this, but White and McMullin were killed this morning."

Lance stared at Hall. "Killed?"

"Yeah, a real freaky thing. They collided on the runway, taking off."

"Oh, shit!" Lance pushed himself fully upright, pulling his knees to his chest. "I heard the explosion."

"Yeah, they're the first." Hall sighed. "We've been lucky. But we've got a long way to go, Fuller." He pulled on his flight cap, firmly tugging the bill. "You get yourself healed up pronto, and get your ass back over here, all right?"

"Sure." Lance nodded at Hall. "I'll be back before you get the chance to miss me."

CHAPTER THIRTY-SIX

"You'd think this would have gone down by now," Janelle said to Emma, pushing her face closer to the mirror above her dresser, examining the puffy black-and-blue splotch on her cheek.

"That's a terrible bruise, Janelle. A week is not enough time for an injury like that to heal." Emma raked her nail file over her thumbnail and lifted her eyes to Janelle. "You should have called the police on that man."

Turning her back to the mirror, Janelle sighed. "And what about Perry?"

"What about Perry?" Emma asked. "If John Gray was going to kill him, don't you think he'd have done it by now?"

"How do we know he hasn't?"

"I hate to admit it, but what Dalton said last night is probably true. Gray was bluffing."

"Hmph!" Janelle dismissed Emma. "That man was deadly serious. The authorities will probably come knocking on my door any minute, telling me that Perry's body has been found floating in a creek or smashed to pieces by the side of the road. I'm so nervous, Emma. I have to appear before the judge at the end of this week, and who knows what's going to happen? I wish I had been able to talk to Perry. I wonder why he didn't call back."

"Probably scared. I gave him the number and told you were alone." Sympathy for Janelle's mounting troubles softened Emma's tone. "I wish you had been the one to take his call. He was frightened. I could tell. He mumbled real fast. I hate to think of him alone out there . . . a fugitive." She felt a surge of sadness. "Perry's not that strong. This thing could break him, you know?"

A whispered warning came into Janelle's mind. If Perry was desperate, no telling what he might do. "I know. Even if he showed up at our door right now, Emma, what could we do? Hide him? Help him? Get ourselves arrested, too?"

"Put that out of your mind. Gray was bluffing! That's what I think." Emma set aside her long metal file and began buffing her nails. "It wouldn't surprise me if Perry's left the area."

"I don't know why, but I have a sense, a strong feeling that he's not far. Emma, he wants to see me. I know it."

Emma remained quiet, considering Janelle's predicament. "Maybe John Gray was the one to run. Maybe he's cleaned out the company's bank accounts and fled."

"Not a chance," Janelle replied hastily. "He's not going to abandon Keystone. It's been in his family for almost a hundred years. No," Janelle decided, "he'd stand and fight." She picked up her hairbrush and began stroking her hair, searching for a plausible explanation. "But how and when will he strike? That's what we need to know, Emma."

The bold, jazzy sounds of Duke Ellington's band drifted from the radio on the dresser and filled the room but did nothing to lighten the mood.

"Speaking of making a move," Emma said, "what is Dalton doing about the boy? Can he help Deacon spring him from the orphanage?"

Wishing she didn't have that sticky problem tucked into the back of her mind, Janelle said rather testily, "The paperwork is a nightmare. Getting Lance's grandfather approved as guardian will take longer than we thought. But Dalton is hopeful. At least it's in the works."

"What about the five-hundred-dollar fee?" Emma curiously raised an eyebrow. "Who's going to cough that up?"

"Don't worry. When the trustees of the orphanage approve Deacon as guardian, he'll get custody of Al. Somehow we'll work it out."

"We? Somehow?" Emma said, surprised. "Somehow five hundred dollars will just . . . appear?"

Janelle kept brushing her hair.

Emma pressed the issue. "I hope you are not planning on using your money."

"I have more than enough. I could help," Janelle said.

"Well," Emma replied, "you have yet to get a disability check. You could use up all that money you inherited by the time you get your compensation."

"Have a little faith, Emma." Janelle put her off, not wanting to admit how uneasy she had become about her involvement in bringing Alabama home. "Wait until after the Keystone case. Then Dalton can concentrate on helping Deacon get custody of Al. The NAACP has a fund. If the case warrants, he might be able—"

The sound of a tap on the door interrupted their conversation. Janelle glanced at Emma, hairbrush in midair.

"Probably Miss Grace," Emma said, slipping off the bed to answer the door. As expected, their diminutive landlady stood in the doorway, a yellow piece of paper in her hand.

"Miss Grace, come in," Emma said.

"No, no, I'm on my way to church. The Western Union man just came and gave me this for Janelle." She handed the telegram to Emma, who thanked her and shut the door.

"Janelle!" she called from the front of the apartment. "Telegram for you."

Janelle froze. The dreaded messenger had arrived: the thin yellow slip of paper, the sterile, impassive notice that could easily shatter her future.

Entering the living room, the blue plastic hairbrush still in her hand, Janelle stared at the envelope, making no move to reach out and take it.

"It's Lance, I just know it." The yawning black hole opened wider. Janelle teetered dangerously at the edge.

"Maybe not," Emma said softly. "Might be a message

from Perry. Maybe he's made it out of the country. He'd want you to know." Emma turned the envelope over in her hands, held it up to the light. "It could be from your mother. She's sent telegrams to you before."

Pushing back her fears, Janelle inhaled, gathering strength from the realization that both Lance and Perry were now immersed in the most dangerous circumstances of their lives. How dare she tremble and quiver and bite her lips over facing a thin piece of paper?

She measured her odds, uneasiness flickering across her face as she took the envelope and tore it open. She read the two lines aloud: "Am at Camp Shanks. On my way home. Don't worry. I am fine. See you next week. Monday or Tuesday morning. Love you, Lance."

Janelle sank down on the sofa, spasms of relief coming over her. "Lance is on his way home. He'll be here next week!"

"Why?" Emma asked, perplexed by this unexpected homecoming. She sat down beside Janelle, took the telegram, and read it again. "He must have completed his allotment of missions."

"I don't think so." Janelle slowly folded the message. "He must be hurt, Emma. There's no other reason they'd let him come back, not with the Ninety-ninth in the middle of the Sicilian campaign."

"Hurt? How could that be? Wouldn't he have been transferred directly to the field hospital? I haven't seen his name on any of our lists. We're not expecting him on base." Emma placed her arm over Janelle's shoulder and squeezed. "He's traveling. He says he's fine. Let's not get ourselves all jittery and conjure up more than there is to this."

Weakly Janelle murmured her agreement, but she could not dispel the agitation the news produced. Something was wrong, very wrong.

Emma told her, "Don't turn yourself inside out over this. When I get to the hospital in the morning, I'll find out why Lance Fuller has been returned stateside. You can be sure somebody at Tuskegee knows what's happened."

Perry curled himself into a tight ball, settling firmly against the hard slats in the sagging wooden fence. The moist evening air seeped into his clothing, covering him like a thin damp blanket. He put one hand under his cheek, glumly watching shadows in the dark alley where two men poked at a fire they had started in a tall metal drum. One of them kept pacing away, then turning back to look at him. Perry was getting nervous.

Just a crazy wino, he thought, relieved that most of them left him alone, ignoring his presence in their haven of decay. Only the one in the denim coveralls seemed nosey and bothersome, always hanging around.

The hobos and mindless bums who had tried to run him off when he arrived three weeks ago now accepted him into their fraternity of lost souls. By firmly refusing to be run off, Perry had forced their respect for his right to the grubby plot of land under the huge gum tree.

Sniffling, Perry wiped his nose on the sleeve of his shirt, wishing the pounding in his head would stop. For three days now the dull, persistent ache had plagued him, spreading from the base of his neck to the middle of his forehead.

Maybe I'm dying, he thought impassively, accepting the pain as a pervasive, hungry cancer born to punish him for killing that German, for running away, for letting his family down, for making a mess of his life.

As the acrid smell of burning trash entered Perry's nostrils, stinging his eyes, he stiffened convulsively, then relaxed, throwing off the newspapers that covered his legs.

I had a home once, he reminded himself. *A nice home filled with love. I had my own room and a closetful of clothes.* With alarming clarity the lemon-fresh smell of the stiff clean sheets his mother had put on his bed every Saturday morning every year of his life intruded on his rambling self-pity.

Too ashamed to allow himself to cry, Perry swallowed stoically, determined to push aside the emerging memories. But they wouldn't leave him alone. He remembered sitting in the kitchen in the house in Oakwood Alley, his mother, his father, his sister at his side. The way the whole house used to rattle with the boom of his father's voice. The outlandish stories he loved to tell.

Janelle had always hogged the corn bread, he recalled with a smile. And his mother had always made them divide the last piece, no matter how small it might be.

Scratching at the itchy rash now blistered in painful welts on the backs of both hands, Perry tried to picture Janelle. He had never seen her in her Army uniform, he realized. He'd never had the chance to "talk Army" with her, comparing experiences, telling jokes about their training, sharing the common thread of their military lives.

I've got to see her, he decided, knowing his luck might be running out. *I'm going over to Tuskegee as soon as I scrounge up some decent clothes and clean myself up. I don't want her to see me looking like the bum I guess I am.*

And after I see her and hold her and tell her how much I love her, I'll turn myself in to the military police at Tuskegee Airfield and be finished with this hellish nightmare.

The decision brought release, and Perry locked the fingers of both hands beneath his head. Lying on his back, he searched the ebony sky for confirmation in the stars. Detached from his miserable surroundings, he floated calmly, absorbing the long-awaited sleep that folded over his weary soul.

When Janelle entered the lobby of the Atlas Hotel, she was glad to see Dalton just inside the door, waiting for her. She hadn't heard anything more from John Gray, but after a week of being anxiously keyed up, she was glad the hearing was scheduled for the next day.

The past five days had slipped by in a blur of apprehension as she waited for the phone to ring, alternately fearing she'd hear from Gray, while praying for Perry to call.

Since neither had contacted her, Janelle could only hope that her brother was still alive.

Dalton greeted her with a calming smile. "It's almost over, Janelle. I just want you to know what to expect tomorrow morning."

Janelle didn't stop walking but hurried alongside Dalton up the stairs toward his room on the second floor.

"No word from Gray, I take it?" She was beginning to believe Emma might be right. Maybe he was too much of a coward to face the judge tomorrow.

"No," Dalton said, taking out his key to unlock his door. "But I'm not surprised."

"Do you think he'll show up?"

"Yeah," Dalton said. "He'll be there. There's too much at stake for him not to make an appearance. Besides, Judge Allen is rumored to be nearly as upset about this movement to integrate Keystone as Gray himself. The judge probably has a bunch of relatives on the payroll."

Janelle didn't like the sound of that. Could the legal system in Macon County handle this case in a fair, just manner?

Dalton opened the door, then hung back to let her in.

Instantly a man stepped out of the cloistered doorway across the hall. A flashbulb popped in their faces.

"What the hell are you doing?" Dalton snapped, moving between Janelle and the reporter.

Jock Taylor crouched down, snapping another picture, catching Dalton with his mouth wide open in surprise.

"Thanks," the grinning reporter called out. His rubber-soled shoes squeaked as he ran down the corridor and disappeared down the stairs.

"I'm sorry about that," Dalton said, entering his room behind Janelle. "That man has been dogging me since the day I returned from Texas."

"He's with the *Tribune*?"

"Yeah. He's been nosing around the Keystone case. Guess he got what he wanted to finish up his story." Shrugging, Dalton went to the table near the window and sat down, waiting for Janelle to join him. He opened a thick manila folder and spread a sheaf of papers on the table.

"I want you to tell me, again, just the way you are going to tell the judge, how you came to be in possession of these papers."

"All right," Janelle said, wondering for the first time if Louise Richards had successfully made it out of Alabama.

After going over the details of the evidence he was going to present, Dalton concluded he was as prepared as he could possibly be.

"Remember," he cautioned Janelle, "don't let anything John Gray says throw you off. You can be sure he is going to lie . . . and lie very well. He's had years of practice bamboozling the authorities."

"How long do you think it will take?" Janelle asked.

"If the judge is on the ball and truly wants to settle this, he should be able to make a decision pretty quickly on whether or not Keystone has violated the executive order. It's a clear-cut case, as far as I can see." Dalton folded up the papers and closed the file. "If we start on time, at nine o'clock, we ought to be finished by noon."

"Or it could drag on for days, weeks?" Janelle asked, not sure she would be able to stand the pressure of going back to court again and again.

"Sure." Dalton gave Janelle a level look. "And the longer it takes to settle this, the more tense everybody is going to be. There could be trouble tomorrow."

She let Dalton's warning sink in. "A riot?"

"Could be." Dalton had seen angry crowds gather in front of courthouses for cases much less serious than this one. "The question is, Will the local authorities do anything if violence breaks out? It wouldn't surprise me a bit if the sheriff did nothing to control the crowds that I'm sure are going to be there."

The thought of blacks and whites, roaming the streets, screaming hate-filled obscenities at one another made

Janelle wish she had never agreed to help. "Are you worried?" she asked Dalton.

He was silent for a moment, then replied, "Worried for me? No. Worried about you? Yes." He leaned over the table. "As soon as court is over, I've got to catch a train to Texas. I must be back in Fort Worth by evening." He rubbed his chin, watching Janelle closely. "I don't like leaving you behind. No matter how this case turns out, somebody is going to be very angry."

"It's all right," Janelle murmured. "I'm not afraid."

"You should be," Dalton said firmly. "It might be a good idea for you to go out to California and visit your mother. Stay a month or longer . . . until things calm down and the folks get used to the changes this decision might bring."

"I can't leave. Lance is coming home. I have to be here when he returns."

The news caught Dalton by surprise. "Oh? What's happened? Was he wounded?"

Biting her lip, Janelle nodded. "Emma found out his plane took a hit, but he managed to land. With some glass embedded in his face."

"God, Janelle, I'm sorry to hear that. Truly. How bad are his injuries?"

"Not so bad. He's expected to recover fully. If he doesn't go back into combat, he'll stay here at Tuskegee and teach."

Dalton relaxed, a hint of jealousy on his face. "Bet that would suit you just fine," he said.

"Maybe, maybe not. It will just about kill Lance if he's grounded. I don't know if he or I could live with that."

"Sure, I understand," Dalton said. "It took awhile for me to come to terms with the fact that I could never serve."

"You are serving, Dalton," Janelle said. "You know that. And you're winning your war."

Embarrassed, Dalton got up and lit a cigarette, his back to Janelle as he looked out the window. "The square is so empty, peaceful. Who could guess that a stream of hatred and ignorance runs a mile wide through this tiny town? Well, it's all going to be exposed when the sun rises over the courthouse tomorrow morning."

Janelle knew it was time to get going. She opened her purse and took out a piece of blue paper. "Dalton?" He turned to face her. "Before you leave for Texas, can you make sure this gets to Montgomery?"

He looked at the slip of paper she held in her hand. "What's this?"

"The money to settle Alabama's release. Can you take care of it for me before you go?"

Surprised, Dalton took the check and studied it silently. It was made out to him for five hundred dollars. "Are you sure this is what you want to do?"

"I'm sure," Janelle said without hesitation. "How can I not help? I saw Deacon two days ago. The man is grieving himself to death, blaming himself for getting sick, letting Ruby take the boy. . . . It's a sad, sad situation. I didn't earn this money, remember? It came to me unexpectedly. Maybe the Lord sent it to me to help someone who was hurting. To give that child an opportunity to have a home, someone to love him. It can't be the wrong thing to do, can it?"

Dalton slipped the check into his leather attaché case. "Of course not. I'll handle it for you, Janelle. I've got to pass through Montgomery on my way out. The least I can do is take the time to put your mind at ease about this. Don't worry. Al will be back with his great-grandfather very soon."

"Thanks," Janelle said, snapping her purse closed, rising to open the door. "I'll see you at the courthouse in the morning."

"Yes," Dalton said distractedly. "Nine o'clock sharp. Get some rest."

When Janelle had closed the door, Dalton returned to stand by the window, waiting until he could see Janelle hurrying across the darkening square toward home. As his eyes followed her statuesque figure, he sighed and shook his head. So Lance was coming home. Janelle's world was finally taking shape. She was going to be happy. He could see it in her face, hear it in her voice, and all he wanted to do was get as far away from Tuskegee as possible and leave her to the happiness she deserved.

Turning around, Dalton reached into his attaché case. He took out the check she had written and calmly shredded it into his wastebasket.

CHAPTER
THIRTY-SEVEN

How disgusting, Janelle thought, folding the morning paper, shoving it across the kitchen table, wearied by the wretched lies in the inflammatory article. Her copy of the Tuskegee *Tribune* fell open again, and the headline story, with a picture of her going into Dalton Graham's room, leaped up in graphic clarity. PROMINENT NAACP ATTORNEY ENTERTAINS COLORED NURSE IN HOTEL ROOM ON EVE OF KEYSTONE COURT CASE.

Disappointed, but not surprised, that such measures had been taken to distort the truth of her relationship with Dalton, Janelle glared at the page.

The reporter craftily painted a disturbing picture of Dalton, depicting him as a womanizing hell-raiser who stormed around the country, taking on cases for colored women in order to gain sexual favors. The writer implied that the attorney's good looks, his debonair manner, and the credibility afforded him by the NAACP allowed him to use his promise of equality in the workplace to seduce attractive black women who were eager to obtain his legal services.

Janelle was branded as Graham's latest conquest, a naïve, unemployed nurse whom he had used to support this case against Keystone, a case the reporter said was so vigorously opposed by local businessmen that the threat of wide-scale rioting hung over the town.

Who in the world would believe such trash? Janelle

wondered, relieved that Emma was not home. This was not the time to have to listen to one of her preachy reprimands, not when Janelle had to be in court within the hour.

I have no reason to feel guilty about my relationship with Dalton, Janelle reflected defensively. Nothing obscene or ugly or shameful had ever occurred between them—not in Columbus, at the base, or in Dalton's hotel room, though Lance had certainly misinterpreted their relationship, jumping to the conclusion that she and Dalton were having an affair.

Dalton Graham is in love with me, Janelle admitted, *but he has willingly sacrificed his feelings to protect me from people who think just like this reporter.* The fact that Dalton was leaving Tuskegee immediately after the hearing saddened Janelle. She'd miss him, but it was best that he move on. It was time for him to untangle himself from the cords of her life.

After glancing at the clock, she headed for the bedroom. Janelle groaned. Eight o'clock. In a few hours the dreaded hearing would be behind her.

Pulling her most conservative dress from the closet, Janelle felt a spurt of nervous tension begin to weaken her resolve. What if the picketers from Keystone did show up, primed to start trouble? What if the colored people who had been denied jobs appeared, giving her their support? Janelle gritted her teeth. Regardless of Judge Allen's decision, the reporter was right, the situation was potentially explosive.

As Janelle slipped her navy blue dress over her head and reached around to zip it up, she thought of Lance—on his way back home—to be greeted by news that she had helped Dalton Graham, with her picture smeared all over the front page of the paper. *He's going to be furious with me for doing this,* she thought, *but I don't care. I'm doing this for me . . . for Dalton . . . for all the people John Gray crushed and denied the right to earn a decent wage. If*

Lance can't accept what I've decided to do, maybe we don't have a future after all.

Dalton stubbed out his cigarette in the blue ceramic ashtray on his dresser, balled up his copy of the Tuskegee *Tribune,* and stuffed it into the wastebasket.

"Rotten racist bastard," he growled, giving his knotted tie a final yank. What Jock Taylor had said about him was upsetting, but he'd had worse things written about him—and his work—in much more important papers than the four-page Tuskegee *Tribune,* and by reporters whose by-lines carried weight across the country.

Dalton shoved his legal brief into his attaché case and pulled on his beige suit jacket. He could take whatever slanderous garbage any newspaper wanted to throw his way, but dammit, why did Taylor have to go after Janelle?

Dalton snapped his heavy suitcase shut and picked up his room key, ready to check out and get over to the courthouse. At the doorway Dalton paused, looking around the dismal green room, a tightness gathering in his throat.

I hope my knack for choosing the wrong women ends right here at Tuskegee. As soon as Judge Allen makes his ruling, no matter which way his decision comes down, I'm getting on the first train out of this town and out of Janelle's life forever.

Lance raced alongside the slow-moving train, and grabbed a handlebar to swing himself up. With a thump he landed on the platform between cars. He paused for a few seconds to catch his breath. He'd made it. This was the first train from Montgomery to Tuskegee, and he was two days ahead of schedule. If he'd missed it, he'd have had to sit around the Montgomery station until at least two o'clock in the afternoon.

Grinning, hardly able to contain his excitement, Lance shouldered his way through the crowded Jim Crow car. In less than an hour he'd be back with Janelle, back in the soft embrace of the woman he loved. And as soon as he hit the tiny town square, he'd find someplace to buy her a dozen red roses, even if it broke him—he only had six dollars.

An elderly gentleman got up, offering Lance his seat.

"No, no," Lance protested, insisting the man sit back down. Touching the patch over his right eye, he said lightly, "This looks a whole lot worse than it is."

He tossed his bulky duffel bag into a corner and settled down, blocking out the swirl of noisy chatter filling the car. *And the first thing I'm going to do when I get Janelle alone is come clean about Al. I've got to.* He glanced at the faces of a group of young soldiers headed back to the base after a night on the town. *Well, maybe the second thing,* he admitted, feeling his desire for Janelle begin to rise, warmth spreading through his groin.

Lance reached into his inside pocket and pulled out his last letter from his grandfather. As he reread it, his eyes teared up. The boy meant so much to the old man. The thought of abandoning the child to the dungeonlike cells of the colored orphanage was too much for him to live with. *If Janelle loves me, she'll accept Alabama. She's just got to, because I can't live with myself if I abandon the boy.*

The tall column rising from the middle of the turreted brick courthouse towered above the crowded town square. Its huge round clock rang nine times, the resonant gong hanging in the air long after the final strike. The sudden signaling of the hour momentarily seemed to calm the restless, suspicious men and women gathered at the courthouse steps, as if the bell-shaped tones were ushering in the commencement of a ceremony that would determine the fate of their town.

The hush didn't last very long, and as Perry lowered his eyes from the moon-faced clock to the throngs of agitated citizens milling on the street, he tensed, balling his hands into fists as an indignant farmer, clad in dirty overalls, hurled a stream of curses at the blacks standing calmly on the other side of the esplanade. Immediately the anger that

Perry had known was going to break out rose in a chorus of hate-filled threats that shot back and forth across the square.

On either side of the yellow brick courthouse, clumped in front of its two octagonal wings, two distinct groups of citizens stood shouting: the blacks on the west side, the whites on the east.

The crush of people spilled down the white granite steps out onto the grassy, shaded square. As Perry cautiously inched a little closer, he caught a glimpse of Janelle.

The melancholy of their estrangement began to hurt fiercely. For so long he had struggled to keep images of his sister as far from his conscious, waking thoughts as possible. Now, seeing her, watching her, he found his fears slipping into nothingness, intense pride replacing all apprehension.

There she was, as lovely as ever, his sister, head high, pushing past the meanspirited people shouting racial barbs at her. She regally mounted the steps and disappeared inside the building.

Perry unfolded the newspaper he had crushed between both hands and reread the front-page story.

What a pack of lies, he thought, scanning the page, his mouth set in a firm, thin line. *Dalton deserves better than this. Janelle, too.*

There was a time when he had been the one on the front lines, eyes wild with hope, boisterous and proud. Perry rose on tiptoes to get a better look when his friend Dalton started up the courthouse steps. Perry watched him shrug off an angry hand, pushing his way determinedly through the restless mob, going in the door right behind Janelle.

Oh, yes. Perry relished the biting surge of adrenaline that coursed through him now. He had felt the same heady rush of energy on each picket line he had marched in, at each corner where he had handed out flyers, at each microphone on each lectern he had been lucky enough to stand behind to preach his fiery words of struggle.

Running his blistered hands over the front of the nearly

clean shirt he had managed to con from one of the hobos in the alley, Perry drifted in memory. So long ago it seemed: shuffling through banks of snow in Cincinnati, shivering under leaky umbrellas in freezing rain in Cleveland, staying up half the night nailing cardboard signs to long wooden poles at the kitchen table at the house in Oakwood Alley.

The Lantree protest had worked, too. Not a week after Perry was drafted, Dalton had sent him a newspaper article. Howard Long had relented and hired fifteen colored engineers. Now that was a victory he could claim.

Cautiously moving to the far west side of the square, Perry found a spot beneath a shade tree and sat down to wait. He didn't dare show his face in the courtroom, but as soon as Janelle completed her testimony and walked down those granite steps, he'd go over and hug her and tell her how proud he was. Then he'd turn himself in to the authorities. It was a great feeling to finally start setting things straight.

With Dalton sitting stiffly erect at her side, Janelle felt a small measure of comfort, though she had kept her eyes straight ahead since the hearing opened, unwilling to glance either left or right for fear she'd see John Gray. Luckily Judge Allen had ordered a private hearing on the evidence, allowing only those directly connected to the case to be present as he listened calmly to what both sides had to say.

"Miss Roy," the judge said, peering over the edge of his bench to see her, "from what I understand, these documents were given to you by a Louise Richards, a former employee at Keystone?"

"Yes, Your Honor," Janelle replied.

Judge Allen leafed through the papers one more time, then folded his portfolio closed. Clasping both hands atop his desk, he lifted his chin, pondering his decision, then let out a long, loud sigh.

"Mr. Gray, I have spent many hours carefully reviewing

the documents Mr. Graham submitted to me earlier this week. It is quite clear from the evidence presented here that you have systematically prevented many, many qualified Negroes from securing gainful employment at your plant, while misrepresenting your company to the federal government." His level, nonjudgmental tone prompted no reply from Gray. "I see thirty-seven qualified applicants were turned away since the first of the year."

Gray pulled his hulking shoulders up around his ears, nonchalantly dismissing the judge's observation.

"Our nation is at war," Judge Allen said. "We must have plants like Keystone operating at full capacity, providing the supplies the War Department needs." He paused, adjusting his wire-rimmed eyeglasses.

Janelle leaned back against the hard bench, feet flat on the floor, fearing Judge Allen's opinion of John Gray's maneuvers was in line with the beliefs of the rowdy agitators who had hassled her outside the courthouse. She glanced at Dalton's rigid profile, unable to read his expression.

"The Keystone Company has a long history of defense supply," the judge continued. "My own grandfather was a welder on the line during World War One. My grandmother lost a part of her index finger under a needle sewing uniforms for our boys in France. Keystone has always played an integral part in the defense of our nation."

Dalton pulled in a deep breath and slowly let it out, reaching over to grasp Janelle's hand.

"But," Judge Allen went on, "it is your responsibility, Mr. Gray, to ensure that every citizen who is qualified and capable has the opportunity to work for the country's defense ... regardless of color or religion or national origin. The evidence presented here is very disturbing." For the first time, a flicker of perplexity passed over Gray's flushed face. "I have no intention of dragging out my decision ... or shutting Keystone down. Time is of the essence here. Our country needs what Keystone can produce." He picked up a pen, and made a notation on the document before him. "Mr. Gray, please approach the bench."

John Gray, flanked by two attorneys, reluctantly got up and went to stand before Judge Allen.

"It is my decision that the federal contract be granted to you." Judge Allen rendered his verdict in an authoritative tone. "However, these are the conditions: All qualified Negroes who were turned down for employment by Keystone in the last six months will be contacted and offered positions. You are to bring your number of Negro personnel to at least ten percent within thirty days and pay a fine of ten thousand dollars." Hunching closer to the men standing before him, Judge Allen added, "You do know that what you have been doing, Mr. Gray, is cause to give you a pretty stiff sentence. I could sentence you to federal prison for quite some time, but in the spirit of national defense, I am going to let you stay to run your company. Your expertise is needed, but as of today I am ordering you to step aside as president of Keystone. You will still be in charge of operations, but overseen by a board of directors approved by the Fair Employment Practices Committee."

Janelle watched the thick red veins in John Gray's neck grow fat, near to bursting, as he fumed under Judge Allen's stern eye. Dalton went limp, squeezing her hand. It had worked. This fight was won.

"The FEPC board will remain in place as long as you are under contract with the federal government." Judge Allen looked from Gray to each of his lawyers, to Dalton, then Janelle. Banging his gavel, he pronounced, "This case is decided. Bailiff, you may clear the courtroom."

Dalton turned to Janelle, beaming. "Any regrets now?"

Janelle hugged him tightly, then sat back. "None. This feels wonderful. Accomplishing what we set out to do. It's the most important thing I've ever done."

"Quite an experience, isn't it? Making a difference?"

Janelle nodded, smiling. "Thank you, Dalton. This day will stay with me forever. I've learned a lot, believe me."

Dalton stood and waited for Janelle. They walked toward the courtroom door. "You don't have to explain it to me. I was hooked a long time ago."

At the double arched doorway they paused, cautiously watching John Gray engaged in heated conversation at the foot of the steps, his protruding belly bouncing up and down with each furious gesture he made to the crowd.

"Stick close behind me," Dalton told Janelle. "Looks as if he's trying to whip up some sympathy. Don't look at anyone. Don't speak. Just keep walking."

Janelle fell in closely behind Dalton, hurrying down the steps, his body shielding hers.

"You get your Yankee nigger-loving ass back up north where you belong!"

Dalton inched his way grimly through the crush of enraged onlookers.

"Keystone will burn before niggers work the line!"

Janelle felt a rock hit the pavement at her feet.

"You traitorous bitch. You whore to the white man!"

The rising voices paralyzed Janelle. Confused, she stopped, unable to believe how much hatred was swelling through the frenzied mob.

Dalton turned back, frowning, and grabbed her by the arm. "Come on! Don't stop." He yanked her forward just as somebody fired a rifle over the square. The loud crack made the crowd scream and scatter, but they quickly resumed their taunts.

"We're not fighting this war for you darkies. This ain't your war. Stay home!"

Oh, God, no, Janelle panicked, digging her fingernails into Dalton's wrist. "They're going to kill us, Dalton."

"No, they're not. Come on," Dalton yelled, pushing a thick-necked man in a blue plaid shirt out of his way. The man swung back to hit Dalton, who ducked quickly, letting go of Janelle's hand. She screamed, terrified when Dalton disappeared into the throng. In an instant the irate citizens had closed in behind him, blocking her off.

Shocked, Janelle screamed again. "Dalton!" He had vanished. A white woman with her hair tied up in a kerchief pushed her thin, contorted face in front of Janelle's and spit. Smirking, she turned away.

"Dalton!" Janelle cried, praying he could hear her above the chaotic upheaval that had broken out all across the square.

Whites and blacks, armed with sticks, bricks, shovels, and clubs, attacked one another in what seemed a desperate attempt to kill. They yelled obscenities, screamed racial threats, flew at one another in a bloody frenzy. A whizzing sound streaked overhead. Then a smoke bomb exploded at the edge of the square.

In a panic Janelle put her arm to her forehead, lowered her face, plunged forward. Someone grabbed her arm. She tried to pull free, but the man shoved her roughly to the side.

"Janelle."

Uncovering her face, she saw Perry. Bearded, thin, eyes lost in misery, but it was her brother, Perry. She gasped in surprise. "Perry!"

He threw one arm across her shoulder while kicking at a teenager who was beating his leg with a stick. "Hold on to me," Perry told Janelle, using one hand to flail at the boy. They burst from the violent mob and dashed across the street toward safety.

As soon as they stepped onto the curb in front of the Atlas Hotel, Janelle turned to embrace her brother. The look they shared dissolved the pain and misery of the past few months. A shot rang out. Janelle yelled in fear, cowering against the brick wall.

Looking up, she saw that the bullet had struck Perry in the forehead, right above his left eyebrow. Blood ran from his head.

"No!" Janelle screamed, lunging to grab him just as his body jerked backward.

With a thud Perry collapsed at her feet—a pitifully frail imitation of the muscular, handsome brother she remembered.

"Perry!" Dropping to her knees, Janelle watched in horror as her brother's blood seeped from the front of his head. Should she run for help? Run for cover? Would the gunman make her his next target?

Crouched on her knees, frantically wondering who had done this, Janelle scanned the tangle of angry citizens who continued their brutal attacks.

Forcing herself to get control, she ran her shaking fingers over Perry's neck. She could not find a pulse. Automatically she covered his mouth with hers, blowing, desperately trying to force life from her lungs into his. She checked again. Still no pulse.

In a panic Janelle dragged his thin, lifeless body up against the building, and cradled his bleeding head in her lap. "Oh, Perry," she moaned aloud, her grief too sharp to shed tears, "why did you come back now?"

The sound of shattering glass and a burst of gunfire spurred Lance faster toward the square. *What's happening?* he thought, tossing aside the newspaper he'd picked up at the train station. He had hoped to read some news about the recent movement of the 99th in preparation for the assault on Anzio Beach but had been greeted by the most shocking photo he'd ever seen: his fiancée's picture on the front page of the Tuskegee *Tribune*! And he had trusted Janelle to keep her promise. God damn her! Going into that man's room! He raged silently, walking faster. She sure as hell had gotten herself in over her head this time.

The closer Lance got to the center of town, the more convinced he was that a riot had broken out. It sounded as if he'd entered a war zone. The clamorous pitch of loud voices, the smell of gunpowder and tear gas that pervaded the air jolted his thoughts away from Janelle's betrayal.

He sprinted down Main Street, crossed Spring, and Lee, then rounded a corner in front of the Alabama Exchange Bank. From there a grisly sight unfolded before his eyes. Two overturned cars lay flaming, their rubber tires melting in the red-hot fire, billows of sooty smoke soaring skyward. One uniformed deputy took his pistol from his holster and shot into the air, dispersing the out-of-control rioters. In seconds the confrontation dissolved into a one-sided battle between three deputies and a few resistant blacks as the rest of the people moved back.

Lance cringed, restraining himself as a white officer raised his billy club and cracked the skull of a colored man who had fallen, facedown, to the ground. The crowd, which had gradually divided itself into two restless groups, created a semicircle to witness the subjection of the last of the feverish agitators.

But the sight that captured Lance's attention, that sucked his breath from his lungs was Janelle, crouched on her knees in front of the Atlas Hotel, rocking a crumpled, bleeding body. He went to her instinctively, his anger forgotten.

CHAPTER
THIRTY-EIGHT

"Miss Roy?" A white-gloved gentleman approached, elbows waist high as he bowed. The solemn set to his face, the blank calm in his eyes were indicative of the message he had come to deliver. Janelle crossed her ankles, priming herself for the encounter, waiting until the gray fringed curtain had fallen into place behind the undertaker before she responded.

"Yes, Mr Forney?" Janelle said, hoping she had signed the last piece of paper, had completed the final detail concerning the disposition of her brother's body.

Standing above Janelle, sympathetic eyes on her puffy face, the owner of Forney-Locke Funeral Home gently asked, "Would you like to view the body before the casket is closed?" Lips puckered in prim correctness, he lowered his eyes as he waited for her answer.

"Yes, I would," Janelle said, nodding in thanks to the undertaker.

When he left the room, Janelle turned on the red brocade chair, first to Lance, then to Emma, thankful both were there.

"Want me to come with you?" Emma murmured, the strain of Perry's death cloaking her voice.

"Oh, Emma!" Janelle smothered a sob with one hand, her body hiccoughing as she tried to keep control. It was no use. Her grief erupted in a torrent of tears, and as she wept aloud, Emma placed a damp cheek to hers.

"Janelle, this is the darkest time of your life. You go ahead and cry. I'm here."

"Why Perry? Why? He didn't deserve to leave us like this."

"No, he didn't," Emma said softly.

Janelle rested in Emma's arms, wondering if Mr. Forney had been able to repair the ghastly hole in Perry's forehead and flesh out his skeletal face, change him back to the robust young man she remembered.

Calmly Janelle pulled from Emma's embrace, wiping her eyes as she pulled air into her lungs. "I'm all right. I want to see Perry now."

"Are you sure you don't want me to go with you to the station?" Emma asked.

"No, Lance and I can manage. You go back to the house. Get some rest."

Emma gave Lance a light hug, then left.

Searching Janelle's face, Lance worried. Creased from lack of sleep and unstoppable tears yet still magically beautiful to him, her face was testimony to the loss she had suffered. He had not left her side since he found her on the sidewalk, and he knew she was operating on raw nervous energy. He helped her up, and watched her walk stiffly through the gray fringed curtains into the hushed viewing parlor.

Janelle gazed down at the body in the coffin. Realizing Mr. Forney had done the best he could on short notice, she was hardly able to recognize her brother. The Army wanted Perry Roy's body out of Tuskegee as soon as possible.

The undertaker had repaired the gunshot wound in Perry's head, and the pancake makeup used to camouflage the gash had lightened his face two shades. The rich chocolate brown complexion, like hers and her father's, was now a pasty, dull beige with yellowish undertones. Mr. Forney had shaved Perry's face clean. That was good, Janelle thought, glad the beard was gone. Now he appeared much more like the Perry she remembered, but he still remained a stranger.

"Why? Perry. Why? What pushed you to kill that prisoner?"

Wishing desperately she had been a better sister, Janelle asked his forgiveness. With the blue satin pillow beneath his head, Perry appeared at peace, freed from agitation—perhaps for the first time in the past two years.

"Excuse me."

An Army captain holding a pasteboard box in his hand stepped into the room. "These were the personal items taken from Private Roy whiled preparing the body. The Army has no need of them now." He handed the box to Janelle. She opened it to find a rabbit's foot with a thin piece of leather attached to it, two books of matches, a pack of Lucky Strike, a slip of paper with her telephonc number on it, and the dog-eared notebook she knew without opening was one of his journals he had always kept. She closed the box and addressed the captain.

"Thank you." Tears from a childhood long ago, far away, welled up. She was very grateful to have these few meager remnants of her brother's short existence.

The captain stepped back smartly, saying, "As soon as you're finished viewing the body, it will be taken to the train station."

"May I go with him?" she asked.

"Certainly, ma'am. You can follow in your own vehicle, if you'd like."

The last two days had passed in a blur of uniformed Army officers, first parading in and out of her second-floor apartment, then coming into the somber funeral parlor. Always pushing papers in front of her to sign.

She had answered their brusque, interminable questions as completely and politely as possible. For hours military investigators had pressed her for information about Perry's whereabouts since the day he fled Camp Livingston.

Hoping to charge her with conspiring to harbor a fugitive, the men had even searched her apartment for letters from Perry. Of course, they found nothing and grudgingly apologized for all the damage they had done to her personal belongings. Janelle wondered why they were spending so much time searching her home instead of searching for the gunman who had shot Perry. There was little discussion of that subject. The Army quickly and curtly dismissed the shooting as an unfortunate result of the frenzy on the square, expressing relief that the case of AWOL Private Perry Roy had come to a swift conclusion.

Having Emma there, supportive, gently urging her to eat, sitting at her bedside as she groped for the elusive release of sleep, had been Janelle's salvation. And throughout it all Lance had never stopped reassuring her that she need not blame herself for Perry's misfortune. His circumstances had been far beyond her control.

And in the midst of the tragic aftermath of her court appearance, Dalton Graham had quietly slipped out of her life. She had not even had the chance to give him a real good-bye; he'd left the same day on the 6:52 headed straight to Fort Worth, Texas. Dalton and Lance had separated with a handshake, both acknowledging the fact that Janelle's decision to assist in the Keystone case had played a most important part in the victory. A cluster of supportive well-wishers had taken up vigil in front of her house.

Now the arrangements to send Perry's body by train to California were complete, yet the chilling wail of her mother's anguish still shrilled inside Janelle's head. The two women had talked off and on, seemingly every hour, since Janelle had called with the devastating news. Burying Perry near his mother in Southern California was not what she had wanted, but Janelle understood. If it were up to her, she would have placed him at rest beside their father in the Greenlawn Cemetery in Columbus. Too exhausted and distraught to make a fuss, she had kept her mouth shut, honoring her mother's wishes.

In the car lent to them by Mr. Forney, Janelle clung to Lance's arm, remaining silent as they wound their way through town to the tiny Chehaw station.

"I never dreamed my homecoming would be under such painful circumstances." Lance stroked the back of her hand with his thumb, knowing there was still much to be said, acknowledged.

"Lance," Janelle began, "as difficult as losing Perry is, I don't think I could have survived if you had turned away from me for helping Dalton." She hesitated, then added, "And Al."

Lance leaned back to catch her eye. "Al. My son." Now he choked back tears pressing inside his chest. "I *was* angry at first, Janelle. I was furious with Pop. And you. Not because of what you did but because I was not involved. Being so far away, I felt out of control. The letters from Pop—telling me he was sick and couldn't care for the boy—cut me down low. Made me feel like the heel I have been. I wanted to come back and explain it to you. Make everything right."

"Lance, I never hated you for fathering a child."

"But you hated me for withholding the truth."

Janelle snuggled closer, placing their entwined hands in her lap. "Hate? No. Disappointed, yes."

"Can you forgive me?"

"I did that long ago. I just pray you'll be able to claim your son."

Lance kissed her gently and held her for a moment. Then Janelle opened her purse and took out the tattered notebook, the size of the palm of her hand.

"I'm so glad I have this. It's like a piece of Perry. His thoughts, his dreams, even his troubles are probably documented here."

Easing the first page into view, she smiled to see Perry's delicate, precise handwriting. She clearly remembered Perry sitting on the floor in front of the radio, their father helping him learn to form his letters. Over and over their father had made him practice, telling Perry, with an authoritative voice, that a colored man might be judged at some important juncture in his life solely on his ability to write a clear hand. Perry had taken his father's injunction to heart and had practiced long into the night.

Janelle held the faded words close enough to read. Perry had always been one to write down his thoughts. Even put them in the newspaper or read them into a microphone whenever he got the chance. She relaxed. That was Perry—always center stage.

"Listen to this, Lance," she said suddenly, after having been immersed in the journal for some time. " 'How could I have killed a man? All I've ever done is work for peace. Now peace has turned from me. With the slip of my finger, the odd tilt of the gun, my future is lost. How could I have hit him when I aimed high above his head? Fate has conspired to make me a fugitive in my own country.' "

"See?" Lance reached over to hold the edge of the page. "It was an accident! Perry didn't intentionally kill that prisoner."

Sobs of relief burst from Janelle. "I knew there was more to it than the captain told me." She wiped her eyes and continued to read: " 'It is the nature of war to test man's tolerance and determine exactly who he is. It's the soldier's burden to bear up to the test and carry out his orders. The way is tangled and steep—who helps me along this treacherous path? Who holds my hand on this lonely journey? Not my family, not my fellow soldiers, not my enemy, not even my country. I have no one fighting for me. I applaud those who will reach their destinations in pride, but I fear I have lost my way. June 1, 1943.' "

Lance put his arm around Janelle, urging her head onto his shoulder. "God, he was suffering," Lance said, curling Janelle to his chest.

She wept against his jacket, and he held her, his chin resting on the top of her head.

"He was so alone, Lance. So completely alone."

"Hush," Lance said comfortingly. "He's at peace, now, thank God."

At the train station they waited for more than two hours before finally getting the casket on board. Once all the paperwork was cleared and the captain said she could leave, she and Lance turned from the maze of track, crossed the platform, and walked toward the station.

Janelle paused, then tugged on Lance's arm.

"What?" he asked gently. "Is something wrong?"

"No," she said, "but I think we know that little boy."

"Where?" He looked in the direction she was pointing.

"Over there, standing with the porter."

The crowd thinned, and Lance immediately saw the frightened face of Alabama Easter—small, anxiously searching the crowd, gripping the porter's hand. Lance swung around to face Janelle. "Yes! It's Al!"

"He looks as if he could use a friendly face," she said, her voice firm with the expectation of happier days to come.

At that moment, after sending her only brother off to be buried thousands of miles away, Janelle knew in her heart that family was all that mattered, all that lasted, not a blessing to be taken for granted.

Lance broke away from Janelle and began walking faster. She held back to watch Lance kneel to eye level in front of Al and take hold of his small brown hands. She noticed that Al had been outfitted in new Levi's and a striped T-shirt for his trip from the orphanage.

"Do you know who I am?" she heard Lance ask.

"I think so," Al chirped clearly. Opening one hand, he revealed a scrap of a photo, frayed and smeared. He studied the picture of Lance. "Grandpa Deacon gave this to me. He says you fly airplanes and you're my daddy."

Lance clasped the child to his breast, then rose. He thanked the porter for escorting the boy.

"You Deacon Fuller?" the suspicious porter asked.

"No, but I'm his grandson," he said, showing the white-jacketed man his military ID. "I'll take care of the boy from here."

"Right smart boy you got there, Lieutenant." The porter beamed a wide smile. "We had us a fine time on the ride up from Montgomery. Didn't we?" He ran a hand over

Al's close-cropped hair, then reached into his white coat pocket. "The man who asked me to bring the boy back gave me this here letter." He held it out. "For a Miss Roy." He looked at Janelle. "That you?"

"Yes," she said, puzzled. The orphanage didn't know about her. She opened the envelope. Inside was a note from Dalton Graham, folded over a check for five hundred dollars.

She silently read: *Janelle, have a wonderful life. Use this to fix up that little cabin where I know you and Lance and the boy will find happiness. Always, Dalton.*

Janelle folded the note and put it in her pocket, then slipped her arm through Lance's. He kissed her on the forehead, put his flight cap on Al's small head, then took his son by the hand.

"Well," Lance said with a sparkle in his voice as they walked to the car, "let's shove out!"

Janelle tightened her arm about Lance's waist. "Do you mind if we take the long road home? I'd like to visit Wild Embers."

AFTERWORD

World War II was a major force for change in the lives of all Americans, challenging them to examine closely their definition of freedom. As the nation fought to liberate those oppressed by the Axis forces, it did little to promote the economic, social, and political equality of black men and women at home. But African Americans rushed to enlist, answering their country's call to duty, expecting to share in the dividends of peace.

Black soldiers fought a two-front war, at home and abroad. With admirable persistence, they challenged the racial prejudice and hatred facing them in every city in the United States, while remaining fiercely determined to carve out their place in the ranks of the United States armed forces.

Those who participated expected to be rewarded, hoping the erosion of Jim Crow laws would open up avenues of achievement with better jobs, housing, education, and a generally higher standard of living.

Toward the end of the war African Americans had been fully integrated into most defense industry facilities, and more than 900,000 had been inducted into the Army. At the time of the Japanese surrender, black military aviators trained at Tuskegee Army Airfield near Tuskegee, Alabama, numbered 996. Nearly half these pilots fought in aerial combat, escorting bombers over North Africa, Sicily,

Italy, southern France, and central Europe, distinguishing themselves by never losing a single bomber to enemy fire.

Throughout the war black nurses lobbied against the quota system, determined to serve wherever they were needed. Shortages, rising casualties in the field, and pressure from the National Association of Colored Graduate Nurses eventually forced the Army to reexamine its policies. By July 1945 there were approximately five hundred nurses in the Army Nurse Corps, serving at home and abroad.

If you enjoyed *Wild Embers,*
you will love
Anita Richmond Bunkley's
marvelous new novel about
two contemporary African-American
sisters caught up in a bitter
rivalry over their
family's legacy, which stretches
all the way back to their
roots in Africa.

Turn the page for
a special preview of
Starlight Passage,
available in the Spring of 1996
from Dutton.

PROLOGUE

1839
The Gold Coast
West Africa

The howl of a spotted hyena shrieked up from the floor of the densely forested valley, its maniacal echo breaking Ijoma's concentration. More annoyed than startled, she frowned, then placed her hands firmly against the wall, pressing her palms flat against the dark mahogany poles to create a sliver of an opening between the tightly tethered pieces of wood. Cautiously, she inched her small brown fingers inward, the golden bands beneath each knuckle scratching the wall as she forced the sections apart. With her shoulders locked rigidly in fear, she listened for the familiar sound of Tabansi's footsteps as she fit her right eye against the tiny peephole and stared.

"So many of them," she murmured in hushed surprise, her eye flitting over the gathering of bare-chested men squatting in front of bulging camelskin bags. Like a colony of scarabs picking through a dung heap, Ijoma thought.

With brazen delight she studied the pincher-like arms and chiseled faces of the *Wangara* traders as they meticulously weighed and measured their hordes of gold. A tall spire of flames, held in check by a circle of water-filled clay pots, roared in the center of the walled clearing, etching the fast approaching dusk a flat yellow hue. As the somber gold merchants prepared for the next day's trading, the hiss and crackle of burning wood was the only noise coming from the compound.

Ijoma grinned, delighted to witness a sight that no other girl in her village had ever laid eyes on, though a tinge of disappointment did flare as she assessd the scene in the rapidly darkening courtyard.

Why weren't the men dressed in white robes, turbaned and upright, draped in necklaces and armbands of gold, ambergris, and saffron? That's how Tabansi had told her the *Wangara* would look. But here they were, sitting on their haunches like fat tiger beetles, wearing no more than the Ashanti warriors wore to protect their private parts. Ijoma's heavy golden earrings brushed her wine-dark cheeks as she shook her small head back and forth in disbelief.

Suddenly, the strong shoulder upon which Ijoma sat shifted, threatening to throw her off balance.

"Hold still, Sekou!" she hissed, settling more firmly onto the smooth warm flesh of her accomplice. "You will make me fall."

The young man supporting her slight frame struggled to recapture his balance. Ijoma teetered precariously above his head.

"Stop moving!" Ijoma urged, her tense whisper resounding in the humid twilight. Reluctantly, she turned loose the poles to steady herself by grabbing Sekou's head. The pieces of wood snapped back into place with a crack. Ijoma froze, then jumped to the ground and ran.

"Wait!" Sekou called, the word no more than a frightened breath. "Wait, Ijoma!"

But Ijoma kept going, fleeing into the leafy forest as Sekou hurried after her, his bare feet making flat, muffled thuds along the path.

"What did you see?" Sekou asked, grabbing Ijoma's arm, forcing her to stop.

"Not much," Ijoma whispered quickly. "You should not have moved." She pulled Sekou beneath the low branches of a silk cotton tree, then leaned against its trunk.

"Was it beautiful?" the young man asked. "Were they dressed as kings? As the *Chibale* would dress?"

Ijoma straightened her brightly colored lappa, then replaced the gold-threaded headwrap that protected her elaborately braided hairdo from the eyes of non-royals. If Gram-Ma-Ma knew Ijoma had been out of the compound with her head uncovered she'd never hear the end of it.

"Beautiful?" Ijoma replied sharply. "No. Not at all. You should see for yourself how common they are. Half naked! Heads uncovered! The *Wangara* look more like the beetles we torture with sticks at Lake Volta than traders in gold."

"Common? The *Wangara*?" Sekou's full lower lip turned down in disbelief. Suspiciously, he tilted his flat ebony face to the sky, sniffing as if searching for a scent. "Maybe we are at the wrong compound. Maybe these are not the gold traders at all."

"Oh, no," Ijoma said, now inching back toward the mahogany wall. "This is the right place. The gold is piled high. In camelskin bags. And I could see the salt blocks lining the courtyard. This is the place all right." Ijoma stepped forward, then turned to look at Sekou. "Let's go back. Lift me up again. I want to see more."

Sekou raised one shoulder in question. "Why tempt our good fortune? I promised I'd take you to see the *Wangara*, and now you have seen them. Let's go, Ijoma. Please! Tabansi will pass by soon."

"Old Tabansi?" Ijoma intentionally injected disdain into her voice to remind Sekou of her royal status. "He does not frighten me. He is only a servant. My father would never allow Tabansi to punish me."

"Maybe not, but Tabansi has acquired much power through allegiance to the Kante clan. Your father allows him much control."

"True," Ijoma admitted, "but Tabansi is still only a servant, and he is getting old. He takes his job of protecting the secret location of the *Wangara* much too seriously."

Sekou placed a long finger under Ijoma's chin and

gently lifted her face toward his. "Just as seriously as he takes his job of protecting the *Chibale*'s daughter."

Now Ijoma squinted, weighing Sekou's remarks against her own knowledge of her father, the ruler of their village. The natives of Bwerani considered her father a just ruler, a patient soul with plenty of time to listen to their problems. Ijoma had witnessed his somber posture while he quietly received his people, but when it came to his only daughter, he had no time for her at all! He shut himself away, letting old Tabansi make all the rules, allowing him to hover over her like a wary lioness.

Sekou tries to be such a know-it-all, Ijoma thought, wishing she could put him in his place, yet not hurt his feelings. "Sekou!" she said, pulling back her delicate shoulders in courtly assertion, "I think you have forgotten that Tabansi must serve me, too."

"Ha!" Sekou threw back at her in a loud guffaw, playfully slapping his hands at her. In the dusky twilight, his richly beaded corset shimmered on his ebony chest. "Then why did I see you doing the picking of the rushes while Tabansi carried the basket when you were at Lake Volta yesterday morning?"

Scowling, Ijoma pushed past him, turning deeper into the forest that she knew as well as the network of lines on the back of Gram-Ma-Ma's hands. Taking long strides up the narrow trail, she clamped her lips shut, both angry and pleased by Sekou's question. "You spied on me at Lake Volta?"

Sekou fell in step beside her. "I wasn't spying. I only said that I *saw* you."

"You didn't make your presence known," she said, annoyed that he hadn't had the courage to step forward.

"Why get Tabansi all riled up?" Sekou replied. "He doesn't like anyone who is not Kante coming around. The word has traveled far across the lake. He will never accept me as worthy of your attentions."

"You worry too much, Sekou. I told you Tabansi has no

say about who I spend my time with. You should not be so frightened of him."

Ijoma's haughty tone belied her inner joy that Sekou had come looking for her. For the past three moons they had been secretly meeting at the cove on the lake, and her mind was made up—Sekou would be her husband.

If only he would show more courage, she thought. Who knows? The *Chibale* might be impressed enough to accept him as a son-in-law even though he isn't Kante. Besides, she had already lain with Sekou, more than once, and her body craved only him. She couldn't imagine lying with any other man.

"I am not frightened," Sekou muttered in protest, easing his arm around Ijoma's waist, "I only wish I could be with you all the time, Ijoma. I'm not spying. Don't ever think that." He splayed his fingers along her side and stroked the warm flesh that peeped out above the waist of her lappa. His voice deepened as he told her, "I only wanted to see you."

Ijoma smiled, lids lowered as she stole a glance at the muscular young man beside her. "It won't be long. Only four more moons until my sixteenth season. Then my father *will* agree to our union."

"Did he say this?" Sekou asked warily, his grip tensing on Ijoma's waist. "Will he let you join with my tribe?"

"Well, I'm not certain . . ." Ijoma hedged, "but I feel he is coming around. In four days Asesima will speak for me. I am certain he will not refuse Gram-Ma-Ma's request."

Sekou hugged Ijoma closer. They continued up the leaf-covered path in silence, then bent low to duck into the bushy green ferns that camouflaged the trail to the *Wangara*. Emerging, they paused at a fork in the road. Sekou turned to face Ijoma, his eyes fastened on hers.

"Will you be at the lake again tomorrow?" he asked.

"Yes, and everyday until the harmattan ends. The royal basket weavers need many rushes. They are creating the most exquisite ceremonial pieces for the celebration of Asesima's fiftieth season. Gold threads will be woven with the rushes to create a most rare type of basket. More delicate than those created in any other village—far superior to those made in Bambuk. Everyone in Bwerani will attend."

Sekou nodded. "Then the rushes must be gathered before the rains are upon us once more." He let out a deep, contented breath, edging closer to Ijoma. "I wish the baskets were for our marriage ceremony."

Ijoma stroked Sekou's bare shoulder, facing him, almost dutifully lifting her lips toward his. At this same fork in the road he always kissed her good-bye before returning to his village on the other side of the lake. "Soon," she whispered. "Have patience, Sekou."

"Yes. Yes. Until tomorrow," he murmured, kissing her lightly, affectionately, with a great deal of respectful restraint.

Ijoma touched the back of Sekou's hand, lowered her eyes, then hurried up the path to the royal compound, hoping she hadn't been missed.

Morning came very quickly and Ijoma woke easily. Her eyes popped open, her mind cleared in the space of a moment, and she was immediately flooded with a sense of victory. She felt smugly grown-up to have seen the *Wangara,* and to have managed to slip into her sleeping chamber without running into Gram-Ma-Ma or one of her nosy servants.

The pale wash of daybreak nudged her against the slatted window as Ijoma wrapped a fresh lappa about her hips and placed her heavy cowrie-shell collar around her neck. In quick movements, she twisted a length of white silk cord through her braids, then pulled a roll of thin banana-leaf parchment from a waist-high basket near the door. Reaching deeper, she retrieved two small pots of indigo paste, a sharpened quill, and several long-handled, finely tipped brushes. If she hurried she might be able to get in an hour of sketching before Tabansi rattled her door to drag her off once more to the thick stand of bamboo at the edge of Lake Volta. Why the basket makers insisted that the reeds be cut by the family of the *Chibale* escaped her. They *were* excellent artisans, but entirely too superstitious.

"High God of Patience remain with me today," she grumbled in prayer, making up her mind that this morning, *she* would carry the basket and order Tabansi to wade out into the murky water and cut the prickly rushes. No one would know the difference.

During the next hour, Ijoma practiced drawing the intricate designs of the Kante tribe on brittle, pale banana leaves. The pattern of the horned dogs, with their scrolling tails and tongues, was her favorite. When the elongated animals were drawn very close together, the fluid shapes blurred into a circular linkage that made them appear to be moving. Ijoma had instructed the royal dressmaker to weave the dogs into Asesmia's new ceremonial skirt.

The pattern, consisting of diagonal blocks of bold stripes separated by tight little spirals, was difficult but not nearly as hard to master as the flat oval fish, with their butterfly tails and tiny mouths bursting with sharp little teeth. There were concentric circles overlapping each other, triangles set closely together, and feathered sunbursts that represented cascades of shooting stars. And then there were the weeping gods with their sorrowful faces, flat and round, covered with plump long teardrops.

Of the forty-seven traditional designs of the Kante, Ijoma had only mastered twenty-three, and even those were not so easily drawn. No matter how hard she tried, her lines never came out straight and her circles were always wobbly. The weavers, she knew, would not welcome her into their chamber to work the golden threads until all the designs could be recalled and woven perfectly and quickly. They would have little patience for her sluggish hand. If the gold could not be placed precisely onto the design, a piece could be ruined in the space of a second.

Sighing, Ijoma dipped her sharpened quill into the pot of rich blue paste, curled her tongue over her bottom lip, and began inscribing a series of eight-pointed stars with hollow centers on the blank banana-leaf scroll. She was determined to master the royal designs—as Gram-Ma-Ma and her mother had done.

Soon sunlight streamed through the bamboo curtains, crept across the hard dirt floor, and touched the edge of her straw mat, signaling the end of her morning practice. Ijoma scanned her work, then nodded, the early morning ritual was beginning to pay off—she had completed three more passable designs. Now it was time to meet Tabansi at the front gate. The smell of boiling peanuts and wild bananas drifted into her chamber, but Ijoma knew there would be no breakfast for her until the rushes were gathered.

With a towering multicolored basket atop her head, eyes vacant in regal indifference, Princess Ijoma made her way through the village of Bwerani. Proudly arrogant, Tabansi led his charge from her walled home, through the dusty assemblage of thatched huts and meandering cattle, to the road leading out to Lake Volta. No one dared to call out or approach Ijoma as she proceeded on her royal mission, for all the people knew of her part in the upcoming ceremony for the fiftieth season of the *Chibale*'s mother. Excited speculation grew as the villagers discussed what might be fashioned by the secluded artisans who worked in gold, leather, and even glass.

Stepping briskly to the thumping cadence of Tabansi's finialed walking stick, Ijoma took two steps to each of his.

He is trying me, she thought, determined to say nothing until they reached their destination. Then I'll let him know who is in charge. Nearly giggling aloud, Ijoma imagined the old man's astonishment when she ordered him into the lake.

Emerging from the wooded trail, Ijoma grimaced in disappointment to see a wispy fog hanging over the flat, still water. On a clear day Ijoma could see across the lake directly into the Oda village where Sekou lived and communicate with him using hand signals, letting him know how much she missed him. Not so today.

Lowering the basket to the ground, she inhaled, trying to settle the quaking sensation in her stomach. Hesitating a second, she summoned the courage to give Tabansi a royal command.

"Stay close to the shoreline, Princess," Tabansi began. "And be sure to cut above the waterline. The weavers have no use for soggy reeds."

Ijoma stiffened her spine and raised her chin until the flawless brown skin of her neck was taut and smooth. "Tabansi," she started, peering down her nose at him, "I think it is time you understood—"

"Listen!" The graying servant stopped her. "Do you hear?" He cupped one hand to his ear, leaning so far from the shore that the hem of his white robe sank beneath the water's surface.

"Yes!" Ijoma answered, turning to look back at her village, then across the lake. She *did* hear the sound of drums—a faint and hollow resonance, the talking drums of her people.

"Shh." Tabansi put a finger to his lips and listened. "There are strangers in the area. Evil strangers. The white man's hunters have returned." He waded deeper into the water.

Ijoma gasped. "Those who raided Diomo last moon?"

"The same," Tabansi uttered lowly, motioning for Ijoma to stay put. He crept farther out—until the rush-filled water came up to his knees.

A thick curtain of milky white mist shrouded everything. Only the faint drumbeats coming across the lake penetrated the barrier. Ijoma began to shake.

"What do they say, Tabansi? What?"

Tabansi didn't answer, but quickly turned around, stumbling onto the bank to grab Ijoma by the arm. "We must go back!"

The look of surprise that came to Ijoma's face was not brought about by the rough manner in which Tabansi had spoken to her but by the sudden appearance of a huge Sosi warrior who materialized out of the fog.

"Tabansi!" she warned as the hunter shook his arrow-tipped spear up and down, advancing on her servant's back. With a swift stroke, the slave hunter knocked Tabansi to the ground. Ijoma fell to her knees beside him, only to be jerked upright. The warrior tried to bind her hands with a length of jute, but she struggled, pressing against the hunter's slick, wet chest. Ijoma cried aloud, digging her fingernails into his arms. With a snap of her head she bit down on his sheening black flesh, tasting the warrior's bitter blood on her tongue. He tried to pull his arm free, but she clenched her jaws, holding on, her head lolling back and forth until her silken cords fell from her braids and landed in the dust.

The painful clamp of the hunter's hard fist over her skull forced her to let go.

"Stop! Turn me loose!" Ijoma pleaded. But the slave catcher wrapped her body in rough hemp, cutting her slender arms as he shoved her down on her knees. Raising his spear, he growled, then thrust it into Tabansi's chest. Withdrawing it, he waved the dripping lance at arm's length, spinning the old man's blood into the air, splattering Ijoma's face.

Sickened with fear, Ijoma doubled over, watching in horror as a band of slave catchers rushed from the forest and thundered toward her village. Within seconds, bright orange flames rose in the distance and the screams of her people clawed at the sky. Lowering her face to the ground, Ijoma let the soil of her land fill her mouth.

"Oh, Gram-Ma-Ma . . . oh my *Chibale*," she whispered, "help me."

But she knew that neither her grandmother nor her kingly father would hear her cries for rescue when a callused hand closed over the tender skin at the nape of her neck. With a grunt, the slave catcher pulled Ijoma to her feet, heaved her over his blood-soaked shoulder, then sprinted away from Bwerani.

* * *

The gentle splash of waves lapping against the ship calmed Ijoma and nudged her into a welcome half-sleep. The slaver had docked hours ago, and Ijoma's sensation of continual motion was finally beginning to subside. For weeks, the curling sound of the ever-present water had seemed like moving pictures inside her head, like the fluid Kante designs she had memorized. Into the never-ending darkness she had mentally etched the swirls and points of the long-tailed dogs, the bold diagonal stripes of the Ghanaian sunset, the spirals and spinning circles of her ancestors' markings against the pitch-black span of her journey. She wondered if Gram-Ma-Ma had lived to wear her ceremonial skirt. Had Sekou survived the massacre? Only visions of the intricate Kante designs had kept Ijoma imagining, remembering, sane.

She pulled her left foot an inch forward, grimacing as the iron cuff scraped her flesh anew. At least the ship had docked—where, she did not know. And for the first time in ten weeks, Ijoma no longer smelled the stench of death or the rancid reminders that some in the hold were still living. Her senses had fortunately become immune to the pervasive odor of rotting flesh, excrement, and fear.

After five weeks in the holding pen at Cape Coso and ten more weeks at sea, she was grateful to be alive, thankful that her body had been small enough to allow extra space in her eighteen-inch berth, leaving sufficient room to shift now and then and keep her circulation going. The woman chained to her left arm had not been so lucky, and Ijoma wondered how much longer it would be before the captain ordered the corpse removed.

Now that the journey seemed to be at an end, Ijoma felt the grip of fear. A nervousness that she had managed to keep at bay during the passage resurfaced in galloping waves. What would await her in the bright sunlight of this far-off land? What manner of people would she now live among? Surely they must be a most savage tribe to have created this barbarous way of bringing others to their shores.

Ijoma swallowed dryly, tasting the foul odor of her fellow travelers in her mouth. A spasm of nausea surged up, but instead of frowning, she smiled. If she had been able to move her hands, she would have lovingly stroked the swell of her belly, but instead, she offered up a silent prayer of thanks to the gods who had watched over her during her journey. Sekou's child had survived the trip.

"I will call you Adiaga, the first daughter," Ijoma decided, certain it was a girl child struggling to grow inside her bone-thin body. "You will be strong like Mama, Gram-Ma-Ma, and all the Kante women of Bwerani. As soon as you can hold the quill, I will teach you every one of the Kante designs that I have brought in my head from my village, and you will never forget where you came from."

ONYX

ROMANCE FROM THE PAST AND PRESENT